Tisha + David

~Harada

AN ALLEGORY OF THE TIMES

Toward a Greater Awareness

J T SAWADA

Order this book online at www.trafford.com
or email orders@trafford.com

Most Trafford titles are also available at major online book retailers.

Print information available on the last page.

ISBN: 978-1-4907-8599-8 (sc)
ISBN: 978-1-4907-8656-8 (e)

Trafford rev. 01/30/2018

 www.trafford.com

North America & international
toll-free: 1 888 232 4444 (USA & Canada)
fax: 812 355 4082

CONTENTS

THANKS

Thanks to my wife Norma for her suggestions and feedback.

DEDICATION

To: Norma, Joe, Shelly,

Ayako

&

Fellow Earthlings

INTRODUCTION

This novel was written
For the curious
And open-minded
                          Seekers after truth
With a bent for asking
Provocative questions
Which challenge the intellect
And stimulate the imagination
To look for answers
Compatible with a level
Of cognitive awareness
Relative to the prevailing
Mentality
          Consequently
This is not an ordinary story
Of pathos and glory
It is an allegory
Of the times
Presented as a murder-mystery
With a complicated history
Confounded
By a chaotic crime scene
And a most disturbing crime
Without rhythm or rhyme
Besotted by
Reason and commonsense
Often used in the defense
Of the guilty

Seeking justice
Until proven innocent
By a jury of one's peers
Sitting in judgment
Over the years
                    Providing
Further verification
For the startling revelation
That...
          Ever since
The human species became believers
It was not unreasonable to expect
That they would behave
At a level of awareness
Commensurate with their beliefs.

PART ONE

TELLING IT STRAIGHT

CHAPTER ONE

MURDER IN THE FIRST DEGREE

Is there anything more illuminating
Than the truth?

PRELUDE

"*They need to know the truth!*"
"*Indeed they do.*"
"*However you look at it... it is a strange and unusual predicament. They believe they are being punished. The believers reduce themselves into being tragically flawed specimens in dire need of redemption. It has very few, if any, positive aspects. It is like a contagion, a sickness unto death that since 325 AD has afflicted billions with an institutionalized disease, something like a vast psychosomatic illness.*"

"*I know. It is very disturbing to say the least. They have developed an exceedingly negative mindset. It has metastasized into a grand religious neurosis. It is a mortal malaise: the consequences could be catastrophic. Time is of the essence. Unfortunately, it seems that the vast majority are still not ready; they are not quite um... aware enough. We need to find a way to uh... set the record straight - before it is too late!*"

"*We need to find a way... Hmm... Who was it that said, 'The play's the thing'?*"

"*Shakespeare. That fellow knew a thing or two.*"

"*Perhaps we could present the message like a-a drama: a grand, universal morality play - an allegory of the times?*"

"*An Allegory of the Times? Are you serious?*"

"*Is the Pope a devout Catholic?*"

* * *

The stage was set in realistic shades of autumn greens and browns. A beautiful flower bloomed for its own sake: a late bloomer. It was precious. The audience was hushed and expectant. The drama began to unfold as in a dream from which one was unable to awaken...

"Lenny here," he said after he had ascended the speaker's platform and adjusted the mike, "Lenny the Bruce."

He gazed out with solemn eyes at the multitude assembled before him. A mortal moment disappeared into eternity. He inhaled deeply of the crisp autumn air. Upon exhaling he commenced speaking, with clearly enunciated words and phrases, to the restless mob milling before him like a herd of wild-eyed cattle about to stampede.

From a distance it looked ominous: a single frail-looking individual with electric strands of unkempt hair protruding from under the edges of a sky-blue cap standing alone before the elements. He leaned forward as if valiantly attempting to withstand the onslaught of a menacing rogue wave by the use of nothing... nothing but words, words, and more words.

"My God," he muttered to himself, "What is happening?"

"Lenny the... who?" The question echoed malevolently in the maelstrom.

Was there was anyone out there who understood what he had been saying for the previous ten - or was it twenty minutes? Anyway it seemed like forever... standing up there like an over-aged nerd with his stylish Toronto Blue Jays baseball cap perched precariously upon a slightly elongated skull, shouting into the wind that blew in from the vastness of the Pacific Ocean. It was unbelievable. Irrational. Unnerving. Terrifying!

"Get him!" George Webster Brown was beside himself. The blood roared in his ears. The moment was at hand. He yelled at the top of his voice, "Get that little bastard!"

The crowd surged forward. The mike was ripped from Lenny's hand. Chaos ensued. Something that his *nocturnal advisor* had once intimated echoed in his subconscious as angry hands pushed him from the stage. A pointed shoe connected with his groin.

"Mercy..."

He fell precariously into the abyss. His head hit the ground with a thud. The light grew dim. A heavy boot landed upon his back and his breath whooshed out into the salty air seeping in from the thin edge of the western horizon.

There was an unearthly silence. The solid ground absorbed every vibration. He lay spread-eagled where he had fallen. His left cheek made a shallow imprint on the hard-packed earth. There was a cool dampness, as if Mother Earth had begun to weep.

"Bam!"

The sound reverberated amongst the milling throng out at Garry Point Park. It sounded much like a firecracker, the kind sold in the mid 1950s at local convenience stores for the convenience of rowdy boys looking for excitement. It was not an uncommon noise in that era. Once, a tall, gangly, pockmarked Russian youth had a bunch of firecrackers in the right front pocket of his trousers. The fuse was dangling out. A mischievous sneak lit the fuse as a joke.

George Webster Brown was there when it happened. He laughed hilariously. It was amusing. The skinny lad, who had a funny sounding name that few people could pronounce, sustained serious sulfur and powder burns to the front of his right thigh. The doctors spent two months grafting skin from other parts of his body to re-cover that thigh. It left an ugly patch of scar tissue that the unfortunate lad habitually rubbed as if it were perpetually itchy.

George claimed that the incident was simply an accident; others said that it was the careless act of an ignorant youth. Nevertheless it happened.

"Bam!"

The sound reverberated amongst the multitude. Only in this instance it was not a firecracker. It was a gunshot - the sharp report of a bullet being projected from the muzzle of a German luger into the back of a human skull.

"Bam!" Just like that… Lenny the Bruce was shot dead.

* * *

Pardon me. I did not mean to sound offensive. I-I was…ah-ah momentarily quite out of it. Quite out of it! Beside myself! Irrational!

Forgive me. I should have said something like-like… 'Namaste'. It is the proper greeting of one human being to another. The divinity within me acknowledges the divinity within you.

Such divinity cannot be expunged, like the fecal matter that clogs your intestines and makes you feel nauseous and constipated. It radiates from you like an aura of invisible energy.

I can see by the shallowness of your aura… that you have been repressing it. That takes its toll. There are side effects. Serious side effects. Ever heard of the 'sickness unto death'?

You look disconcerted. Perhaps shocked. Confused? I know. I know how it is. You thought you knew?

Perhaps my seemingly esoteric remarks got you rattled... stirred up some old animosities, some latent feelings of remorse that lay deeply buried like the bones of all those hapless heathens your forefathers so righteously persecuted over the ages with their bitter tongues?

'Get him!' you yelled as if demented. Remember?

The mike was ripped from my hand. The speaker's platform collapsed. Pandemonium ensued. I was just there, consumed by the insanity, a muffled sound amidst the fury. Someone kicked me in the groin. The pain penetrated like a Roman spear shattering my delusions. I whimpered, 'Mercy!' You were merciless.

And the lunacy of it all was that you did not know me from Adam! You thought you did, you with that black leather jacket and shiny bald head... wearing those old leather army boots as if you were still in active service.

You only knew me like information on a printed page, something amenable to your five receptor senses, something you thought constituted objective evidence, hard evidence, empirical evidence. You knew me like that.

Sorry to say - you did not know me from Adam.

You did not know my karmic state of conscious awareness, my unspeakable embarrassments, my mortal shyness, my frustrations, my deep-seated insecurity, my sense of inadequacy, my longing for affection and understanding, my unending search for the truth, my yearning for freedom... my humanity.

* * *

Lenny Bruce looked up at the crystal blue sky with a sigh, and a cry of existential angst. He had been conceived, born and raised in a little town called Steveston situated near the estuary of the south arm of the Fraser River. The town was later incorporated within the city of Richmond. Steveston lost much of its distinctive identity when it was absorbed into Richmond. Things changed... and so did Lenny.

On nice days Lenny liked to go for slow meditative walks around Phoenix pond to think and reflect upon the past. He frequently felt like a comedian who never was. Was it because he tried so hard to be funny? There was a kind of wry poetic humor in the way his life had unraveled throughout the years. There always seemed to be some kind of prose or poetry involved, a kind of rhythm and rhyme that emulated a movement - and a rest.

Sometimes he danced ethereally to the music of the spheres – and at other times he lay in bed bestially fornicating to the beat of the little drummer boy. It was all there stored in the archives of his infinite memory to be retrieved and relived in retrospect when the meaningless took on new meaning. It seemed as if it had always been thus… as far as he could remember forward and backward throughout time immemorial. Rack his feeble brain as he might, he could not recall a time when he was not aware… of being aware. It was a conundrum.

There is something poetically prosaic about the human condition, something oxymoronic, like being immortally mortal. Mortality drifted by year after year as if it were immortal, until… as a matter of routine precaution due to his ever-advancing years, Lenny with his spouse Lana in tow, went in to see his medical practitioner for a routine checkup.

His doctor did the usual: weight to height, blood pressure, eyes, ears, and throat, heart condition… he even asked Len to cough while he held his testicles. All seemed fine and so he gave unsuspecting Lenny a requisition to have some blood work done at the Life Labs across the street.

"Routine for a man of your age," the doctor had said.

For an old pensioner, Lenny the Bruce seemed to be in fine shape.

Lenny began to feel a little more mortal than immortal on the day his doctor revealed the results of his PSA test.

The doctor leaned forward and stared Lenny in the eye, "Your PSA level has spiked unusually high," he quietly stated.

Lenny had no idea what the doctor was talking about. "PSA, ASA… what was the difference?" he thought. He just sat and stared at the doctor.

"Your prostate specific antigen is about fifty."

"Is that good?"

"Sorry. It indicates that you might have … cancer."

"Prostate cancer?"

"It's only an indication, like global warming is an indication that something could be wrong with Mother Earth," the doctor insinuated.

"I get your inference. This could be very serious!"

"Indeed. A biopsy is the only way we can determine whether your PSA test indicated the presence of a cancer."

"How is this done?"

"It is relatively simple: a surgical tool is inserted into your rectum; twelve tiny needles puncture the wall of your colon and penetrate into your prostate which is about the size of a large walnut, and samples are extracted for examination."

"Are there any negative side effects?"

"Afterwards there could be some internal bleeding... and also the possibility of an infection."

"Is it worth it?" Lenny asked with a rising sense of disbelief... and dread.

"It is good to know one way or the other... you know, for your own peace of mind."

"But if I hadn't had the PSA test in the first place... we probably would not even be having this conversation – right?"

"Sometimes ignorance is bliss. If by chance – instead of an aggressive life-threatening variety - you had a slow developing form of cancer, you would probably die of other natural or unnatural causes before the cancer came into play," the doctor leveled.

"Natural or unnatural causes?" Lenny inquired as if baffled.

"Yes, possibly a heart attack or stroke, an accident," the Doctor clarified.

"I see," Lenny sighed. He sagged back into his chair and exhaled as if it were his last breath. "I'd like to discuss this with my wife first. I'll get back to you." He stood up as if to leave.

"I would suggest that you at least consult a urologist and get all the information you can before making any rash decisions", the Doctor paused and stared compassionately into Lenny's eyes: *"After all, it is your life!"* he solemnly added.

When Lenny talked it over with Lana that evening she said, "Trust your Doctor; he knows way more than you do about this."

Lenny checked out everything he could on the Internet. Later that evening when he came to bed looking haggard and resigned to his fate, he informed his spouse. "Okay, let's do whatever is necessary."

And so – after they did *whatever was necessary* - it came to pass that... after his last successful radiation treatment at the Cancer Agency in Vancouver, Lenny paused momentarily under a sprawling maple tree in a nearby park adjacent to the sidewalk that led to the rapid transit system.

The combination of the hormonal injections along with the radiation treatments left him frequently feeling nauseated, fatigued and slightly depressed. With a deep sigh of resignation, he sat down despondently on a dampish-grey cedar bench, and meditated.

It was only a brief moment in eternity, but in that infinite interval he suddenly became aware of the magnanimity of the macrocosm and his microcosmically vain and self-serving existence within it. The moment gave rise to a profound existential question: *What difference would it have made… if the treatment had been unsuccessful and the cancer had been terminal?*

The question was enough to inspire Lenny to a serious reconsideration of what he thought had been his *good intentions*. The problem with his *good intentions* was that they always seemed to remain *good intentions*. Why?

"Why?" Lenny asked himself. Perhaps it was because his *good intentions* only existed in the invisible realms of his *mind*. But, in the visible realms of the real world, was that enough?

"Was that enough?" The question sat like an immovable object upon Lenny's conscience. He felt suffocated. He attempted to draw in a deep breath but his lungs refused to cooperate. He coughed and hacked for air. He looked up to the sky. He looked at the trees, the grass, the dandelions, and the earth beneath his feet.

Was it enough? Enough to lessen the cancerous pain and suffering being inflicted daily upon Mother Earth by the silent majority, the uncommitted, the uncaring and the ignorant… people like himself?

In his own nerdish manner Lenny decided that he would attempt to speak out a little more vociferously - that he, Lenard Bruce Jr., would become a voice of rationality in a society where the vast majority of his fellow human beings took the miracle planet for granted as a place to be used, abused, polluted, discarded, and burnt to a cinder as if it were their God-given right to do so.

He was here – not to desecrate the earth – but to help the people to better understand and appreciate the wonderful opportunity they had been given to learn a simple karmic lesson. A lesson they were incarnated here to learn, a very basic and fundamental lesson vital to their own soulful survival as a unique life form upon this miracle planet.

What lesson?

* * *

By the time Brad Bradley, lawyer for the accused, George W. Brown, really got to know the victim, he had been cremated and his ashes scattered out at Garry Point Park. The victim's life was a matter of public record.

"Born to die, just like everyone else," Brad wryly reflected, *"survived by his wife Lana, a daughter and grandson."* To the ordinary citizen it seemed like just another meaningless murder. But Brad was not your ordinary run-of-the-mill busybody. He was a lawyer of some repute: a somebody.

What made Brad into a somebody was his obsessive interest in a poem originally conceived and written in around 1909 by T.S. Eliot (1888 – 1965) called *The Love Song of J Alfred Prufrock*. At the time Brad was an impressionable undergrad at the fledgling University of Alberta in Calgary, before he was accepted at UBC for Law. He felt the dramatic monologue was speaking to him when the poem opened with the lines:

> *Let us go then, you and I*
> *When the evening is spread out against the sky*
> *Like a patient etherized upon a table.*

Brad was reminded of the glorious Southern Alberta Chinook skies. He identified with the simile, 'like a patient etherized upon a table'. It was like that, vaguely irrational – yet he went along... *into the evening sky, old J Alfred and I...* he accidentally rhymed. Even at such a young age, he could relate; it made him feel mature beyond his years. Sometimes he felt his life was a reflection of things past redeeming. In later years it drew him to cases like the gruesome murder of Lenny Bruce.

Few cases intrigued Brad like this one. This one tweaked his intuitive interest in psychological and existential matters. It was exactly the type of case that interested him, the kind that enabled him to integrate his imaginary role as an armchair psychologist into his legal practice. He also was one of the few barristers who professed an avid interest in matters considered to be beyond the pale of rational deliberations, making him susceptible to Carl Jung's babblings about the collective unconscious. He even had purchased a copy of Jung's long awaited *Liber Novus*. He ordered it from Amazon.ca for $152.00.

It was a huge red, hard-covered publication – sometimes called *The Red Book* - that weighed a ton. It sat prominently on the left side of his maple coffee table at home. He bought it after he heard that Lenny Bruce had had one. He thought that it might help him to better understand the life of the victim. It opened his mind to spiritual influences that went beyond the mechanistic logic of Newton.

It was hard to tell just by looking at him that Brad had a philosophical turn of mind that sometimes made his rudimentary form of logical analysis seem, at times, painstakingly hard-to-take for his partners and associates at the law firm. In addition to his intellectual mannerisms, he had this embarrassingly uncouth child-like habit of unconsciously picking his nose when he was on the verge of revealing a profound insight, a nasty habit which made it difficult for listeners to focus on anything but the tip of his right index finger... making the profundity of his comments seem rather juvenile. But in the final analysis he was probably the smartest barrister at the legal firm who ever picked his nose in public. He brought in more money to the office than half the other partners combined. This enabled him to take on the *pro bono* cases that piqued his interest: cases like the killing of Lenny Bruce.

As far as Brad was concerned, it was practically impossible to account for the whys and wherefores of human behavior. People had long tried to rationalize the irrational, to make sense of the behavior of humankind. During the early nineteen hundreds Sigmund Freud and Carl Gustav Jung attempted to make a science out of the study of human behavior. They, along with a host of others, attempted to apply the scientific method to an intelligent species aware of being aware. They primarily used the old mechanical cause and effect formula. Was the neurotic behavior that was rampant in the culture in which they found themselves, the *effect,* produced by a longstanding religious tradition as convoluted and as baffling as say, *ancestral sin?*

Organized religion, the founder of psychoanalysis had insightfully pronounced, *is a collective neurosis.* Freud had hit the nail on the head. The question that then arose was: *Why this neurosis?* The evidence was obvious in the repressive psychological behavior of his patients. Something had caused them to suppress their basic erotic yearnings, or eros.

What was there in the undeniable spirals of DNA that linked Sigmund Schlomo Freud to his ancient Jewish heritage that predisposed him to spend a mortal lifetime attempting to rationalize his subconsciously repressed reproductive instincts and innate longing for freedom? What existential angst was manifested by the dissonance reflected in the beady eyes, inset behind a full darksome beard reminiscent of the ancient Hebrews who toiled as slaves in the desert sands of antiquity?

Unfortunately the *life-negating ideas* of the early Judaic fathers were visited upon the sons and daughters of future generations. Free spirits, like Sigmund Freud and his open-minded associates, felt stifled by an institutionalized religious dogma that transmuted man from being a divine expression of mortal life to being a tragically tainted specimen who required the intervention of a higher power in order to be 'saved'... from his sinful self. Little wonder Freud proclaimed the effects of such an organized religion to be a *collective neurosis*.

In his attempt to justify this conjecture, Freud hypothesized that there had to be a cause that went *Beyond the Pleasure Principle*, the title of his famous work that delineated a psychological model that provided the foundation for his basic conceptions of a consciousness which consisted of the *conscious ego, the moralistic super-ego, and the instinctive id*. This astounding work along with the publication in 1929 of his most controversial work, *Civilization and its Discontents*, elevated Freud beyond the rudimentary understanding of the many practitioners who attempted to follow in his footsteps.

Psychoanalysis tweaked the public's prurient interests in sexual matters. Their curiosity was aroused. *Libido* became a catchword. And so like peeling back the wrinkles of an old foreskin, practitioners thought that eventually they would discover the root cause of human behavior. The root cause, according to Freud, was sexual in nature. Sex was the brute, primordial instinct that drove man to behave in a sinful manner consistent with his underlying desires. Repression of such a basic instinct resulted in the most neurotic and deviant of behaviors. Sometimes it produced vile, grotesque and embarrassing manifestations of abuse, rape, torture, sadism, masochism, delusion, psychosis, and... contrary to Darwin's expectations re the *survival of the fittest*: celibate priests. All of these life-negating traits were encapsulated within a grand facade promulgated as being the consequences of disobeying a punitive and authoritative Father-like persona called THVVH.

In so rationalizing man's behavior, Freud and his pre-eminent disciple, Carl Jung, became aware that the root cause of man's behavior was buried in the deepest archives of his memory: in his conscious, subconscious, personal unconscious, and in the collective unconscious. And most important of all, these memories consisted of mythological images and primordial dogmas that pushed them from behind to behave in a manner compatible with such life-negating predilections. The ramification of this led to the subtlest implication of all: the man-made reality in which sentient beings exist was only a reification of these ideas… indeed civilization was simply the evolution of man's unconscious being, made manifest via his behavior. *Was it really a collective neurosis?*

There was something obliquely dogmatic about that concept that in Brad's scholarly opinion, enabled Jung to realize that perhaps they had put the proverbial cart before the horse, and it was this inversion that created the dissonance. Jung became aware that there seemed to be a divine component to man's nature: man did not need to be bullied, or pushed from behind with dire threats of eternal damnation. Rather there was something spiritual that attracted man like moths to a lantern. Human behavior could be explained by this pull or attraction toward an ideal. The logic was teleological.

"*Teleological!*" the idea registered in Brad's consciousness.

"Brute existence cannot be denied, but it can be rationalized," Brad had sagely hypothesized. "Perhaps Lenny was just a funny little guy with a penchant for telling tragic stories with a humorous punch-line that few people, used to being threatened, bullied, and pushed from behind - could appreciate. You could say that he unwittingly brought his own misfortune upon himself," Brad informed his wife, Elizabeth, just before he rolled out of bed.

"You don't say?" Elizabeth replied, raising her plucked eyebrows.

Brad was diligent. He took the time to familiarize himself with the victim. He found out that when he was alive, Lenny had often tried to be funny like his namesake, the outspoken Jewish American comedian, social critic and satirist, Leonard Alfred Schneider… who came into this world on October 13th, 1925, and passed away on August 3rd, 1966. He was also known as Lenny Bruce, a stand-up comedian who during a short and much maligned career waxed eloquent on themes such as moral philosophy, politics, patriotism, religion, law, race, abortion, drugs, the KKK, and Jewishness. Unfortunately his satirical views on such sensitive subjects did not exactly endear him to the authorities who worked on behalf of those in influential political, economic, social, and religious positions of power. Somehow Lenny Bruce, had managed to alienate them all.

Like his American counterpart, Lenard Bruce Jr. of Richmond, British Columbia, Canada, sometimes attempted to be humorous at the most inappropriate times. If he could speak from the grave, he'd probably say something ironic like, *May my passing hasten your awakening...* or, *Let this be a healing experience.*

"Good old Lenny the Bruce... was he funny or what?" Brad Bradley, attorney for the defense, eulogized on his way to the courthouse.

* * *

The sky was clear for once, a beautiful pale blue with just a hint of vapor on the western horizon. The icy sidewalk crackled underfoot as passersby hurried toward the old brick and stucco-sided building. It was ten a.m. The glass front doors of the courthouse swung open automatically. A man wearing a long grey overcoat entered carrying a brand new patent leather attaché case. Inside on neatly typed sheets of quality bonded white paper was his defense. His team had worked on it for months. There was something ambiguously insidious involved that challenged their moral and legal sensitivities and impinged upon the fiber of their own integrity in the matter. There were some loose strings and even *loose cannons* that kept the gentleman's blood pressure up - but he had had worse cases. "Nothing to worry excessively about," Brad reassured himself as he stepped confidently into the foyer.

Sarah Brown had seen her husband's defense attorney, an elderly fellow with a slightly humped back, walking meditatively toward the courthouse. She was on her way there too. The sidewalk was somewhat treacherous underfoot. She picked her way gingerly.

Brad Bradley had informed her some time ago that he was going to call her as a character witness. When she first met him she was reminded of Brando, the movie star; there was a slight resemblance, perhaps it was the jaw line. His mannerisms gave her confidence.

They had carefully rehearsed what she was going to say in an effort to deflect the expected attack on her husband's character by the prosecution. He would feed her leading questions. She would simply tell the truth.

"George has never during our married life been unfaithful, as far as I know; he has always done his best to provide for us. Most Sundays when he is at home we attend church services… we are good Christians. George is a considerate and gentle person… he has never hit me. He is not a violent man!" Sometimes it felt as if they were overdoing it. George Webster Brown was no saint.

When the automatic doors of the courthouse opened, she entered quickly. In a way the drama was playing out in the prosecution's favor. It seemed as if the Press was on their side. They published the most gruesome photos of George they could find, their favorite being the one showing him standing over Lenny with that luger in his right hand and a dark scowl on his face. That picture was worth a thousand words. It had *guilty* written all over it.

"Poor Georgie," Sarah lamented, "How could he have been involved in such an unfortunate mishap?" It was inconceivable. She drew in a deep breath and hustled upstairs toward the courtroom.

* * *

When George Webster Brown first met his lawyer, he stared at the evidently older than middle-aged man with the long grey coat and patent leather briefcase and thought, "Who asked for him?"

"I've been assigned to defend you. My name is Brad Bradley. You can just call me Brad."

George looked over the stocky gentleman who stood before him like some hack lawyer in a low-grade murder-mystery movie. There was something vaguely familiar about him as if he should have been cast as a fat cigar-smoking, greasy-looking mafia don. But he was neither fat nor greasy-looking and he did have a friendly demeanor… and he had said, "You can just call me Brad," as if friendship was a real possibility.

George shook his head as if suspicious of his first impressions. "I can't afford to pay you much," he stated morosely, as if anticipating the quality of legal service he could expect.

"Relax; I've been assigned by the Court. It won't cost you anything. In this country, everyone is allowed a proper defense."

"I served in the Armed Forces, you know," George stated succinctly, establishing his status as a veteran with a veteran's right to a proper defense.

"Then... you've earned the right."

Brad's forthright response set George at ease. He leaned toward his defender and cautiously suggested: "Have I met you somewhere before?"

"Not that I know of."

"You kinda remind me of someone I used to know... a long time ago." George shook his head as if attempting to jog his memory.

"Some people say I sort of look like Marlon Brando... you know, the movie star?"

George liked Brad's disposition. He did sort of look like Brando in profile. He liked the way he took off his overcoat, sat down beside him, rubbed his hands together and said, "We've got work to do."

They talked and talked for days, weeks, and months... until Brad squeezed George's shoulder one evening as he was departing and said, "I believe we have a case."

"I believe we have a case!" The words washed over George like a baptism of faith. Months of anxiety, insecurity, and dread receded into the background as a faint glimmer of hope shimmered like an early dawn upon a dark horizon.

When he lay alone on his prison cot at night that sentence brought George a semblance of solace. "*I believe we have a case.*" It was the word *believe* that drew George closer to his defender. He related to Brad as if he represented his savior - and he was an abject sinner confessing to someone who had the power to save him.

They had many confidential discussions that required much soul-searching. It seemed to take ages before Brad's relentless probing eased off... and he once again reiterated the words that planted the seeds of hope in George's heart: "*I believe we have a case.*"

There was one conversation during that interval that stuck in George's memory because it gave him a feeling that there was much more to his case than he could have ever imagined. It began when Brad raised his eyebrows and stated: "There is no point in arguing about whether or not you shot Lenny Bruce. What we need to concern ourselves with here is your intention. Is that okay with you?"

George shook his head as if bewildered by the obtuseness of the question.

"You must be unequivocal about that."

"Like I said, it… it happened so - so quickly it still seems unreal. People were pushing, shoving, yelling, swearing, and cursing…. It was chaotic. It-it was like as if I was in the eye of a storm and being carried along by a-a…"

"Tide of events?" Brad ventured.

"Yeah… over which I had no control… like as in a bad dream. I – I have only a vague recollection of even being there."

"Were you under the influence of alcohol or some other kind of drugs?"

"No!"

"Okay." Brad grimaced and ran his left hand through his wavy brownish-grey hair. "There is no doubt that you had the opportunity. You also were in possession of the murder weapon. The prosecution will be very clear about those two facts. There were plenty of witnesses."

"It… made me sick when I saw him lying there. It was like I was a-a bystander or stranger, or something… like… like in a dream."

"I know, you said that before," Brad pointed out, feeling slightly annoyed by his client's vagueness. He scratched his head on the left side and thoughtfully asked: "You served time in the Army… right?"

"Haven't we been over this before? I joined when I was just a few years out of high school."

"I know…" Brad paused and cogitated. "Didn't you mention something about participating in some kind of secret project back then?"

"I was told that it was my patriotic duty to keep such information to myself… for-for security reasons," George admitted reluctantly.

"Hey, we are talking about *murder in the first degree.* I need to know everything. Everything! Got that?"

"You're the boss."

"Did you ever participate in any clandestine or secret activities where drugs or mind control were being experimented with?" Brad asked, playing a hunch.

"I spent some time at the Allan Memorial Institute in Montreal way back in… in the sixties."

"I've heard about that place. Some rather weird and far-fetched stuff went on there. You were there – eh?" Brad queried.

"Yeah."

"Hmm… you were actually a-a patient in that institution?"

"I wouldn't say 'patient'… I was more like a volunteer. I did it to help out. I was told they needed people like myself, patriotic servicemen who wanted to serve their country."

"Who told you that?"

"The personnel officer in charge of admittance to the top-secret project. He said I was lucky to have been selected, that it was a privilege."

"Did you say top-secret project?" Brad's ears perked up.

"Yeah."

"What top-secret project?"

"I'm not allowed to say… I swore an oath."

"Come on now, we are talking about murder in the first degree – remember? I need to know the facts."

"Between you and me… it was referred to as MKUltra."

"Did you say MKUltra?" Brad asked in disbelief.

"Yeah. I think it was project number sixty something. Maybe sixty-eight?"

"Hmmm," Brad cogitated, his brain attempting to relate to the information he had just gleaned. "I've got some homework to do," he announced. "We'll discuss this further next Thursday."

Brad did his homework. There was very little factual information about MKUltra available to the public. He'd have to get what he could from George. Thursday rolled around. The first question Brad asked was: "Have you ever heard of the Manchurian Candidate?"

"What?"

"Okay. Forget that."

"Forget what?"

"I just mentioned it because I thought you might be able to relate to it."

"Never heard of it," George confessed.

"Anyway, getting back to MKUltra. When you were a participant in that top-secret project, were you ever hypnotized?"

"Several times…"

"Were you ever given post-hypnotic suggestions?"

"Post what?"

"That is where someone is programmed to carry out an assignment at a future date." Brad stared at George as if he represented the fragmentized bits of a puzzle that needed to be put back together.

"At a future date?" George asked as if in disbelief.

"There is usually a trigger word or something that initiates the hypnotic command," Brad explained. "It's uncertain how long such post-hypnotic suggestions might last, if inadequately or incompletely erased... or both? We know so little about the potentiality of the human mind."

"Huh?" George shook his head and looked at his lawyer with a bewildered expression.

Brad paused reflectively. "To be honest, we don't have much of a case... yet," he cogitated, "but you know... this kind of stuff could be *dyn-a-mite*." He syllabized the last word and paused yet again. "Would you mind if I checked into this matter a little deeper and perhaps consulted with your spouse and appropriate military personnel to get further verification?"

"Sarah was there with me in Montreal when it all went down. I am sure she'll vouch for everything I've said."

Brad leaned toward George and spoke in a lowered tone as if sharing a confidence. "They were messing around with mind-control and other psychological stuff back then that could have had far-reaching consequences for the guinea pigs involved."

"I wasn't a guinea pig."

"Never mind. If you were, you probably wouldn't remember it anyway. But it is something that we need to keep in mind because... it could prove problematic for the prosecution when it comes to the matter of establishing motive."

It was a *stretch*, but Brad was aware that in this day and age where conspiracy theories abounded and a sensitive public became incensed with just about anything that smacked of a cover-up... where there was smoke... there could be fire. "I think we just might have a fighting chance," he looked up confidently at George.

"I get your drift," George acknowledged. "Motive is important."

"Yeah, the prosecution's case seems vulnerable... when it comes to the fuzzy matter of clarifying your state of mind at the time of the murder. What headspace were you in? Were there any other extenuating circumstances? There are so many unanswered questions... that may be ultimately unanswerable. In a case like this, circumstances related to your mental state of awareness could be crucial. Without a clear cut motive, it will be very difficult for the prosecution to prove beyond a reasonable doubt that you are guilty of *murder in the first degree*."

"I was just a guinea pig," George acquiesced.

"*A state of awareness*? What is that?" Brad cogitated the day after George had admitted to being a guinea pig. The combination of the word 'state' with 'awareness' produced a phrase that sounded like something far-fetched... like a charge the thought police or Big Brother in George Orwell's masterpiece *1984*, might bring. To Brad's mind it elicited the question: To what extent does 'covert mental life' exist?

It was a fascinating question. It hung like a dark cloud over Brad's head for weeks. When he went to bed at night the question hung there. He couldn't sleep. One night he got up and perused the mound of papers stacked on the lower shelves of his study that represented the thoughts of the late Lenny Bruce as published in a pamphlet called *Final Draft*. "Radical!" he thought. He spent days and days reading those pamphlets. Somehow they spoke to him about a state of awareness that... awoke him from his dogmatic slumbers. "This Lenny was nobody's fool!" he proclaimed.

"What if...?" The question typified the kind of simple-minded curiosity that came naturally to inquisitive minds like Lenny's, free from the restraints of religious dogma. Throughout the ages the great unwashed were reluctant to ask such a simple question because it represented a blasphemous affront to blind faith. It took a certain kind of intrinsic courage – like that demonstrated by poor old deceased Lenny the Bruce!

Lenny seemed to have had a reformer's sense of intellectual and spiritual fortitude, the kind required to complete the 'What if?' *What if man's essential nature was not tragically flawed? How would this change his attitude and outlook on life? What if man was a divine expression of a 'karmic soul' progressing toward a greater understanding of altruism?*

These were the kinds of annoying but cogent ideas and questions that in the cultural time in which Brad existed, were almost never considered - let alone answered. Where did George W. Brown fit into this historical and cultural framework? What subconscious psychological influences distorted his mental outlook? What collective neurotic tendencies had he inculcated? What was he aware of when he robotically removed a German luger from the right hand pocket of his black leather jacket? To what extent did *covert mental life* exist when George, on behalf of the great unwashed, pulled a gun on Lenny the Bruce?

Could it be said that in the coherent collective unconsciousness of that mortal moment, his client had committed a compassionate act of *euthanasia*? Brad had a funny sense of social justice; some would even use the word bizarre: in this case it somehow seemed appropriate.

Brad looked up the term euthanasia in the dictionary in case he wanted to use that term later in court. Euthanasia was succinctly defined as being: *the deliberate painless killing of persons who suffer from a painful or incurable disease or condition, or who are aged and helpless.* It could be said that Lenny was aged and helpless and suffering from some kind of an incurable condition when, according to the prosecutor, he was *deliberately dispatched.* Would it be in the interests of his client if the foul deed were referred to as *euthanasia* or a mercy killing carried out on behalf of the public good – instead of *murder in the first degree*?

* * *

To look at Brad Bradley with his reading glasses dangling, soft grey-brown hair combed forward to cover the balding spot on the crown of his head, it was all too easy to overlook the magnificence of his ever-curious intellect. Without a doubt he was one of those underrated, taken for granted, public defenders who, as he graciously devoted his time defending clients like George W Brown, did not receive the credit he deserved for bringing to the court his lofty notion of justice.

"What is justice?" Brad had often asked himself when he was a law student at UBC. He saw the evolutionary reality about him as a work in progress. His interest in the collective unconscious led to a continuing interest in the insightful work of Carl Gustav Jung.

Jung was born on July 26th, 1875 in Kessewil, Switzerland. His father, Paul, was a county parson of the Swiss Reform Church, and his dutiful mother, Emilie Preiswerk Jung was the parson's wealthy and long-suffering wife. At the age of eleven, young Carl realized with sudden clarity that he was the *existent-essence* or the intrinsic source of the awareness that enabled him to be conscious. It was the turning point in his life that set him on the path that became his life's work and gave the fledgling study of psychoanalysis another mentor besides Sigmund Freud.

Jung went beyond Freud and delved into the spiritual realm of the *collective unconscious* where terms like *synchronicity* and *archetypes* helped to further explain the whys and wherefores of human behavior. Because Jung's point of view regarding human nature seemed to coincide with Brad's personal assessment of the human condition, he found Jung's *teleological* approach where human beings were led or pulled ahead by ideas, and his *dynamics of the psyche,* immensely helpful in deciphering the behavior of the populace from which he drew his clientele.

Such knowledge helped Brad to get a better handle on what he considered to be the most complicated case he had ever tackled. It was a case that, in his mind, represented the ebb and flow of what constituted the social intercourse of the milieu. He liked the term 'intercourse' because it represented a give and take, a coming together of disparate parts to yield a complicit action. In every murder case there was the murderer and the victim. There was this social, psychological, and existential intercourse between them that created the event. They were, in a manner of speaking, both victims of the circumstances that produced the result: in this particular case, the gruesome killing of Lenard Bruce Jr.

Brad Bradley leaned back in his padded leather armchair in his office and sighed, "Sometimes we shoot the messenger because we are overly concerned about the radical implications of his ideas." He thought of some famous seekers after truth like Socrates, Jesus, and Gandhi. "We associate a man with his ideas… because ideas per se cannot exist without the thinker who thinks them up." He could understand why Socrates was poisoned, Jesus was crucified, and Gandhi was shot - but a virtual *nobody* like Lenny Bruce?

Outside the Courthouse about a dozen people were carrying placards; one read: "We want Justice!"

* * *

There was a hush in the courtroom, the kind that precedes a tsunami wave just before it hits the shoreline. The tension was palpable. Sarah Brown, the stoically contrite wife of the accused, could see it on every face. The Prosecution was neatly arrayed, confident and anxious to start proceedings. The Defense looked bedraggled. They all stood. The Judge entered. He sat down. They followed suit.

The gavel hit the hardwood like a gunshot. Court was in session. All eyes were riveted on the judge who seemed to be enjoying his vital role in the legal proceedings. When the appropriate moment arrived he gazed down from his lofty perch and stared solemnly in the direction of the accused.

"In the matter of George Webster Brown versus the Crown, how do you plead to the charge of… murder in the first degree?"

"Not guilty, Your Honor."

A murmur spread throughout the crowded courtroom. "Not guilty?" those present looked at one another in disbelief. *Not guilty… my ass! That skinhead deserves to be drawn and quartered and pissed upon. Ha, not guilty, what a laugh!* They turned to look at George. What did they perceive? Did they see a fellow human being of infinite worth… like themselves?

"*Pathetic!*" they exclaimed in disgust.

What culmination of antecedent social, psychological, and historical events brought about this sorry state of affairs? How did this collective state of awareness become manifest in this particular manner… in a courtroom where a skinhead was on trial for shooting a defenseless old pensioner in the head?

"Not guilty, Your Honor."

Unreal!

Days turned into weeks before the defendant got his chance to tell it like it really was. George W. Brown, the accused, got up in the stand and stood tall with his shoulders pulled back, a proud ex-serviceman. He swore an oath to tell the truth and nothing but the truth "so help me God". He had a strange feeling that God was on his side. He smiled his crooked little smile in spite of his lawyer's sage advice: "Don't smile, George, it makes you look sly and avaricious". George never asked what avaricious meant.

"*Did you intentionally shoot and kill Lenard Bruce Jr.?*"

They had rehearsed it for months. George knew his lines by heart. Who knew he was such a good actor? He imagined he was like Jack Nicholson on the stand in the movie *A Few Good Men*, a brave soldier being denigrated for doing his duty. He wore his hair in a brush-cut like Jack's and pretended that his drab prisoner's garb was an officer's uniform. He looked directly at the twelve carefully selected members of the jury, and in a voice modulated with humility and compassion replied: "I am truly sorry for what has happened."

He gazed over to where the victim's spouse, Lana Bruce, was sitting and recalled what his lawyer, Brad, had told him: "It is imperative that you demonstrate remorse. How can you expect the jury to forgive you, if you cannot convince them that - even though you are innocent - you are truly sorry for what has happened?"

George clasped his hands together as if in prayer. "I am a simple man," he began, "I can only tell it like it was. I had no intention... I repeat, no intention of shooting that poor man. It all seems so vague, so hazy. I have no recollection of-of what exactly happened. I've seen the photos. It looks bad, I know. Perhaps I-I was just threatening? Believe me... I had no intention to shoot him. I was just standing there... and then someone must have jostled my arm and the gun went off. It was an accident... an accident," he repeated as tears of remorse rolled slowly down his pale cheeks. "I am so sorry," he lamented, bringing his hands to his face, "so very sorry," and the sorrier he felt the easier the tears flowed. Between his fingers George could see that there was a kind of stone-faced empathy etched upon the faces of the six men and six women who sat in judgment of his coldblooded crime.

It was not easy for Brad to build up the circumstantial case that tended to make the defendant look less guilty than he seemed to be. There was an inherent built-in logic to the way things unfolded, that from Brad's legal point of view enhanced George's chances of 'getting off'. He developed the *Leviathan theory of culpability*: George was only a small part of the 'monster' that dispatched poor Lenny Bruce. It was a hard sell, but Brad did his legal best. He called up many eyewitnesses who testified on George's behalf. It was like putting together a giant puzzle; each additional piece made the picture more impressive, and most important of all, more believable as the amorphous leviathan took shape.

Brad looked at it this way: George represented only a small cog in a very large wheel, or the period at the end of a long and convoluted story that began at the Allan Memorial Institute in Montreal and ended at Garry Point Park. It was a story that involved the collective state of mind of a generation of gullible converts looking for a fall guy: someone who could be blamed for carrying out their hidden agenda, someone at whom they could point and say: "He did it!" while washing their contaminated hands and pretending they were innocent.

"George was not the only one at Garry Point Park on the fateful day Lenard Bruce was killed," Brad had pointed out. "There was a large, angry mob there that acted like an irrational monster. The monster was comprised of all the individuals who made up the mob. George was just part of the monster: the monster had many heads, legs, torsos, arms, hands and feet. George... unlike Lee Harvey Oswald, did not act alone," Brad added, knowing the jury could relate to that comparison.

"Someone yelled, 'Get him!' like some demented banshee with a grudge. Someone else yelled, 'Let's teach him a lesson he'll never forget!' Someone else knocked over the wooden podium that was subsequently smashed to smithereens. Someone else pulled Lenny from the stage. Someone else kicked him in the crotch. Someone else punched him in the stomach. Someone yelled, 'Kill the little bastard!' as he fell awkwardly to the hard-packed ground. The *Leviathan* placed its boot on Lenny's back. The *Leviathan's* finger twitched... and 'bam!'" Brad surveyed the solemn faces of the twelve jurors.

"But only George was arrested and charged with the murder of Lenard Bruce Junior," Brad concluded.

"Skinhead may walk", the papers shouted the next day. The public was outraged.

The trial dragged on day after tiring day. Every day George sat in court, a model of humility and remorse. Except for one unforeseen incident when George appeared to hallucinate while on the stand, all seemed to unfold according to plan. During those days, ironic as it may seem, George actually became humbler and more contrite. It was as if the experience gave him the opportunity to change... for the better. But would it matter in the end? All that was left was the summation. If he had any chance at all, it would depend upon how Brad summed things up.

As the trial drew to an end the stress began to show on Brad's face; his left eye began to twitch involuntarily. He had witnessed many stirring summations on HBO where the lawyer cunningly saved his best performance until the end. It made for great theatre. But this was not a movie and he was not an actor. He was Brad Bradley, lawyer for the defense. A man's life hung in the balance... and as his lawyer, it was definitely time for him to give one of those heroic summations. The problem was... he felt inadequate, stymied, and frustrated – at the very time when the actor on TV was shuffling the papers on the table and preparing to stride confidently up to the jurors and lay it on the line. "Lay what on the line?" was the only question that came to Brad's mind as the trial wound down.

George could sense Brad's feelings of anxiety and insecurity as he sat stoically beside him at the table reserved for the defense. He turned sideways and stared at the man who represented his last hope, and as he did, the remaining vestiges of hope convulsed in the pit of his stomach resulting in a sickening feeling of nausea. He thought of the biblical phrase: *Sickness unto death.* It made him feel worse. He stared morosely at his lawyer. "Ready for the summation?" he asked hopefully.

There was one point in the prosecution's cross-examination of his client that, in retrospect, often set Brad to wondering: "Have I misjudged George? Is he actually far smarter than anyone has ever given him credit for?"

The dicey situation arose about three-fifths of the way through the trial when George was on the stand and Brad had clumsily sat back down. The prosecutor - a tall, gangly fellow with a slightly pockmarked sallow-looking complexion, who called himself "Russ" strode forward confidently and peppered the defendant with a torrent of accusative questions that made George appear incompetent and confused. Near the end he paused for a moment, and then in a loud voice suddenly asked: "Do you believe in God?"

The question caught both George and Brad off guard. George just glared inanely at the prosecutor. Brad sat dumfounded at the table for the defense. He should have jumped up and yelled: "I object Your Honor, to this line of questioning," – but instead he just sat there.

George leaned toward the prosecutor as if on the verge of responding. He opened his mouth, but no sound ensued.

The moment took on a surreal texture. Brad's mind flashed back to a moment many years ago when the great pioneer of modern analytical psychology, Carl Gustav Jung at the ripe old age of eighty-four, was being interviewed for television at his retreat in Switzerland. Near the end of the session the interviewer leaned forward and asked point blank: "Do you *now* believe in God?" There was an awkward moment of silence before the feeble old man muttered: "Difficult to answer... I know...I don't need to believe... I know."

"Do you believe in God?" the prosecutor asked in a louder and more demanding tone of voice.

George sagged back with a puzzled expression on his face and cautiously replied, "Difficult to answer..."

Brad's jaw dropped open. It was as if Jung's concept of synchronicity was in play.

"Before I reply I need to know two things." George continued. "First, what do you mean by 'believe'? And second, what do you mean by 'God'?"

The seemingly innocuous response suddenly seemed to turn the tables. The jury sat up expectantly and looked to the prosecutor.

It was the prosecutor's turn to look dumbfounded. He opened his mouth as if to respond, but no words of clarification issued forth. Finally he uttered with a hostile demeanor: "I asked you a simple question... and I demand a simple straightforward answer!"

The jurors turned back to George. He cleared his throat, swallowed and contritely replied, "How can I answer your simple question... when you do not seem to understand what you yourself are asking? Just tell me what you mean by 'believe', and what you mean by 'God'... so that I may respond in a simple and straightforward manner to your question."

On the surface of it, it probably seemed like a reasonable request... to the jury. They turned once again to the prosecutor.

He rubbed the back of his neck as if to stimulate the blood flow to his brain. He appeared to be stymied by his own question. He frowned and paced back and forth. He glared malevolently at George as if it were his fault he was in such a predicament. At long last he heaved a heavy sigh and tentatively began, "To believe means to-to know... yes, to know something profoundly... to believe something is true... to have conviction that something is true. Yes, that's it: to have conviction that something is profoundly true."

"To have conviction that something... is profoundly true," George reiterated. "And what is it that is profoundly true?"

"God," the prosecutor practically shouted.

"Could you please explain what you mean by that three letter word? Is it simply dog spelled backwards?" A wisp of an enigmatic smile flickered ever so briefly upon George's countenance, "Or does it have some deeper significance?" he asked humbly.

"You know..." the prosecutor looked flustered, "that word is very difficult to define. It means so many different things to different people. It is just something that we believe in... something called God."

"Are you referring to the God the terrorists prayed to before crashing the airliners into the twin towers on 9/11?"

"That was ah-ah Allah. I'm talking about the one and only true God... the all powerful, invisible God of everything."

"Everything?"

"Yes, everything there is. Period," the prosecutor concluded with finality.

"Are you asking me if I believe in some all-powerful invisible *God* who created everyone and everything... including Allah?" George paused melodramatically. "Or," he glanced reverently toward the jurors, "are you asking me if I believe in..." he bowed his head humbly, "our Lord and Savior, Jesus Christ?"

The question just hung there between George and the prosecutor as if awaiting a response. There was none. The prosecutor turned and slowly walked back to the table for the prosecution. "No further questions," he said.

* * *

It was probably one of the most unorthodox summations the judge and jury had ever heard. On behalf of the defendant, George Webster Brown of Richmond, British Columbia, Canada, Brad Bradley rose slowly from his chair dressed smartly in a grey three piece suit with dark grey tie to match, and with a somber expression of subdued confidence, sauntered thoughtfully toward the panel of jurors. He was not the condemned, but in many ways, given the predilections of the great unwashed to pre-judge clients like his, he felt as if he too were condemned... to failure before he started. It was therefore vital, if his summation was to have any effect at all, that he somehow get them to listen empathetically to what he had to say.

Up until a few weeks ago he had no clear-cut, persuasive idea what to say in defense of his client that would appeal to the empathy and sympathies of the jurors. The prosecution had all the ammunition including the smoking gun. What did he have? A guilty client… or so it seemed. Then, as if by providence, he bumped into the deceased victim's spouse, Lana Bruce, at Tim Horton's where he had gone to ponder his client's fate. He was sitting alone by a window seat beside the garbage stand where brown plastic trays were emptied and stacked, when Lana Bruce sat down at a table next to his. He recognized her immediately. He coughed loudly to draw attention to himself. When Lana looked up he asked, "You're Lenny Bruce's wife, aren't you?"

"You mean, the late Lenny Bruce, don't you?"

"Yes… the wife of the deceased… the-the victim's spouse," Brad stammered, his face growing red with embarrassment.

Lana looked around and saw that they were the only two people in that area. "If it is appropriate… you can join me, if you like?" she suggested in a friendly tone.

"Sure," Brad moved over to Lana's table. "I'm Brad Bradley, lawyer for the defense," he introduced himself formally while extending his right hand. "I am deeply sorry about what happened to your husband."

Lana shook Brad's hand politely, "I know," she said looking up at his face. "You have a compassionate face," she commented.

"I do?" Brad replied quizzically.

"Yes. The accused… I mean George, is lucky to have you in his corner."

The unexpected compliment caught Brad off guard. "Th-thanks," he muttered self-consciously.

"You know… there is something about your client that I find rather ah – ah… pathetic," she pointed out.

"Pathetic?"

"Yeah, I felt the same way about Lee Harvey Oswald."

"You did?" Brad raised his eyebrows in surprise. "He's the one who shot JFK."

"Right. George has that same pathetic, helpless, wasted, anemic look about him."

"He does?"

"He looks like a lost soul…"

Brad cleared his throat, "Ah-hem!!" It had the desired effect. The sleepy jurors raised their collective heads. "Ladies and Gentlemen of the jury," he began, and reiterated what he had stated at the beginning of the trial with extra emphasis on the word *fair*: "All I'm asking for on behalf of my client is that he receive a fair hearing from you... that he be believed innocent until he is proven guilty... that he receive a fair trial."

The jurors sat up indignantly, as if being accused of the remote possibility that they could render a verdict that could be considered to be unfair. They stared malevolently toward the aging defense attorney with eyes that asked, *who do you think you're talking to?*

At the prosecution table Ruskolnikov Kublinsky smiled self-indulgently.

Brad intuited that he had somehow offended the jury. Sweat oozed from his forehead. He dabbed at it with his white cotton handkerchief.

At the table for the defense, George sat stoically staring up at the judge. His hands were clasped together so tightly his knuckles gleamed. He turned and gazed solemnly at the man in whose hands he had placed his life. He grimaced as if in pain and bowed his head to hide his anguish.

To disguise his discomfiture, Brad turned away from the six men and six women who comprised the jury. The blood drained from his red face leaving it pale and anemic. He pulled his shoulders back, drew in a deep breath, raised his head and composed himself.

He looked deeply humbled and almost on the verge of tears when he turned back to face the jurors. He slowly exhaled and, with a sigh of regret so deep that it even registered with the judge, began in a timid voice that required the jurors to lean forward with ears perked.

"My client is accused of murder in the first degree," he whispered. "The evidence against him is compelling. The prosecution has provided you with what may seem to be an open and shut case. They have proven almost everything except..." Brad paused to inhale, as did the jury, "except for one thing... they have not established a clear-cut, straight-forward, unambiguous motive.

"Why did George Webster Brown murder Lenard Bruce? What was his state of mind... at the time of the incident?" Brad lowered his gaze and shuffled back and forth as if pondering that very question.

"As you know, ladies and gentlemen, my client has pleaded 'not guilty'. He has only a vague recollection of what happened. I know that it is a simple deductive leap to assume, as the prosecution has, that in the face of such a serious charge as murder in the first degree... my client might be inclined to forget, or develop a selective memory, or fake amnesia or... let's face it... lie through his teeth." Brad candidly laid out the barebones of the situation.

"But the fact of the matter is, ladies and gentlemen of the jury, the prosecution has failed to provide you with any kind of a clear-cut and convincing motive. My client stands accused of a most heinous crime... for which there does not seem to be any apparent motive." Brad paused to let the jury cogitate upon what he had just pointed out.

"In times like these... ideas can be much more potent than bullets. Lenny was a man of ideas. I have personally read selected portions of his work that some might call inflammatory. Lenard Bruce was a messenger with a powerful message. In our short and beleaguered history we have developed a penchant for killing the messenger in hopes of eliminating the message and preserving the status quo." Brad paused to draw in a much-needed breath before continuing.

"I submit that Lenny Bruce was murdered because of his message. In the cause of social justice... someone must pay for such a crime. Someone must be held responsible – so that the rest of us need not feel... accountable." Brad squeezed the tip of his nose with the thumb and forefinger of his left hand. "Have you ever heard of the word 'patsy'?" Brad asked the jurors. They all nodded.

"That is where someone is set up to take the fall for the guilty who pretend to be innocent. We usually associate patsies with organized crime and conspiracy theories, but when you consider all the nefarious undercover activities associated with secret service agencies, like the CIA for example, the term 'patsy' becomes alarmingly ominous.

"Let's take a look at some very well known historical figures who were all dispatched by groups or individuals in order to preserve the status quo of their times. In ancient Greece, Socrates was accused of corrupting the youths and forced to drink a deadly poison made from hemlock juice. We blamed the ignorant individuals who acted on behalf of the ruling class. When Jesus of Nazareth was accused of corrupting the youths and subsequently crucified, we blamed the Jewish High Priests." Some jurors leaned forward in their chairs.

"However, in more recent times when wise and enlightened individuals like Mahatma Gandhi, John F. Kennedy, and Martin Luther

King Jr. were eliminated, we blamed some hapless fanatics representing the lunatic fringe who hardly anyone ever heard of before.

"Many questions come immediately to mind regarding these matters. What did these murdered individuals have in common? Why were they dispatched? And who ultimately was held accountable? Think about that." Brad paused to give the jury time to think.

"Let me attempt to answer these questions," Brad continued. "Those late, great murdered individuals were all ahead of their times. They were courageous, intelligent and sensitive human beings who were not afraid to speak out in the face of a powerful and entrenched establishment. Why were such wise and enlightened individuals dispatched? From their small-minded point of view, the establishment perceived them as being a clear danger to the status quo." Brad pensively paced to and fro.

"And after they were dispatched who was held accountable? Who was held responsible for the gruesome murder of Mohandas Karamchand Gandhi on January 29th, 1948? A little-known fellow named Nathuram Godse was found guilty of shooting three fatal bullets into Gandhi's chest. Who took the blame for the assassination of John Fitzgerald Kennedy? After a prolonged ten months investigation the government-appointed Warren Commission concluded that Lee Harvey Oswald acted alone when he shot and killed the President, and moreover that Jack Ruby, who killed Oswald before he could stand trial, had also acted alone. And who was charged and found guilty of the murder of Martin Luther King Jr.? James Earl Ray, a fugitive from the Missouri State Penitentiary was arrested and deemed to be the one who shot and killed Reverend King in Memphis, Tennessee on April 4th, 1968." Brad paused to let these poignant facts soak into the curious minds of the jurors.

"There are many not-so-notable or famous individuals who have had the courage of their convictions to speak up on behalf of the human race. They are the unsung heroes no one hears about… until they are dispatched. They are the Lenny Bruces of their times."

Brad surveyed the sombre faces of the jurors assembled before him. With the instincts and cunning of an experienced old lawyer massaging the emotional proclivities of his fellow seekers after truth, he returned to the singular example that seemed to resonate sympathetically with the twelve men and women in whose hands the fate of his client depended.

"John F. Kennedy, as you know, was considered to be a great American President because he represented an enlightened view of the public good. Unfortunately there were powerful vested interests whose views of what constituted the public good were at loggerheads with his," Brad suggested. "It is no secret that there were a handful of influential Americans who wanted John and his younger brother Robert out of the way.

"When John was assassinated, Canadians mourned his passing as much as his American countrymen. There was a massive public outcry. Someone had to pay for this heinous crime. Lee Harvey Oswald with his old bolt-action type rifle was summarily arrested and charged. He claimed to be innocent. He even referred to himself live on television as being a patsy.

"Unfortunately – or was that fortunately? - Jack Ruby was able to brazenly murder Oswald, also live on national television… before Lee got his chance to testify in a court of law. Consequently he did not get to tell his side of the story. Nor did he receive a fair trial before a jury of his peers… unlike my client," Brad added craftily.

"Did anyone care? Did anyone feel sorry for Lee Harvey Oswald? Would he have been found to be innocent – if he had received a fair trial before a jury of his peers?" Brad paused to draw in a sober breath.

"Was justice really done?" Brad continued. "Was Lee Harvey Oswald guilty? Or was he just a patsy - a throwaway victim of the circumstances, used and abused by the establishment for their own selfish purposes?

"The official government investigation undertaken ostensibly to prove whether or not Oswald had acted alone was able to convince the gullible that a single magic bullet fired from Oswald's old bolt-action army rifle had done the job." Brad smiled at his own witticism. "Of course the controversy and conspiracy theories continue to this very day. *To this very day!*" Brad repeated as he looked up at the jurors.

"What do you think?" Brad asked, knowing that most Canadians had serious doubts regarding the official government account of what happened at Dealey Plaza, Dallas, Texas on Friday, November 22nd 1963 at 12:30 pm CST. He paced sombrely back and forth before the panel of jurors with his hands clasped behind his back like an old Oriental sage practicing walking meditation.

"What do you think?" he repeated. "Is George Webster Brown guilty of *murder in the first degree?*" He gazed searchingly into the eyes of every jury member before continuing.

"Or - is he just a patsy, a throwaway victim of the circumstances like poor Lee Harvey Oswald with his frightened anemic countenance and incriminating old-fashioned weapon? A startled, hapless animal caught in the headlights of an onrushing eighteen-wheeler?"

* * *

Twelve weary jurors re-assembled back into the courtroom after seven agonizing days and nights. There was some gossip about the possibility of a hung jury. George was led back into the courtroom for the last time to be sentenced. Whatever the outcome, it had seemed like a born-again experience. It was not the same George who had smiled so avariciously on opening day. It was a man who realized that his life now hung in the balance. Either – Or. All he could do was stand there impotently and look up at His Honor as if he was god almighty.

The night before, George had penitently gotten down on his knees and prayed, and prayed, and prayed. Somewhere way out there, was anyone listening? Did anyone care what happened to a desperate soul groveling on the dirty floor of a prison cell in abject humility? In the Great Beyond where such prayers reverberated in a void of infinite potentialities, was there a spark of hope for one such as he?

It gave George pause. He looked up at the ceiling, at the walls, and at the floor. He was alone. There was no going back. Lenny was dead. Dead! For Lenny Bruce there was no second chance.

He could see Lenny lying there in the dirt with the blood oozing from a bullet hole in the back of his head; his white hair had turned crimson. George curled up fetus style on the dirty concrete floor.

He became Lenny lying supinely on the trampled hard-pack. "Mercy!" he pleaded before losing consciousness.

Dawn found him lying nearly comatose on the cold concrete floor of his sparse prison cell. His eyes fluttered open momentarily and then closed. In his semi-conscious state he gradually became aware of a ghostly apparition of himself standing before the judge waiting to be sentenced, a ghastly figure with graying hair and pale hands dangling limply at his sides like those of a condemned man. His head was bowed as if in perpetual mourning. He stood as countless other craven souls charged with murder in the first degree, had stood. Who would have ever thought that his miserable life, such as it was… would come to this?

The judge in his magnificent black flowing robe looked down pathetically at George. He cleared his throat and looked at the paper the foreman of the jury had handed to him. He handed the note back to the spokesperson for the jury. "On the count of murder in the first degree… how do you find?"

"The jury finds the…"

George closed his eyes; he stood as if frozen with dread. He could hear voices, a multitude of voices yelling: *"Get him! Get the little bastard!"* He felt the cold steel of the handgun. He saw the hot crimson blood oozing from the bullet hole in the back of Lenny's skull. He could smell the dampness.

It was a nightmare… he ascended the gallows; he was standing expectantly upon the trapdoor with a hangman's noose tightening around his neck. He could hardly breathe. His bloodshot eyes bulged from their sockets. Every nerve in his body was tingling with expectancy.

The courtroom was deathly silent. All eyes were riveted upon the accused. George Webster Brown opened his eyes, drew in an agonizingly slow breath and gazed up at His Honor with eyes glistening with repentance. Silent tears of regret dribbled helplessly.

The Judge slowly raised his gavel, held it omnipotently in mid-air, and brought it down with conviction. "Bam!" the gavel resounded throughout the courtroom…. The accused dropped to his knees and sobbed uncontrollably.

* * *

In the immortal silence
Of the mortal moment
There were compassionate vibes
That resonated empathetically
In the crystalline tears of the forsaken
Overlooked
      By the shifty eyes of the gullible
Darting hither and thither
Righteously extolling the virtues
Of those who have made a ritual

Of awakening
           As they have always awakened
With a yawn at the dawn of a new day
And taken for granted the miracle
Of the morning sun that envelops them
With a golden aura
As if they were divine beings
Of infinite worth.

- L B

CHAPTER TWO

THE GREAT UNWASHED

Who knows why
The great unwashed
Remain unwashed?

The man in charge of the prosecution was the Crown Prosecutor, the formidable Ruskolnikov Kublinsky. He was all the more formidable because he represented in his own mind that vast unappreciated mass of humanity often derisively referred to as the 'great unwashed'. In Russia the term 'proletariat' was used to designate the same class of hardworking, salt of the earth folk.

He identified with the common folk because of his cultural sensitivities and ideological convictions stemming from Rousseau and Marx. But in his Canadian homeland, nature and nurture combined to produce a self-conscious citizen who was embarrassed by his foreign-sounding name. Consequently like thousands of others like him who were born of immigrant parents, Ruskolnikov affected an English accent, shortened his name to "Russ" because it sounded more Anglo, and attempted to blend into the great Canadian mosaic.

His parents were old school Belarusians from a central area in the old USSR known as Kharchav. The family had emigrated from Russia to Toronto where they lived with their sponsor, a professor emeritus at the University of Toronto referred to as the "Polish Jew" – although he was neither Polish nor a Jew. He was related to Russ's father's elder brother's wife, who was a so-called White-Russian. No one knew for sure what the designation 'white' meant other than as a directional indication like 'north'. Some uninformed folk assumed it had racial implications that had to do with color. Historically, the Tsar was often referred to as the "Great White Tsar" which somewhat explained why Russ's relatives who survived the 1917 Revolution espoused Tsarist sympathies in the anarchic period immediately following that event.

After residing in the Roncesvalles neighborhood of Toronto for three years, the Kublinskys moved to a Ukrainian village in Alberta just northwest of Edmonton where some spelled their last name 'Kublinski. From there they departed two years later and ended up in Vancouver along with their one and only son.

Ruskolnikov, or "Russ", emerged into the new cultural environment of southeast Vancouver, British Columbia, Canada, transformed from an old-world cocoon spun from Communist and Bolshevik threads, and spread his wings in a reality manifested from 'funny money' and Social Credit theology secularized as liberal politics. It was to be a whole new experience for a fledgling soul blessed with a beautiful purple birthmark below his bellybutton. Was it a sign of future greatness? Or just a meaningless blot or stain on a sea of pale white skin?

Ruskolnikov Kublinsky matured into a gaunt, slightly, hawk-faced, six foot seven inch white-Russian Canadian giant. He could have been a professional wrestler or a basketball player, or even a slow-skating, stay-at-home defensive-defenseman on the local hockey team. But alack, he wasted his prodigious size advantage by taking up law at UBC.

It was assumed by his freshmen peers at the university that the Canadian giant had a penis that was commensurate with his gigantic size. Alas, nature had compensated in his case by endowing him with a penis that was in inverse ratio to his physical mass. Consequently throughout his public life he shunned sports and activities that required communal showers or nudity of any kind. When he had to urinate in public washrooms he usually used the enclosed toilets rather than the open urinals. However his "little bud", as he called his penis, rose to the occasion on his wedding night to deflower the girl of his wet dreams.

He met his wife in a third year Sociology class. She sat just ahead of him in the fourth row from the front. Never had he seen such a beautiful young woman. She was petite, slender, graceful, and exotic – just the opposite of what he saw when he looked in the mirror in the morning. Near the end of the fifth week he worked up the courage to pass a note to her as class ended. The note read: "My name is Russ. I would like to make your acquaintance. Could we meet in the hall right after class?" He signed it: "An ardent admirer".

They met after class. Her name was Michiko Kuriyama. Her folks had been interned in New Denver during the War. She was a Buddhist. Six months later Russ said, "I'll become a Buddhist if you will marry me." She replied, "I will marry you because of your compassionate heart." That single comment reverberated within Russ's heartstrings for the rest of his life along with her Quatrains.

Mitchiko Kuriyama was a budding poet. She gave voice to her religious sentiments via her Quatrains. The poetry was simplistic. Four lines did not leave much room for beating around the bush.

Russ had memorized the Quatrains that Mitchiko had presented to him the week after he had said he would become a Buddhist. It was entitled: *Our Buddha Nature.*

I

It is good to be open minded
And look at both sides of important issues
That might have religious implications
Which could impact upon human nature.

In the beginning there was light
That in the Rig-Vedas
Was distinguished by the ancients
As being the opposite of darkness.

In between the light and darkness
Mortality became self-evident
As the consciousness
That lit up the cosmos.

Where did such an awareness come from?
When we contemplate upon
The singularity of this question
We become aware of our Buddha Nature.

One does not need to be a Buddhist
Or a Muslim, a Christian, or a Jew
To realize their Buddha Nature;
One only needs to be conscious.

II

Siddhartha Gautama was an Indian Prince
Born in Northern India of wealthy parents;
It took him almost a lifetime
To realize his Buddha Nature.

He became aware of the infinite and eternal
Altruism that leads away from pain
And human suffering
And yields only happiness.

He was filled with compassion
For those who were not aware
Of this self-evident truth
Realized as enlightenment.

After his passing
His disciples told the story of his life;
It was the story of a young man's search
For the ultimate answer.

Many have attempted to emulate his journey
But they are not he;
They are not Siddhartha Gautama
But they have the same Buddha Nature.

III

Jesus of Nazareth was born in a manger
On the outskirts of Bethlehem
Where, in those days, the unclean and unwed
Gave birth to the illegitimate.

All newborn babies
Illegitimate or not
Are incarnated with a Buddha Nature
Just like Siddhartha Gautama.

Every newborn child in the world
Is a mortal manifestation
Of a divine expression
That is inherent in every human being.

Jesus, like Siddhartha
Realized his Buddha Nature
And became a mortal manifestation
Of an enlightened being.

There is a deep yearning
Within the heart and soul
Of all sentient beings
To realize their true nature.

Siddhartha and Jesus are examples
Of the immortal freedom
That makes us all worthy
Of being called 'divine expressions'.

Ruskolnikov Kublinsky and Michiko Kuriyama got married in Steveston at the Buddhist Church. There is a wedding picture that still hangs in the White-Russian's office. In it there is this anemic looking giant standing amongst a bunch of pygmies wearing dark colored suits. That photo reminded Russ of the important insight he learned on his wedding day: *He too was a divine expression.*

In later years when he approached the Bench, he shuffled along in a monk-like meditative perambulation enshrouded in a flowing black robe that ironically, made him resemble a throwback to the Inquisition. He was both an imposing and formidable representative of the legal authority of the Crown.

Perhaps it was his karmic destiny to prosecute George Webster Brown. Perhaps it was just dumb luck. Few of Ruskolnikov's cases were of the variety that he considered 'open and shut'. This was one of those rare instances. He felt very confident – except for what he called the *loose cannon probability*: when there is a loose cannon aboard the deck of a swaying ship – who knows what to expect? From day one, he had a premonition that this would be a very special case.

And to make matters even more complicated, the attorney for the defense was that irascible old fart who seemed to get off on pro bono cases. Kublinky's record against his nemesis was not impressive. He had no bragging rights there. Nevertheless in this particular case it certainly appeared to be a slam-dunk, if ever there was such a thing in legal matters. George Webster Brown was apprehended with the smoking gun firmly clutched in his right hand! However one looked at it, it was a no-brainer. And yet, that crafty old fox, Brad Bradley, had accepted George as his client. What did he know? For sure, he wasn't that stupid – or was he?

Of course when it came to a trial by jury there were always the imponderables. Ruskolnikov often wondered in past cases which he had considered to be 'too close to call', whether his overbearing presence had turned the jury against him at the end.

He tenderly scratched the hairy mole on the left side of his face and attempted to force a pleasing smile upon his pallid countenance as he casually took his place at the table set up for the Crown's Prosecution.

"What Crown?" he often asked himself as he sat down gingerly and began removing papers from his black leather briefcase. Why, of course, the *British* Crown. Tradition had to be respected: stiff upper lip and all that stuff. Ruskolnikov Kublinsky had grown a stiff, wiry mustache under his nose somewhat like Hitler's. It made him look like a no-nonsense, hardnosed, humorless British military officer: the 'pip-pip' type. Yet strangely enough, his colleagues appreciated him for his ribald sense of army barracks humor – though he had never served in the Armed Services. In his own mind he felt that such off-color jokes made him more acceptable to the great unwashed; consequently he tediously punctuated his vernacular with all the clichés and homespun colloquialisms he could think of.

Ruskolnikov knew which side his bread was buttered on and who buttered it. He was a 'smart operator' as his peers noted. He played his cards close to his shiny bronze-colored vest with the outside watch-pocket from which dangled a golden chain that was attached to a gold-plated timepiece within. It had stopped ticking years ago, but he left it there for effect. Every once in a while when a witness became long-winded, he would take it out and pretend he was checking the time.

Over the years he had kept his nose clean and close to the political grindstone. His timing had been fortuitous as well as pragmatic. One does not get to be the Crown Prosecutor without proper connections. He was proud to represent the Crown's lofty sense of justice and fair play in the province of British Columbia, the westernmost part of the mighty Dominion of Canada.

In the case before him, it was his responsibility to make sure that justice was not only done, but was seen to be done. Public scrutiny of trials like this were important because they gave the people the feeling that there was a sense of integrity involved, that there was always hope for the so-called underdog. All the close relations, friends, and public supporters of Lenard Bruce Jr., would be there, and they would expect nothing short of a proper outcome: that in the end, justice had indeed prevailed. It was not an uncommon expectation held mostly by the idealistic and the romantic.

Ruskolnikov Kublinsky turned sideways in his chair to better survey the courtroom audience. All eyes detected the movement and came to rest upon the purveyor of the movement. It was only a moment frozen in time: a drop in the bucket. But Russ remembered it like it was forever: the hope-filled look on the faces of all of Lenny Bruce's friends and relatives, those expectant eyes. How could he fail them?

Ingrained within the gigantic White Russian was a deep-seated sense of proportion that harkened back to his childhood in Russia when he was a gangly boy of five, or was it six? Even at that age his parents dressed him like a little man: he wore a neat double-breasted wool coat and flannel trousers. Ruskolnikov Kublinsky stood out amongst the shabbily dressed proletariat.

People noticed him, and in a self-conscious manner, he became aware of the life-negating gleam of hopelessness reflected in the dark eyes that stared at him as he passed by. It happened on the occasions when he stoically trudged along behind his parents, down a dusty path that led to an opulent looking farmhouse – it seemed opulent at the time - where his uncle lived.

The eyes that noticed him belonged to the serfs, who in turn belonged to the land upon which they existed like parasites upon impoverished soil. They were dirty, poor, smelly and ignorant. That was their lot. They were born into it, matured, grew old, and died... without ever experiencing the luxury of a real bath.

There was something out of proportion there: a fundamental inequity between those who owned the land or had money – and those who had neither. Usury dictated the terms; inflation was built in; money begot more money. The ones with the land or money had something to look forward to with hope – while the unfortunate looked on with stark, empty, hopeless eyes.

In between lay a heartless disparity as desolate as the baleful eyes that noticed a gangly little child trudging stoically down a dusty road behind his parents. Unlike the little boy, the hapless peasants were not going anywhere: born to wither upon the parched earth and die ignominiously as if their lives were worthless.

It irked Ruskolnikov when the not-so-well-off lower socio-economic class in British Columbia scoffed at the impoverished street people and said, "They're just a bunch of lazy bums looking for a hand-out." The pecking order seemed to have no bottom in a country where everyone received a free public education. In such circumstances it seemed to be difficult, if not impossible, to experience the abject hopelessness of having 'nothing'.

Indeed, it was admirable when two or three rich individuals volunteered to sleep out on the streets in cozy sleeping bags for one night… to find out what it was like to experience poverty. Poverty to them just meant *the lack of money*. Sure, their pockets might have been empty, but they knew they had thousands in the bank. Still, they were trying to understand – but they were not serfs.

A serf has nothing. Nothing! No land, no money, no knowledge, and no education. A serf is illiterate. Where is the hope that springs eternal in the human breast?

"Most Canadians just do not get it!" Ruskolnikov Kublinsky exclaimed to himself. "They take their public education for granted. They complain about the teachers' salaries and the quality of the learning experience. If only they could look through the eyes of a serf standing on the side of the dirt road with no land, no money, no education… and no hope - then they might be better able to appreciate their many blessings."

Knowledge and information is food for the mind. It nourishes the soul with ideas. It gives meaning to the word 'hope'. That is the essence of what it means to be 'educated'. *Education* is what was lacking in the hollow eyes that gazed out sadly at the world; the divine spark that once resided in the eyes of the newborn baby had been reduced by grinding poverty… to a hopeless stare.

"The country with the most enlightened view toward public education will be the first to eliminate poverty from the midst of opulence," Ruskolnikov Kublinsky professed to himself as he reflected back. "If the trillions of dollars spent on armaments and weapons of mass destruction that fan the flames of continued economic inequity, intolerance, hatred, greed, and terrorism, were to be spent on providing food and schools for the poor and destitute… hope might then begin to sparkle in the smiling eyes of Mother Nature's children."

"What biased mentality prevents the opulent from sharing the bounty… and motivates the 'haves' in opulent capitalistic nations of the world to endeavor to make tax cuts for the rich permanent?" Kublinsky asked himself. It was the kind of self serving attitude that perpetuated the disparity.

It was appropriate that the Crown Prosecutor had, during the fledgling years of his youth, developed a profound awareness of proportion. It tempered his lofty notion of justice with a down-to-earth sense of fairness. Such a unique disposition enabled Russ to develop a soft spot in his heart for the underdog.

"We're representing the common man here," he had pointed out to Lana Bruce at their first meeting. "We need to make sure that justice prevails for the good of all Canadians."

"Lenny will be glad to hear that," Lana had replied as if her husband were still alive.

"Ah-hem!" the Crown Prosecutor coughed and broke the spell. He habitually rubbed the remnants of scar tissue remaining on his right thigh, evidence of a past juvenile misadventure, as if it were perpetually itchy. He turned to face the judge while exuding a confident and self-satisfied smile.

"All stand!"

The Crown Prosecutor stood at attention, all six foot seven inches of him - a beacon of reason, fairness, and justice.

* * *

It was a comforting feeling to know that the beacon of reason, fairness and justice was on her side. As far as Mrs. Lana Bruce was concerned, it was both a privilege and an honor to have a man like Ruskolnikov Kublinsky prosecute the case. He seemed like the sort of human being that Lenny would have approved of; he had a kindly demeanor and gave off a vibe that was not unpleasant.

But Lenny was not there. She was. It was up to her to help the Chief Prosecutor defend the integrity of the deceased. What about the deceased? What about the unfortunate victim, Lenard Bruce Jr.?

He became quite well known, in retrospect. Suddenly a 'nobody' of little public significance became the spark that strove to illuminate the dogmatic darkness that enveloped the four dimensional membrane of forces that existed in the modern capitalistic world as, 'reality'.

People became curious. They wanted to know who this quiet, humble but outspoken character from Steveston, British Columbia, Canada, was. *"Lenny the who…?"* they asked.

Lenny the Bruce was a beautiful person – but few who saw him would use the adjective 'beautiful'. He looked more like a nerd than anything else. What distinguished him from most of the other human beings was something that was invisible to the naked eye: *the level of his state of awareness.*

Lenny's state of awareness was influenced by a near-death-experience when he was just an infant. What is a near-death experience? It all depends… on who experiences the inexplicable, the mysterious, and the miraculous. It is relative to the individual who undergoes the experience.

In Lenny's case his near-death experience magically enhanced the interface between his biological brain and the infinite *mind…* giving him access to the paranormal. It wasn't anything that anyone could have anticipated. It just happened as if it was supposed to. It contributed to Lenard Bruce Jr. becoming the thinker with the unorthodox ideas that may have led to his untimely demise.

When one thinks of a 'thinker', most people imagine the robust image of the marble statue known as *The Thinker*. However in Lenny's case the image that came to mind was that of the world- famous Englishman, mathematician/cosmologist, Stephen Hawking, author of *A Brief History of Time*. Why?

Perhaps because they were both afflicted contemporaries who due to their afflictions, lived mainly in their heads? Whatever the case, there was no doubt that as far as Lenny was concerned, the comparison was flattering, to say the least.

What can be seen in a face? At a casual glance and with a name like Bruce, one imagined images like the Scottish Highlands, bagpipes, plaid kilts and haggis along with squinty eyes, a wrinkled forehead and flared nostrils. But there was more, much more. Lenard Bruce Jr. was no ordinary Canadian Scotsman.

His father, Lenard Bruce Sr., was descended from a long line of Scotsmen who could trace their Canadian identities back to the days of Sir John A. MacDonald. Yes, all the way back to the birthplace of Confederation: Prince Edward Island.

There was a Scotsman living there at the time who could honestly say he saw Sir John A. MacDonald with his own two eyes; in fact he saw all of the so-called Fathers of Confederation… and it was not in a picture. He worked on the boat that ferried them to and from the fabled island with the red soil, the place made famous by *Anne of Green Gables*. His surname was Bruce, as was his first name; but his wife's maiden name was Arsenault and she was a French-speaking Acadian. Lenard Jr. inherited all these wonderful genes from his father's side.

Lenard's mother's maiden name was Okuda. Her ancestors on her father's side could trace their descent all the way back to the hairy Ainus who resided on the northern island of Hokkaido, Japan. Her father took a wife who was a Métis - that is half Haida and half Caucasian, who had been born in the Queen Charlottes, now called Haida Gwaii. Yes, Lenny had some Aboriginal genes in this DNA.

Anyway, all that nit-picking aside, Lenard Bruce Jr. was a bona-fide *Canadian*.

A closer look into the genetic heritage reflected in Lenny's refined countenance spoke of a hybrid vigor that produced a brain of unequalled receptivity. It attracted the paranormal wisdom of generations of fellow human beings who had travelled down this mortal coil before him, and upon looking back, spied a kindred spirit following in their fading footsteps, valiantly attempting to stay in tune with the higher frequencies of their greater awareness. It was there, etched into the fabric of his existence and reflected in the ever-deepening twinkle in his eyes. As he grew older he became more and more conscious of his mortal predicament, and it made him feel slightly anxious to know that his time on earth was… limited.

* * *

There was a solid wooden bench adjacent to a wooden viewing platform that jutted out over Phoenix Pond. It was built there so that people could sit there and contemplate the serene beauty of the flora and fauna that surrounded the placid waters of the pond. White gulls sat in rows on the floating logs while blue herons stalked the shores looking for tasty morsels to eat. The light showered down in a cascade of muted pastels that brought to mind a hazy watercolor painted by a master. Across the pond a sturdy footbridge spanned the entrance where the waters ebbed into the estuary of the south arm of the Fraser River.

The setting was idyllic. Luscious green lawns and paved footpaths replaced old canneries that used to line the shoreline when B.C. Packers Ltd. used to own the fourteen-acre site. Now there were no roads, no automobiles zooming by, no buses, no police cars with sirens screaming, no fire trucks followed by ambulances, and no noise pollution – just people casually sauntering along carrying little white plastic bags following an assortment of big and little dogs on retractable leashes.

"It's a dog's life," Lenny often remarked to himself. He lived nearby in a small condo. At times it felt a little small and claustrophobic. It helped to venture outdoors and make use of the many benches spotted here and there along the manicured pathways.

Lana was proud of their new address in Richmond, B.C. They lived in an area that once comprised the historic old fishing village of Steveston, where in 1941 all the citizens of Japanese ancestry were rounded up like cattle and temporarily housed in cattle stalls at the Exhibition grounds while awaiting either deportation or relocation to internment camps scattered throughout the country.

Ever heard of Otokichi and Asayo Murakami? They used to live in house No. 40 alongside the boathouse and little flower garden... up-rooted like enemy aliens and shipped off to an internment camp. Everything they owned was confiscated and auctioned off to pay for the internment. In those days this was known as poetic justice. Lenard read all about it shortly after he retired as a custodian with the School District, in a book entitled: *Once a Proud Canadian* that he got out of the Steveston public library down on Moncton Street beside the park. It provided him with the background information that made living in Steveston a more poignant experience.

The sagging wooden walkways had been reconstructed and some of the derelict old buildings preserved as historical sites. On warm sunny days both Len and Lana liked to stroll along that reconstructed wooden walkway and pretend it was 1941. "It must have been tragic for those poor *Japs*, as they were called back then," Lenny had once commented, mindful of his own Japanese heritage from his mother's side.

"People were much more uh – uh bigoted in those days," Lana had replied. "The 'enemy aliens' were innocent Canadians... just like us. Most of them never returned. I guess in some remote way you represent them in spirit."

Lenny and Lana were sensitive to such things. The vibes impinged upon them like whispers from a not so distant past and made them feel sad and sympathetic. Whenever they walked down the boardwalk they felt as if they were following in the fading footsteps of little Oriental men, women and children who used to smile and admire the colorful flowers blooming in Asayo's tiny garden as they clomped by... *ghostly shadows fluttering in the wind like the gossamer wings of wounded angels.*

Lenny's parents had lived on Number Two Road near Williams. His father, Lenard Sr., was a school principal and his mother, Helen, was a stay-at-home housewife who operated the small vegetable farm that Lenny's father had acquired for a song, after it had been confiscated from the Tanaka's, who were uprooted and shipped off in a boxcar to an internment camp in New Denver. Very few people were willing to share such information – it was not something one was proud of.

There were many others like his father who had acquired farms and fishing boats for next to nothing. His father had explained to Lenny that immediately after the boat-auction, local rednecks who had spoken the loudest and made the most patriotic noise were seen driving their new gillnetters up and down the Fraser tooting the horn and waving the Union Jack. Lenny's father felt somewhat guilty for acquiring the farm in the manner in which he did. But that was the way it was in those days. *"No Japs from the Rockies to the Pacific"* some politician had mouthed, and the Prime Minister of the day, Mackenzie King, concurred by invoking the War Measures Act... and making it a reality.

"Unconscionable", Lenny's father had once sympathized. "This house was built by one of those *enemy aliens.*"

"We owe them a debt of gratitude," his mother had chimed in pointing out the obvious. "Be cognizant of your heritage. You are a

Canadian. We all are proud Canadians. We cannot change the past – but we can help build a better future."

His mother had an indelible influence on him from the earliest days. She had this attitude that reflected the Golden Rule; she in fact seemed to personify the Golden Rule. To Lenny, his mother was golden. Some of that gold must have rubbed off on him.

"My God, he's beautiful!" Helen exclaimed when the young doctor placed Lenard Jr. in her motherly arms.

Lenard's father strode into the room. "What a handsome baby boy," he proudly announced.

It was an auspicious beginning. Lenard Bruce Junior came into existence as a mortal being incapable of performing one of the most basic of life-sustaining functions: photosynthesis.

Without this ability he was forced to rely upon the generosity of other mortal life forms. He needed to learn how to care for those other life forms upon which he was totally dependent. Why had he been placed in such a situation?

Lenard Jr. peered out blindly into a four-dimensional reality membrane of forces into which he had just been born. He had no idea that he was a *parasite*. Indeed, he was as ignorant as any newborn babe! No court of law could convict him of all the heinous crimes committed against Mother Nature by all the hoards of greedy parasites that had preceded him down the Great Chain of Being. He was innocent.

Had he been incarnated here to become more aware, and to learn an essential lesson that would embellish his karmic destiny? Was there purpose and meaning in being a parasite? Perhaps it was not a *sin* or a punishment – rather, it was a divine opportunity!

And so when his mother smiled demurely and asked her proud husband who he thought the baby resembled, she was pleasantly surprised when he paused thoughtfully and said: "He kind-a looks like a… a baby Buddha.*"

* * *

The baby Buddha nearly died two short months after his parents brought him home from the hospital. No one could have foreseen it. No one was to blame. It just happened as if – as if it was supposed to. Baby

Lenny was asleep in his crib with just his white flannel blanket over him. A night light was left on in the hall. His exhausted mother had gone to bed, while his father was watching the Toronto Maple Leafs lose to the Montreal Canadiens on their new Admiral twenty-three inch stereo television set.

There was a loose safety pin that had accidently fallen off one of his cloth diapers; it lay embedded in the folds of his white flannel blanket. It was unlatched. Lenny's baby fingers clutched the blanket and pulled it left to right across his chest. The loose pin fell onto the mattress beside his left arm. After the Leafs finally scored to make the score three to one, Lenny's right hand reached out and grasped the safety pin that was no longer safe. A minute later the Leafs scored again! Lenard Sr. could hardly contain himself. Baby Lenny's mother was snoring.

Lenny put the pin in his mouth. He swallowed. The pin stuck in his throat. He coughed. It was a feeble cough. Blood began to ooze from the left side of his mouth. He cried as loud as a baby could with a pin stuck in his throat. He coughed and coughed. The more he coughed, the more the blood gushed out. The white blanket turned pink with crimson patches. The Leafs pulled their goalie.

Chaos ensued. No one scored. The Leafs lost. Lenny's father climbed upstairs despondently to check on the little guy. He peered into the crib. He nearly passed out. "Helen!!!" The scream shattered the silence.

Helen was there in a panic. How much blood is there in a nine and a half pound baby? The white flannel blanket was soaked through. Time was of the essence.

The baby! The carrying-basket! The car! Out the door! The busy road! The traffic lights! The Emergency ward! Hurry, hurry, hurry! Lenny arrived comatose. He wasn't breathing. Was his heart still beating? Was there blood enough?

"He needs a transfusion now!" the Doctor ordered.

Lenard Sr. rolled up both sleeves. The rubber transmission tubes swelled.

The stuck safety pin was removed with the deft use of surgical tweezers. Massive doses of vitamin K were injected to cause the blood to clot. The Doctor looked up to the ceiling for no reason. Lenny's father was white as a sheet. Baby Lenny's life hung in the balance.

Helen prayed with all her might. *"Please dear God... God of all Gods... please, please provide a breath of life for this little baby and- and I will gladly forfeit ten years of my adult life."*

Was it enough?

There was an eternity of silence. The Doctor despondently whispered, "I've done everything I can."

Three mortal beings looked down upon a pale little baby with his eyes closed as if in sleep - or in death. Is there a difference? Of course there is a difference. The difference was the *cosmological constant*: the singularity was filled with light, all the light of the universe. It only looked dark from the outside.

Lenny saw the inside... he was conscious of the light. Space vanished into time. Infinity into Eternity. Immortality loomed...

He opened his eyes.

His parents wept.

And so Lenny the Bruce came back into the world of the living, the benefactor of having had a near death experience. It provided him with a unique outlook on things. He knew things very few others knew. He vaguely recalled memories others had long forgotten. The brain specialist said there might be some small vestiges of brain damage due to a momentary lack of oxygen to the brain, but all in all he seemed normal enough.

As he grew older Lenny developed a heightened degree of extrasensory perception: his biological brain was attuned to his cosmological mind. He was one of a kind - a unique person who seemed to be normal most of the time.

He grew up on the fringes of society where such individuals find solace... solace in being left alone. But being left alone brings loneliness. And loneliness provides the lonely with time - time to think and meditate upon what-is.

As a youth Lenard walked alone to school. And he walked home from school alone. After school and on weekends he liked to go fishing in the Fraser River that meandered along about a mile south of his home. He talked to the fish he never caught. He felt sorry for the ones he caught and took home for supper. He developed idiosyncrasies that caused some people to think that he could be slightly backward – but he wasn't.

Some kids thought it was cool to make fun of Len. But Lenny developed thick skin, and what fun is it to tease a person with thick skin? You might as well be talking to a watermelon. So they mostly let Len be – except on Halloween when they plastered him with eggs. They tried their best to make him cry – but he remained stoic. He never retaliated. He just hunched up his shoulders and skulked off into the bushes that grew next to the baseball field. Eventually a few more sensitive kids began to feel sorry for him because Lenny's father was the principal of the school they attended. They even came around to where he lived and said they were sorry they had picked on him. That made Len feel really good. He smiled. There were some kind people out there.

He made it through his primary years. He wasn't stupid when it came to academics. He was actually quite smart. He demonstrated what some folks refer to as paranormal insights. He just knew things that others classified as being beyond the pale. Most did not even know what paranormal meant but they pretended they did when they said, "Lenny's just being his paranormal self." Anyway, who cared?

At the request of his fourth grade teacher, and with his parents' consent, Lenny underwent a battery of psychological assessments. It was like shifting through mounds of gravel looking for some tiny specks of gold. The results were as baffling as Lenny himself. "Some savant-like tendencies," the lady with the puffy pink dress and hairy legs suggested, "may account for his outbursts of brilliance." "Actually, he is quite bright for his age," the pipe smoking counselor with grayish-brown Harris-tweed sports-coat added thoughtfully. The classroom teacher wearing a purple gabardine skirt with matching jacket, who asserted herself as the spokesperson for the assessment team, concluded: "He has some minor idiosyncrasies for sure, but we think it best to just treat him as if he were normal." What a relief it was to his concerned parents to hear that word *normal.*

In Junior High school Lenny gained a bit of notoriety because he once predicted his father would win a raffle. The raffle was for a brand new bike with all the bells and whistles attached. It was displayed in front of the principal's office. "My dad will win it," Lenny had stated matter-of-factly to the vice-principal.

"You don't say?" the vice-principal responded, lifting an eyebrow.

"Just one of those things," Len shrugged, "It happens."

It happened. The vice-principal drew the winning ticket at the Christmas concert. When he drew the ticket, he paused. He could hardly believe his eyes. "Mr. uh – uh B-Bruce," he stammered.

The evening after his father won the bike, Lenny overheard his parents talking in hushed tones in the kitchen while washing the supper dishes together.

"Did you know that Lenny had predicted I would win the bike?"

"I would not be surprised if he did."

"Something astonishing must have happened to Lenny when he nearly died as a baby," his father had intoned.

"He always has had that halo-effect that gives him that shiny appearance. Remember when he was born? You called him a baby Buddha?"

"I think all babies are born as such. It wears off as they become older. They gradually forget their Buddha nature and become acculturated to the norm."

"Somehow it has not worn off; Lenny is still aware of his Buddha nature. To him it is natural," his dear mother surmised.

"He must feel out of synch with the reality that surrounds him. Sometimes I can feel his loneliness… his suffering."

"Remember as a young child when he used to just wander about the house like a phantom? He was so very quiet. He would just appear here and there. I'd say 'Where are you, Lenny?' And he'd say 'Right here.' And I would look down, and there he'd be looking up at me like a lonely little puppy with its tail wagging. I should have paid him more mind."

"You did your best, Helen. We did our best. I think Lenny knows. He knows you gave up ten years of your adult life so he could live. He knows I gave him my blood. He knows we love him more than we love ourselves. He knows we try to live by the golden rule."

That conversation stayed locked in Lenny's memory. It gave him solace when the world seemed mean and savage. It gave him a sense of purpose. He had been so lucky to be born to such loving parents. Most of the time he had just taken them for granted. They were always there, being concerned. They cared. They shared. They did their best. Lenny's parents were filled with loving-kindness. Somehow he had inherited those unselfish genes.

Those unselfish genes manifested themselves in Lenny Bruce Jr. as a tendency to remain aloof from the harsh reality of selfishness and greed. He floated about like some Socratic half-wit asking silly questions that brought annoying stares... implying: *What are you asking that for?* Like the water-boy on a team of professional mercenaries, Lenny was relegated to the sidelines. He stood on the sidelines like an interested bystander observing the passing parade, a quiet, shy, introspective little kid looking out at the world as if to say... *What am I doing here?*

Right up until he entered grade seven, he was a bystander most of the time. He had discovered that if he camouflaged himself as a half-wit with a silly grin reminiscent of a Charlie Chaplin mime, people gave him credit for being somebody. Humor was a very human expression of joy and happiness. People loved to laugh... at someone else. Thus Lenny the Bruce emerged like a butterfly from the shelter of his self-made cocoon into the harsh light of day... and attempted to flap his gossamer wings.

* * *

Lenny flapped his flimsy wings a lot when he was just a kid growing up in the Richmond, B.C. During his kid years some mighty big concepts began to coagulate in his maturing mind. He had a keen intellect and that gave him a leg-up on matters where physical size was not an important factor.

When he was a kid with an ever questioning mind, Sunday morning did not mean getting up at 9:30 am and getting ready to go to Sunday school. It meant lying in bed and reflecting on the notion of a supreme deity.

'God'. It was a novel concept.

Where did such an idea come from?

Did it came from his parents, his friends, the teachers, and the society he participated in as a member of the great Canadian cultural mosaic that was being manifested before his very eyes? Wherever it came from, for a short time it made somewhat of a 'believer' out of him. At the age of eleven going on twelve Lenard Bruce Junior had inculcated enough information to enable him to ask himself: *Who created all this?* It was a heady question for one so young.

It seemed natural in such an epoch to believe that the creator of 'all this' was an external force, a mysterious Creator with dictatorial authority over everything. To an intellectually curious kid with psychic abilities, the grand notion tweaked an interest in attending Sunday school... like many of his public school peers did.

So on May 8th at 9:00 am Lenny got up and put on the Sunday clothes his thoughtful parents had set out for him the night before when he had casually announced: "Would you mind if I went to Sunday school tomorrow?"

At the time his mother had looked at him kind of funny as if to say, "There he goes to join the flock". It wasn't really a *funny* look – it was a look of motherly concern that belied an inner apprehension.

So a youthful and exuberant Lenny Bruce went to Sunday school to find out about God Almighty. But he did not find out a whole lot about that mysterious force everyone talked about as if they knew what they were talking about when they said "God bless you," or "God damn you," or "God help me." They uttered the latter at times when they had committed some God-awful sin. Lenny was interested in finding out as much as he could about such a personal God.

Unfortunately no one knew much about such a God. They just talked about him as if he were real. *What if he wasn't really real? What if he was just a figment of the imagination?*

That question was rarely asked amongst the offspring of the great unwashed. But to Lenny the Bruce the question reverberated as if in a hollow space where it echoed around and around.

He must be real because millions of Canadians prayed to him as if he were real. He had to be real because he had a real family of sorts. Billions thought of him as a being their 'father'. "Our Father," they prayed, "Who art in heaven...." Indeed, it seemed he was a father, and he had a family of sorts.

In this family there was this surrogate mother called 'Mother Mary' who conceived without the necessity of sexual intercourse, sexual intercourse being one of the most disgusting sins anyone could participate in. Apparently God's sperm was implanted immaculately without Mary's or her betrothed Joseph's, knowledge or consent. To a prepubescent kid it seemed sort of like an alien abduction scenario where the abductee has no memory of the mysterious implantation.

Joseph must have been flabbergasted – but he never complained, not once. No one could come up with a reasonable explanation as to why all this hanky-panky was even necessary... to an all powerful, chauvinistic God-father.

Would not all this hanky-panky have made much more sense if God were... say... *homosexual*? And was loathe to have intercourse with Mary?

It was a horrendously blasphemous thought – but what if it was true? *What if God was indeed 'gay'? Would not 'celibacy' as a preferable status, then, make a whole lot more sense? Would not the 'gays', especially in the Roman Catholic Church, feel more empowered... as if they actually represented the chosen few?*

Anyway, the offspring of this 'immaculate' conception was a boy named Jesus. But, *what if the child had been a girl? What then?* Lenny's imagination went rogue. He had a vivid imagination along with the curiosity to inflame it.

In the Biblical version of events, God is imbued with the kind of chauvinistic prejudices that are particularly loathsome to women. Perhaps God was biased in his preference for a son... given his mistreatment of poor Eve, her being created as an afterthought from Adam's seventh rib and portrayed as a sensuous temptress tempting innocent Adam into committing the very first abominable 'sin': *disobedience.*

How so? The question reverberated within Lenny's precocious mind. Adam must have had 'free will'. FREE WILL. He chose *Freedom*! Freedom from the controlling, authoritative, vindictive, chauvinistic influence of a fearsome father figure who for no apparent reason righteously vented his wrath upon those who decided to exercise their freedom to choose. *Adam chose Eve.* To Lenny the kid, Adam was a hero – not a sinner.

Would a simple down to earth *caring-sharing father* in a fit of vindictive rage, have vengefully condemned and disowned his own son because his spouse had courageously dared to share the truth with him? *Yes, she had eaten of the tree of knowledge!* What was Adam supposed to do? Remain ignorant, and forsake his spouse?

Would a compassionate and caring Father have sent his children from the safety and comfort of their home out into the wilderness, and cursed them with a vile and despicable fallen nature? Was that how all fathers should treat their sons who venture forth with their helpmeets to seek a life of their own?

Thank God, that imaginary persona is not my real father! Lenny reflected at the time the matronly Sunday school teacher with the dark horn-rimmed glasses related the tragic story of Adam's tragic fall from grace.

"And now let us pray to God's only begotten Son," the Sunday school teacher intoned.

God's only son? The question rose like an impossible discrepancy into Lenny's inquisitive mind. "Why didn't God acknowledge Adam as being his first son?" he insightfully asked after cogitating on the relationship between Adam and Jesus.

The hefty woman with the thick ankles and long purple gown with white satin trim removed her horn-rimmed spectacles and glared at Lenny with a disapproving frown. "I don't know," she admitted.

"Was Jesus... Adam's step-brother?" Lenny followed up demonstrating his boundless curiosity. It was the kind of question an only child who wishes he had a brother... thinks of. The intention was honest and hopeful.

"Could you just listen and keep quiet like the others?"

"I think the others would like to know too," Lenny persisted. The others all nodded in agreement.

"Can't you just keep your mouth shut?" the perturbed Sunday school teacher demanded as if it was beyond her dignity to answer such a foolish question.

After that Lenny learned to sit quietly and keep his thoughts to himself. He reminded himself of that old adage: *It is better to keep one's mouth closed and be thought a fool, than to open one's mouth and remove all doubt.* Nevertheless his Sunday school days were not a complete waste of time. He learned that righteousness was very important to those who pretended to know the truth.

To a sensitive and perceptive child of eleven going on twelve the adult world of religious ideas was a fascinating theatre of the absurd. As a curious youth Lenny pictured himself as being something like Jesus was... when he questioned the priests at the synagogue and was chastised for his impudence. All he did was to ask: Why?

The adults who took religious matters seriously knew why... because they had access to the literal truth: it was written in the King James Version of the Holy Bible. It was the Word of God, they said, and there were millions of them... and only one of him. And they were very righteous. Besides, they had the power and the economic clout of all Western Christendom on their side - so who was he to be so impudent?

He was a curious young boy who due to a near-death experience could see beyond the façade. He could not bring himself to accept the Creed on blind faith just because the Sunday school teacher had said he would go to Hell if he didn't.

From the open-minded intellect of a prepubescent youth searching for the truth, it seemed odd that so many smart grown up folks like doctors, lawyers, professors, presidents and prime ministers ... could be so gullible! But they were.

On the Sunday after he had dropped out of Sunday school, a concerned young boy lay in bed contemplating his blasphemous fate. Surely he was hell-bound. Why?

Because on that last and fateful Sunday School class after he had confessed with all due humility that he just could not accept the Creed on blind faith, he had politely asked the members of the class: "Do you really think that a compassionate and loving God would send me straight to-to... Hell?"

Before the sympathetic class could respond to Lenny's question, the unbelievable happened! The Sunday school teacher, in righteous indignation had involuntarily farted out loud, turning her face beet-red with embarrassment. She quickly reacted by demonstrating her most foul disdain for such an unspeakable utterance. "Get thee behind me!" she had demanded like the Protestant reformer of old, Martin Luther, as she turned her ample backside toward poor Lenny - who thought that the gist of his question was not all that offensive.

Only an inexperienced boy with the undaunted courage of a youthful seeker after truth would have dared to give voice to reason and logic in a place where doctrine and dogma ruled supreme.

"An utterly thoughtless, obnoxious and uncalled-for question," the Sunday school teacher had fumed on the occasion she paid a visit to the Bruce household accompanied by Reverend Edward Brighton. To the righteous, Lenny's behavior reflected the irresponsible attitude of an immature and ignorant little troublemaker.

"It was not only blasphemous, it was a sacrilege!" they informed his apologetic parents who made a twenty dollar donation to the Church on the spot. Of course little Lenny the Bruce felt deeply humiliated to the point of tears. He felt like an innocent little child who had been wrongfully sent to the Principal's office to get the strap.

It was the beginning of his soulful journey of self-discovery.

So it came to pass that the idea of 'God' began a gradual spiritual metamorphosis in Lenny's curious mind from being a personified extrinsic tyrant somewhere way out there – to being a spiritual essence, a compassionate presence that simply existed.

"God," an immature Lenard Bruce Jr. prayed on Sunday mornings when he lay curled up fetus style in bed feeling vulnerable, insecure, and uncertain of himself. "Why am I here... at this particular time, and in this specific space?"

And the answer came back in a flash as if sent telepathically by an old mentor who had predeceased him: *To do good.*

* * *

"How quickly we grow old," Lenny thought as he gazed at his aging countenance in the wall-sized mirror above the bathroom vanity. He splashed cold water on his face, toweled it dry, and sauntered out into the living room where his spouse was waiting for him on the sofa.

"You know, Lenny," Lana sighed as she got up from the micro-fiber sofa in the living room, "I'm going to make us a nice cup of green tea." She shuffled off into the kitchen area.

"That'd be nice," Lenny replied, sagging into the adjacent dark green leather rocker. "I'm so lucky that I have someone to commiserate with. If it weren't for you I'd have no one to talk to."

After Lana returned with two cups of green tea, which she set down on the coffee table, she got out her journal and began writing down ideas they had discussed during the night. "Got to get this stuff down before I forget it," she said.

She diligently kept notes on anything the least bit profound that her husband uttered. She developed the habit shortly after Len graduated from UBC with a BA in Philosophy, which enabled him to nail down a job as a custodian with the local School District.

"Nice of you to be so conscientious."

"The world needs to hear from you. What you're saying is vital to the formation of a new caring attitude that will enable us to share and harmonize with Nature."

"You are an eternal optimist."

"You're a gem, Lenny, a one of a kind. You can see the forest without having to cut down the trees."

"I often wonder why I know what I know, and see things the way I do. I wonder why it is so obvious to me… and so obscure to others."

"You're just a little more aware… not much, maybe one or two incarnations worth. I know it can be difficult. Throughout history people who are ahead of their time are resented and even scapegoated as heretics, witches, blasphemers, and false prophets. Some are killed: stoned, burnt at the stake, drawn and quartered, crucified, hung, shot and uh…" Lana ran out of examples.

"That is reassuring!" Lenny joked as he reached for his green tea and took a long swallow.

"Poor old Socrates had to drink hemlock."

"I wonder what hemlock tastes like?"

"Maybe it tastes like green tea. Hey, don't look so glum. I was only kidding. Humor is good medicine."

Len smiled. "Speaking of humor…ever heard of my namesake… Leonard Alfred Schneider?"

"Who?"

"Leonard Schneider, aka Lenny Bruce, the Jewish-American comedian… he's deceased now."

"You mean there was actually another Lenny Bruce?"

"Yeah, he was born in the state of New York on October 13th, 1925 and passed away on August 3rd, 1966 at the age of forty."

"Jesus was only thirty-three," Lana pointed out.

"I fail to see the relevance of that tidbit of information," Lenny muttered under his breath, "Anyway… at the age of seventeen he joined the US Navy and after serving in Europe was discharged three years later in 1945. He became one of the first American stand-up comedians to speak openly about social issues that were considered to be taboo or unacceptable. His outspoken views attracted a growing audience with open-minded, avant-garde attitudes - a development that the moral majority began to view with increasing alarm. In a scant two-year period, beginning in 1961, he was arrested no less than fifteen times – yet he refused to be censored. He just liked to tell it as he saw it."

"Something like you, Len," Lana commented.

"After a performance at Carnegie Hall, Albert Goldman wrote in his liner notes…" Lenny disappeared into the bedroom and emerged carrying a creased piece of paper from which he read: *"His ideal was to… take the mike in his hand like a horn and blow, blow, blow everything that came into his head just as it came into his head with nothing censored, nothing translated, nothing mediated, until he was pure mind, pure head sending out brainwaves like radio waves into the heads of every man and woman seated… he would finally reach a point of clairvoyance where he was no longer a performer but rather a medium transmitting messages that came to him from out there."*

"Except for place and time, and the fact that you are not Jewish… he could have been talking about you!"

"A bit of a stretch there, I'd say. Unfortunately, by 1966, the year of his demise, he had been blacklisted by nearly every nightclub in the US of A."

"The home of the brave and the land of the free," Lana added satirically. "Did he have any children?"

"Yeah, like us, he had a daughter named Kitty… she could still be alive."

"No kidding? Some coincidence – eh?"

"Perhaps that is why I insisted that we call our daughter by the same name… who knows? Anyway, his wife was called Hot Honey Harlow. It's the alliteration on the 'h' that makes it work."

"I'll bet she was really something… especially if you change the 'honey' to 'horny'."

"Poor Leonard Alfred Schneider died of a drug overdose in the bathroom of his home. In the end, after all the jokes, the satire, the righteous condemnation and the public outcry… in the silence of the funeral home where last respects were paid… did anyone care?"

* * *

The little known fact that Lenny nearly died as a baby had far reaching repercussions in his later life. Near-death experiences are little understood and poorly explained primarily because they are considered to be paranormal. There is too much Judeo-Christian-Muslim misinformation. Who has seen the fabled pearly gates or a host of harp-playing angels? Who has met St. Peter, sat on the golden throne, and returned to verify such experiences?

Many survivors have described *an all-consuming brilliant white light, ultimate freedom, overwhelming compassion, a loving kindness... and an abiding altruism.* What did Lenny experience? Because his infant brain was uncontaminated by dogmas, prejudices, and biases, it was open to what some refer to as the "wisdom of the ages". Something happened to his infant mind and to thousands of genes that constituted his genetic makeup, something that made him slightly *more aware.*

Imagine a realm in which the most brilliant minds that ever existed were stoically sending out signals into an earthly Ethernet of psychosomatically flawed, short-circuited, non-receptive receivers. And then, out of the blue, to detect an open receiver! What excitement! What exhilaration! What joy to be able to share with the most needy... the collective wisdom of the ages!

As he grew older and wiser it gradually dawned upon Lenny that he was aware of ideas others found to be baffling or inconceivable. And like those from whom he received the information, he felt a compassionate need to share the wisdom that had been shared with him.

Sound improbable? But so is life itself. The life-story of Lenny the Bruce morphed into a complicated existential narrative filled with humor, irony, tragedy, murder, and mystery.

* * *

A *murder-mystery*, some called it - especially those fond of reading gruesome who-dunit novels. Such readers understand that there is very little humor in murder. It is not a laughing matter. It is a nasty business: to kill another human being in cold blood, to snuff out a precious life like one snuffs out a candle.

And then to be caught red-handed, manacled and pushed down into the back seat of a police car and driven off to jail without a *Get out of jail card* – this isn't Monopoly; this isn't a game.

Imagine standing before the judge in grey prison garb, immobile and silent while the jury hands over its verdict to the man wearing the black flowing robes of justice, and to look up with unseeing eyes to where god sits on his throne with his mighty gavel poised to ring down your eternal fate. How does it feel to stand there like a frozen zombie while your life ticks by second by second – and all you can do is wait?

Is it like a near-death-experience where you have arrived prematurely, your mortality fragmentizing all about you at the speed of light while you struggle valiantly to breathe your last breath? Is it a breath of immortality? Does it take forever? In that mortal moment what are you aware of? The beating of your telltale heart?

Of course your feeble heart still beats on and on as if – as if suddenly aware that it can beat on and on... as if it knows something that is innate within the primordial DNA of your genes. You were incarnated into that mortal moment for a purpose... just like everyone else. But you are not "everyone else": you are George Webster Brown.

What did the judge say? You see the gavel fall like a distant tree in a virgin forest. Did the tree make a sound? Yes, of course it must have made a sound – logic demands it – a loud crashing sound as it hits the ground. "Bang!" the sound ricochets about the courtroom. It shocks you into realizing the truth. *Lenny is the fallen tree.* His life is oozing into the ground... silently. And in your right hand you hold the axe, which has morphed into a German luger.

Below on the damp ground, crimson red blood spurts from the back of a shattered skull. Who is that man? His body quivers spastically and more blood oozes and oozes. Life silently ebbs onto the trampled soil and pools about your shiny black army-boot like an enormous footprint. You suddenly feel cold as ice and sick to the pit of your stomach. Your eyes blink. You see him in your mind's eye. A dying human being. A fellow mortal... *born to die.*

It is that mousey little fellow who calls himself "Lenny the Bruce". You know him well. You have stalked him for months. For months! It seems you have done little else. You were delusional, obsessed, paranoid, driven. *Driven*, that's the word.

Somehow your right index finger had twitched... involuntarily?

A black hole! Nothing.

Beads of cold sweat form on your forehead. You begin to shake and shiver. You vomit on Lenny's head. The big guy with the black Stetson mouths some expletives and does his patriotic duty: he makes a citizen's arrest.

The police arrive on the scene. Handcuffs are applied. Your rights are read. Your head is pushed down forcefully as you are shoved into the back seat of the police cruiser. You crumple into the back seat behind the screen. Sirens wail. You close your eyes. You try to pray.

The police car arrives at the police station. You are led up a flight of steps to the booking office. Name? Address? Spouse? Next of kin? Your pockets are emptied, wallet taken, and shoe laces and leather belt extracted. Fingerprints recorded. You are allowed a phone call. You call your spouse and tell her to contact a lawyer. You are led to your cell. The iron door squeaks open. You walk in. The heavy door clangs shut. *Clang*!

Everyone leaves. You sit down on a hard mattress. You hold your head in your hands. You are alone in the universe. It seems as if nobody cares. Nobody. And you gave up your freedom. Was it worth the sacrifice?

The next morning your wife arrives. Such a shrunken little woman. She cries and cries and cries. You tell her to go home. She leaves with her black coat wrapped about her hunched shoulders. She reminds you of one of those wizened old women doing penance in an old Spanish Cathedral.

Her name is Sarah Brown. She straightens up as she leaves the front door of the police station. She draws in a deep breath and stares up at the overcast sky. She shivers and pulls her coat tightly about her. She can hardly believe it. She shakes her head sadly and hurries along the barren sidewalk with a vacant expression masking her inner anxiety.

Only two days ago she and her husband had enjoyed a late evening supper out on the wharf. It was beautiful. They caught the last rays of the setting sun and the rising sliver of the cresting moon. George had ordered a litre of their favorite red wine. They toasted each other's good health. They dined on fish and chips. They went home and made love like any other normal retired couple of their age: George took Viagra or was it Cialis? It lasted almost four hours with no noticeable negative side effects. She smiled at the thought. It was nice.

And now what? Nothing. A black void. Death. Cold blood. Murder in the first degree. Saah sobbed all the way back to their modest two bedroom townhouse. She went directly into the master bedroom, removed all of her clothing, and with a sigh, crept into their queen-sized bed with pillow-top mattress. She dreamt of the dead man.

She had met Lenny and his wife once before at one of those open forums George insisted they attend. The master of ceremonies identified them as Lenny and Lana Bruce. "Such a humble couple," Sarah recalled. "Why would anyone want to hurt them?" She remembered that Lana had worn a navy blue skirt with a flowery pink silk top. She was very shy. She declined to go up on the stage when her husband did. She sat by herself in a seat on the far right, second row from the front.

Lenny gave a rather interesting speech, she thought, about the meaning of *Pi*. "Where does he get such knowledge?" Sarah wondered at the time. He seemed so much more refined than the righteous religious radicals who ranted and raved on the rightwing TV channels that her husband loved to watch.

Compared to Lenny, George appeared crude and ungainly like a throwback to the good old days when the righteous were right. When George was right, he was right; there was no middle ground.

Some evenings when there was nothing else to do, George liked to lie on the couch and listen to the radio with his eyes closed. He could relate to the voices of the most charismatic preachers who spoke of Jesus as if they personally knew him as their "Lord and Savior". He liked the way they claimed ownership: "My *personal* Lord and Savior". He liked that. It sounded so exclusive. It made him feel like repenting.

Sometimes after they returned home from Church he felt so penitent he'd get down on all fours and grovel and whine like a whipped dog. "Don't ever leave me," he'd whimpered, "I don't know what I would do without you... you're my angel of mercy... the only person who understands my sinful nature." She tried to understand, and to be sympathetic. It was very challenging and difficult. She did what she could. She was long-suffering to a fault.

"What if he were given a *second chance*? What if by some miracle of miracles George could change his attitudes and beliefs? Would that not change... everything?"

* * *

When Brad Bradley first met Sarah Brown in his posh office near Number three and Grandview, she seemed intimidated by the luxury. "Pro bono," he said, "that means my services are free." This seemed to relax her. She was such a shy, withered-looking little woman with a quivering child-like voice, that he immediately felt beholden to her. He felt as if he owed her a debt of gratitude... for being so contrite and humble. He stared at her for a long time with sympathetic eyes before he said "Please sit down," and pulled up a leather-covered armchair for her to sit on.

He distinctly remembered that visit because it had to do with the ascertainment of motive   or the possibility of establishing some contributory factors that could help make sense out of a seemingly meaningless, random and tragic act. At first the session dragged on monotonously until, as a singular event in the passing parade of the years spent in the armed services, Sarah casually mentioned the word *MKUltra*.

"MKUltra?" Brad eased upright in his chair.

"George was involved in a secret project by that name. We were living in Montreal at the time."

"What can you tell me about that specific period of time?"

"What do you want to know?"

A long and serious discussion ensued.

Sarah Brown proved to be far more knowledgeable about MKUltra than Brad could have anticipated. She used the code word MKUltra as if she knew precisely what she was talking about. She had spent years attempting to make sense of the conspiratorial theories and Machiavellian implications that abounded. There was something sinister about all the cloak and dagger secrecy that particular code word connoted that verged on the diabolical. It sent a chill up Brad's spine when Sarah whispered, "Sometimes I feel scared to death just talking about this."

What could have happened to George W. Brown at the Allan Memorial Institute in Montreal that years later would lead to the killing of an innocent Canadian citizen?

"Have you ever heard of the *Manchurian Candidate*?" he had inquired at the time. "Do you know what a post hypnotic suggestion is... or how long it might last?" He asked dozens of probing questions to which Sarah nodded and smiled and smiled and nodded.

Eventually Brad leaned forward and in a secretive tone of voice quietly inquired: "Do you think your husband could have been reduced to a-a so-called MC?"

Sarah shrugged and stared at him with eyes that opened up as if to say: '*Surely you must be kidding?*'

"There had to be some kind of triggering mechanism involved," Brad had conjectured out loud at the time. "A word, or phrase like-like..."

"How about a name?" Sarah had offered.

"Perhaps the name of some well-known past or present radical who represented an affront to-to... the status quo?"

* * *

What is the point?
Of existing day after day after day
In a meaningless and eternal void
Of nothingness
     As if there really is something
Mysterious that ultimately matters
In the seemingly mundane
Give and take of normal everyday
Social and sexual intercourse
In which billions of sentient beings
Instinctively participate
     Convinced
That if they continue to procreate the species
Incarnation after incarnation
Somehow reason and common sense
Will eventually reveal the answer.

- LB

CHAPTER THREE

MKUltra

Is there such a thing
As the greater good?

George usually lay snoring on the far side of the bed on those lonely nights when Sarah lay curled up fetus style beside him... dreaming of having a baby, a cuddly little baby of her very own. But try as they did in every conceivable position known to man or beast, Sarah remained barren. Barrenness is often seen as a state of being empty, destitute, and without worth as a fecund female human being of childbearing age. But the magic did not happen. The sperm were impotent; try as they did to penetrate the outer wall of the tiny ovum that had descended expectantly into the lower reaches of the fallopian tubes in hopes of being fertilized. Sorry, no luck... and no cigars.

No one tried harder than George to impregnate his wife. Most of his married army buddies had two or three kids, proof positive of their macho manhood. It proved they were not some kind of closet faggot in army drag. They were real men, the kind you could depend on to defend the homeland.

George practically exhausted himself trying and trying, every time he was on leave. It was a relief to get back to the barracks. But months and years past, and George began to suspect that his dutiful wife was incapable of being impregnated: a sterile, barren vessel only good for fornication, copulation, and sexual intercourse. He began to rag on her saying things like, "Perhaps you should see a Doctor?"

In his absence, she did. "There is nothing wrong with you," the Doctor said, "You are a healthy young woman fully capable of conceiving." He paused a moment and then suggested: "Perhaps you should ask your husband to come in?"

Sarah never disclosed this information to George. She just stoically accepted her lot in life as if it was her duty as a spouse. She pretended it was her fault when her husband shouted, "Come on woman... put your heart into it!" He couldn't see the silent tears that ebbed into the pillow... that stifled her sobs when she moaned.

When George was away serving his country, Sarah felt lonely and forgotten. She felt shut out from her husband's cloistered life in the armed forces. He did not like to discuss army business, as he called it. Even during the years when she endured his participation in the Montreal experiment, he remained aloof and noncommittal. She steadfastly supported her husband during the long years when she commuted every week from the rental unit subsidized by the army, to the Allan Memorial

Institute where he was a patient of sorts. In those days everything to do with his incarceration – it seemed like an incarceration – was so hush-hush and secretive. The army had sent George there for "treatments," was all she could find out from the local gossip group of army wives.

Actually George had volunteered. It was near the beginning of the in-between-years bridging 1960-63 when George was informed in strict confidence by his superiors, that the Armed Forces were collaborating with the US Central Intelligence Agency on a top-secret project headed by a Doctor Gottlieb.

The project was code named: *MKUltra*, a CIA cryptonym made up of the digraph MK, meaning the project was sponsored by the agency's "Technical Services Staff", followed by the word *ULTRA*, which had previously been used to designate the most secret/ultra-secret classification of post WWII intelligence. MKUltra was started on order of CIA Director Allen Dulles back in April of '53, supposedly in response to alleged, North Korean, Chinese, and Soviet uses of mind control substances on US prisoners of war in Korea.

Far-fetched as it may sound today, the wider implications included being able to manipulate and control human behavior. The ramifications of such experimentation were of interest to both public and private concerns.

The experiments were exported to Canada when the CIA recruited a Scottish psychiatrist named Doctor Donald Ewan Cameron, of Albany, New York. He was the author of the *Psychic Driving Concept*, which the CIA found particularly interesting because in it he described his theory on how madness could be corrected by erasing existing memories and rebuilding the psyche completely.

Potentially lethal experiments such as the kind required by Doctor Cameron, were illegal in the United States – but in Canada, at that time, they were deemed to be permissible by the powers that be. Obviously such experiments had to be labeled Top Secret.

Doctor Ewan Cameron was put in charge of the Canadian operation identified as MKUltra: Subproject 68. Subproject 68 was jointly funded by the CIA and the Canadian Government.

Doctor Ewan Cameron commuted to Montreal every week to work at the Allan Memorial Institute in conjunction with McGill University. He was paid around $69,000 per year from 1957 to 1964, to carry out

MKUltra experiments there. In Montreal Doctor Cameron could carry out *potentially lethal experiments*... the kind that could only be tried on non-US citizens... like patriotic army volunteer, George Webster Brown, Canadian.

George was proud to be of service to his country. He gladly signed all the documents waiving his rights without even reading them. *For your own protection*, he was informed. He felt honored to have been selected.

No one told George that one of the project's goals was to produce a truth drug for use during interrogating suspected Soviet spies during the Cold War, and in general to explore any other possibilities of mind control. The recruiters also forgot to inform George that the experiments often took on a sadistic bent. Project head Dr. Gottlieb of the CIA was said to torture victims by restraining them in straitjackets and locking them into sensory deprivation chambers while dosed with LSD... and to make tape recordings of the patient's most self-degrading statements and play them over and over through headphones.

George was not the only one to be hoodwinked into participating in such a clandestine endeavor on behalf of the CIA and the Canadian secret service. Other military personnel, government employees, members of the general public, aboriginal people, mental patients, and even prostitutes were recruited, and without their knowledge or personal consent, given LSD. It was all done in defense of a secretive ideology, *to protect our democratic right to freedom*, George was told.

George was proud to have played a small part in such a glorious undertaking. On the day he left for Montreal, escorted by army personnel in plain clothes, he felt uniquely blessed to be one of the chosen few.

Of course, as the old adage goes, all good things must come to an end. Project MKUltra was first brought to the public's attention in 1975 by the Church Committee of the US Congress. The resulting outcry resulted in a Gerald Ford Investigative Commission. However, two years prior to the investigation, Director Richard Helms had ordered that the most incriminating of the MKUltra records be destroyed - giving the general public the erroneous impression that the secretive program had been abolished and was no longer in operation. Destruction of the most incriminating of the MKUltra records was better than classification because it is permanent. Consequently it is now impossible to have a complete understanding of the more than one hundred and fifty individually funded research projects sponsored worldwide by MKUltra and related CIA programs. Speculation abounds that MKUltra is still in operation – only under another code name.

A young and gullible patriot eager to serve his country was there in Montreal in the early sixties, proof positive that such things do happen -and continue to happen - right under our noses, and all we, the great unwashed, can do is grin and bear it.

George grinned like a fool, Sarah thought. "Changed my whole life," was the only summary of that experience she could get out of him. She did not know he had been sworn to secrecy. "He must think he's still working for the CIA," Sarah had muttered to herself, "Doesn't he realize that that is an *American* outfit?" She did not understand that the CIA has very long tentacles that reach anonymously into very deep pockets that provide financial support, and direction.

Shortly after his discharge from the Army for 'mental instability', George, driven by his spouse's incessant nagging, took it upon himself for personal reasons relating to flashbacks as he described them, to look into the properties of the hallucinogenic chemical known popularly as LSD. What he discovered was yesterday's news.

He discovered that LSD was first synthesized by a Swiss chemist by the name of Albert Hoffmann on November 16th, 1938. At that time Hofmann was working for Sandoz laboratories, now known as Novartis, located in Basel, Switzerland. However it was not until five years later on April 16th, 1943 that the psychedelic properties of the drug were discovered. Lysergic Acid Diethylamide or LSD is considered to be an *entheogen* because it can catalyze intense spiritual-like experiences during which some users feel they have come into contact with an otherworldly or cosmic presence.

Knowing this made George feel a little better about what happened to him; it sort of put things into a more positive light. He was particularly gratified to discover that in 1962 one of his favorite movie actors, Cary Grant, had told *Time Magazine* that he had been taking LSD with his psychiatrist since 1958. Mr. Grant was so pleased with the results that he publically endorsed psychedelic therapy as a treatment, during a lecture to curious students at UCLA. "Cary Grant," George had enthused at the time, "imagine that!"

There were many properties about LSD that intrigued and fascinated George. It was a powerful hallucinogen; it took only a very small quantity to be effective; it was almost tasteless and odorless; it did not seem to have any physical side effects, and most importantly, it was not addicting. Its virtues had been eloquently extolled by a Harvard Professor named Dr. Timothy Leary. There were so many worse drugs like cigarettes and alcohol with far worse side effects… and yet the government banned LSD. George was baffled. The more he thought about it, the more frustrated he became. In his frustration he wrote a letter to the leader of the country he had so gallantly tried to serve: the Prime Minister.

"Dear Mr. Prime Minister" he began:

You should have banned cigarettes instead of LSD. Cigarettes are a proven carcinogen that causes cancer and death. Why spend millions on a war on drugs and then allow the legal sale of one of the worst killers of all time? Cigarettes have absolutely no – zero – positive benefits. They stink, and pollute, they taste awful, and cause all sorts of respiratory and other physical ailments. And they inflict huge costs to our medical system. Can you name one single health benefit the average citizen reaps from the smoking of cigarettes? From my point of view it is a no-brainer if there ever was one. Can you do something about this tragic oversight?

Sincerely,
George Webster Brown
Canadian citizen

Who would have thought that a person like George had a social conscience? There can be a lot more between the covers of some dog-eared and dilapidated old books… than one might expect.

* * *

Lenny Bruce used to smoke the odd cigarette now and then in his teenage years due to peer pressure, sheer macho vanity, and gullibility. It was all there in the marketing. It paid off in humungous profits for the tobacco industry. But that was before Len became aware that the harmful side effects far outweighed any possible benefits. He quit before he became thoroughly addicted. He had better things to do with the money he earned.

It also had a lot to do with his attitude toward his health and wellbeing. Sometimes he felt frail and vulnerable like a tiny flower attempting to grow amongst a tangle of oppressive weeds; it was suffocating. Cigarettes symbolized that sense of suffocation brought on by personal ignorance.

"Existence is such a wonderful thing: *ephemeral, and magical; a melding of Yin and Yang… it is a divine experience.*" he thought on the day he quit cold turkey. For some odd reason pertaining to his youth and inexperience that memory stayed with him long after he had given up smoking. Sometimes when he saw young teenagers hanging out just off school property attempting to look cool by puffing on white paper-covered cylinders of tobacco, it took him back, like a recurrent dream, to a cold dawn on June thirtieth.

The day before, he had inhaled deeply from a Lucky like a tough weather-beaten hombre in a B Western, before grinding the butt into the ground with the left heel of his leather boot. He visualized it in his mind's eye: *The Last Cigarette…* the opening title to a new saga marking the beginning of his manhood.

School was out and the summer holidays were just beginning. In the evening his father had insisted that they rise the next day at crow-piss, as he called it. That was the time just before the sun peeked over the eastern horizon and cast a thin line of white light between earth and sky.

They were up by then, just he and his dad hustling around in the kitchen with the lights on. His dad cooked bacon and eggs for breakfast. The smell never left him. He sat at the round kitchen table with his dad, hunched up over his plate feeling cold and sleepy. He was fifteen years old… no longer a child…an adolescent growing into a young man. He was nearly as tall as his father.

It was grey dawn when they packed the car, a black third-hand '46 Plymouth sedan. There was plenty of room in the back seat to fit three suitcases and the battered old acoustic guitar that he was just beginning to strum with some finesse. The engine started with nary a sputter. Lenny watched his father shift into low gear. The clutch engaged and the car lurched forward. He could hear the crunch of the wheels on the gravel as they left the yard. It stayed with him: the early rising, the dawn, and the quiet departure.

The mist was just rising off the fields as they made their way toward the Trans Canada Highway. There was hardly any traffic. The steady hum of the engine, the vibration of the wheels on the road, the sound of the wind rushing by provided an ambient cocoon within which two human beings sat stoically, moving along at sixty miles per hour. They were headed for Pincher Creek, Alberta.

It was about seven a.m. when they got to a little town called Hope. They stopped for gas at the Esso station. Both Lenny and his dad got out to use the washroom and stretch their legs. What remained with Lenny was the smell of the gasoline. For some reason he always liked that smell.

From Hope they headed east on Highway No. 3 through Princeton and other small villages that dotted the beautiful southern BC landscape. The highway twisted and turned through the Crowsnest Pass, past Coleman, Bellevue, and Blairmore toward Lundbreck and Cowley. It was a long trip, over twelve hours. But the days were long and the sun had not yet not even begun to set when they turned off No. 3 Highway at Pincher Station and drove three miles south toward their destination: Pincher Creek, Alberta, Canada.

They drove in slowly, down a winding hill and over a short bridge toward Main Street. At the intersection there was a gas station and drug store on the right, and Jackson's Hardware Store on the left. They turned right and drove west up Main Street, gawking at both sides as they crept along. They pulled over in front of the City Café and parked. "Hungry?" his dad asked.

"Starving," Lenny replied.

They got out of the car and pushed open the door to the café. There were several booths to the left and a paying counter to the right behind which sat a Chinese gentleman wearing a white jacket. Lenny selected an empty booth near the front window. They slid in on opposite sides of the table. A young Chinese waitress came by with menus and two glasses of water. She stood by patiently while they looked over the menu. "Special today is hot beef sandwich," she informed them.

"Sounds good to me," Lenny responded.

"I'll have the same," his father replied.

"Two hot roast beef sandwiches," the waitress reiterated as she wrote down the order.

"Say," Lenny's dad spoke up, "Is there a Japanese barber in town?"

"Yes there is."

"My wife's father used to know him. I thought I'd get my hair cut there before I left."

"There are actually two barbers in town. If you go up the street about half a block, you'll come to a T-intersection. The road to the left goes up over a hill toward Waterton Lakes National Park. On the corner is a two-story sandstone building housing the Royal Bank. Beside the bank is the barber shop you're looking for. You'll see the red and white barber's pole out front. Across the street is the other barbershop."

"Thanks, I'm sure we'll find it."

The roast beef sandwiches were delicious. They ordered apple pie for dessert, and coffee to keep them alert.

"Your aunt lives in a little bungalow somewhere close by," Lenny's father remarked as they left the café. "She gave me instructions over the phone," He extracted a crumpled piece of paper from the left pocket of his jacket. "Hmm, here it is... just a few blocks away."

They got back into the car and drove to Lenny's aunt's residence. It was four square and solid with a gabled roof over the front porch-entry. Faded white paint peeled off the horizontal siding and dark green asphalt shingles adorned the roof.

Long afterward Lenny recalled that old house with nostalgic twinges. After all, he had painted the whole thing. A fifteen year old remembers things like that. It was a poignant experience, made all the more poignant after they both got their hair cut the next day, and as they stood awkwardly in front of the barbershop his father extended his hand. After they shook hands, man-to-man, his Dad quietly said, "Do what you can to help her out – eh," and drove off.

"Do what you can... to help out." The words echoed in his mind like a stuck record.

It was the first time he'd ever been on his own. Just him and his matronly old aunt, alone in a little foothills town inhabited by about twelve hundred or so down to earth folks... where the wind blew and blew and the dust particles swept down Main Street with a ferocity unique to Southern Alberta.

There was an old CCM bicycle parked in the little lean-to shed behind the house. It was maroon in color with fenders over the front and back wheels. After he lubricated the moving parts, inflated the tires, and cleaned it up, it became Lenny's main mode of transportation for the summer. He rode it everywhere.

He was the new kid in a town where every new kid was a novelty. Because he had a bike he was asked by the owner of a magazine and candy shop if he wanted to deliver papers for the summer.

"Some of my boys are away on holidays," he explained, "I could use someone for about six weeks."

Lenny accepted the job. It gave him extra pocket money and a legitimate reason to ride his bike all over town.

One of the local residents that Lenny encountered while delivering his papers was an old gentleman named Andy Foot. He had a long scraggly white beard, weather-beaten face, and glistening dark eyes. He was the one who informed Lenny about how Pincher Creek got its whimsical name.

According to Andy in 1868 a group of prospectors lost an instrument called a pincer, used to trim the feet of horses, in the small creek at this particular location in Southern Alberta. Six years later, in 1874, the North West Mounted Police arrived in Southern Alberta, and miracle of miracles, one of the Mounties discovered the rusting pincer in the Creek. The Mounties named the area Pincher Creek. In 1906 when Andy was just a kid, the little foothills community was incorporated as a town.

Andy's claim to fame was that he had actually worked on the magnificent Prince of Wales Hotel in Waterton Lakes National Park just thirty miles south of town. He told Lenny, "Be sure you go up there to see it before you leave."

The following Saturday Lenny hitched-hiked to Waterton to see the edifice that Andy had worked on. "Impressive!" he said to himself when he first set foot inside the grand lobby. The grand vista of the upper Waterton lakes that connected Waterton to Glacier National Park in the US spread out before him like a mirage. He gazed up at the towering log beams overhead… and imagined Andy dangling by skimpy ropes attempting to secure them in place.

The hotel was built by the American Great Northern Railway to attract thirsty American tourists and encourage them to venture north of the border during the prohibition era. It was named after the Prince of

Wales who later became King Edward VIII. The Architect was Louis W. Hill. It opened to the public on July 25th, 1927.

"What a treasure," Lenny said to himself as he wandered around examining every detail as if he himself had had a hand in the construction. The hotel gave off an ambience that made him feel a sense of wonder and awe at what the combination of man's ingenuity and nature's magnificence could produce.

When one is fifteen and horny as the day is long, there is a tendency for the eye to be constantly on the lookout for comely females. It is a natural inclination. There is nothing sinful about it. As he rode his CCM about town Lenny became aware of many young girls about his own age. There were several, but one in particular caught his eye. The reason she caught his eye was that the first time he saw her she was wearing a form-fitting one-piece bathing suit. It was crimson red with a white logo above the left breast. He couldn't make out what the logo was. It looked something like a dove or a person diving. He found out later that it was a person diving.

At the west end of town, where the main street turned into a footpath that wound its way over a mile of meadowland to a rocky bend in the creek, the water swirled about into a deep pool. The local kids called the spot 'the Canyon'. On hot days some kids made their way up to the Canyon to swim and cool off. By bike it was about a fifteen minute ride.

The first time Lenny rode his bike up there, he didn't take his swimming suit. He just went up there to check it out. Being the new kid in town, he was mostly a loner. The path to the Canyon ended at the brow of a rounded knoll that descended down toward a flat rocky outcrop, beyond which swirled a rippling pool. On the other side of the creek was another outcrop that projected into the pool area and was used as a diving platform. When Lenny came over the knoll, she was poised on that outcrop preparing to dive into the water. She was wearing a red bathing suit. Even at that distance Lenny noticed the logo. He had good eyes. *She looked nice*, Lenny recalled years later. She was just there... and so was he.

The next time Lenny rode his bike to the Canyon he took his blue bathing suit. He fed the right handle bar through the leg holes and let the swimsuit dangle. On the way back it dried in that manner. He just left it there on his bike practically all summer... so he wouldn't forget it. Almost every hot day he went up to the Canyon to swim and cool off – but if the girl with the red bathing suit did not show up he always felt disappointed. One day he casually asked one of the other boys who was taking off his wet bathing suit in the boys changing area behind a bunch of bushes beside the creek, "Who is that girl wearing the red bathing suit?" That night he dreamed about her.

It was a strange surrealistic type dream. It felt as if it was not supposed to be happening – but it was. She was poised on that rocky outcrop preparing to dive. And then she vanished! He looked everywhere. She had disappeared. Suddenly he was on that rocky outcrop. He was diving into the water. He searched and searched. His breath grew short. He felt near to panic. Where was she? Where had she gone? He heard a desperate sound... like a call from afar: *"Help me!"*

He could hold his breath no longer. His head burst from the water. He saw the blue sky. He was free.

He drew in a deep breath of freedom... and when he exhaled he felt her suffering: *her suffocation!* Tears flooded down his face. He was overwhelmed with impotence, grief... and an abiding sense of melancholy.

"Drowned in the tears of grief and compassion," he thought just before he awoke.

The feeling stayed with him. It was persistent. Some days it filled him with anxiety. He felt helpless. What could he do? He went to the Canyon. He stood on that rocky outcrop. He visualized her submerged just beneath the surface. He dove in. He would save her if he could.

It was just a premonition... and the summer was long.

Years passed. Lenny aged. The girl in the pink swimsuit – or was it red? – faded into the background. There were many other attractive girls who turned his head. Adolescent whims turned into infatuations, and then back into whims. Time moved on relentlessly. And there was Lenard Bruce Jr. growing up like a dandelion amidst the weeds. He could have been mistaken for a flower. It could have been a laugh. He was here like all of us are here: maturing, aging, and growing older. Sometimes at the oddest times of day or night a submerged question emerged from the fringes of his subconscious: *What if I had gone back? What then?*

But he did not. He could have... Perhaps he should have... his life would have been so different. Sometimes he felt it as if... it was a crying matter that was synchronized from afar.

And here and there in quiet moments when no one was looking... Lenny looked. And there in the dark spaces of a swirling pool as ominous as the Milky Way galaxy, a teenager once heroically dived in... to save a kindred spirit. And in the time and space that intervened, sometimes there was a melancholic yearning that endured like a memory that refused to be forgotten.

* * *

It was camouflaged under a mundane grimace, but sometimes Lana saw it when Lenny did not know that she was lurking about. Sometimes Lana caught a glimpse of it and... and she was filled with such compassion and love that it overflowed from her like a silent spring. *Lenny was a quiet hero.*

It happened something like that on the day after Christmas in the year their only daughter left for university and they suffered the loneliness of the empty nest syndrome. Lenny was sitting on the couch watching the football game on TV. Lana decided to go out for a breath of fresh air.

The winter air was bracing. Lana breathed in deeply to expel the stale air in her lungs. She sauntered meditatively around Phoenix Pond and quietly returned home.

The television had been turned off. There was a silence in the room. And yet there was this ambience... like a musical interlude, as if the room had vibrated with a melancholic vibe as evanescent as a spiritual communion that defied space and time. She could feel the resonance: it felt like the *music of the spheres.*

There was Lenny staring out the front window. Beside him on the couch was a box of Kleenex. He had been crying. She just knew it. He turned and looked at her. There in the dark pools of his eyes she could see it. He had been weeping for every hopeless hope, for every devastated dream, for every unrequited love. It was there like the dark spaces between the stars: the awareness, the looming event horizon, the loneliness of the singularity.

She saw it there for an instant... before he smiled and said, "Oh, is that you Lana?" and got up and shuffled off into the bathroom like a decrepit old man. After that she could sense it from time to time in quiet moments when there was nothing to say. It just hung there like a premonition of things to come. It was just a feeling.

It was a feeling like no other that brought two disparate entities like Lana Lamb and Lenny Bruce together as man and wife. Their coming together was indeed a rather fortuitous event. It seems that some things just happen as if they are supposed to, like Lenny's near-death-experience. It helped to shape an individual with paranormal capabilities into a nerd in need of a sensitive, caring and open-minded spouse like Lana. There was real significance in that, more than most people realize.

People like Lenny know things others do not. They can tune-in to vibes others don't even know exist. They are like a sponge soaking up esoteric information that is often in contradiction to what passes for infallible religious dogma. Who can one share such insights with? Fortunately, Lana was a very good listener. She had an ability to tune-in her husband's vibes. She resonated with his vibrations. She knew Lenny was special.

Shortly after they retired, to help capture and preserve the verbal essence of the resonance shared, she bought a Sony tape recorder to insure she got the message right. In her spare time she diligently typed the information into a journal she called *Final Draft*. "Incredible!" she often thought as she typed. "What kind of a brain is capable of such ideas?"

The fledging roots of this symbiotic relationship between Lana and Lenny began in the last year of Junior High School. They were both in grade ten. He was fifteen. Lana scarcely knew Lenny existed. He was just that quiet kid who sat at the back of the third row, the one who always got the highest marks. However, from his rear view, Lenny could not help but notice Lana because of her refined eroticism. He couldn't help himself in those days. He was horny all the time. The *little head* kept asserting itself even during class time when the *big head* was pretending to be cool. Sometimes he dreamed about her.

On the other hand, Lana never once dreamed about Lenny. She dreamed about fun things like picnics and farm animals. She liked lambs because they reminded her of her surname and were so nice and cuddly. She also liked boys, but no one in particular. If anyone had asked her back then who Lenard was, she would have said, "Lenard who?"

The boys hovered around Lana with their *little heads* interfering with their rational judgment causing them to act goofy and outlandish. It seemed they all had a one-track mind – except for the quiet-spoken kid who sat at the back of the class and said practically nothing. He was unusually intelligent in spite of his appearance to the contrary. Perhaps that was why, out of an adventuresome sense of curiosity, Lana developed an interest in that slim, mousey-looking character.

He was always so self-conscious when she passed him in the hallway. "Hi there," Lana once acknowledged.

"Hi La-Lana," he stammered, as if in awe.

That was the beginning of the erosive impact that Lana had on his platonic attachment to the girl with the red bathing suit he had met in Pincher Creek. She was *there...* and Lana was *here*. Was it that simple?

Once they had actually conversed with each other, Lenny's relationship with Lana grew day by day. They just met at school and chatted whenever they had time to spare from school studies and athletic activities. Lenny was too insecure to ask her out for a date for fear of being rejected. That would have been devastating. So he contented himself by just hanging out with her at school and dreaming about her at night. By the time they reached high school and she began flirting with other good-looking boys, his anxiety grew so intense he frequently became depressed.

"Snap out of it," he admonished himself at such times, "Is being sad and depressed helping?"

Lenny discovered the power of meditation when he most needed it. It just came to him as if it were a natural reaction to stresses and strains out of his control. His parents had some books at home about the Buddha. He read them. They were very consoling and enlightening to a high school teenager in emotional distress. Lenny thought the Buddha was cool... nothing seemed to frazzle him.

"Why?" Lenny wondered when his little head, swollen with desire, asserted itself needlessly – when his bigger head struggled to put two and two together and attempted, through reason and logic, to produce a result worthy of both heads.

As he became older and wiser, and much more sophisticated in his thinking, Lenny began to understand that he existed as a mortal being in an infinite, eternal, and therefore immortal universe. Why was he not aware of the altruistic reality of such a miraculous state of being? Was he too enamored with his own sensate human desires, needs, and insecurities to appreciate the miracle represented by his own brute, undeniable existence?

"You idiot!" he once admonished himself, "You are so utterly selfish and self-serving you continue to sow the seeds of your own pain and suffering. You reap the whirlwind of your own ignorance. Smarten up!"

The high school years drifted by in spasmodic dribs and drabs of pseudo-memorable: *should'a-could'a-would'as*. If only one could relive those years! In retrospect the past always seems like a litany of missed opportunities. "Too late smart," Lenny often thought with a sense of regret.

The end of his public school education loomed nearer and nearer. Grade twelve was exciting, but also sad; there would be a parting of the ways.

Two months prior to graduation Lenny summoned up all his manly courage and asked Lana if she would like to attend the prom with the valedictorian. It was Saturday night. He phoned her. That made it easier. He was just a voice on the line… and so was she.

He recalled the moment. His heart was beating frantically. He was hyperventilating. Before dialing he put the phone down. He composed himself as if he were The Buddha. He dialed the number on the phone pad. The phone rang.

"Guess who?" he asked

"Uh – uh… say that again."

"Guess who?"

"Sort of sounds like –like you Len… is that you Lenny?"

"Yeah. They asked me if I would be valedictorian."

"Congratulations. I knew they would. Nobody else is nearly as smart as you."

"I – I was wondering if – if you would consider attending the prom with the – the valedictorian?" Len stammered nervously. He worded it that way so that it would seem as if someone of note, rather than an intellectual nerd was asking her.

"Hmm, well now, no one else has asked me… yet."

"Is that so?" Len queried as his hopes faded. There was an awkward silence on the phone.

"Tell you what… if no one else asks me by next Saturday I might go with you… okay?"

"What are you saying?" Len felt humiliated. Even nerds have feelings. He paused and waited for clarification.

Somehow the hurt was communicated. Lana suddenly felt very small and contrite. She visualized that shy smiling face withering into sadness. There was actually something quite endearing about him, some vibe that could not be repressed or hidden emanated from that smiling face. At that moment there was a movement in her heart… and a rest.

"On second thought," she replied, "Len, yes, I would be proud to be your date."

On the other end of the line there was stunned silence. A simple-minded nerd shed a tear of gratitude. "Thank you," he said with such deep-felt sincerity Lana remembered it for the rest of her life.

Lana wore a beautiful white satin dress with tiny pink roses around her neckline on graduation night. Lenard wore a neat charcoal-black suit with double lapel. They led the prom dance. Some snide onlookers commented: "Beauty and the beast." They were just jealous. Sometimes the nerd gets the girl. It is just the law of averages. Who knows when it could happen again? It happened then – that was all that mattered: Lenny and Lana, like two peas in a pod. It was wonderful.

Actually, in a world filled with the most bizarre occurrences, it really was nothing to write home about. In the entire Milky Way Galaxy did anyone else care? How about the entire universe? And yet just like the ever-evolving decimals of *pi*, they carried on as if it made sense… as if it really mattered.

Actually it mattered that so many decent, kind-hearted, and compassionate people living in Steveston during that epoch actually thought of themselves as being Christians. They loved Jesus. Consequently it mattered that Lenny had a rather unorthodox take on the biblical story concerning baby Jesus. He came to this understanding, in a manner of speaking, quite naturally, for one with paranormal inclinations.

From the moment he was incarnated into a predominantly Christian society, he had no option but to accommodate himself to the physical, psychological, social, and spiritual reality in which he was by accident of birth, simply born. It was as if he had been gifted with a miraculous freedom - in a land where the inhabitants did not feel themselves to be worthy of such.

He imagined that baby Jesus had been born into similar circumstances. He had been incarnated into a society where everyone around him believed they were innately flawed, and consequently behaved in a manner commensurate with such an identity. Unfortunately, the people with the greatest spiritual, moral, social, and political power, condoned, reinforced and perpetuated the delusion.

Baby Jesus was born just like all human babies are born: free. He was very precious to his mother Mary and father Joseph. They did not want their son to be tainted by the sins of their ancestors. His dear mother, socially ostracized in a 'manger' on the outskirts of Bethlehem where the *unclean* could give birth to the illegitimate, informed her precious son when he was old enough to understand that... his birth was a miracle: a divine gift from his *Heavenly Father*. "If she had not told him this - who else would have?" Lenny had conjectured.

What mother would want her precious son to be tainted for life as being an illegitimate child: *Joseph's bastard son*? Surely Mary had informed her son Jesus that he was pure and innocent – that he was not a sinner who needed to be saved. Indeed, in his early childhood years Jesus demonstrated the moral integrity required to remain aloof from the spiritual malaise that lingered over his kinfolk like a psychosomatic illness to which they seemed to have little or no immunity.

Those afflicted with the spiritual *sickness* were assembled in the Synagogue on Sundays to hear an edifying message of salvation. If one humbly accepted one's fate... with the blessings of the High Priests, one might be restored to health *in the hereafter*.

Miraculously, young Jesus remained free from the contamination all about him. He grew up to be a healthy, happy, curious child with a heightened state of awareness that enabled him to see - that although Moses had led the enslaved tribes of Israel to freedom – *they still were not free...* from the dogma that had enabled them to survive over four hundred years of ignominious slavery.

In his mind's eye, Lenny could see Jesus as a young boy listening intently to stories of how Moses so courageously led the tribes of Israel out of captivity. How he stood defiantly before the Red Sea with staff in hand commanding the waters to part. How the waters parted! And how he led the Hebrew people to freedom. Freedom!

Lenny could hear Jesus precociously asking the high priests: "So why does it feel as if we still are not free? Why have the offspring of the tribes of Israel not been able to shed the superstitious beliefs that in the past enabled them to persevere as slaves – but now, are not only debilitating but no longer relevant for a free people?" Lenny imagined Jesus as a young lad of twelve pestering the religious authorities with such questions, and being chided and reprimanded for his blasphemous attitude and heretical behavior.

Lenny felt stifled and suffocated just thinking of how Jesus must have been treated: *like an ignorant sinner who needed to be saved.* But Jesus was not a sinner! Nor was he ignorant! He was a free spirit, a divine expression of life. However, in the society in which he grew up as a boy, the people did not behave with the psychological exuberance of a 'free' people. Rather, they behaved as if they were still afflicted with a slave mentality that held them captive to an outmoded religious dogma.

In the chambers of his mind Lenny could hear Jesus questioning the high priests: "Why are we not yet spiritually free?" Imagine, a twelve-year-old boy challenging the authority of the religious hierarchy responsible for maintaining the status quo! Who did he think he was?

The outer world did not mesh with the karmic needs of such a free-spirited soul. Dissonance filled Jesus with an existential sensation akin to anxiety, angst and suffocation. His brain attempted to make sense of his predicament. Was he the only one who was so aware?

What could a young lad of twelve raised in such a life-negating environment do to shelter himself from an archaic concept of sin to which he could not relate? His loving parents spent long evenings worrying about what would become of their precious young son. They remembered the three Magi from the East and what they had offered.

A twelve-year-old boy left his homeland and disappeared. Where did he go? And what did he do? Lenny scoured the Holy Roman Bible. The Gospels are mute. Had all the historical evidence been deliberately destroyed at the Council of Nicaea? Why?

When he returned eighteen years later Jesus was thirty years old. What had he learned? Why did he return? He had not forgotten. He nostalgically recalled his childhood years. He remembered Moses. He had come back home to complete the mission that Moses had begun: *to free his people.*

Lenny found it easy to identify with the man who all his Christian associates referred to as 'the Christ'. But to Lenny he was Jesus, the *son of man*: a young man, who as a child was baptized in the Jewish faith and vociferously argued with the priests in the Synagogue. It was his mission to free his people from the archaic chains of a religious dogma that kept them subjugated to outmoded beliefs that kept them beholden to the High Priests. Jesus encouraged his Jewish peers to leave the stifling synagogue and follow him out into the sunshine and fresh air of a mountainside to drink wine and break bread. He had a powerful message that resonated with the suppressed and downtrodden of his era.

Follow me! Be like me: a free spirited soul, a divine expression free from sin. A free man!

It was a dangerous message. If the people followed this upstart heretic Jew – then would not the High Priests... become redundant?

It was a scary thought... to the High Priests.

Lenny admired the spirit of the young heretic Jew. He liked his courage in the face of a powerful religious establishment. He particularly related to the manner in which Jesus dared to share his ideas in social circumstances where he was a minority of one.

It was easy for Lenny Bruce to pretend that he too was a *free spirit*... that he was in tune with the person who called himself the *son of man*. Because, was he not also... a son of man? It was in this sense that Lenny and his spouse Lana accommodated themselves to the Judeo-Christian-Muslim hegemony in which they were ensconced.

* * *

Her name was Catherine Schneider - no relation to the Jewish-American comedian with the same surname who became famous as Lenny Bruce.

It was just a coincidence that she lived in the same area as Lenny and Lana Bruce. Cathy lived on the fourth floor. She owned a two bedroom and den, two bathroom, 1086 square foot luxury suite with a lovelyview out over the Fraser and the Pacific Ocean, all the way to the Gulf Islands.

People envied the view that Cathy got to admire from the comfort of her Italian leather swivel rocker with padded armrests that was positioned in front of her large living room window. The view was just there. All she had to do was look at it. "You can't eat a view," she once remarked to an envious neighbor from across the hall. She had a practical way of putting things in perspective.

Cathy had become a bit of a recluse in her later years, a bit of a hypochondriac in some ways. She began worrying excessively about the state of her soul ever since her husband, Bill, was killed in a freakish accident while riding his bike along Steveston Highway on the evening of June 7th at precisely 7:35 pm. He was making a left turn. His left arm was extended out horizontally to indicate he was turning left. The traffic light was green. He was hit and killed instantly by an ambulance on the way to an accident. The driver of the ambulance was very defensive, "How was I to know he was hard of hearing?" he lamented. "There should be a law prohibiting such hearing-impaired persons from riding bikes."

Fortunately Cathy's husband had the foresight to have purchased a very lucrative insurance policy in anticipation of such an accident. Some people are very perceptive. Cathy was the sole beneficiary. The settlement was just. It enabled Cathy to purchase the beautiful suite without batting an eye with regards to the ridiculous asking price. Out of respect for her deceased husband Cathy never spoke about the amount of the settlement. She had more than she needed. She anonymously donated some of the settlement to her husband Bill's favorite charities in hopes that it would bring him good karma. Although he had passed on, Bill was probably there in spirit.

Cathy believed in karma. It added another dimension of meaning to her lonely existence. Sometimes when she was admiring her million-dollar view, she would sigh and say, "Too bad Bill isn't here to see this."

Cathy met Lenny when he was sitting on the bench adjacent to Phoenix Pond and she was out walking her fluffy grey poodle on a retractable leash, with white plastic bags in hand. Fluffy, the poodle, always came over to sniff Lenny's left leg, which was crossed over his right. "Nice dog," he commented the first time it happened.

Cathy smiled as if the comment had been directed at her. Some people resemble their dogs. "Isn't he a dear?" she gushed.

Lenny reached down and patted the dog's head. "Good boy," he said.

"You live around here, don't you?" she asked. "I'm Cathy. What's your name?"

"Lenny Bruce, or Lenny the Bruce as some people call me, because of my strange sense of humour."

"You mean as in… Lenny Bruce, the Jewish-American comedian?"

"Yup."

"He and I share the same surname: Schneider!" Cathy exclaimed.

"You don't say?" Lenny responded in surprise.

"Yeah. What a coincidence, eh?"

"Well I'm glad to make your acquaintance… and believe it or not, my name actually is Lenny Bruce. I suppose we were destined to meet."

And so it began: two retirees sitting on a wooden bench shooting the proverbial shit with a dog sniffing Lenny's left leg. It was a hoot. That is how it started.

One day when Cathy joined him on the bench, Lenny noticed that she seemed a little depressed so he inquired, "Something getting you down?"

"I didn't win," she replied.

"What didn't you win?"

"The Lottery."

"Oh, what was it worth?"

"Eight point two million."

"Were you close?"

"I had two numbers."

"You buy many tickets?"

"Every Saturday I buy ten dollars worth."

"Hmm, that amounts to five hundred and twenty dollars a year. Nothing to worry about if you can afford it."

"I know, but it's always a downer when you don't win."

"Do you expect to win?"

"Of course. That is why I buy the tickets. Everyone who buys lottery tickets expects to win. It gives them hope."

"Every ticket is a potential winner, eh?"

"Something like that. Every Saturday I get a new surge of hope for only ten dollars."

"Is that enough?"

"Better than nothing. I started buying right after my husband passed on. He used to buy them. I guess I'm really buying them for him. Actually it is quite addicting, like gambling."

"Do you always play the same numbers?"

"I play, Bill, my husband's date of birth. He's always brought me luck. He was a Buddhist."

"And you?"

"I'm a Buddhist too. I became a Buddhist after I met my husband at UBC. We were both students there. He was an intellectual Buddhist; by that I mean that he read a lot of books on the subject, which he said made a great deal more sense than any other religion he could think of. He gave me a few books to read. I read them. And you know what?"

"What?"

"He was right."

"So you're a lottery- playing Buddhist?"

"Yup. Do you play?"

"I play once in a while when the pot becomes ridiculously large. I play my wife Lana's date of birth. She brings me luck. She's still above ground."

The lighthearted banter relieved Cathy's depression. "You know… gambling is a sin," she commented. "I used to teach Sunday school," she stated, suddenly changing the topic.

"You did?"

"I am of Jewish descent, but when I was young – before I became a Buddhist - I attended a Protestant Church. I was a staunch Christian."

"What was that like?"

Cathy paused to ponder the question. "At first I was very prim and proper - you might even say pious. I was the spitting image of what a devout church-going Christian soul is supposed to look like."

"But looks can be deceiving, eh?" Lenny prompted.

After a reflective silence Cathy thoughtfully replied: "We used to have these Sunday school comics. In one issue Eve was portrayed as this evil temptress who conned Adam into partaking of the forbidden fruit. The little girls in my class were being brainwashed with this extremely negative self concept."

"But weren't you brought up to accept this without question as being true?"

"Yes. I was groomed to be a trustworthy and dedicated Sunday school teacher. I was supposed to indoctrinate the children in my class with the doctrine of Original Sin. The ignominiousness of the situation did not occur to me until that moment, as I studied the wanton way Eve was portrayed: reaching over and handing Adam that apple after she had already bitten into it. Suddenly I was filled with revulsion! There was nothing divine about that story in Genesis. That stupid myth had absolutely nothing to do with me! I was not some after-thought helpmeet chauvinistically created from Adam's seventh rib. I was a natural born woman. I was innocent!" Cathy lamented, her voice breaking with emotion.

Lenny gazed at Cathy with empathy; her forlorn appearance compelled him to search within for consoling remarks. "According to Sigmund Freud, religion has tamed our innate instincts and created a sense of community around a shared set of dogmatic beliefs, exacting an enormous psychological cost by making the individual perpetually subordinate to a primal father figure."

The remark seemed too intellectual to be consoling. Cathy simply nodded and said, "I have read some of Freud's works."

Lenny could feel Cathy's sense of hurt and frustration, particularly with those who strove to perpetuate such a sense of degradation upon their fellow human beings. "I understand," he said gently, nodding his head. "I know a few people who have undergone similar epiphanies."

"You do?"

"Apparently it can be a very difficult as well as an exhilarating moment; the realization is so profound!"

"You know, sin is an internalized belief, as powerful as any psychosomatic illness. The sinner actually convinces herself that she is in some way flawed, and consequently subconsciously behaves as though that were true," Cathy explained.

"I can imagine the dissonance and the anxiety involved."

"You have no idea how freeing it is to be rid of such a self-imposed burden! Poof! It disappears like a bad dream. Once the realization hits, it is like turning on a thousand watt bulb in a darkened room…." Cathy's voice drifted off. She gazed upward as if seeking divine inspiration, and continued in a contrite tone. "I went to see the Pastor. He was married with two young children named Mary and Eve. They were both in my Sunday school class. I showed him the pamphlet, the one that contained the comic version of the Fall of Man. 'Do you condone this view of women?' I asked. Guess what he said?"

"It is only an archaic myth, so don't worry about it?" Lenny offered.

"'God condones it. Who are we to challenge the word of God?' He reached for his Bible and showed me the passage in Genesis where it was written. 'God has made you the way you are,' he said."

"What did you say?"

"I said, 'If God has made me the way I am… then He has created a woman who is an expression of His divinity – not some chauvinist's egotistical image of subservience and degradation.'"

"That took real courage," Lenny exclaimed.

"The pastor just shook his head and walked away. After that I quit teaching Sunday school. But, you know, the lure of the Church is very powerful in this culture. I still attend the odd service now and again when I feel the need for fellowship and community."

"The Church does play a significant role in that regard."

"There are a lot of good folks who attend Church on a regular basis. They find solace and communion there, especially in their later years. I must admit, there is a feeling there that is consoling. People tolerate the dogma in exchange for the social security."

"If only the dogma was more enlightened!"

"It is very difficult for a child brought up in our society to break out of the mould. Each of the three main religions is theoretically based on the word of God. It seems ironic, but the worst bickering seems to occur amongst these three related religions - in spite of the fact that their respective adherents all pray to the very same God," Cathy pointed out.

"Unfortunately, they seem to concentrate on their differences rather than their similarities. They have apparently forgotten that the Creation myth is simply about 'a movement… and a rest'. Sounds oxymoronically simple – eh? Nevertheless in all Eternity that is all there is: homeostasis, resulting from an eternal movement and an eternal rest. The meaning and significance of this movement and rest is relative to the Cosmological Constant as Einstein theorized, or in layman's terms: the beholder," Lenny elaborated.

"Sounds like you're quoting from some ancient Greek philosopher or some obscure eastern mystic."

"Actually, he was a seeker after truth," Lenny clarified.

"Who?"

"Jesus."

"Who?" Cathy repeated.

"Jesus of Nazareth. Jesus said it. It is actually written in the Bible. The Bishops back in 325 AD probably had no idea what he was alluding to. Otherwise it might have been culled out."

"I don't recall Jesus saying anything like that," Cathy skeptically replied.

"Check it out for yourself," Lenny advised.

"I will. He was that profound?"

"After Jesus returned from his long sojourn in another land, he returned to share his enlightened views with his fellow Jews… somewhat in the fashion that the enlightened fellow in Plato's Allegory of the Cave returns to the shadowy confines of the cave to share his knowledge of the real world of light."

"Good analogy," Cathy approved.

"Unfortunately, the residents of his homeland, like the residents of the Cave, were not ready to hear the truth. Jesus paid dearly for sharing his views with his countrymen who clung tenaciously to the cherished beliefs that in the past had provided them with the hope that sustained them when they were dehumanized as slaves in Egypt. He was, in his own way, trying to free them from an obsolete doctrine that kept them captive in the religious chains of a slave mentality," Lenny asserted.

"Too many of us still retain that same mentality!" Cathy lamented.

"Did I detect a hint of frustration there?"

"I suppose I'm still bitter about the place of women in Western Christendom. In such an environment it seems we will always be second-class sexual appendages created as an afterthought. Does anyone in Western Christendom really care?"

Of course Cathy knew that no self-respecting Jew, Christian, or Muslim would condone such blasphemous views, no matter how much common sense they actually made in the rational light of day. In the olden days people like her who espoused such ideas would most likely have been burnt alive at the stake as witches, or stoned to death… or worse. What could be worse?

The social snubbing, the condemnation, the snide remarks, the holier than thou glances, the relegation to Purgatory - perhaps they weren't worse but it was hard to take day after day after day. It was such a relief to be able to talk with someone like Lenny. He seemed to understand exactly what she was talking about.

* * *

It is happening and there is nothing you can do to stop it. You are standing erect with your unclad feet clinging desperately to the ground. You are toppled over like an uprooted tree. They are forcing you to lie down on a crudely hewn cross of rugged timbers. They stretch you out on the cross and spread your arms out like branches. Helpless.

Clunk! Your head snaps back. Your arms and feet are being held firm. You are vulnerable, totally at their mercy.

It is happening. It is not a dream. You cannot stop it. You cannot wish it away. You cannot deny it. It seems surreal – but it is real. You see the clear blue sky. You feel the rough-cut timbers. You hear the labored breathing. It is not yours. You cannot breathe.

It is happening…

A cup of cold water is splashed upon your face. The numbness fades. Your muscles quiver; your face twitches. What are they doing? Those determined creatures with mallets and spikes? What do they think they are doing!

That sound? Like nails being driven into wood. Through your hands! God forbid. Your feet! The mindless, merciless pain: unbearable. God let it pass. Let it pass!

It is passing…

The earth moves. The wooden cross is planted upright like a tree being rooted to the good earth. Your blood intermingles with the sap from the wood. It coagulates. There is silence. You look down. You see the faces! The sweaty expectant faces of the creatures glorifying in your pain and suffering. What have they become? Your kinsmen, your friends, the ones you came to free from an archaic sin! How can they do this… to a fellow human being?

You vaguely recall your prolonged sojourn in a foreign land. You arrived as a child. They welcomed you. You matured from a child into a man. It took eighteen wonderful years. You emerged from the cocoon of your Hebrew heritage out into the sunlight: a divine expression of hope. You spread your spiritual wings and took flight. It was like a dream. It was magic: you were free!

You had to return, like the enlightened soul in Plato's Allegory of the Cave, and share the good news. Was it not your duty... to go back down into the shadowy cave and share your enlightened views with those struggling vainly to see the light?

You are thirty and three. In between thirty and three you dared to share. You dared to descend back down into the shadowy realms of dogmatic religious beliefs. You made the ultimate sacrifice... for their sake you had dared... to return.

"Save yourself!"

You hear the pitiless sarcasm. The words pain you more than the nails.

"Save yourself!" The taunt rings out like a spear thrust to the heart.

Don't they understand? You are mortal. Just like them you will die – if they do not spare you. Had you not said: 'Treat thy neighbor as thyself'? Did they not understand what you meant? They stare up at you with expectant faces. What do they expect? A miracle?

They wait...

A vinegar-soaked sponge on a long stick is thrust up to your parched lips. It stings. The fumes sear through your nostrils and your eyes water. You blink away the tears. The clarity is instantaneous.

They were not ready!

It is not their fault. They cannot help themselves. Four hundred years of abject slavery cannot be erased as if it never happened. It happened. It is engraved upon their collective memory. It is who they are. It is their identity. They are only being true to themselves.

They could do no other. There is an irony there... an irony of historical proportions.

"Forgive them for they know not what they do." The words are spontaneous, the sentiment sincere. "Forgive them... for they know not what they do," you whisper to yourself, as your vision grows hazy.

Was it karma?

You had tried. You had encouraged them to emulate you, to free themselves from the outmoded dogmas of the past, to be free...just like you.

"Follow me," you said. "Treat thy neighbor as thyself," you patiently reiterated. "You are free spirits like me," you implored time and again. But they were not ready.... Will they ever be ready?

You stare down at the shiny faces of the rabble. What are they doing there? There is something disturbing submerged just below the surface, something irrational. You close your eyes.

Surely this cannot be happening. You must be dreaming...
The Roman spear ascends. It penetrates.
Mercy!

And now it is just a memory of another life in another time kept alive by the sadness, the guilt, the injustice, and the rabblement's personal sense of remorse. Instead of *following you* – they *worship you*!

* * *

"In God We Trust". There it was emblazoned on the filthy lucre as if to sanctify it. Did it? Lenny was baffled.

The motto first appeared on US coins in 1864 and on US paper currency in 1957. What was the mindset of those who passed a law in July 1956 in a Joint Resolution of the 84th Congress that declared *In God We Trust* must appear on US currency? What had God to do with money? Had money suddenly become deified by a simple act of the US Congress? In corporate America and in the global world of capitalism, was it now acceptable to worship at the altar of the Almighty Dollar?

The question was certainly thought-provoking. It motivated Lenny to register for an Adult Education course. It was an evening course called *Corporate America*, taught by a lecturer named Ms. Sandra Kuntz.

Ms. Kuntz was standing at the front of the classroom writing her name on the chalkboard when Lenny arrived. She wore a sensational one-piece red dress accentuated by matching three- inch heels to give her extra height. After writing her name she thoughtfully replaced the chalk on the ledge and began methodically pacing about the front of the classroom like a caged tiger: back and forth, back and forth. It was mesmerizing. "Her feet must be killing her," Lenny thought.

According to Ms. Kuntz it had taken nearly a millennia to reach the sophisticated state of affairs manifested as *Corporate America*: the birthplace of the most powerful corporations ever created by ingenuity, parasitic opportunism, and greed the planet ever had to contend with. By a twist of fate, these American corporations morphed into profit-seeking leviathans unlike any human creation that had ever existed before.

The amazing thing about these corporate leviathans, Sandra pointed out to Lenny's amazement, was that not only were they mandated by law to make a profit for the stock-holders, they had been able to assume all the rights and privileges accorded by the 14th Amendment to the once enslaved *Black Americans!* "Their existence as 'persons' is the stuff of legend and myth," Sandra declared.

After several minutes of pacing and pontificating about the relationship between money and corporations, she pounced: "American Corporations," she said, "are a fascinating entity, are they not?" She glowered at Lenny because he had the stupidity to sit in the front row. "You sir," she demanded, "What do you know about corporations as persons?"

Lenny sagged back in the desk he was sitting in. He felt intimidated and insecure. If he had been in grade three he probably would have wet his pants. But he wasn't in grade three; he was a senior citizen taking an Adult Education class in order to keep abreast of things. He summoned up his courage and spoke: "Why don't I take that as my homework assignment and report back next week?"

"That's the spirit!" she exclaimed, "Yes, why don't you do just that?" Sandra smiled at Len. "Class dismissed," she announced. "See you all back here next Thursday. "I'm looking forward to your report," she said encouragingly to Lenny as she picked up her tattered briefcase.

The following Thursday Lenny showed up at class with paper in hand. Sandra was happy to see him because she had been too busy to prepare a proper lesson for the occasion. She consumed about fifteen to twenty minutes wasting time with little-known anecdotes about Alan Greenspan and the Chicago school of economics. All this time Lenny sat waiting with his hands clasped together as if in meditation. He was composing himself. When Ms. Kuntz finally said, "And now we will hear what Mr. Bruce has to say about American Corporations as legal persons," Lenny was ready.

Lenny walked up to the front of the class and spread his papers out on the lectern that was available there. He looked over the class that was comprised of fifteen women and sixteen men. "Corporations are a man-made entity," he began. "By man-made, I mean they would not exist if man had not conjured them up out of his imagination and breathed life into them for his own purposes. Let me provide a comparison that might give you some idea of what I'm talking about. Consider Superman."

There was a smattering of amused laughter.

"Superman is a creation of the human imagination. He is not real. He is not a real person. Clark Kent as you know, is the mere mortal in plain clothes who pretends he is not Superman. Clark Kent represents the stockholders who own the corporation. Superman is the corporate persona, the powerful entity who makes Clark Kent into a 'somebody'. There is a symbiotic relationship: the one is the other in disguise. Is Superman a real person?"

The rhetorical question vibrated as if it needed an answer, until Lenny responded by saying: "Lawyers are needed; and lawyers as you know are ordinary people like you and me with a certificate conferred by other human beings to discuss matters pertaining to the laws of the land. How these corporations became entitled as *legal persons* is a fascinating story."

He paused to give the class time to consider his opening remarks. He certainly had caught their attention. Lenny glanced over toward Ms. Kuntz who was sitting on a side chair with her legs crossed, before continuing.

"Up until 1886 corporations in the USA were treated as companies with business interests that were subject to the laws of trade and commerce. They were organizations that were constituted to achieve specific objectives for which they were granted a charter by the government. The charter could be revoked after the objectives were achieved.

"The vestiges of such charters are exemplified here in Canada by the big six Charter Banks: The Royal Bank of Canada, The Bank of Nova Scotia, The Canadian Imperial Bank of Commerce, The Bank of Montreal, The Toronto Dominion Bank and the National Bank of Canada which operates mainly in Quebec. One of the main objectives of these six Charter Banks is to distribute the man-made money printed or minted by the Bank of Canada to the people of Canada. How does this work? The money is made available to the Charter Banks at the prime rate (set by the governor of the Bank of Canada), and in turn is loaned out by the Charter Banks at prime plus two or three per cent, or whatever the market will bear. Theoretically, this gives the Bank of Canada some ability to control inflation, by raising or lowering the prime rate."

This foray into the workings of Canadian Charter Banks prompted Sandra to remark. "Please try to stay focused on the topic at hand". Lenny nodded, and continued.

"In the United States an anomaly of sorts occurred in 1886 that transformed corporations into legal persons. It happened during a simple court case that took place at that time, called *Santa Clara County vs. Southern Pacific Railroad.*

"The County wanted the Railroad to pay taxes on land demarcated by a fence that ran along the right-of-way. Southern Pacific Railroad refused to pay the taxes. The case reached the Supreme Court. What was the Supreme Court's ruling?

"The decision was unanimous. Justice Harlan ruled that *the State of California (Santa Clara County) had illegally included the fences running beside the tracks in its assessment of the total value of the railroad's taxable property.* The conclusion?

"The County could not collect taxes from property that it was not entitled to collect taxes from in the first place. Make sense?" Lenny looked over the class. Many heads nodded.

Just to make sure they really did get it, he repeated himself: "The County of Santa Clara representing the State of California, could not collect taxes from property that it was not entitled to collect taxes from. Get it?" Many more heads nodded. "That should have been the end of the matter – but it was not. Why?"

The entire class looked up with bated breath, including Ms. Kuntz.

"The case becomes quite convoluted at this point so please bear with me. The decisions reached by the Supreme Court are dispensed to the legal community by way of books known as the *United States Reports.* Preceding every case entry is something called a headnote. What is a headnote? Pay close attention to this.

"A headnote is a short summary note in which the court reporter summarizes the opinions as well as delineates the main facts and arguments of the court. Such headnotes have been defined as *not the work of the court, but simply the work of the Reporter, giving his understanding of the decision prepared for the convenience of the profession* (United States vs. Detroit Timber Lumber Co., 1906).

"In the headnote regarding the case under discussion, Court Reporter, Bancroft Davies wrote: *The court does not wish to hear argument on the question whether the provision in the 14th Amendment to the Constitution, which forbids a State to deny any person within its jurisdiction the equal protection of the laws, applies to these corporations. We are all of the opinion that it does.*

Lenny paused dramatically as if he knew what he was doing. The class leaned forward in their desks. "Note the last sentence: '*We are all of the opinion that it does.*' That *opinion* presented future lawyers, politicians and learned judges with the opportunity to bend the law to serve pecuniary interests. To what Amendment of the Constitution was the Court Reporter Bancroft Davies referring? The famous *Fourteenth Amendment.*

"Previous to the 14th Amendment to the Constitution, Negro slaves were excluded from the rights and privileges accorded to persons born in the United States. The 14th Amendment provided all persons born in the USA with the rights and privileges of an American citizen. Slaves now became, for purposes of the law, persons, like everyone else living in the USA. Persons, as such, had equal rights and protection under the law.

"The Fourteenth Amendment had nothing whatsoever to do with the case under discussion, or with the Supreme Court's deliberation on the case - except that the Court Reporter, Bancroft Davies, a former president of Newburgh and New York Railway, mentioned it in the headnote. Why did he do this?"

"Why?" Ms. Kuntz queried on behalf of the class.

"This comment regarding the 14th Amendment could have been, or more properly, should have been omitted from the Headnote… because it had absolutely nothing to do with the case at hand! And furthermore it was only an opinion. But, for reasons inexplicable, it was not omitted. And based upon this insinuation, bolstered by the monetary interests of the people involved, and augmented by the persuasive arguments of the most influential lawyers… corporations in the United States inherited all the rights and privileges previously withheld from Black Americans!"

"What?" a man sitting in the second row expostulated.

"Let me repeat that for clarity. In the United States of America, all the rights and privileges previously withheld from Black Americans… were also accorded to American corporations."

"Incredible!" a gentleman wearing a padded grey vest exclaimed.

"And to add insult to injury, more legal expertise, money and court time has been spent to date defending the rights and privileges of Corporations - than of Black Americans!"

"Only in America!" a young man in blue denim exclaimed.

Lenny drew in a deep breath and stepped back from the lectern. Some members of the class looked upward and shook their heads as if in disbelief. "In this nefarious manner," Lenny concluded, "Corporations became legal persons in the United states of America with the same rights and protections under the law as any real citizen! In short Clark Kent went into a phone booth and took off his clothes. When he emerged he was no longer a puny, ordinary mortal - he had transformed himself into a super-man."

Lenny looked over toward Ms. Kuntz. She was smiling and holding two thumbs up. He wanted to end on a positive note so he wistfully added, "Corporations are not necessarily selfish, greedy, and amoral; after all they are beholden to the stock holders. And who are the stockowners? Probably many of them are kind, decent, church-going religious folks." Lenny paused and looked out over the class as if they represented the congregation and he was ministering unto the faithful. "Perhaps corporations could be more like Superman: *heroic.* The world is in dire need of such heroes. Super-corporations could be a real force for good, because unlike Superman – they are not imaginary entities - they are real, legal persons."

There was a polite smattering of applause from the class. Lenny had been hoping for a standing ovation. "Probably, some of them didn't quite get it," he rationalized as he gathered up his papers.

As he was about to exit the classroom Ms. Kuntz came over. She stood tall in her three-inch heels. Her form-fitting red dress looked alluring. She was smiling. She shook Len's hand enthusiastically. "Well done," she said. "You should have been a lawyer."

Lenny pulled back his shoulders. That was heady praise for one who had spent his productive years sweeping the floors of public schools... in search of wisdom.

* * *

Unbelievable
Some said in retrospect
When the honesty
Was surreptitiously removed
From between the lines
And replaced with opinions
Astutely interpreted

And seamlessly insinuated
Amongst the twisted intertwining spaces
As legal rights for persons
Wearing expensive suits
Pretending to be black slaves
In dire need of protection
From those entitled by the motto
In God We Trust.

                    - LB

CHAPTER FOUR

SECOND CHANCE

What makes the ignorant
So gullible?

It was true... obviously George had been given LSD at the Allan Memorial Institute in Montreal. Colloquially known as "The Allan," the prestigious institute is located on the slopes of Mount Royal adjacent to McGill University. George was in a group of seven. "The group of seven" they were called, something like the famous Canadian painters.

Why seven? So, there would never be a tie. Four out of seven was pretty convincing, as evidenced in the World Series and the Stanley Cup.

However, now that most of the evidence has supposedly been destroyed... it can only be surmised that it had something to do with brainwashing and the development of a truth serum.

Researchers eventually dismissed LSD as being too unpredictable as a truth serum. In Operation Midnight Climax for example, the CIA actually set up several brothels to provide a selection of men who normally would be reluctant during interrogation to talk about sexual matters, an opportunity to shed such inhibitions. The lucky fornicators were given LSD with the hope that the LSD would diminish their self-control, weaken their will power, and enable them to freely discuss their embarrassing experiences.

Unfortunately, the most marked effect was just the opposite of what the researchers were looking for. The subjects became more resolute in their convictions! They felt, with absolute and utter certainly, that they would be able to withstand any form of interrogation attempted... including physical torture. Some truth potion! Imagine administering LSD to enemy spies so they could become even more able to withstand any kind of conventional or unconventional interrogation, including physical torture! Little wonder the government banned the substance from public use. But in secret - was it being used for more sophisticated and diabolical brainwashing and mind-control techniques?

George was one of a few lucky Canadians who were able to enjoy many legal doses of LSD. Unfortunately the Group of Seven were not provided with prostitutes and observed through two-way mirrors. Instead they were interrogated like common spies. They were asked the most intimate questions that could be asked about their private sexual behavior. Of course George was too inhibited and embarrassed to share much information. They asked such questions as: "Did you ever perform cunnilingus?" George was unable to answer that question because he did not know what cunnilingus was. They thought he was lying or just being stubborn so they kept him on LSD for three days. He was later informed that a selection of volunteers had been kept on LSD for seventy-seven days straight. It wasn't a threat, they said, just a fact.

Actually George found his trips on acid to be rather transformative... especially his first trip. It actually changed his outlook on reality. Mind-set and setting had a great deal to do with the outcome - mind-set probably being the most important factor. One important factor that affected George's mindset was that he was disposed toward introversion. In his earlier days in the Army this disposition had led him to idle away his leisure time in the little library adjacent to the Army pastor's residence. The pastor, a gangly fellow with horned-rimmed glasses, befriended him. For a man of the cloth, he had a philosophical turn of mind that George felt rather refreshing. There was little talk of sin or other religious dogma. They talked mostly about the Old Testament and the thoughts of the ancient Greeks. After a month or so the pastor showed up one day with a thick volume entitled *A Brief Summary of Western Philosophy.*

"Here, you can take this book with you. Read that section on page 207 about the First Mover," he suggested. George took the book back to the barracks and with furrowed brow read that section twice over. *A First Mover?* The concept caught George's fancy. The logic seemed simple and straightforward. Of course there needed to be a 'first' mover. Wasn't it obvious?

In his own mind, George W Brown was a lot smarter than most folks gave him credit for. 'Sneaky-smart' some would say when condescending to give some credence to his intellect. He frequently found it irritating when others dismissed his opinions out-of-hand as if they were worthless.

In discussions with the other six members in his group, George ascertained that the depth and direction an acid trip took was contingent upon the tripper's psychological inclinations. Some just reported hallucinogenic trips like being able to see through walls, morph objects into various shapes and sizes, and float sublimely on fluffy clouds in the sky. George, on the other hand, had a much more profound experience.

Who knew what crazy ideas and notions were buried deep in his subconscious? *First Mover!* Unbelievable! Who could have known? That idea took George on a trip that no one could have ever foreseen. It just happened as if it was supposed to. It took him back and back and back.

He paced round and round and around beyond the Milky Way Galaxy, round and around… "And it just takes one more step…" he thought, "just one more step…."

On the occasion of their first clinically monitored experiments with LSD, each member of the Group of Seven was isolated in a small room. The room that George was isolated in was furnished with a couch along one wall, an easy chair in the corner, and a round table with two folding chairs to one side. The floor was covered with a nine by twelve brownish-grey rug.

George was standing in the middle of the room when a nurse dressed in a starched white uniform came in carrying a small tray. On it was a glass full of water, and beside it was something that looked like an aspirin that had been cut in half.

"Please sit down on the couch," the nurse directed.

George sat down feeling a little apprehensive. "Am I supposed to take that?" he asked, pointing to the white substance.

"Yes, wash it down with the water."

George did what he was told to do. "What did I just swallow?"

"Oh, nothing much. It will make you feel… ah – ah rather nice. Just give it a few minutes. You'll see."

George sagged back into the sofa cushions. "Nothing much yet," he thought and relaxed. Minutes past and he began to feel a bit light-headed. He stared with fascination at the tables and chairs across the room. Did the chair move? Yes it did! Amazing. The chairs moved. The table moved. Interesting. Profoundly fascinating. More minutes silently passed, unnoticed.

George stood up. He slowly began to pace about the room. The sunlight streamed in through the walls illuminating the room with a warm sunny glow. It reminded George of his old room in their old house on Number 3 Road when he was a kid… when the golden sun streamed in through the window at half past six in the morning. It felt just like that: quiet and pristine. The sun streamed in through the east wall as if it were transparent. Solidity became permeable as if it were just an illusion. There were no physical barriers between him and what was out there. It really wasn't out there; it was all… in here. "All in here," he thought when the nurse returned carrying another glass of water.

She had shrunk in size. She had morphed into a three-foot roly-poly dwarf wearing a white uniform. "Here, drink this," she demanded, "You need to keep yourself hydrated." Her voice invaded his space. "Drink some." He reached out with a robot arm and clutched the glass. "Drink some," the dwarf repeated.

He could not block out the sound. It intruded into his wondrous reality like an unwanted phantom. "Drink some!" He could see through walls, morph objects, feel the warmth of the sun – but he could not control the sound. "Please drink the water!" He drank. The added electrolyte was electrifying. He became oblivious to his physical environment; there was no such thing. Only awareness.

Like magic, he was way out there in the cosmos.

There were stars and dark spaces. He walked round and around the room, which was not a room – it was a space in the universe. Further and further he went in search of the ever-elusive "First Mover." One more step... just one more....

Round and round he went deeper and deeper into the abyss. It was cold in the dark spaces... cold and dark. And still his curiosity was undiminished... he needed to know. Undeterred, he plodded on placing one foot ahead of the other as if treading on an infinite treadmill into eternity. Where was the First Mover? He kept moving on and on and on... toward a consciousness so vast his awareness turned inward upon itself and he realized he had gone... *too far!*

The *singularity* was all that was left. The loneliness was absolute. There was no *other*. Just *me*. Just *myself*. Just *I*... alone in the universe. There was no going back. It was a singular moment in Eternity. He was the only one who knew. There was no going back to the mundane comfort of *not knowing*. He had arrived at the source of the eternal reality: *Here and Now.*

He was always in the Here and Now! It was as real and finite as consciousness, and as infinite and eternal as an ever-expanding universe of *awareness.*

"It is always *here and now*. Always!" The realization shattered his ideas of heaven and hell as being *somewhere else* - when it was all here, now. He was creating his own heaven or hell... here, now. It just took one more step. Just one more... one more... *step.*

George Webster Brown stopped. There was no need to take one more step... or a million, or a trillion. He stood as still as eternity: an infinitude of one. A singularity. One wholesome being... *Being.*

And then as if by magic he was back in the mundane comfort of a take-it-for granted phenomenological four dimensional space-time, standing in the center of a brownish-grey nine by twelve rug in a little room at the Allan Memorial Institute in Montreal, Quebec, Canada. He had been given a *second chance*!

Why?

Second Chance permeated everything. Everything. There was no denying it. He had gone beyond.... And now paradoxically, he had been given yet another! Another second chance... *to get it right.*

Gratitude flooded his consciousness with every beat of his heart. He was ever so thankful for every atom of reality, for everything he had previously taken for granted, for every little insignificant, mundane moment.

George crept gratefully toward the old easy chair in the corner and slowly sat down. He was crying. He could not stop. It felt so good to be back... so very, very good. The warm glow from a single naked incandescent light bulb dangling from a ceiling cord illuminated the room. It was a miracle.

He was in it. He basked in the glow. It was so real, so illuminating. Never had he so appreciated... *the light.* George sat as still as a mouse uncertain of its surroundings. His eyes surveyed the environment.

"Welcome back," the nurse said casually.

George looked up as if surprised to see the nurse sitting on the couch. She had regained her original stature. She was gazing at him like a mother looks at her wayward but only child: with loving-kindness. He felt at home. The familiarity was comforting – but her casualness was confusing. She had no idea how wonderful it was to be in the light. She just took it for granted as if – as if she were oblivious of the miracle.

George shook his head slowly. "It is so nice to be back," he said with heartfelt sincerity.

"You were way out there, George," the nurse said quietly. "You were out there for a long, long time."

It was reassuring to hear the sound of the nurse's voice. It was empirical evidence... that he was not alone. His senses perked up.

"Yeah, I know. I was way out there… way out there. I'm so-so glad to be back." He dried his tears with his right sleeve.

"Here," the nurse offered him some Kleenex.

He accepted, and blew his nose. "This is it!" he stated knowingly.

"What?"

"This! This is the *here and now!*" George shook his head as if astounded by his own illumination. "You can never go beyond… the *Here and Now*. There is nothing else - zero. This is it. That is why we are *here, now*. That is why it *exists*. That is why it *is*," He emphasized the 'is', "because it *is* everything!" George felt stymied by his inability to express himself adequately. He lapsed into an apprehensive silence, uncertain as to whether or not the nurse understood what he was attempting to convey. "Make sense?" he asked hopefully.

"Each to his own," the nurse commiserated.

"What do you mean?"

"The effect is unique to each individual. Most folks experience something much more mundane. The effect will eventually wear off… the ordinary reasserts itself."

"What wears off?"

"The hallucinatory effects of the LSD. You were given LSD… you know?

"So that is what that white substance was?"

"Yeah. There will be what we refer to as residual effects that could last for years," the nurse stated sympathetically. "What you experienced was what we call a window of illumination. The experience varies from person to person – but there is some commonality. There is this spiritual aspect that confounds scientific investigation… something like what you probably experienced. Such profound experiences can be sometimes hard to handle and could last a lifetime."

"A lifetime?" George parroted back in a daze.

"What is happening to you has something to do with the brain-mind interface or something like that; it is part of a secretive American project dealing with the psychodynamics of such relationships."

"You don't say?" George inquired shaking his head.

"The Director reports back to his boss in the USA. As far as I know some things that are being done here would be illegal down there."

"Illegal?" George responded with a baffled stare.

"That is why you had to sign all those papers. We're all sworn to secrecy. This is a top-secret operation. Didn't anyone tell you that?"

"I don't recall...."

The nurse shrugged indifferently, suddenly realizing that she was sharing information that was irrelevant to the outcome of the experiment, but could compromise her own security status. She looked George over with a critical eye, "You really flipped out," she commented.

"I'm so glad to be back," George repeated soberly.

"We were a little concerned for you when you stopped communicating. Who knows the limits of the mind – eh? For a while there we were afraid... we might have lost you. The Doctor became quite agitated. 'How much did you give him!' he demanded – as if it was my fault. We should have given you a much smaller dosage."

"Who is 'we'?"

"The CIA, I suppose... in conjunction with the Canadian component. It's all hush-hush. No one seems to know who is ultimately in charge. It has international, perhaps world-wide, ramifications."

"Really?" George shook his head in confusion.

"Here," the nurse handed George some pills.

"What are these?" George asked suspiciously.

"Just vitamin C. Take them." She picked up a glass of water from the round table and handed it to George.

George accepted the glass and the vitamin pills. He slouched back on the easy chair and tilted his head back. He inhaled deeply as if inhaling the universe... and exhaled in the here and now.

A mortal moment passed. George got up and moved over to the couch. He felt the fabric. It felt so nice and smooth, so familiar. The whole room felt so familiar and reassuring. He wanted to share his experience with the nurse. He wanted to say, "I went too far. I went beyond the pale. I can never return to what-is, or rather what-was."

He had gone beyond the shimmering membrane of forces that held the four dimensional space-time dimension together. He had seen right through it. It was nothing: just a membrane of forces vibrating as if it were really substantial. It had become manifest while he had vibrated within it - but he had gone beyond in search of the first mover.

He had moved… and the first mover had moved with him. It was all about relationships, the relationship of the singularity to the whole. How does one explain that to someone who has not been there?

"I was away out there," George repeated once again, "away out there."

"I know you were," the nurse commiserated as best she could. "I'm so glad you're back."

George felt like an alien who had no business being there. He stared at the nurse once again hoping to see a glimmer of real understanding. He peered into her blue-grey eyes, "Have you ever taken LSD?" he inquired.

"Yes, we nurses were encouraged to try it so we could understand our patients better. I've tried it a few times."

"And what did you experience?"

"It was nice," she replied guardedly as if wondering what to say. "I-I felt I was floating about on a fluffy pink cloud. It was real dreamy-like."

"Is that all?"

"Like I said, it was nice. Everyone has their own experience… it all depends…"

"On what?"

"On – on who they are."

George knew she would not be able to relate to what he had experienced, so he replied, "Sounds like you enjoyed it."

The nurse smiled.

How could she possibly understand how lucky she was to be so unaware. She could still accept all of this, and take it for granted. She belonged here. To her all this was… real. "God bless you," he said.

Something very weird happened as soon as he said that. The nurse got up and seemed to levitate about the room as if gravity had no effect upon her.

"After such knowledge – what forgiveness?" she pronounced as she levitated out the door. It seemed natural, as if she always had been levitating and he hadn't noticed. Had he underestimated her? Was she just pretending to be ordinary?

George got up and returned to his eight by ten room. He lay down on his cot and closed his eyes. He was alone in the universe of his mind. "Just me, myself, and I" he thought. He fell asleep.

The nurse looked in an hour later and whispered, "We'll try it again when your mental state stabilizes. Sweet dreams."

It was all part of the process. Brainwashing took a great deal of time, patience, and perseverance. The human brain was like a microcosm of the universe: it was always here, now.

In all eternity, who knows how long a moment is? The day George returned home on a permanent basis, his wife, Sarah, greeted him at the front door of their rented residence.

He had arrived in a taxi. His hair was disheveled and his khaki army-issue jacket was thrown over his left shoulder. He stood on the front step as if he wasn't sure what to do. He was skinny and haggard. He held out his right hand as if expecting someone to shake it.

"Welcome home, George," Sarah said, and hugged him.

He began to quiver and shake. It was the first time she saw him break down and cry silent tears of happiness. "Poor Georgie," she thought, "What have they done to you?"

* * *

Lenny's *near-death experience* impacted him in unexpected ways as he matured and grew older. It made him sensitive to incoming vibrations and dreams that seemed to pop up out of nowhere as if someone else was involved... as if someone else was dreaming too.

As Lenny grew older he continued to feel a connection with an experience that occurred when he was a teen-ager that seemed to validate Jung's theory of synchronicity. It began with his father saying, "I have an older sister who lives in Pincher Creek. She called the other night."

"The one who sends me money on my birthday?"

"Yeah, your aunt Ethel. Her husband recently passed away from a heart attack leaving her with a little house that badly needs painting and a garden that sorely needs tending. She has no children. She is feeling slightly overwhelmed, lonely, and downhearted. When she phoned yesterday, she sounded quite depressed."

"Why don't you visit her, Dad," Lenny suggested.

"Good idea. I think I will." It was mid June and the summer holidays were looming. "Would you like to come? We could leave as soon as school is out."

"Sure."

So it came to pass that in the early dawn as the sun broke over the eastern horizon, they drove to a little ranching and farming community of about twelve to thirteen hundred people nestled alongside a creek called *Pincher* in the foothills of the Rockies.

As it turned out his father only stayed for a couple of days, but arrangements were made for Len to remain at his aunt Ethel's until the end of August when his father would return to pick him up. Lenny would keep his aunt company, paint the house, tend the garden, and do whatever other chores needed doing. For this his aunt Ethel, who was reasonably well off, would pay him fifty dollars a month, not a bad salary in those days.

Who knew what memories would be created by such a whimsical visit? What started off being a compassionate mission of assistance and loving-kindness for a bereaving widow, turned into a romantic adventure; it just happened as if it was supposed to.

Lenny could not recall another two months when he had been so idyllically happy. The memory was locked in his adolescent brain and tingled in his heartstrings. It lasted long after his father had picked him up in the old Plymouth and driven him back home.

On the last day of August when Lenny's father arrived back in Pincher Creek to pick up his son, a solemn looking teenager doing his best to appear cheerful, greeted him.

"Everything okay?" his Dad asked, sensing an air of dissonance and sadness emanating from Lenny.

"I guess so." Lenny looked his father in the eye. "Do I really need to go back?

"Of course. You need to go back to school. Why do you ask?"

"I met this girl here… that I kinda like," Lenny confessed. He shuffled his feet and drew in a solemn breath. "Perhaps I could stay at Aunt Ethel's and attend school here?" he asked hopefully.

"I-I really did not expect this," his father replied indecisively. He stepped back and stared at his forlorn looking son. "You know… that might be too much to ask of your old Aunty," his father thoughtfully responded. "Perhaps you can come back next summer?"

"That is such a long time…" Lenny's voice trailed off.

"Yes, I know," his father commiserated. Did he really grasp the significance of the moment? Did he feel the romantic palpitations of an adolescent heart in turmoil? Did he understand the depth of the existential relationship that existed between a pretty teenaged girl and a heroic young lad who had dived into the watery depths, carried her ashore and frantically performed mouth-to-mouth resuscitation? He had not heard his son's crying prayer: *Oh my God, please, please, please let her breathe!* He gazed intently at the adolescent longing etched on the face of his only son. "Perhaps you should stay..." he relented. "Should I ask your aunt Ethel?"

"There are so many things out of my control," Lenny stated matter-of-factly. "I do not want to be a burden." He drew in a deep breath and gazed at his father. "Perhaps it is best... that I go back home?" he asked indecisively.

"I know what you mean. Perhaps it is best." His Dad stepped closer, and spoke in an understanding and compassionate tone. "Hopefully everything will work out... in time."

It was a sombre and pensive return trip because Lenny was practically in tears all the way back. When they arrived back home Lenny said, "Maybe after I graduate I'll go back there."

He never did.

There are some images that are so powerful they impact upon similar moments in our lives, like déjà-vu. Often when Lenny walked along the beach or beside a river or a stream he could see the girl with the red bathing suit laying there on the sandbar with dark-red blood oozing from a gash on her head turning her blonde hair crimson.

He could see her gracefully diving into the Canyon pool. She made nary a ripple as she disappeared into the water. He waited with anticipation for her to surface. He waited and waited. She did not come back up. Had she hit her head on the rocky bottom?

He remembered instinctively rushing down to the rocky shore, diving in, pulling her out by the hair, and carrying her limp body to a flat sandy area on the shore. He wrapped her head with his beach-towel and frantically gave her mouth-to-mouth. She remained comatose. He redoubled his efforts; he willed her to breathe with every breath of life he blew into her lungs. He prayed with all his might. He was nearly exhausted and crying with desperation when she shuddered, coughed up water, and began to breathe. "Thank you," he whispered wiping away his tears of appreciation.

When she opened her eyes she mumbled, "Who – who are you?"

"Lenny."

She focused her eyes upon his face... in that mortal moment it was imprinted forever on her memory: those compassionate eyes that seemed to be staring into her soul. As she drew in another shuddering breath she slowly raised her right hand to her head. She slid her hand beneath the towel and felt the matted gash beneath her hair. When she withdrew her hand it was covered with sticky red blood. The sight of it caused her to close her eyes and shiver uncontrollably.

She remained as still as death except for the slight rise and fall of her breast. After an eternal moment she quivered and slowly opened her eyes once again.

Lenny stared at her anemic face; his gaze disappeared into the infinite depths of her sky-blue eyes. He felt like a kindred spirit. They had both survived a near-death experience.

Time per se has nothing to say. It just passes relentlessly. Things change. Lenny changed. After he had returned to Steveston he fantasized for a time about the girl in the red bathing suit. But in the grand scheme of things, he did not see himself as being heroic. After all who was he? Just some insecure teenaged kid trying to be 'cool.' But there is a world of difference between simply being cool and being heroic.

In the eyes of a teenaged girl in Pincher Creek he was her *savior*: if he had not been there... she would have drowned. But he was there, and she lived. She remembered that face: those deep dark soulful eyes. Unforgettable. It was just that simple. No big deal. And yet, after all was said and done, it was a very big deal... to her.

Sometimes for no reason at all Lenny would get a flashback, as if it were a reminder to him that something significant had happened that summer, something significant and lasting that resonated in his memory like a distant dream of nirvana relinquished. It was an ache and a joy combined with sadness and happiness.

"Mortality makes us all so vulnerable," Lenny reflected on those romantic moments when he lay upon the fluffy comfort of his pillow-topped queen sized mattress nostalgically recalling how she looked *when the sunlight turned her long silky hair golden, and her eyes sparkled with gratitude and loving-kindness.* Who could ever forget such memories?

It had happened long ago. No one else needed to know. It was very personal. It never left him. It gave a melancholic tinge to his life as if a kindred spirit in Pincher Creek was reaching out for him in a dream that happened yesterday, and he was not there... because in reality it was... today. Sometimes he could hear the music of the spheres vibrating in the ether as if someone hundreds of miles away was playing a melancholic melody intended just for him.

Yes, sometimes in the aging synapses of his subconscious memory, when the future faded into the past and the past into the present... *today was yesterday.*

* * *

Life had its ups and downs for everyone: there were sad times and happy times, and all the times in between when the here and now seemed to be devoid of meaning. It helped to have good friends of like mind. Such friends helped provide the intellectual spice that made Lenny's life seem to be somewhat palatable for one who had lost his sense of smell ever since he began taking eye-drops for his glaucoma.

They were a motley crew, the five of them: Lenny and Lana Bruce, Rabbi Letenberg, Father Bertolli, and Catherine Schneider. They went by the name of the Motley Five. What made the Motley Five such a unique group was its composition, and their collective appreciation of the quatrains written by Mrs. Mitchiko Kublinsky, the Chief Prosecutor's wife.

She had shared the quatrains with Cathy's late husband who had befriended her during his university days. They must have made an impression upon him for he kept them amongst his most important papers: the bundle held together with red elastics. After his passing they fell into Cathy's hands... and in this roundabout way came to the attention of the Motley Five, upon whom they resonated as if they had been written by some obscure oriental sage. The Motley Five referred to the quatrains as 'M-Qs' or Mitchiko's Quatrains. They were simple, but elegant.

> *Karma arises when the soul*
> *Becomes conscious of memories*
> *That cannot be forgotten*

Because they are forever being remembered.

All expressions of spiritual happiness great or small
Arise from virtuous actions
While all expressions of spiritual suffering great or small
Arise from non-virtuous actions.

Due to the Law of Attraction
It is impossible for authentic happiness
To arise from non-virtuous actions
Or for spiritual suffering to arise from virtuous actions.

The consequences of actions done
With non-virtuous intent
Can be ameliorated with virtuous actions
Compassionately contemplated.

Never fear… justice is always near
What is sown will be harvested
Even if it takes several incarnations
For the memory casts a long shadow.

Examine and evaluate your own behavior
In the light of these principles
And there will be less pain and suffering
And more happiness.

Happiness. What an elusive state of being. Just when you think you should be happy you feel this annoying sense of angst as if the last laugh was not on your side. The only thing on your side is the sense of being aware of being aware that you are not happy. That is how Rabbi Letenberg felt on the days his wife, Rebecca, asked: "What is wrong, dear? Are you not happy?"

Like most other rabbis, who had ventured forth and multiplied as dictated by the Law, as the Torah was known, Rabbi Letenberg had copulated with the fervent intent of producing a son and a daughter. He tried mightily in his fertile years – but to no effect. Six devastating miscarriages were enough. Was it penance? For what? Happiness was not to be found in the smiling eyes of the children... who were never born.

After his wife passed away Rabbi Letenberg retired to the west coast of British Columbia. He was a reasonably contented Jewish scholar of some note. As he aged he became much more mellow. He usually dressed up in black garments like a throwback to the old days when it was thought all Jews looked like Shylock the moneylender. He had a long brownish beard with grey streaks that emphasized a pale white complexion, beady brown eyes and a beak-like nose that lacked the hooked feature commonly associated with Hebrews. If he had shaved and had worn ordinary clothing no one would have suspected he was a Jew. He could have passed unnoticed as a white Anglo-Saxon Protestant.

In his flagrant youth he did just that. Why? Because his hypersensitive parents – may their souls rest in peace – pretended they weren't Jews. They even contemplated changing their surname from Letenberg to Letenbury because the first question social snobs asked was: "Letenberg? Isn't that Jewish?" The question was usually accompanied by a condescending attitude as if to say, "You should be ashamed of yourselves, you Christ Killers!"

But Henry Edward Letenberg, named after British royalty, had accepted during his tumultuous college days that he was a Jew... and proud of it! He accepted the thirteen basic principles of the Jewish faith: (1) there is a G-d, (2) there is but one G-d, (3) G-d has no physical body, (4) G-d is eternal, (5) only G-d may be worshiped, (6) G-d communicates with human beings through prophecy, (7) Moses was the greatest of the prophets, (8) the Torah came from G-d, (9) the Torah is the authentic word of G-d and may not be changed, (10) G-d is aware of all our deeds, (11) G-d rewards the righteous and punishes the wicked, (12) the Messiah will come, (13) the dead will be resurrected.

Of all these principles only one agitated the good Rabbi's sense of credulity and commonsense: number nine. What if number nine was simply Judaic dogma? What if the Torah was not the authentic word of G-d... what if it had been written by a host of pretentious scribes... and surreptitiously presented to Moses on Mount Sinai? If so, like everything in the world of flux, was not it, too, susceptible to the immutable laws of change and evolution? Could one remain a devout Jew and harbor such a question?

This was Rabbi Letenberg, one of the Motley Five.

Father Bertolli was cut from a different cloth. It was made in Italy and worn like a papal shawl. He too, like his good friend Rabbi Letenberg, had grown wiser and more open-minded with age. He probably should have been a philosopher or social worker, or some big-shot public servant in the Department of Human Resources for the provincial government. Instead he became a priest.

As he was the only son of immigrant parents, this decision was a mortal blow to their concept of mortality. Who would pass on the precious Bertolli DNA that had been handed down parent to offspring for billions of years along the Great Chain of Being? Would it all end with their only son Alberto? Other couples with many children would have been proud to have a member of the family receive the call of religious duty.

Alberto – Anglicized to Albert – felt sorry for his parents; they did their best to disguise their disappointment while doing what seemed natural, to lure young Albert into changing his mind. On Sundays they would frequently invite the next-door neighbors to join them for supper because they had a beautiful dark-haired daughter with sparkling eyes, long shapely legs, and a face like Barbie's. She was always seated next to Albert. Sometimes she smelled better than the food and she had eyes for the young seminary student. It was tempting, but young Albert was resolute. His precious DNA was wasted in the bathroom. It might not have been… if he had known at that time that some evidence showed that his Lord and Savior had been married and had begat a son. But at that time who knew that the mighty Roman Catholic Church had so many skeletons in its closets?

One of Father Bertolli's favorite sayings was "Too late smart!" In his later years he became an outspoken seeker after truth. His superiors frowned and attempted to muzzle him with threats of excommunication. He said: "Why are you afraid of the truth?"

Father Bertolli was not afraid of the truth – even if the truth seemed to undermine his religious convictions. There was one unique experience that he had when he was in the ninth year of his ministry at an isolated parish in northern Ontario that actually shook his faith in the Christian religion. Perhaps it was the isolation? Perhaps it was his guilty conscience? Perhaps it was his self-doubt? The disturbing experience stayed with him throughout his long career with the Catholic Church. He could not shake it off. The convoluted vision persisted, and persisted…

He was sitting peacefully on a white marble bench just outside the left side door of his red-bricked rectory. The evening rays of the sun were streaming radiantly through the low hanging branches of a towering oak tree. A dark cloud slowly drifted into view. Inch by inch it gradually blotted out the golden rays of the sun and cast an ominous shadow upon the once sunlit landscape.

Suddenly the air grew noticeably colder. He shivered instinctively. He strained to see beyond… beyond what seemed like a 'shadow of death'. The phrase turned his once shiny countenance into an ashen pallor. He closed his eyes. The light grew dim as darkness approached. The surreal became real, and the real a mirage. He could see himself reflected, along with others, as in a hologram.

In his black robe he looked like a ghoul, a hooded vulture looking for carrion.

"That is not me!" He recoiled in fear.

But there he was pretending… he was not one of many hooded creatures carnivorously eating the flesh and drinking the blood of an all too human being whom they had crucified and resurrected as a deity. And as in a nightmare, he heard peals of irrational laughter. When the laughter receded he heard a raspy voice whispering as if within the confines of a confessional: 'the earth is a god-forsaken place over which you have dominion; it is yours to possess and do with as you please… eat heartily and rejoice, my sinful ones. I am pleased.'

"That is not me," he thought. He looked toward the heavens. "I am not one of those sinful creatures!" he declared with righteous indignation. Suddenly the ominous clouds dissipated and he could see the miraculous sun.

The experience had a profound affect upon the young priest. At first Father Bertolli was afraid to share his vision. It had shaken his faith in his Faith. "Could we have gotten it all backwards?" he asked himself. "That is not me!" he reiterated in his mind, "I am not one of those sinners." And yet… he was.

However, as the years passed, time and again he was inundated with an anonymous feeling that he was not alone in his doubts. Many of his brethren seemed to have presentiments of sacrilegious blasphemies that they were loathe to give voice to, doubts that were etched upon their faces in lines of acute psychological distress.

And then one day the Bishop made a timely visitation. His surname was Ferlinghetti. In the past he had always proven to be a very supportive and positive influence.

On the night before the Bishop's departure Father Bertolli had the feeling that he should share his vision with the open-minded priest. Consequently when the opportunity presented itself... he dared to share his misgivings with the kindly Bishop.

They met at the same location where Father Bertolli experienced his vision. They sat on the same white marble bench just outside the left side door of the red-bricked rectory. The sky was foreboding and the atmosphere spoke of the need for confidentiality. It was with an inner sense of relief that Father Bertolli unloaded the burden that nearly suffocated his soul.

Upon hearing what Father Bertolli dared to share, Bishop Ferlinghetti inhaled deeply, and closed his eyes. When he opened them he gazed steadily at the young priest as if looking for signs of trustworthiness before admitting: "Believe it or not, I too have had a similar vision," he said calmly.

"You have?"

"At first I thought I was unique... but now I understand that such visions are far from being original or unique. Dozens have dared to share, as you have. I have given this matter a great deal of thought. I just cannot get it out of my head. As a matter of fact it has been an obsession of mine for years. I cannot explain why so many of us are so afflicted. But I must admit it is deeply troubling and-and unsettling!"

"What exactly are you saying?" Father Bertolli inquired with a look of consternation.

The Bishop shook his head as if attempting to clear away the confusion. He stared at the good Father. The irony of what he was about to say caused him to stutter with embarrassment: *"Ha-have we-we been duped... into doing the Devil's work?"* he whispered.

The question hung in the silence. The silence endured into what seemed like an eternity. Father Bertolli's robust countenance turned ghostly pale.

At long last the Bishop rhetorically responded in a quavering voice as if harboring grave misgivings: *"Who would deliberately depict us as being innately flawed creatures in dire need of being saved?"* He paused before answering his own question with yet another question. *"A righteous persona bent upon destroying this god-forsaken planet… because of his own vanity and personal glory?"*

"Who?" Father Bertolli asked expectantly, holding his breath.

"It must be either…" Bishop Ferlinghetti's lips moved and his utterance became a movement of air: *"the one and only righteous God – or someone else."*

"Who could that someone else be?" Father Bertolli queried.

"It must be… dare I even think it? Some diabolical personality," Bishop Ferlinghetti whispered as if sharing a secret so profane it had the power to undermine the holiness of the Pope and the Vatican.

"Either - or?" the good Father's voice had diminished into an audible thought.

Ferlinghetti frowned, looked up and deliberately made eye contact, before asking in a barely audible tone: *"Could they possibly be… one and the same?"*

It was an impossible question. The ramifications were beyond contemplation. *"One and the same?"* Father Bertolli blanched as if suddenly overcome with nausea.

The Bishop looked upward as if seeking divine inspiration. "I cannot explain why so many of us have had these experiences," he began in a carefully modulated tone. "I must admit it is profoundly disturbing. Profoundly. Like you, I too, have been shaken to the core," the Bishop confessed. "However I feel we have a sacred duty to keep our misgivings to ourselves," he added authoritatively.

"A sacred duty?" Father Bertolli queried.

"A sacred duty!" Ferlinghetti solemnly repeated. Hundreds of millions of devout converts believe in the sanctity of the Church. We are after all, *defenders of the Faith*. Please follow my example and keep this matter to yourself," he implored. "The ramifications are too-too much for the masses to contemplate… especially at this time," he leveled.

Father Bertolli complied, but the experience had changed his attitude… and made him into the open-minded individual who in his retirement years fit right in with the Motley Five.

Since their respective retirements, Rabbi Letenberg and Father Bertolli had become very good companions. They usually appeared together at some of the public speaking forums and seminars on religious freedom that Lenny and Lana participated in. They related to each other on a spiritual, social, and intellectual level.

One evening after the Rabbi and Father left the Seniors' Center where Lenny had been speaking, some snide onlookers quipped, 'What a heavenly couple,' implying some homosexual connotations. They said it on the occasion that Lenny, Lana and Catherine Schneider were walking immediately behind the odd couple on Moncton Street.

"Pay them no mind!" Lenny stated. "I've seen those obnoxious types around here before. They have nothing to do but stand around looking tough and harassing the meek and vulnerable. See that one there with the black leather jacket? Haven't we seen that one somewhere before?"

"Yes, that skin-head looks somewhat familiar," Lana responded. "It is hard to tell them apart."

"Just keep walking," Cathy urged the two elderly gentlemen just ahead of them. "Ignore them."

"Thanks," Father Bertolli replied turning around to face his supporters. "We are on our way to the corner café for coffee. Would you like to join us?"

That was the beginning of their association as the *Motley Five*. They met mostly at Father Bertolli's residence. He had a grand office space filled with shelf upon shelf of esoteric books surrounding a large mahogany table around which five comfortable fabric-covered armchairs were arranged. Usually Father Bertolli, being the host, acted as moderator, while Lana made herself useful by bringing along her note-pad and trusty tape-recorder and recording whatever information she deemed necessary.

When the Motley Five first met, Father Bertolli set the tone by asking: "What are we here for?"

It was such a general open-ended question it caught everyone by surprise. After a thoughtful moment Lenny replied. "We are all mortal beings. We all have that in common," he paused to see if there was any reaction. Seeing only bland faces he continued, "Could it be that our sense of being mortal is at the source of all religious sentiment?" He paused to let the question sink in.

It sank in deeply. Rabbi Letenberg stroked his long beard and adjusted the little round cap on his head. "Ah," he muttered, "a simple but profound question."

"Indeed," Father Bertolli agreed, "it gives us a common starting point, a common purpose. I guess we are here because we desire to gain a greater depth of understanding of what it means to be mortal, human, spiritual... and religious. Are we all in agreement?"

Everyone nodded.

"An awkward silence ensued," Lana noted on her notepad.

Rabbi Letenberg cleared his throat: "Hmm, I think I can provide a well-known historical example of the human condition that we are struggling to express. To do that we will have to go back before the year 70 CE because after that date there has been no single leader, like an Abraham or Moses who presided over the entire Jewish Diaspora. Let us begin by examining the mortal struggle for existence of the people from whom I am descended." He paused deliberately before asking: "What do you think? Are we all in agreement with this suggestion?"

All heads nodded.

"The good Rabbi has made an excellent suggestion," Father Bertolli responded supportively. "It is an existential topic to which we can all relate. We are all mortals growing older and more decrepit with each passing day, senior citizens contemplating the vagaries of life while attempting to make sense of the Judaic- Christian- Muslim-dominated society in which we live."

"We will need some time to think about this. How about we meet back here in about two weeks?" Cathy suggested.

Again all heads nodded. They bustled and smiled with genuine happiness as they emerged into the cool night air. The Motley Five had something exciting to look forward to... with hope.

* * *

Was it the insatiable lust?
Or the smoking that ruined his health
And pock-marked his face with the signs
Of decadence that caused him to hesitate
When he inserted a tailor-made
Into a diamond studded cigarette holder
Refracting the ambient energy of the sun
Through the gratuitous smoke that he inhaled
When he struck the match

That illuminated his life...

A tragically flawed self-made billionaire
Lounged in his posh penthouse suite
Alone in the armor of his own skin
Overlooking a man-made heaven
Sparkling like stars in a vast universe of dark spaces
Filled to overflowing
With an insecurity so profound
All the filthy lucre in the world would not suffice.

He is eighty-three years old today
And feeling desperately despondent
Because his feeble health is failing
And his eyesight has grown so dim
He could scarcely make out the candles
Twinkling on his birthday cake
Like the sparklers he was unable to blow out.

With nicotine-stained fingers
He casually lifts a smoldering cigarette
And slowly inhales the sins of his ancestors
That glow haphazardly in the darkness of the room
Like danger signals at a crossroads
Where he has arrived late in life
To contemplate his longevity.

Anxiety coils and rattles in his stomach
Like the hunger pangs of the impoverished
Whose blood and sweat he has greedily harvested
And secretly hoarded in a Swiss Bank
Where countless millions of Euro-dollars
Accrue interest anonymously.

His tired heart trembles as he gazes
Into the dark confines of his conscience
Illuminated by the biblical zeal of solicitors
Searching frantically in between the lines

Of every obscure passage
For the quantum mechanical conveyance
That would enable a camel to pass
Through the eye of a needle.

Who is so unforgiving and hard-hearted
As to be incapable of harboring
Even the tiniest twinge of compassion
For the seemingly gullible and ignorant
Who remain resolute?

"Ah-so!" he exclaims and attempts to rise
Above the reticent memories that clog his brain
With the misgivings that have come home
To roost upon the carrion of his dreams
Like demonic vultures from a self-made hell
That he had mistaken for heaven.

An ironic little grin gradually appears
On the old man's withered countenance
And tears slowly trickle down the crease-lines
Of his parchment cheeks
Like raindrops on a fractured windshield
Blurring the viability of his vision
As he stares pensively into the void
Attempting to salvage a lifetime spent
As his cigarette smolders into ashes.

- LB

PART TWO

STATE OF AWARENESS

CHAPTER FIVE

THE HUMAN CONDITION

What is more invasive
Than a question?

It was beyond the scope of human understanding, but nevertheless it happened. Eldorado Pena, a native Chilean, came to Lenny Bruce in a dream on October 6th after his exhausted spouse, Lana, had said, "Just let me sleep". Eldorado just appeared as if by magic in the dead of night from a realm of everlasting light, after the discordant and interfering vibes had thinned out. It was precisely 2:32 a.m. Lenny was oblivious of the time. After all he was fast asleep, his eyes moving about as if in REM mode.

Eldorado said, "Pena here... Eldorado Pena. Wake up, you fool, it's 2:32 a.m. and I have something important to share with you."

"Who, me?" Lenny vocalized out loud causing Lana to elbow him in the back, triggering an involuntary roll to the right.

"You are one of the few who is open to receiving vibes from the realm of higher frequencies".

"I am?" Lenny queried.

"Yeah, you nearly died didn't you?"

"My parents said I did... when I was a baby."

"That's all it takes for some. It creates an affinity for the spiritual and provides us with a rare opportunity to share. Sharing is our favorite vocation."

"To share what?"

"A predilection for the unvarnished truth, a common understanding of what you folks refer to as esoteric information... I guess you could call it a shared mission of sorts."

"What sort of mission?" Lenny queried.

"Hold on. I just got here. We'll get to that at a later time. But for now... I'll start with the usual preamble."

"I'm all ears."

"I chose you on purpose because I know you have the kind of uncontaminated mind that is open to the mysterious."

"Thanks."

"Listen to this very carefully. It will help put things in perspective."

"Like I said, I'm all ears."

"In the reality-membrane of Strong, Weak, Electromagnetic, and Gravitational forces in which quantum physicists claim you currently exist, you have physically and spiritually evolved to a level of awareness that enables you to experience the miracle of a reality that consists of three spatial dimensions, length, width and depth, combined with a fourth dimension called time. Now, this experience creates the existential conundrum known as the human condition."

"Human condition, you say?"

"In order to exist in such a reality you have been incarnated as a four-dimensional life-form living in a four-dimensional space-time reality. However, in spite of the fact that your biological form, including your brain, is four-dimensional, your four-dimensional microscopic brain is capable of communing with a multi-dimensional macroscopic Mind. Note I said *capable*. This creates the human condition that makes you rather unique amongst earthly life forms." Eldorado paused and looked at Lenny suspiciously. "Are you getting this?" he asked, raising his eyebrows.

"Slow down a little. Not so fast. Let me get this straight. Can you repeat that last part?"

"Your microcosmic four-dimensional brain is capable of communing with a multi-dimensional macrocosmic Mind. This interface creates the human condition that makes your species so unique."

"Unique – eh? How unique?"

"You have been incarnated there because it corresponds with your karmic level of development. You have evolved to the point where, in your spiritual progression toward perfection, you are ready..."

"Ready for what?"

"Readiness is crucial. When the soul is ready, it incarnates into a reality membrane of forces that coincides with its level of karmic readiness... in your case to experience the condition which most of you just take for granted."

"You mean our human condition?"

"It is indeed a most mysterious and incomprehensible condition to those incarnated at such a level of awareness. In an infinite, eternal and immortal Universe... you have been incarnated there to experience the miracle of being four-square."

"You call that being 'unique'?"

"Your four-dimensional space-time environment leads you to believe that you exist in a finite membrane of forces subject to Newton's laws of physics, Einstein's theory of relativity, and most recently, M/String theory. All of this information convinces you that the universe has a beginning and an end, and that eventually, you are going to die."

"Of course. We are mortal – aren't we?"

"All the hard evidence seems to indicate this. But consider this: Have you ever died?"

"Not yet."

"Do you have any recollection of ever having died?"

"None that I can remember."

"All you have to go on is information derived from your five receptor senses known as empirical evidence. You look around yourself and see a four-dimensional finite space-time reality where death seems natural, so you assume that you will die as well. You convince yourself that you too are going to die - even though in all eternity you have never died - only passed on. If, in all eternity you had actually died – then, you would not be here… now. Get it?"

"I see. Dying is an important aspect of the human condition. Knowing that we are going to die convinces us that we must be mortal - while 'passing-on' suggests something else. I have always surmised something like that – but I have mostly kept it to myself."

"Good. So you really have nothing to worry about except worry itself."

"That is reassuring."

"In your realm, it is important to believe you are mortal. Mortality makes it possible to exist in a meaningful and significant manner. Birth and death provide the finite bookends within which mortal experience occurs… as if the interval is everything."

"Everything, you say?" The question hung in the space between them.

"There is something that I nearly forgot to mention," Pena resumed. "Another reason I chose you is because you can communicate in English. Before you, I was in momentary contact with a very sexy young woman in Brazil – perhaps that is why I selected her - but her English was atrocious. And before that I had a short conversation with a Jewish bloke in New York City who spoke impeccable English with an intellectualized Harvard accent; unfortunately he was too vain.

"So… you chose me of all people!"

"Yeah. I hope you don't mind?"

"I am truly flattered," Lenny replied with all due humility.

"At this time in your earthly sojourn, English seems to be the language that best enables us to share the information that we have become aware of… by using *words* to describe and explain."

"Describe and explain what?" Lenny queried.

"Describe, explain, and make sense of *what-is* or *everything-there-is*. In order to communicate your understanding and awareness of *everything-there-is*, it is necessary to magically transform your interface with reality into... abstract symbols that represent memes of meaning called 'words'. Your ability to communicate your cognitive understanding of *what-is*, is relative to your level of awareness. Without 'words', how could you and I communicate the vast storehouse of information available in our respective karmic memories?"

"Good question," Lenny stated as if he understood what Pena was talking about.

"You have developed this affinity for the use of the English language that enables us to communicate relatively easily and to share... what we know. I used to communicate mostly in Spanish... but times change... Sharing is so-so enjoyable... for the likes of me... having once experienced the same mortal interval that you are now experiencing. What is the point of having knowledge, if one is unable to share one's awareness or understanding of *what-is* with others?

"What else is there?"

"That mortal interval contains all the so-called 'information': all the stories, myths, theories, thoughts, ideas, and dreams a human brain incarnated in a four-dimensional space-time reality is capable of... becoming aware of."

"Slow down, my good man!" Lenny exhorted. "You are beginning to boggle the synaptic connections in my feeble brain with-with excessive verbosity."

"Sometimes I forget who I am talking to... and-and get carried away. You are quite right. You know, you are actually somewhat brighter than I originally anticipated – but not *that* bright, eh? My fault entirely! Please accept my most humble apology."

"No need to overdo it," Lenny grumbled.

"Sharing is one of my most gratifying experiences. I often get carried away..." Pena's voice faded into silence.

"Sharing is also one of my most enjoyable pastimes," Lenny piped up, hoping to be worthy of Pena's estimate of his cognitive abilities.

"You know, you are very perceptive... I think you can comprehend the complexity of what I am about to share with you."

"Please carry on. I'll do my best to hang with you, but like you said we are limited by the use of words to communicate... so I would appreciate it if you would choose your words carefully," Lenny humbly replied.

"That's the spirit. I knew I had a live one in you. Do you know how incredibly unique and remarkable biological life forms like you are?"

"Unique – but certainly not scarce. As far as I know there are over seven billion of us human beings on the face of the earth."

"It took zillions of years of karmic evolution for you to become the biological species that you currently are."

"That long – eh?"

"Consider this: of the infinitude of biological life forms available in Eternity, somehow a two-legged, upright creature like you emerged into the light of day as being the highest form of life on planet Earth. What Master-Creator could have conjured up such an incredibly complicated, spiritually conscious, and mortally fragile biological life form, like you?"

"A fluke of Nature, some might say... an aberration of sorts... a passing whim. Here today – gone tomorrow," Lenny commented self-deprecatingly.

"You've got the hang of it, man. A self-deprecating sense of humor like that is refreshing in this day and age of righteous indignation. Did you know that in your reality, every day is today? You cannot live in tomorrow, and you cannot live in the past. You can only live in the eternal now, realized in your realm as today. Today you are a warm-blooded, intelligent, rapacious carnivore struggling to survive amongst a myriad of other life forms."

"That sounds so-so repugnant," Lenny objected.

"Today most of you will get up, breathe the air, drink water, and greedily devour other vulnerable life forms without a pang of guilt, remorse, or gratitude," Pena followed up.

"You said most of us?" Lenny asked hoping that excluded the likes of him.

"There are a number of you – perhaps more than you think – that are acutely aware of their *human* nature. They have developed a more caring attitude. Unfortunately, every day the vast majority of you will mindlessly kill, devour, devastate and waste millions upon millions of other precious life forms... in order to maintain your own."

"At least they could display a little humility and-and gratitude, eh?"

"It is all about awareness and attitude. Who was it that said: *If you change your attitude that changes everything?*"

"Someone said that in a TV commercial."

"Anyway the fact of the matter is… you really have no option."

"No option?"

"You cannot perform photosynthesis."

The profundity of the statement caused Lenny to smile his simpleton's smile. "True enough," he admitted.

"Unfortunately, you cannot perform photosynthesis like grass and other simple life forms – so you must kill and devour other organic life forms in order to indirectly ingest the life-sustaining energy from the sun that is stored in such organisms. In short, you have evolved into the most dangerous killers the earth has ever realized. You must kill and consume the flora and fauna around you in order to sustain and enhance your own mortal life."

"Sounds ominous. I really haven't given that much thought."

"Think about it. It is as plain as the nose on your face. A greedy, uncaring carnivorous species, if not controlled, will soon eat itself out of house and home. It appears that most of you selfish, egotistical, and greedy types are well on your way toward doing just that! You have devised an economic system that condones greed and hoarding. Less than two percent of the greediest of the greedy hoard and consume the vast majority of the earth's precious nonrenewable resources. Consequently millions of your fellow human beings suffer from malnutrition, starvation, and disease… while the earth is being plundered, polluted and laid to waste."

"You sound a tiny bit exasperated."

"I must admit… stupidity irks me!"

"Me too."

"So, what is wrong with this attitude and behavior?"

"It is life-negating?" Lenny guessed.

"I knew you would get it. Precisely. It is counter-productive to your best interests. You have been incarnated on that miracle planet as a human being for a very specific reason."

"You don't say?" Lenny responded as if overwhelmed by the sudden prospect of learning a vital existential secret about himself.

"You have been incarnated there," Pena paused and gazed solemnly at Lenny, "to learn the importance of *sharing.*

"What?"

"You look a little startled. Isn't it self-evident?"

"According to our behavior, apparently not!

"Let me reiterate this vital point. You have been incarnated on earth as human beings to learn a very important karmic lesson: *Sharing*. It is just that simple."

"Sharing and… caring, I'd say," Lenny cautiously proposed hoping that Eldorado would get a favorable impression of his capacity to understand such concepts.

"You are actually a lot smarter than you look. Yes indeed, caring is important. It is imperative that as the most dangerous species of life on earth, you care enough… to-to realize that you are totally dependent upon the altruism of other life forms for your existence. *You need them - they do not need you!* Think about that."

Lenny drew in a deep breath as if refreshing his brain.

"Demonstrate a little respect and gratitude. These other life forms share their lives with you – and what do you do in return?"

"Massacre, ravage, waste, pollute and kill, as if we are totally ignorant of our own stupidity," Lenny exclaimed. "We do this on purpose and, believe it or not - think nothing of it because… well, because millions of us believe that God has given us dominion over the earth, to pillage and plunder Mother Nature as we please - because in the end… she will be burnt to a crisp, anyway." Lenny lamented. "And, at this time in our spiritual evolution, there are probably millions of such two-legged marauders who just do not care!" he added for emphasis.

"But it is catching up to you. You reap what you sow; it is a universal karmic law. Already you have triggered climate change. Catastrophes will occur, as sure as night follows day."

"It is so-so obvious!" Lenny exclaimed.

"But sorry to say… like you said, most of you still do not get it. You are not aware that you have been incarnated on that miracle planet as a parasitical species that is totally dependent upon other life forms for your survival. You are there to learn how to share, and care for your host, Mother Nature, who provides you with everything you need."

"Everything?"

"Everything necessary… to enable you to progress toward a higher karmic level of awareness - or sadly, regress. You reincarnate at the existential level according to your karmic level of awareness. It may not seem like it, but the essence of this grand idea is altruistic in nature."

"Try telling that to the millions in the Middle East who have reduced themselves to a tribal level of religiosity."

"I'm telling you."

"Why me, of all people?"

"You are Lenny Bruce, aren't you?"

"Yes."

"I chose you because, of all the billions of human beings residing on Planet Earth, you are truly unique. You are special; very few humans have been endowed with such clairvoyance. We need to work together so we can help to set the record straight."

"What record?"

"The prevailing record... of knowing. You've already been doing it subconsciously... as if by instinct."

"I have?"

"Your thoughts and ideas are very important to us."

"Us? Who is 'us'?"

"Mostly, just me and my good friend Issa... you know him by another name..." Eldorado hesitated as if his memory needed jogging. "Anyway he noticed that you seemed to be a rather shallow breather, and wanted me to mention it."

"Why?"

"Your health is important to us. However, most of you just take breathing for granted."

"You know, I believe you are correct!" Lenny admitted, suddenly cognizant of his shallow breathing.

"Proper breathing is of the utmost importance to your health and well-being."

"How so?" Lenny asked, playing the fool.

"Breathing enables the human body to chemically metabolize the fuel it ingests that produces the miraculous fusion-fission dance of the atoms that creates the vital force that animates."

"Interesting."

"To illustrate, what is known as pranayama breathing is an important aspect of meditation and yoga; it focuses the mind upon the essential along with the spiritual. Your aura shines through the opaqueness of the material with every breath. Be conscious of your breathing... it really is literally, *the breath of life.*"

"I'd say proper breathing is not only the key to good health, it is essential for survival and longevity," Lenny commented.

"I am impressed by your astuteness. Take care of your health. Maintain proper posture, and concentrate on breathing properly! We are counting on you." A long silence ensued. It seemed as if Eldorado had taken his leave.

Perhaps he did depart and then returned a mortal-moment later. It was impossible to tell. Lenny waited stoically in the dark.

"Ahem," Eldorado cleared his throat revealing his presence.

"That you?"

"Who else?"

"Who... exactly, are you?" Lenny demanded as if he needed to know.

"They call me Eldorado Pena. My friends call me Peenya. Before I passed on I resided in the geographical area you now refer to as Chile. My early ancestors were aboriginals. I am a hybrid descendent of some of those spiritual wanderers with slightly elongated skulls who in the distant past crossed the land bridge from Northern Asia to Alaska. Some time after that, as you probably know, some European explorer looking for a short-cut to the Orient landed by accident on some islands off the east coast; he mistakenly called the inhabitants 'Indians' because he thought he had landed in India... and the name stuck. See how unreliable history can be?"

"I suppose it all depends on who is writing it. I'm sure it would be a vastly different story if you or your ancestors had written it."

"I have some of that syphilitic Spanish blood in me – but I consider myself to be a native Indian or aboriginal... and am damn proud of it. Anyway to make a long story very short, the Spanish came just to get our wealth. They cared nothing for our culture or the people. They pretended to be religious; they had guns, smallpox, syphilis, and Hey-sus. We had bows and arrows, spears, and gold; we were massacred and decimated."

"I know. Imagine what would have been your history - if the Europeans had not come?"

"A momentous question which I have yet to contemplate. Indeed, what would have been our history?

"No syphilis, no small pox, no rape of Mother Nature, no reservations, no vast polluting cities of concrete, no sin," Lenny rattled off.

"I cared a great deal for the good earth, and still do. That is probably why I sometimes get sentimental and nostalgic... and tune in and interfere in your karmic business."

"It is regrettable... what happened to your people," Lenny commiserated.

"As you know, history is full of examples of man's inhumanity to his fellow man. I guess I've become something of a stoic. Patience is perhaps my strongest suit. Perseverance has enabled me to withstand information that... could have shaken my optimistic outlook and rendered me an eternal pessimist."

"What information?"

"Ancient memories of a tragedy worse than the disappearance of-of Atlantis. Like, for instance, things that happened long before my sojourn on earth: millennia ago in an area you now call Bolivia."

"What happened?"

"Ever heard of Puma Punku?"

"Puma what?"

"Punku, the place where ancient visitors built a sacred site out of gigantic H blocks of solid stone. It seems they sort of got hung up on the optics of geometric shapes. You could say that being too materialistic has its limitations. The H blocks are still there - hard, undeniable, empirical evidence that someone was once there."

"Are you referring to alien beings?"

"They really weren't aliens, as you folks say."

"They weren't?"

"They were just ordinary mortals like you and me who were a little more advanced than the earthly inhabitants they encountered. In the superstitious minds of the ancients who met them, they morphed into superhuman beings that they revered as giants."

"Giants?"

"In the Torah they are mysteriously referred to as *Nephilim*."

"Where'd they come from?"

"The heavens, from their perspective. Essentially it is a matter of time, relativity, motion... and logic."

"Logic?"

"For instance, over two thousand years ago a Greek philosopher named Zeno logically reasoned that before one could cross a river, one must first cross half of it. And before one could cross the remaining half, one must first cross half of the half and so on ad infinitum! Logic informs us that since it takes an infinite amount of time to travel across an infinite number of halves, it would be impossible to cross the river!"

"Yet, in spite of such impeccable logic we cross the river!"

"Indeed you do. And as your awareness has grown... you now understand why such logic is only a word-game that sets out the parameters of your four-square mentality, making you susceptible to the irrational dictates of religious dogma. Using calculus, it can be shown that an infinite number of points can be crossed in a finite amount of time... making motion theoretically possible. Suffice it to say, as your awareness expands, so does the reality of your universe, and your understanding of it."

"Revealing. There are so many paradoxical mysteries that have confounded the minds of the most brilliant thinkers amongst us."

"It will always remain so because your awareness has no finite limitations. In a very short time your 'understanding' of reality has expanded from a flat earth in the center of a finite universe, to parallel worlds in an ever expanding multiverse of dark and light matter and energy."

"Believe it or not - you are making sense. Indeed, I am amazed by your commonsensical explanation of what seems to many of us as being... logically absurd," Lenny commented.

"Consider this from the point of view of the logically absurd. Suppose, in a few centuries or so, you evolve to a point where you are biologically and technically capable of space travel. You leave the earth and travel abroad at hyper-speed. During your absence the earth revolves around the sun thousands of times. When you return to the earth it has aged thousands upon thousands of years – but since you have not been on the earth, you have only aged a few years. You find that relative to you, the people on planet Earth have *regressed* to a primitive stone-age state. How would they relate to you?"

"As children to *Nephilim*? I suppose the people would be in awe of the space ship and me. They might think that I am an extraterrestrial being, or an alien - or perhaps a god."

"Yet, you are an earthling. Planet Earth is your home. You are one of them - returning home after a sojourn into outer space."

"I have never conceived of extraterrestrial beings in that context."

"They were there at Puma Punku and elsewhere on planet Earth where ancient remains speak of alien encounters."

"The evidence is indisputable. It is just there... and yet we puzzle over it as if it is a great mystery. Our memory fails us. We have long forgotten."

"Like I said, they were one of us... with our frailties and foibles"

"One of us?"

"I suppose I could have said... *we are one of them*," Pena paused and smiled his self-effacing little smile before asking, "Do you know what Ethics is?

"Why do you ask?" Lenny replied with a blank expression."

"I'm trying to ah-ah clarify this rather complicated matter... by the use of an illustration," Eldorado looked exasperated.

"Well I suppose Ethics deals with matters of right or wrong behavior."

"How do you know what is right – and what is wrong?"

"Many folks are guided by their religious beliefs."

"And would they be willing to die for such religious beliefs?"

"A great many devout and true believers would. Belief is such a powerful thing. In fact the righteous would be willing to-to righteously destroy the entire world!"

"Why?"

"Because, they are just not aware enough at this time... to know the difference?"

"And who is to say it has not happened... once before?" Eldorado sagely queried.

"Could an unspeakable tragedy like that have happened at... at Puma Punku?" Lenny cautiously inquired.

"Well, believe it or not... you have asked the right question!"

"The right question, eh?" Lenny replied with a confused stare.

"Indeed I do believe you are aware enough... to-to ascertain the difference between being righteous – and being right," Pena responded enthusiastically.

"Most people... probably won't get this," Lenny predicted.

"But you are not one of *them* – you are one of *us*," Pena stated confidently before he left.

* * *

The Public Prosecutor, Ruskolnikov Kublinsky was one of *them* — but he had potential. He stood out because of his size. He was well over what could be considered average in height. In his stocking feet he stood about six feet seven inches. And there he was, standing in front of the Courthouse door with his grey polyester suit, tan leather briefcase, and his left hand on the door handle. He was about to enter, when he paused to briefly reflect upon what had brought him there. In all eternity it seemed odd that persons of such diverse lineage as a White Russian, and a deceased hybrid Scotsman named Lenard Bruce Jr. should have anything much in common. But they did. He turned the door handle and proceeded to his office.

The gigantic Prosecutor for the Crown also had some traits in common with the portly lawyer for the Defense, the inimical Mr. Brad Bradley. They had developed a similar philosophical outlook on life that made their respective interests in the case similar — but different from a legal perspective. The two had attained a modicum of awareness that enabled Kublinsky, the Chief Prosecutor, to feel personally motivated in prosecuting the murderer of Lenny the Bruce — while his beleaguered counterpart struggled valiantly to defend the accused, George Webster Brown... with equal enthusiasm.

In preparation for the case the chief prosecutor had read most of the writings of Lenard Bruce. "Who thinks of these things?" he asked himself at the time. He was impressed. It felt like he had discovered a kindred spirit of sorts. In subtle ways his beliefs and even his attitude had been modified... *for the better.* He was one of a few who could appreciate many of the controversial subjects that had been published in *Final Draft*.

Like Lenny, Ruskolnikov Kublinsky knew what it felt like to be different. "You are a White Russian Jew," his mother, who had a penchant for keeping track of the family tree, informed him when he was old enough to formulate some vague understanding of who he really was.

When Ruskolnikov reached adolescence, he deduced that he was the product of a biological act known as sexual intercourse that took place between a young man from the Belarusian hinterland and a comely maid whose ancient ancestors had participated in the great Jewish Diaspora that resulted in the dispersal of the historical Jews from their homeland in the Middle East. The couple got married so that their only offspring would not be labeled a bastard. Nevertheless, in public gossip gatherings, the little boy who retrospectively bore the family surname was referred to as 'Kublinsky's bastard son'.

In Canada, as in the rest of the capitalistic world where the Judaic-Christian-Muslim faith exerted its influence, sinners were abundant. Thus it came to pass that a young lad who, in the minds of the great unwashed, had been conceived in sin, born in sin, and raised as 'Kublinsky's bastard son', felt right at home. It was relatively easy to come to grips with the possibility that he was in reality and in deed, Kublinsky's, or was that *Kublinski's?* bastard son. In Canada the misspelling was no big deal. Besides, who cared if he was Russian or Ukrainian – weren't they both part of the USSR? And, after all... wasn't he Canadian?

No one cared. But the amorphous notion of also being a 'sinner' grated upon young Kublinsky's inner sense of self-respect. He read the King James Version of the Holy Bible. It seemed more convoluted than holy, but he persevered. He was particularly fascinated with the first part called Genesis, which began: *In the beginning God created the heaven and the earth.* "What God?" thought *Kublinsky's bastard son.* The archaic creation-narrative undermined any inherent sense of reason and justice he harbored as an adolescent. In secret he began to have serious doubts about the whole dogmatic concept.

It was not until he reached university that the Public Prosecutor dared to unveil his blasphemous views. In his final year at UBC in a course on Ethics, his ever-curious and questioning mind posed questions like: "*Why are we sinners? Do we really deserve such a status?*" Ruskolnikov attempted to address such questions in a term paper required by his Ethics Professor.

The gargantuan Prosecutor got up from his desk and sauntered over to the filing cabinet and opened the third drawer from the top. Under 'E' he extracted his old term paper on Ethics. He took it back to his desk and with a sense of self-satisfaction began to read what he had written as an undergraduate student hoping to become a big-shot lawyer.

In his term paper Russ had deduced that approximately seven weeks after the Exodus from Egypt, on the sixth day of the month Sivan, in the year 2448 of the Jewish calendar, G-D had *revealed* Himself in an awesome cloud of thunder and lightning at Mount Sinai to a great multitude of Jewish men, woman, and children. How did this mysterious entity with an unutterable name *reveal* Himself?

A curious Ruskolnikov Kublinsky imagined God standing before a full-length mirror and staring at his own gargantuan image - the image in which he supposedly had created the first human being: Adam. What did he see? Did he see an intelligent, free-willed man with a head, two arms, a torso, two legs, a penis, and testicles?

Why would a celibate God or for that matter, Adam, need testicles? Russ was reminded of the parched, anemic faces of the celibate priests standing forlornly outside the parish church smoking cigarettes. They had useless testicles too. Was God that obtuse?

It was a simple question asked by a curious youth mindful of the religious ethos of the times in which he had been born and raised. Unbeknownst to himself at that time, he had inadvertently given expression to a conundrum that seemingly had been overlooked by those who studied the Torah as if it really was the *word of God* – and not the 'word' of some secret chauvinistic clutch of ancient scribes pretending to be holy.

The Crown Prosecutor exhaled while stretching out his legs. He had read the Old Testament. He could see why a pre-law student of Ethics would be perturbed. What happened to reason and logic?

The term paper went on to say that the mythological *Children of Israel* were being punished by the One and Only True God because they were descendants from the first man, Adam, who had unwittingly committed the first mortal sin: *disobedience.* Why? *Because he had been created with testicles and testosterone?* Who's fault was that?

In a moment of mortal weakness Adam had let Eve tempt him with the 'forbidden fruit'. And furthermore, after being dispatched from the Garden of Eden as a punishment, Adam sinfully fornicated with Eve and produced the sinful offspring from whom the early ancestors of the Twelve Tribes of Israel were descended. Did not descendants with such a lineage deserve to be vengefully punished? It was their lot to do penance and ask God Almighty to forgive them for the terrible sins of their ancestors.

Was there method in all this righteousness? The timeline and the chronology of events were convoluted, but eventually Adam's descendants, the enslaved children of the Twelve Tribes of Israel, were given a second chance, so to speak, to redeem themselves in the eyes of God! If they persevered and humbly atoned for their *ancestral sins*, they would be rewarded with life-everlasting. Justice would prevail.

In the second part of his paper Russ attempted to explain the rationale behind the retrospective application of the myth known as the Creation Narrative. Could not such a narrative be used as a rationale to justify the existential status of any beleaguered group of human beings who by simple accident of birth were born into a life-negating environment like say... a miserable disease-ridden slum in a destitute third-world country, a deplorable refugee camp in the Middle East, an exploitive work camp in south-east Asia, a wretched cotton or sugar cane plantation, or in any such existentially challenging situation? Would not children born into such circumstances be inclined to look up to their parents with innocent eyes and ask: *What did we do to deserve this?*

The myth concerning the Fall of Man provides the rationale needed to answer such an ethical question.

(1) It justifies the child's status as being a punishment.

(2) It rationalizes the punishment as being an atonement.

(3) It condones the atonement as being meritorious!

(4) It provides the child with hope everlasting in a situation
where everything appears to be hopeless.

The creation myth justifies the pathetic status of the hopeless by providing them with otherworldly hope. The Judaic, Christian, and Muslim faithful hold the Creation Narrative dear. They believe in its authenticity. They believe that it is truly the literal word of God. Their influence is felt in the highest courts of law throughout the world.

Perhaps the most important ethical question of concern to the legal profession and to all adherents of fair-play and justice might be: *Is God's personal behavior as exemplified in the Holy Bible the type of behavior to be admired, glorified, and emulated... as being just?"* a youthful and inquisitive Ruskolnikov Kublinsky had bravely concluded.

The Professor whose name was Mordecai H. Eisendrath, had given him 80%, the highest mark he could bring himself to give to any third year student of Ethics and scrawled on the last page: "A bit convoluted in places, but you have raised some sensitive religious and ethical questions that even I had not previously considered."

* * *

Like his parents George was brought up fearing the Lord his God.

It seemed beyond his mental capacity to comprehend why *fear of the Lord* constituted the *beginning of wisdom*, and why he had been designated as being a sinner in the first place – especially when he did not feel at all sinful.

It was just a simple matter of acceptance: he accepted the obvious biological fact that nine months or so previous to his birth, his dear old parents had sinned, and he was the biological proof that indeed, they had. No one talked about this. It was sacrosanct – but George was not stupid; he knew when to keep his mouth shut. But as he grew older, he was smart enough to feel that something felt somewhat... odd.

When George weighed exactly nine pounds twelve ounces, his parents bundled him up in a blue flannel blanket with little cute ducklings spotted here and there and drove down to an old house on Number Three Road where baby Georgie – without his consent – was baptized in the name of his Lord and Savior. From that moment on George, whether he knew it or not, was, in the opinion of his parents, the preacher, and billions of other devout believers throughout the world, 'saved'. *Halleluiah!*

George's father, Harry, drove a tandem-wheeled truck used for picking up and hauling garbage; he was in fact a garbage collector. Someone had to do it – right? Harry had inbred religious beliefs that he had inherited from his parents who were both devout Baptists and from whom he had inherited the dilapidated old house. To George that old house was home. He did not notice it was dilapidated... until after he had inherited it.

When Harry passed on shortly after his wife died of pneumonia, George officially became a homeowner. Ownership came with its own encumbrances.

George was twenty-one years old at the time and grateful for his small blessings. He spent countless hours fixing up the rundown clapboard house and eventually made it into something approximating a decent two bedroom, one bathroom bungalow, situated on a street lined with such newly renovated homes. George was proud of his carpentry skills. His house looked quite modern with its green shuttered front windows and dark green asphalt shingled cottage roof. It was a home befitting his prospective wife-to-be.

Her name was Sarah Smith. She was not ravenously attractive, but she was pretty in a country sort of way. She had scrawny thighs that George found to be rather erotic. "It is what lies in between..." he pointed out to his vulgar associates at the local watering hole. It made some sense to most of them. They looked Sarah over with renewed interest the next time George brought her along for a beer. But in the end it was good ol' Georgie Porgie who put his money where his mouth was and dropped into Stan's Jewelry and purchased a fabulous zircon that Stan said could fool even the most perceptive of the perceptive.

George, unromantic as he was, presented the fake diamond to Sarah while she was reclined upon the sagging leather couch decorated with soft emerald-green velvet pillows, located in the living room of his refurbished house. The date was October the 19th and the time was precisely 8:37 pm. Unexpectedly, tears welled up in George's eyes when Sarah accepted with a gracious smile.

"It's...it's not a real diamond," George humbly confessed, overcome by the romantic authenticity of the moment. "Some day when we can afford it, I-I will get you a-a... real one." It was a solemn moment.

"It's the sentiment that counts," Sarah replied, gazing into George's watery eyes, "not the monetary value."

Who knew that George Webster Brown was capable of such honesty? Could it be that he really did have a soft spot in his heart for Sarah? One month later on November 19th, George and Sarah said "I do," and George carried his blushing bride over the threshold of his honeymoon home and laid her on the sagging couch. There the marriage was successfully consummated... and George was able to realize his fondest wet dream.

Being right was important to George. He had developed a righteous attitude from his parents. "You are amongst the elect," his parents would say, "Be worthy of it!" He tried. On the elementary school playground when the other children sang out "Georgie Porgie puddin' and pie, kissed the girls and made them cry," little George would scowl menacingly and clench his tiny hands. "Want some of this?" he would challenge holding up his right fist. Usually the smaller kids would scatter, laughing as they ran. This made George feel really quite tough. There was one big kid, however, the school bully, who refused to run. He'd complete the verse... "When the boys came out to play, Georgie Porgie ran away." There were fisticuffs.

"Don't let them bully you," his mother advised whenever George arrived home after school covered with bruises. "Don't worry, some day I will get even," George vowed. "That's the spirit," his father would say after supper when the day's events were rehashed.

Much later, when he turned thirteen, George snuck over to the residence of the aforementioned offender, and started a fire in the back entrance to their house. He thought it might cause the porch to burn with the resultant loss of the bully's bike that was parked therein. Unfortunately the entire house burnt down! "Who would have thought it?" George reflected afterwards with considerable remorse.

The fire chief declared, "Some good for nothing son-of-a-bitch set that fire." George heard him say it. He felt insecure, frightened, and scared out of his wits. Revenge wasn't as sweet as he thought it would be. He was only thirteen. He did what he had to.

The memory stayed with him. It haunted his dreams. He had a conscience.

George's parents had no inkling what their son had done. They thought they were raising a god-fearing son instead of a "son-of-a-bitch," as the fire chief had called the perpetrator of the fire. But of course, like most parents who constituted the great unwashed, they were duly proud of their dutiful son. George was very good at playing that role. Until the age of eighteen he usually accompanied his parents to Church and sat beside them in the third pew to the left. He sang "Onward Christian Soldiers" with fervor and was not shy about declaring himself to be a defender of the faith. He had developed a militant outlook on things. Consequently his father was not surprised when he asked him if he would mind if he joined the army.

"What army?" his dad had joked, "The Salvation Army?" That was the last joke he shared with George. He passed away soon thereafter.

Perhaps George should have joined the Salvation Army; it might have changed the course of his destiny. But instead a year and a half before he got married to his high school sweetheart, George joined the Reserve Army. This enabled him to drink with the other seasoned veterans even though he was slightly underage, and receive a small stipend for the privilege. The experiences whet his appetite for more.

Three years after he graduated from high school and had married his good wife, he joined the regular Armed Forces. He really liked his brand new black leather army boots. He shone them up so brightly his commanding officer once remarked: "That's the spirit!" This made George feel especially proud. He took a picture of his boots and gave it to his spouse. She had the photo enlarged to an eight by ten with the caption: George's Boots, and hung it on the wall adjacent to the bed to remind her of his presence... when he was absent.

Since he had spent time in the Reserves, soon after he joined George was assigned to serve in an Army Cadet Training Camp in the Okanagan. He got to help train the youngsters. He enjoyed making them parade around: left-right-left-right. The officer in charge commended him. George never felt prouder to serve his country. It wasn't work – it was more like being on paid holidays. Every weekend he drove back home to 'take tail' as he called it. It was a lark.

A few years later he was transferred to a camp in Alberta. At that time the political party in power was called the Social Credit Party. "What is social credit?" George wondered. His interest was piqued when he found out what 'funny money' was. The idea of 'funny money' appealed to him; "Yeah, just print off what is needed," he told prospective voters. When elections were called he volunteered to pass out leaflets. He acquired a reputation for being a staunch supporter of the Social Credit Party of Alberta.

George did not mind his sojourn in Alberta because Sarah was able to rent out their bungalow in Richmond and join him. They were fortunate to find a little house close to the army barracks that cost less than half of what they got for the rental of their west coast home. Compared to their army friends the Brown's seemed to have plenty of extra cash to spend. Most Saturday evenings at the Legion, George usually bought the first round, which gave him added status amongst his peers. He liked to talk politics, especially the merits of 'funny money'. If he could have stayed in Alberta his life might have been drastically different. He could have been a real somebody. "You've got potential," his buddies said.

Time passed, as did his potential. He put on some extra weight and his once slim profile began to bulge in the middle. He was never called to serve on any peacekeeping missions overseas. Still he had his own aspirations.

Who knows? If he had been able to stay in Alberta, he might have run for election himself... and become a big-shot MLA in the provincial legislature. He had his dreams – who doesn't? But his dreams were dashed when some higher-ups decided he was needed in the province of Quebec... Montreal, to be precise.

Sarah appreciated her small blessings. She was blessed with good health, a comfortable home, and a husband who conscientiously took home most of his army pay for her to spend or invest as she saw fit. Soon after her arrival in Alberta, she managed to find a part-time job as a clerk at a nearby confectionary store. The work helped to pass the long summer days when she often felt nostalgic for her old B.C. surroundings. In the evenings she diligently watched the CBC news on television to keep abreast of what was going on in the world. She was proud of her knowledge of national and international events. She accepted her place in the grand scheme of things with a stoicism that enabled her to say: "We should be thankful for what God has provided." She helped out at the local Evangelical Church. Most Sundays she generously put a blue five-dollar bill on the collection plate. It made her feel as if she belonged. Life was good.

What more could anyone want?

The slow passage of time and the loneliness of being childless eventually motivated Sarah to take matters into her own hands. When George was transferred to Montreal, Quebec, she decided that she would remain behind until he got things settled. Fortunately the renters moved out of their bungalow in Richmond, BC enabling her to move back... "To be closer to old friends and family," she told her spouse.

"Wait there until you hear from me," George had said. "It might take some time for me to arrange for subsidized accommodations for married folks... apparently there is a waiting list."

Sarah waited and waited. No word. She grew impatient. She did the irrational: she contacted a lawyer who phoned George. "Your wife wants to sell the house," he told him.

"No way!" George replied.

"She is planning on moving down there... to be with you. You could rent the place out – but as you know, it is harder to get good tenants for older houses like yours... and the place might get trashed if no one is here to look after it."

"What do you recommend?"

"If I were you I'd probably sell. The market is very good. You should get top dollar. If it sells, you could invest some of the money into dividend paying bank stocks that will provide you both with a little extra security in your old age."

George hesitated: "Okay, if that's what Sarah wants… fine, go ahead. But tell her not to come just yet. There is sort of a-a secretive type of mission that I might volunteer for that that might take some time."

"Why don't you tell her yourself?"

"Is she there?"

"No."

"Then you tell her."

The lawyer told her.

With part of the money from the sale of the house, Sarah bought a used car, a demo: a bright red Pontiac four-door sedan. She drove all the way to Montreal, Quebec in five days with all their worldly belongings in the trunk and back seat… "To be near my husband," she informed her friends and neighbors.

By then George had gallantly volunteered to serve in a top-secret project no one had ever heard of at that time. The Army's personnel officer, who turned out to be a very kind and considerate person, found Sarah temporary accommodation in a four-story brick building close to the University. "I hope George will like it." Sarah had muttered.

"Didn't you know?" the personnel officer spoke with a French accent. "George has his own place over dere," he pointed toward some distant buildings. "As far as I know… he won't be staying wid-you… so don't worry about it. God only knows how long he will be in dere!'"

"But-but I have come all this way to be with him."

"Where did you come from?"

"Richmond, B.C. It's on the west coast."

"Dat is a long way…"

"What shall I do?" Sarah asked despondently. "Perhaps I should go back?"

"I'm sorry," the personnel officer commiserated. "You might as well stay for a while… since you are here… and I have found you dis lovely place."

On Sunday Sarah went to a nearby Church and prayed for guidance, patience, and perseverance. She had come this far; there was no going back... was there? Sarah looked about at the beautiful stained-glass windows that let in the muted rays of the sun that transformed an ordinary space into a place of worship. A huge wooden cross adorned the space above the pulpit. She closed her eyes and bowed her head.

* * *

"Belief is such a powerful thing!" the old man with the long scraggily beard exclaimed. His dark eyes sparkled with knowing. He knew.

The young lad stood awkwardly before his mentors. There were three of them, three elderly men clothed in silken garments that cast an aura like that of royalty – but they were appreciated for their wisdom rather than their regal status. The eldest with a neatly trimmed white beard sat on a raised dais between the other two; he acted as the chief spokesman. *"They believe they are tragically flawed, imperfect, tainted, and defective human beings. And yet they are no different than you or I."*

"Belief is such a powerful thing!" the old man with the scraggily beard repeated.

"They grovel in the dirt and call themselves worthless sinners. It is so pathetic. I can still see them in my mind's eye, your own kin folk, prostrating themselves before the high priests and crying out in the most piteous voices, 'save us, save us, save us' – as if they are unable to save themselves."

"Belief is such a powerful thing – is it not?" the elderly man who had yet to speak intoned.

The young Jewish lad standing before them bowed his head as if he was ashamed of himself. He was fourteen, small and fragile-looking for his age.

"Your sensitivities make you vulnerable to the suffering of your people. You intuit the dissonance vicariously. You feel their imperfections as if they are your own. Distance and location makes no difference to such vibes. You have taken upon yourself the burden of your brethren – but you are not them. They believe that they need to be punished for the sins of their ancestors. Look what they have become. They have become what they believe they are."

"They have become... what they believe they are! Belief is such a powerful thing," the young lad declared bringing a smile to the faces of all three sages simultaneously.

"We knew. We knew you could not be intimidated and tainted with such dogma. That is why we brought your parents the frankincense, myrrh, and

gold... so they would have the means to send you forth from your homeland to find enlightenment in lands where the spirit is not encumbered by such a self-deprecating belief."

"*I am truly beholden to all of you, Magi.*"

"*You have honored us with your presence. You have come a long way along the Silk Road, but there is still a long way to go. The road leads to the monasteries high in the Northern Himalayas. It will take many years before you will be ready.*"

"*Ready for what?*" the frail-looking teenager inquired.

"*When you reach the Buddhist monastery in Ladakh, India, you will find solace in the wisdom of the ages.*"

"*Ladakh?*"

"*In time you will understand what you must do. You are like that fellow in that... ancient Greek Allegory. You have ascended from the shadowy realm of ignorance, dogma, and sin. It is your journey. It is your life. The road ahead beckons.*"

The young lad stared deeply into the darksome pools of the aged Magi's eyes. "*You are referring to Plato's Allegory of the Cave?*"

"*Yes,*" all three Magic responded simultaneously.

"*I shall leave tomorrow at first light,*" the young lad rose to his feet.

First light came and went. Years passed. And still the feeling never left him; it stayed with him like a stain that no amount of washing could remove - because the stain was not on him. It was on them. He could not shake off the oppressive feeling that followed him around like his shadow. He became slightly depressed. Wherever he went, empathy and compassion followed him. His newfound friends shouted, "*Issa, look at the sun. It shines down upon us with the glory of heaven. Cheer up. Let your sunny disposition shine through.*"

But something deep down inside him drew the dark clouds about him and smothered the light within with a depressing feeling of insecurity and sadness. Where did it come from?

It came from within, from the memories that were layered generation after generation... upon the essence of who he was: a Jew. Why was G-d so important to him? "Why?" the question festered upon his conscience as if he were somehow guilty of a crime against himself. With every step along the path to his destiny, the answer eluded him until...

Perhaps it was always there as he trudged down the Silk Road step after step. And the further he travelled from Jerusalem the more desperate the feeling became. As his twenty-seventh birthday loomed he went to meditate in a beautiful leafy green garden. As he sat quietly on a wooden bench with his head bowed and his hands clasped in his lap, the sun broke through a sullen cloud and bathed everything with a golden haze of divine light.

It was not a matter of belief. It was a matter of gnosis: he knew. It was so obvious! After Moses had led the enslaved tribes of Israel to freedom, a belated history was written that ennobled and justified their former slave status. It provided the rationale that enabled the enslaved to survive an inhuman, life-negating slavery that seemed hopeless.

And now that they were no longer bound in the chains of such an intolerable slavery - *what was preventing them from being free?*

He recalled the Magi saying: *Belief is such a powerful thing.*

Only by freeing *them* – could he in good conscience redeem himself… from the archaic dogma that weighed his brethren down with the sins of their ancestors. They did not understand that just like him, they were free. How could he convince them that they too, were *divine expressions* of freedom incarnate? He meditated in the garden of his altruistic intentions for nearly two years before he knew that it was time for him to go back *home*. Back down into the darksome cave in which his Jewish brethren were enslaved to an outmoded and life-negating religious belief that clung to them like a sickness unto death.

He laced on his leather sandals. He picked up the tattered cloth bag that held his meager belongings. He stood tall amongst the people who called him *"Issa, the best of the sons of men."* It was flattering.

His heart trembled when they tugged at his sleeves and implored him to stay. *"Issa, Issa,"* they cried as if overcome with a premonition that made them all the more vociferous. *"Please do not go. Such a mission is fraught with danger. You belong here… with us."*

"I must go," he said calmly. *"They are my people, my kinfolk. Perhaps they will be able to emulate my example. Follow me, I will say, be like me, a free man. It will be a simple message. Surely they will come to realize that they too are divine expressions of life like us, like you and me… like all sons of men."* He smiled graciously, drew in a sombre breath… and set one foot ahead of the other with a fateful determination. He did not look back.

* * *

Some things went beyond the pale of what most folks understood to be the case. Who knew that the Sanhedrin, chastised, demonized, and put down as they were by latecomers calling themselves *Christians*, nevertheless had a very important role to play in the passing parade of historical events?

Lenny knew. He intuited it through his third or all-seeing eye on Easter Sunday morning when he was hiding the Easter eggs and writing the clues that would lead his daughter, Kitty, to the place where the chocolate bunny was hiding. It came to him when he asked himself a simple question: "What am I doing this for?"

It was as if the Sanhedrin were watching. Why was he hiding... the Easter bunny? Was there some significance to such behavior? It was a very good question.

The fanciful experience got Len to thinking: "Who the hell were the *Sanhedrin* anyway?"

Jesus knew.

When he was praying in the garden of Gethsemane for guidance and reassurance, he could feel their presence. Their spies were everywhere. They had gotten to Judas and to Peter and they were determined to follow through with their trumped up charges against him.

Ever since he had argued with the priests at the temple they had become increasingly suspicious and hostile toward him. What could he do? He was just a child back then. His parents, Joseph and Mary were constantly being intimidated and harassed. Fortunately they had saved the gifts that the Magi had given them upon his birth. It bought him eighteen years of freedom.

The *Sanhedrin,* derived from 'zaddikim' meaning the righteous ones, represented the Establishment. It consisted of a council or court comprised of a selection of priests, scribes, and elders, plus a High Priest who pontificated over the sacred group. There were two types of councils: the Lesser and the Greater. The Lesser Sanhedrin, which was comprised of twenty-three members, presided over minor cases and disputes – while the Greater Sanhedrin, which consisted of seventy members plus the High Priest, dealt with cases of major importance where serious allegations of a criminal nature were involved.

The historical significance of the Sanhedrin is not to be overlooked. In the Torah, God commanded Moses to: '*bring me seventy of Israel's elders who are known to you as leaders and officials among the people. Have them come to the Tent Meeting, that they may stand there with you.'* The Sanhedrin was responsible for the maintenance of the historical and traditional validity of their religious beliefs. It was up to them to defend and maintain the status quo that consisted of their personal involvement as spokespersons for God's fearsome sense of vengeance and retribution, and the validity of the Torah, also called the Old Testament.

Could the Sanhedrin tolerate the blasphemous behavior of an upstart heretic Jew who had driven the moneylenders out of the temple and was undermining their authority and destabilizing the social order?

The Lesser and Greater Sanhedrin were made up of members from two populous groups: the Sadducees and the Pharisees. Unlike the Sadducees, the Pharisees stressed the importance of three major doctrines: the immortality of the soul, the resurrection of the body, and the existence of demons and angels. Both groups were united in their opposition of the tiny minority of the general population who endeavored to follow in the footsteps of the heretic Jew from Galilee.

Amongst the well-known Pharisees was a devout individual named Joseph of Arimathea, who in the late afternoon of the fateful day of reckoning, claimed the body of a crucified brother, and in the cool of the evening with the help of his friend Nicodemus, prepared it for a proper Jewish burial. Also numbered amongst the Pharisees were two religious teachers: Gamaliel, and his famous student, Saul of Tarsus, who later became Saint Paul.

During the interval that led up to the events that culminated with the crucifixion, two men enjoyed the status of High Priest: Caiaphas and his father-in-law Annas. Caiaphas was the High Priest in charge at the time of the arrest and crucifixion. Annas was the High Priest who had preceded his son-in-law to that title. Together they wielded tremendous religious and political power and influence in the Middle East of their times. What happened at Golgotha was unfortunate... was it not?

* * *

The heat was oppressive.

The sun shone down upon Golgotha, known in Latin as Calvary, situated just outside the walls of Jerusalem. Jesus had been forced to drag his own cross up to the top of the hill so all the passersby on the road below could see what happened to those who dared.

Jesus had dared. When the multitude broke bread with him… he had dared. When they thirsted for his wine… he had dared. When they had reveled in the fresh air and freedom of the mountainside… he had dared. He had dared to hope!

He had dared to hope when the Sanhedrin sent him to the Roman procurator Pontius Pilate. The Roman questioned him but could find no fault in him. But because the Jewish High Priest would not accept his assessment, Pilate sent him to Herod for a second opinion.

Herod was no fool. He interrogated the accused at length and drew his own objective conclusion. Anyone could see that the charges were without any basis in fact. The accused was just a humble Jew with a kindly disposition and a proclivity for parables. Herod sent Jesus back to Pilate as if to say: *why are you wasting my time?*

It was not the kind of answer Pilate was looking for. Now the onus was on him to decide. Surely the Sanhedrin would agree with his decision: "*I will chastise him… and let him go.*"

"I will chastise him… and let him go." The sentence was clear-cut and unambiguous. It had the authority of the mighty Roman Empire behind it. It was just: "I will chastise him… *and let him go.*" Pontius Pilate, the great Roman Procurator informed the Greater Sanhedrin.

But the Sanhedrin would not hear of it! *In that mortal moment the die was cast and the blood of an innocent man began to flow into the stream of consciousness from which history is fashioned. What if they had been reasonable? What if they had agreed with Pontius Pilate? There would have been no crucifixion, no martyr to worship, no Nicene Creed, no Roman Catholic Church, no Protestant Reformation… and no Holocaust.*

What were the wise and exalted members who made up the Greater Sanhedrin thinking? Who were they to challenge the ruling of the great Roman Procurator?

They were the descendants of those who had experienced generation after generation after generation of mind-numbing, brutal, meaningless slavery. They were born of an existential insecurity so profound and so irrational it caused the Sanhedrin to overreact to a singular opportunity to free themselves and their kinfolk from an archaic and debilitating slave mentality, an opportunity presented by one charismatic heretic Jew. To them he represented a threat and challenge to the status quo, an affront to the very core of who they were: sinners! The chosen people... *the descendants of over four hundred years of abject slavery!* Their slave mentality and identity as pious long-suffering Jews was being threatened. Consequently they dared to challenge the authority of the mighty Roman Procurator. They dared to demand *justice*!

Had not justice been duly served?

And yet they obstinately refused to accept the obvious verdict: *I will chastise him... and let him go.* Both Pontius and Herod had duly interrogated the accused... and *could find no fault in him!*

The profundity of the insecurity that emanated from the Sanhedrin washed over the mighty Roman Procurator. He was only human. The Sanhedrin pleaded as if... *they could do no other!* What could he do? He called for a basin.

Pontius Pilate washed his hands in public to demonstrate his indifference. Still it was difficult to remain totally neutral. Fortunately, as it turned out, it was the Hebrew custom that on the day-of-judgment a convicted criminal could be released as a sign of benevolence and good will. It was a rare stroke of good fortune! He would leave the ultimate decision up to the people, a kind of jury of his peers. The people would choose. He would make the contrast so ridiculous, the correct choice would be unmistakable. Unmistakable! Surely justice would then prevail?

It was an incredible moment. The jury of their peers stared up at the platform upon which two humiliated candidates stood. The mob blinked their eyes in disbelief that the mighty Roman Procurator would trust them with such a decision. They held their hands up before their sweaty faces to shade them from the glaring sun. The Middle-Eastern sun shone down upon the scene like an all-seeing god.

The soldiers thrust the innocent man forward. He stood mutely before the multitude with a twisted crown of thorns upon his bleeding head, humbled by their tumultuous greeting. Another man dressed in the decrepit garb of a convicted criminal was roughly pushed forward; he stood awkwardly before the multitude with a demented smile upon his face as if expecting the worst.

The unbiased sun hovered over them both with an equanimity that left nary a shadow of a doubt. The Procurator dressed in Roman gowns of despotic power waved his freshly washed hands for silence. The great unwashed stared up at him in awe.

"There is an old Jewish custom that I wish to honor. Today you will be given the responsibility to help promote a sense of democracy and justice in your society. Today you will be given the opportunity to give a deserving countryman his freedom!"

The crowd lapsed into thoughtful silence.

"Two candidates stand before you. The man to the left is known as Jesus of Nazareth. Both Herod and I have questioned him at length, and could find no fault with him. Therefore I had decided that I would simply chastise him and let him go," Pilate paused to let this cogent fact sink in.

The jury of his peers stared at the man wearing the crown of thorns of whom the great Roman Procurator had just spoken, and considered his remarks in the clarity of the unbiased sun.

"But, the Sanhedrin have objected... as is their right," Pilate continued. "The man beside him is a convicted criminal and murderer named Barabbas," the Roman Procurator pointed him out to make sure there would be no mistake.

The great unwashed murmured amongst themselves as if cogitating upon the verdict. Was not the choice obvious? Surely justice would prevail? A chilling silence fell over the multitude as they stood expectantly under the hot blazing sun.

"Whichever man you choose will be set free. The choice is yours."

The sweaty faces of the indecisive stared up at Pontius Pilate. Never before had they been given such a serious responsibility.

Suddenly the shrill voices of the paid instigators planted amongst them could be heard. "Give us", they yelled, "that one!" And they pointed with extended fingers. "That one!" the righteous demanded. An ominous hush fell over the crowd as if in that singular moment sinners could rise above their sinful nature.

The crowd roared the name of the one chosen with a certainty that left little doubt that... *justice was being done.* "Give us Barabbas!" they yelled as if in a frenzy.

It seemed like another lifetime. As if it had happened to someone else. Yet there he was... alone, forsaken, forlorn beneath the cloudless sky. He shivered as if a chill had enveloped his heart, froze it solid in a heartbeat and then began to melt with every slow intake of breath.

It was shocking: the truth. Why had he not seen it? He gazed down solemnly at the multitude - the shiny belligerent faces, sneering, jeering, and laughing.

Tears came to his eyes and mixed with the dried blood that had oozed down from the scars on his forehead. What else could he have expected? What other decision could they have rendered? They were only being true to themselves. *They could do no other.*

A sense of foreboding descended momentarily upon him. *If a sapling is grossly misshapen and insidiously twisted - how can it grow to be straight and true? If they could do this to one who had come to set them free... what dark premonitions might the future hold?*

It was with loving-kindness that Jesus gazed at the people staring up at him with all-too-human eyes. In those eyes he saw the endless grief, the pain and suffering, the confusion and frustration, the sorrow and longing, the sadness and insecurity... he saw a *human-condition* symptomatic of having endured over four hundred years of slavery. He gazed deep into the eyes of his kinfolk. *He saw a psychosomatic legacy of atonement.*

It touched him as nothing had ever touched him before. Compassion filled his heart with an empathy that knew no limits. These were his people, his blood brothers and sisters... *sinners reduced to an insecure mob whose ancestors had withstood four hundred years of mind-numbing and soul-destroying slavery. What was he to them? A chattel, a cut off bit of straw, a nothing?*

For their sake, he had come back from his long sojourn abroad. For their sake he had descended back down into the shadowy cave of the past. For their sake he now stood before them... *wearing a crown of thorns.*

The sunlight was directly overhead. They were tugging at his sleeves. He remembered. *He never looked back.*

If he had he would have seen them standing there with their heads bowed and their hands clasped in prayer. Some were weeping in despair as if overcome with a premonition of something worthy of such a display.

It had been a lengthy sojourn, eighteen years long. Thoughts of his countrymen had stayed with him during the adventurous journey down the long Silk Road winding northward toward the mysterious Orient. For a twelve-year-old boy it had been heartbreaking to leave all his Jewish friends and relatives behind. He remembered: it seemed like such a long time ago.

As he hung silently upon the cross, remembrances of the eighteen magical years he had spent abroad gave him the spiritual fortitude to remain hopeful, resolute, and compassionate in the face of a tortuous and imminent death. If by some miracle he managed to survive, he would go back to where the people called him 'Issa'.

"*Issa, Issa,*" they yelled with happy adoring faces. He liked that name.

"Save yourself!" someone scoffed.

'*Issa, Issa…*' was someone calling him?

* * *

Lenny was breathing hard as he dismounted from his refurbished bike at the bike rack in front of Starbucks. It was January the twenty-third. The male members of the Motley Five had agreed to meet without the women, reducing it to the Motley Three. It was 2:30 pm and on that occasion the sun smiled cheerfully from a frosty blue sky.

"Let's sit outside under the heaters," Lenny suggested, selecting a table in the corner near a heat lamp. They were the only persons willing to brave the chill; it gave the three old codgers the space, time, and privacy needed to discuss a topic that had always intrigued Rabbi Letenberg.

"I'll get the coffee," the good Rabbi offered while the other two selected chairs around the table. He went inside and returned five minutes later carrying three tall cups filled with dark roast coffee, steaming. He set them down on the table and said, "I doctored them up with syrup, chocolate powder, and cream."

Father Bertolli picked up a cup and sipped it. "Not too bad," he appraised. The other two followed suit. The Motley Three hunkered down around the table anticipating something they all enjoyed almost as much as food and drink: a stimulating and open-minded discussion on an interesting and controversial topic. "Shylock," the good Father began, hoping to get a rise out of his old Jewish friend.

"You talking to me?" Rabbit Letenberg responded with a crooked smile.

"Who else responds to that name?"

They all laughed goodheartedly.

"Speaking of stereotypes… is it not all about perception?" Rabbi Letenberg ascertained.

"Ah, yes," Lenny began, "some people have these stereotypes about other people that are mostly based on misinformation and ignorance. We Canadians, for example, living next door to Goliath, perceive ourselves to be the puny but courageous David. Goliath possesses the world's largest arsenal of WMDs – while David has his slingshot. We reside in Goliath's towering shadow in fear and trembling, acting out our fantasies in pubs and coffee shops where once in a while someone slings a bit of verbal mud in Goliath's direction, hoping to smear his vaunted reputation...." Lenny offered, hoping to stimulate the keen intellects and emotions of the two sitting across the table.

"And hide behind the shield of the forty-ninth parallel, righteously passing judgment on our formidable neighbor as if we somehow know better," Father Bertolli chimed in, rising to the bait.

"I enjoy your analogies, Lenny," Rabbi Letenberg commented, "They are provocative and insightful. It has been my observation that living in Canada provides us with a unique and almost privileged relationship with regards to the amazing political and economic development that ah-ah... has flourished in the free enterprise environment created by a bunch of hard-done-by colonists who had revolted against the tyranny of British Rule."

"We live vicariously in their shadow," Father Bertolli added. "They courageously fought a revolutionary war for independence; they fought a gut-wrenching civil war for human rights; they won the west; they remember the Alamo. They appropriated, stole, purchased, annexed, and usurped a vast geographical territory through their blood, sweat, and tears... while we watched."

"We watched as an impotent voyeur watches, with vicarious fascination. We looked through the peephole of our political independence as a sovereign nation flying the Union Jack with a sense of conservative propriety. Eventually we too asserted our growing sense of independence: we designed a bold new flag, a red maple leaf on a white background, and politely asked the British parliament to approve it," Rabbi Letenberg pointed out.

"We still cannot amend our own Constitution without the approval of Her Majesty's government! We are a constitutional monarchy; the Queen of England is our Queen too. We are loath to cut the apron strings entirely. We enjoy our patriotic position as the Queen's loyal overseas subjects, most likely because members of our largest ethnic group can trace their ancestry from British stock. Their competition with the French has resulted in an ongoing struggle to merge the cultural identities of the two founding European nations into a cultural mosaic that represents all Canadians who maintain political control of the lands north of the forty-ninth parallel – with the exception of Alaska which the U.S. purchased from Russia for a measly six million dollars," the good Father responded as if reciting a history lesson.

"You speak candidly, but somewhat self-deprecatingly, as is the Canadian mode of behavior that has evolved regarding our powerful neighbor to the south. It is perhaps a reflex action: we need to put ourselves down first... a kind of supplication before Goliath's might, before we dare venture an unflattering opinion about the blood on his mighty sword," Lenny vented somewhat sarcastically.

"We are a supine lot!" Rabbi Letenberg grinned sheepishly behind his beard. "But who can blame us for becoming such? We are born and raised with our eyes peering south, ever watchful, wary - perhaps even envious of our rich and powerful neighbors with their movie stars and glamorous and heroic celebrities. We sardonically search for counterparts in our own country, reasonable facsimiles with whom we can identify... and find lean pickings."

"Although we may be somewhat reserved," Lenny began hesitantly, "I think most Canadians have more admiration for our American neighbors than any other nation does. Even when we are somewhat critical, it is because we, as pseudo-Americans, want to help them do better. We empathize, sympathize, and agonize with them. We suffer immensely when they do something which conflicts with our noble image of them. We are saddened and traumatized when our heroes next door do things that we ourselves would never do – if we were them."

"Adroitly put," Rabbi Letenberg agreed. "Yes indeed, if we were them, 9/11 would have been handled so much differently!"

"As Canadians, we were there in our living rooms glued to our television sets when the Twin Towers came crashing down. We were horrified. It was as if it was happening to us. It was traumatic."

"And then Goliath, disguised as the Commander-in-chief, raised his mighty sword and smote the evildoers!" Rabbi Letenberg exclaimed. "Goliath raged, 'Either you are with us, or you are with the terrorists.' It was a threat so tangible that it stiffened the backbone of a little guy from Shawinigan, Quebec. He was not David. He was the Canadian Prime

Minister, Jean Chrétien. He was not intimidated. He informed Goliath that he was not with him – nor was he against him. He was a respected member of the United Nations like most of the other sovereign nations of the world that watched helplessly as Goliath, with the assistance of Great Britain, righteously smote the evildoers in Iraq. The only problem was: Iraq had nothing to do with 9/11 - but it did possess vast quantities of oil, and was threatening to destabilize OPEC."

"Destabilize OPEC?" Lenny asked,

"As you know, OPEC oil can only be purchased with US dollars, making US dollars valuable on the international market. Saddam Hussein was considering switching to the Euro," the good Rabbi candidly replied.

"Too bad Saddam Hussein had nothing to do with 9/11, nor did he have any weapons of mass destruction. The war effort could have been rationalized and glorified so much easier – if he had," Lenny lamented on behalf of the great unwashed who would have followed their Commander-in-chief into purgatory, which in retrospect was what the once majestic middle-eastern city of Bagdad was reduced to.

"You know, the grossness of this scenario becomes all the more tragic because… right after 9/11 the entire civilized world sympathized with the United States. The US had a glorious opportunity to demonstrate the sincerity of its Christian convictions. The Golden Rule could have ushered in a golden age of peace and cooperation. If the trillions spent on inflaming the war on terrorism had been spent on the root causes of the economic disparity that fuel envy, jealousy, and hatred, the entire world would have applauded," Rabbi Letenberg waxed eloquent.

"We Canadians, who attempt to make rational sense of the clandestine activities of our southern neighbor, have to scratch our collective heads at times in exasperation," Father Bertolli added.

"Perhaps we are all somewhat culpable," Lenny insightfully began. "It seems that the world economic stage has become a grandiose gambling casino where anything goes. Cheating, conniving, bluffing, stealing, lying, intimidation, and murder are commonplace. At stake are the world's renewable and nonrenewable resources. Everything is on the table." Lenny looked up at his compatriots who were leaning forward in anticipation.

"And?" Bertolli prompted.

"Common greed is the underlying operating principle. To become as wealthy as possible is the objective. Free enterprise is the slogan. It's like a poker game. The players are represented by big privately owned banks and multinational corporations legitimized as persons who hunker around the poker table disguised as statesmen. The stakes are… winner takes all."

"You have a flair for the dramatic," Father Bertolli noted. "I must say it is a creative but perhaps somewhat naïve metaphor," he praised and critiqued simultaneously. "What do the poker chips represent?" he asked, demonstrating his own complicity.

"They represent ownership."

"Ownership of what?"

"A portion of the world's total worth. It used to be that each country had its own respective valuation. However, since the meltdown it is evident that the grand economic system has become so interdependent and interlinked through various international trade agreements that the relative valuation of each country's currency is based purely upon its purchasing power in the world marketplace. The perceived exchange value or PEV of any currency represents the size of the mound of poker chips each sovereign nation has at the table. Each chip represents ownership of a micro-portion of the world's total economic value as perceived by the players. It is in fact a marker or IOU. Its worth depends upon its PEV."

"'Perceived Exchange Value' - an interesting concept," Rabbi Letenberg commented. "So the size of a country's pile of poker chips could inflate or deflate depending upon the PEV of its currency, the value of which is dependent upon the perception of its worth in the world marketplace combined with its poker playing skills… right?"

"I'm no economic wizard," Father Bertolli confessed. "In fact my accounting skills barely enable me to file my income tax. So let me play the fool here. PEV you say? Could you give us one of your simplistic analogies to-to illustrate?"

"Hmm…" Lenny cogitated for a moment. "Suppose there was an explosion aboard a ship at sea and only two people survived. One of the survivors is a young entrepreneur who is blindly driven by greed, while the other is a middle-aged conservationist. Both survivors only have time to take something of great value with them before boarding the only lifeboat still available. The entrepreneur takes a gold plated jewelry box full of precious diamonds while the conservationist takes an icebox filled with bottles of drinking water and dried foods. They paddle safely to a nearby island where they are marooned in a remote part of the Pacific."

"Like in the TV program about people attempting to survive on an remote isolated island," Father Bertolli contributed playing the fool like he said he would.

"On day one," Lenny continued, "the fellow with the jewelry box gloats that the other fellow was stupid to take something of such small value. On day two he is thirsty but still gloating. On day three he is willing to exchange a diamond necklace for one drink of water. On day four he is very anxious to make a deal: the whole box of diamonds for a bottle of water and a box of dry cereal. On day five he throws himself upon the mercy and compassion of the person he once ridiculed as being stupid." Lenny drew in a deep breath and tentatively sipped his slowly cooling coffee as if savoring the aroma.

"Our perceptions are profoundly influenced by our attitudes. Unfortunately those of us who are motivated by the mantra that *greed is good* are prone to act accordingly," Rabbi Letenberg insightfully added.

"Such greed is not to be confused with enlightened self-interest," Father Bertolli clarified.

"The person with the icebox is kind and compassionate," Lenny continued. "He retroactively accepts the offer made on day four and thereafter magnanimously shares the rest of his food and water with his fellow human being. A week later they are rescued. The conservationist, who was denigrated as being stupid, has the remainder of the food and water and the gold plated jewelry box full of diamonds. He gives his fellow survivor a diamond necklace as a parting gift. The young entrepreneur thanks him from the bottom of his heart. He now knows precisely what is meant by perceived exchange value."

"Illuminating," Father Bertolli responded enthusiastically. "You know, we are gambling with Mother Nature's nonrenewable resources. We are like the shortsighted person who took the gold plated jewelry box. When we have ravaged, decimated, and polluted the world... who will provide the food and water?"

* * *

She prayed for all her offspring
Who once rejoiced in the sunlight
And sprouted in the rain
Free from pollution and pain

And the callous disdain
Of greedy parasites
With gluttonous appetites
Unrequited
       She remains
Like a ghostly spire
Of desire etched upon the horizon
Of things long past remembering
When the rivers ran clear
The air was pure
Birds chirped
Children smiled
And she was fecund.

-LB

CHAPTER SIX

BEYOND THE PALE

Dependently – arising
Sin subjectively personified
As a psychosomatic imperfection
Exists as an embarrassment.

Pena had a habit of materializing when the moment was right. He must have been listening in on one of the Motley Five's discussions because he said, "Listen up Lenny. You've got to hear this. It is all about money!" The date was February 6th, and the time was precisely 3:46 am.

"Hold on," Lenny replied spritely. "What on earth are you so excited about?"

"When I develop a rapport with someone... well I guess it-it animates me. We have an affinity for each other's well-being."

"We do?" Lenny inquired with a humble sense of appreciation.

"You have not noticed?"

"Well, not actually," Lenny admitted.

"I had somehow gotten this impression that you were a little bit more intuitive. Anyway there is some unfinished business we need to deal with."

"What unfinished business?"

"A great deal has come to pass since the Nazarene was crucified. There are various consequences and ramifications we need to discuss. As you know, neither Christianity nor Islam would exist if Judaism had not existed first. And Judaism owes its legitimacy to the existence of the Torah as representing the word of God. And when, exactly, was the Torah written?"

"I suppose it came into existence when Moses came down from Mount Sinai carrying all those clay tablets."

"Was that before or after he had led the enslaved Israelites to freedom by crossing the Red Sea?"

"Obviously it had to be after."

"Correct. Before that there was no such document as the Torah, Pentateuch, or Old Testament."

"So what is the point?"

"That retrospectively-written document provides the belated history of the Chosen People. Before that... who knew that such a history existed?"

"Are you suggesting it could have been fabricated?"

"It is confusing, I know. The timeline is convoluted and the genealogical facts confusing. Nevertheless, both Christianity and Islam owe their existence to the rise and proliferation of a mythological concept of a righteous God, along with what could be the most irrational religious doctrine ever promulgated as the truth."

"What doctrine is that?"

"That the One and Only True God denigrated humankind as being 'fallen' – and therefore in dire need of doing penance."

"It is known as Ancestral Sin. Such a relationship to their God makes the adherents feel sort of beholden and of very little worth," Lenny chipped in. "Some will do almost anything to get themselves back into God's good graces."

"You mean to ingratiate themselves... to become worthy?"

"Worthiness is important, especially to those who are told that they are as worthless as the spittle of cattle." Lenny attempted to show off his biblical vernacular.

"How can a worthless sinner increase his depreciated sense of self-worth?" Pena posed the existential problem.

"How?" Lenny took the bait.

"It is a significant question that every self-righteous sinner and or capitalist should consider. Take your time. Think about it."

"Self-worth?" Lenny cogitated. "Hmm... perhaps one could equate one's personal sense of worth with something that was deemed to have value. How about something tangible and material like... the medium of exchange: money?" Lenny brightened up.

"You are nobody's fool, my friend. And what causes money to increase in value?"

"Usury?" Lenny suggested.

"Indeed, you do occasionally surprise me."

"You mean that is correct?"

"Ah-yes. You know there is more to usury than meets the eye. For example, consider a tree. Within a space-time reality it will grow larger and larger with time, because the impetus to growth is innate or owned by the tree. Now take an abstract material concept like money. What causes it to grow?"

"Usury."

"Who owns the growth?"

"The owner of the money. I see!" Lenny exclaimed. "And if the owner of the money is prudent, the sinner's self-worth will grow commensurate with his ability to increase his monetary worth. This motivates the sinner to compile huge amounts of such wealth, far beyond what is necessary for one's basic survival needs. One's social and religious status is relative to one's worth in money."

"The compounding affect of charging interest on the interest on the interest enables the saved to increase their worth many fold... over time. And time never stops – does it?"

"How clever! Putting a monetary value on the passage of time, as if time can be owned! Consider how much value would accrue on a hundred dollars at ten percent over a lifetime?"

"A hundred dollars compounded on a quarterly basis at ten percent interest over fifty years would be worth about $13,956. Within one single lifetime a worthless sinner can increase his self-worth many, many, many fold," Eldorado astutely calculated.

"Essentially, time is money, eh?"

"It is easy to see how a few bucks with a little luck, can be levered into a fortune, and rationalized as being a sign of God's blessing... and that one's worth in the eyes of God has increased with one's growing fortune." Pena replied.

"Intriguing."

"Since the Protestant Reformation the western world has combined the Protestant work ethic with the spirit of capitalism to produce the most potent socio-economic virus ever to affect the modus operandi of those residing under the vast influential shadow cast by the umbrella of the Judaic-Christian-Muslim cultural hegemony."

"Boy, did you ever say a mouthful there!" Lenny exclaimed impressed by his nocturnal friend's insight.

"And as you probably already know, the Rothschild's were amongst the first European money-lenders to understand the pecuniary power involved in the relationship between control of the medium of exchange, simple usury, and time. Today they prefer to operate behind the scene... like a ghost in the machine, so to speak."

"I'm beginning to understand why the concept of usury is so-so... powerful, and so fascinating!" Lenny expostulated.

"Look around. It is the foundation of what has become revered as 'banking'. Consider Goldman Sachs, as a shining example of what can be wrought from unregulated banking practices combined with usurious intentions. From humble origins in the city of New York in 1869, it has morphed into a world-class bank dubbed 'too large to fail', because if it did, it could drag down the illusionary leviathan experienced as modern capitalism. It nearly happened in 2008, but it had enough influence in the secret boardrooms of the most powerful sovereign nations to survive. It is a man-made phenomenon: a reified idea driven by secularized sinners: deluded self-seeking capitalists convinced that greed is actually good."

"You have a knack for telling it like it is," Lenny approved.

"It is incredible what has come to pass since the Nazarene drove the moneylenders out of the temple and especially since the infamous Council of Nicaea of 325 AD," Pena pointed out.

"The collective unconscious attitudes and beliefs of those affected by the amorphous vibes of the Doctrine of Original Sin have encircled the entire world. We seem to have become the tools of a bunch of sinful and greedy moneylenders like the kind Jesus drove out of the Synagogue in a fit of temper," Lenny added.

"And look what happened to him!"

* * *

George's mother's grandmother was of Jewish descent, making George about one-sixteenth Jewish… not that anyone noticed. George's father, Harry, was an uncircumcised English Baptist just like the previous five generations of Browns. He always rose early on Sunday morning and had his weekly shower, whether he needed it or not. His wife, Louise, would have his black three-piece suit neatly laid out on the bed along with a clean, starched white shirt and navy blue tie.

Louise herself usually wore a plain black polyester dress with a smart white jacket with black trim around the cuffs and lapel. George wore a little man's suit, black just like his father's with a navy blue tie as well. He looked just like a miniature clone of his Dad. He also took his weekly shower on Sunday morning right after his father. His dear mother always took her bi-weekly showers on Mondays and Fridays to enable the "men" to have more hot water on Sunday mornings. The trio always looked upright, and as clean as any Baptist family in good standing with the elders.

One time when George was eight and a half years old, Louise wistfully sighed: "Perhaps one day our son will become a minister of the Faith." "Don't be silly," Harry quickly replied, "Georgie ain't cut out to be no saint!"

George could hardly qualify as a saint, especially after he turned fourteen and began to masturbate diligently with sinful hands under the sheets in the early dawn. "Gosh, Georgie," his embarrassed mother admonished on days she washed the sheets, "don't you know that you could go blind?"

Thank god, George did not go blind – but it was not for a lack of trying. Still George felt guilty as hell, and as he grew older and more mature in his attitude toward such things, he attempted to rationalize his new-found interest in triple-X rated hardcore pornography by taking the time to confess his sins in the still of night while ensconced in the security of his own cozy bed. "Dear Lord," he would begin as if dictating a letter, "Please forgive me… for I have sinned. I just can't help myself; the temptation is so great – and I am so tempted. What will become of me?"

It seemed not only unnatural, but also masochistic for George to have willingly of his own free will, and without question, condemned and degraded himself from being a divine expression of God's grace - to being an abject sinner. However, unnatural as it was, it was a self-concept that he just accepted as if it was meritorious to be so classified.

With such an attitude it is little wonder that as a preschooler, immature little George was convinced that as a sinner, he needed to be 'saved'. "Suffer little children to come unto me," George recalled from one of his Sunday school lessons, and like millions of others who constituted the great unwashed of Western Christendom, he willingly came to church on Christmas Eve with his parents to hear the minister proclaim: "You are not alone. We are all sinners. Pray for forgiveness… for God is mighty - and we are like cut off bits of straw or the spittle of cattle…" Little Georgie humbly bowed his head and penitently put his chubby little hands together. His mother often shed a tear whenever she recalled that particular moment.

"It is a miracle!" Harry and Louise exclaimed on the day their only son graduated from high school. No one expected him to actually graduate, especially his parents. George surprised nearly everyone. He made it by the skin of his teeth – but he made it.

In his final year he was particularly motivated to do his best because a girl named Sarah sat in front of him in class. She usually wore loose fitting cotton dresses with a white plastic belt to accentuate her narrow waistline. What intrigued George the most was the way she crossed her legs. Sometimes when he was walking down the aisle and she was already sitting in her desk with her right leg over her left, he would drop his pencil on purpose. Sometimes he could see her fleshy thighs gleaming under her flimsy cotton dress, a sight that contributed to his excessive masturbation on those days. He sat directly behind her, three desks from the back, third row from the left.

Sarah was graduation bound. She was above average in intellect, which impressed George. When the teacher said, "Pass your papers back," when quizzes needed to be marked, George always felt privileged to be able to mark Sarah's. It became a secret endeavor of his to get higher marks than she did, because in his own mind he thought he was much smarter. So he began to study and do his homework diligently. And, wonder of wonders, he passed every exam… and graduated. All because of those erotic thighs! Incredible.

Yes, there is humor even in the most asinine situations imaginable. But let there be no mistake: none of this was funny to George. He was dead serious and deadly earnest. His *little head* spoke to his *big head*; it said, "Please Georgie, please, please find a way to put me out of my misery." What could George do? He just had to find a way.

This business of "finding a way to get the job done," was not new to George. He played hockey right up to the juvenile rep level. He was actually one of the best right-handed shots on the team. He'd streak up on right wing just like the pocket-Rocket and let her go: top corner, stick-side. The coaches were impressed. What impressed the coaches just as much was his attitude: "Don't worry, coach," he'd say between periods when the team was losing, "We'll find a way to get the job done!" And more often than not, they did. They made it to the playoffs in George's final year.

Sarah was an avid hockey fan - sort of a juvenile groupie. She sat behind the player's bench with her legs crossed. What more motivation did George need?

Considering how he ended up in his latter years being charged with murder and all… he did have his moments. Don't we all?

* * *

Unlike her husband, Sarah Brown was abnormally patient, stoic, and longsuffering. It was not evident, but it was a righteous trait not uncommon amongst the females in her family tree. When George took Sarah as his dearly beloved, he had no idea that she possessed the tenacity of a bulldog when she developed an interest in a subject that piqued her curiosity. She was able to post-hole, as they called it, by focusing her attention on a specific subject and digging in deeper and deeper until she got to the bottom of the matter. Some detectives are like that. When certain cases intrigue them, they are able to zero in like a kamikaze pilot over a target.

It was never mentioned, but it was basically because of Sarah's longsuffering perseverance that the marriage lasted and lasted and lasted until George was released from the Armed Forces... and beyond that.

After they had retired, Sarah became increasingly suspicious of the 'confidential matters' her husband refused to speak about that involved what might have happened to him while he was at the infamous Allan Memorial Institute. There were many odd behavior traits that George exhibited as the months and years rolled by that grated upon Sarah's sensibilities like an irritant upon a raw nerve. For example, when George bought a German luger with the grocery money she never received, Sarah said nothing. When he began obsessing over various editions of a pamphlet he referred to as a 'rag', she turned a blind eye. But inside, in the ever-conscious synapses of her brain where no one could see, she was as alert as a housecat on the scent of an elusive mouse. Whenever George took out his prized German luger and meticulously cleaned it over and over at the dining room table, the excessiveness of his behavior caused Sarah to wonder if her husband really had free will – or had his free will been compromised back in Montreal?

Sarah felt stymied, fatigued, depressed and was on the verge of throwing in the towel when she stumbled upon a self-published book at the local library written by a professional interrogator turned rogue, who claimed to have served in Korea and Vietnam. Sarah signed the book out and took it home to peruse. She set the paperback on the side table by the couch and neglected it until she received a phone call from the library reminding her that the book was overdue. She attempted to read the book in one evening.

Near the end of chapter nine Sarah read: "Free will is one of the greatest stumbling blocks confronting those attempting to control the minds of others." According to the author, the way around this problem was resolved: "by allowing the hapless victims to control their *own* minds." Apparently, that was the basic premise upon which the CIA operated their clandestine mind control programs. "The only way the human mind can be controlled," the author pointed out, "is by forcing it to control itself."

"*What do you mean?*" Sarah had blurted out rhetorically at the time of reading.

"Free-will can never be eliminated. Throughout the centuries man has attempted to enslave the minds of his fellow man by use of the most horrific tortures conceivable, without success. Free-will cannot be usurped by another – only by the possessor of it," the author had written.

"*Only by the possessor of it?*" Sarah mouthed.

"We all have free will. It is innate. How do you control something that is innate?"

"*How?*"

"You get the possessors to control their own free will," the author contended.

"*How do you do that?*" The question stuck in Sarah's mind and remained there long after she had returned the book to the library.

It was the answer to that last question that took Sarah's investigation to a new level. When she began, she had no idea it would lead to the infamous Abu Ghraib prison in Iraq, and 'GITMO,' a military detention camp located just off the eastern shore of the US at Guantanamo Bay in Cuba… and beyond. It took her to the gut-wrenching limits of her cognitive ability to process such information. Human rights were routinely violated in the form of psychological and physical torture including rape, sodomy and other types of sexual abuse, sometimes resulting in homicide. Those awful photos she saw of naked Iraqi prisoners of war being paraded around with dog collars around their necks were nauseating. Most viewers who saw them on TV had no idea why prisoners would be treated thus. The authorities concerned wanted the general public to believe that it was just the random activities of a handful of maladjusted military insubordinates.

Sarah would have been content to remain ignorant. She did not have to *know*. Knowing had its own ramifications, side effects, consequences, and existential implications. It could be depressing or possibly enlightening. When one is on a quest for the unvarnished truth, one does not know when, and in what manner, such vibrations will intersect with sympathetic vibes that exist in the minds of others.

"It was done" - as a former FBI operative, who had fortuitously arrived from San Diego to retire in Vancouver BC, had pointed out to Sarah one frosty afternoon after she had explained the sensitive nature of her quest - "to dehumanize them... to render them powerless and impotent. It is an important step in the brainwashing process that is an integral part of the mind-control program... justified as being in the interests of homeland security."

"Intriguing," Sarah had replied in a quavering tone that belied her modest demeanor. "There is a process?"

The longhaired, aging FBI agent was a psychologist who had a Masters degree in social psychology and had undertaken, but not completed, studies towards a PhD. Due to his training in psychology he had been assigned to work with 'the real criminals' he liked to joke, in the CIA. "When you are dealing with the most astute minds in the criminal business, you need to be even more devious than the most devious!" he liked to explain to novices who were finicky about ethical matters. He had spent more than half of his professional career liaising with the CIA, "so that the left hand would know what the right was doing". He had risen fairly high up in the ranks of his fellow employees before retiring. The higher he rose the more disillusioned he had become with the hidden agenda that for national security reasons always seemed to remain 'hidden'.

His name was Kevin Larose. He had some distant relatives who claimed to be descendants from the beleaguered and much maligned group associated with the infamous Riel Rebellion. He was aware that Louis Riel himself had spent some time in the United States, after which he returned to Canada to lead the rebellion... only to be captured and hung by the neck until dead. Larose was plagued with a keen sensitivity for social justice that seemed to be part of his genetic makeup.

The retired agent, and his comely wife Sophie, had moved to Canada to get out from under a suffocating feeling that they were under constant surveillance. Kevin had let his hair grow long and bushy at the back; he wore a black baseball cap with a red maple leaf on the front, dark sunglasses, and white sneakers. They had purchased a two bedroom, two-bath townhome in the same complex as the Brown's. It was a sunny but frosty autumn afternoon when the Browns had helped the American couple move in. George had been particularly helpful with his red steel dolly.

The greying retiree and his spouse had taken a shine to Sarah with her timid mannerisms. After the work was done and George had excused himself to return the dolly to the storage unit, Sarah invited Kevin and Sophie Larose to their place for tea and cookies.

"You have a lovely place here," Sophie remarked upon entering the Brown's townhome.

"Nice of you to say. George and I like the simple things... not too much clutter. And where do you hail from?" Sarah casually asked to break the ice.

"From the US of A," Kevin replied.

"And what did you do there?" Sarah asked after passing around the tea.

An awkward silence ensued before Sophie, hesitatingly replied, "My-my husband used to work for the Federal Bureau of Investigation."

"You mean the FBI?" Sarah clarified.

"We like to keep that information to ourselves," Kevin added.

"I understand," Sarah replied quietly. She studied the retired couple sitting across the coffee table from her. They seemed likable enough. She leaned toward them and proceeded in a quavering voice. "There is something that perhaps... perhaps you could help me with. It has to do with MK... MKUltra," she stammered.

Kevin Larose stood up as if to leave – but his wife stared up at her husband as if to say 'this is Canada... we are guests here... at least be courteous... sit down and relax.' Kevin hesitated and then slowly sat back down on the sofa beside his spouse. "You know," he began in a low tone, "that is a very secretive matter. Can you keep a confidence?"

Sarah nodded, crossed her legs and looked up with innocent child-like eyes, hoping that she looked trustworthy.

"Okay," Kevin began slowly, "what do you want to know?"

"It is about my husband, George," Sarah began in a hushed tone befitting a subject that was 'top secret'. She related what she knew about her husband's incarceration at the Allan Memorial Institute and his seemingly odd behavior.

Sarah's heartfelt anxieties, her sincerity, and her shy manner impacted upon years of stoic silence and awoke a long dormant need in the elderly man to at least appear to be somewhat heroic. For Sarah's sake, he decided to put aside his usual reluctance.

"Have you ever heard of the old movie entitled The Manchurian Candidate starring Laurence Harvey?" the retired FBI agent thoughtfully began.

"Yes. I remember seeing it a long time ago."

"In the movie, it is insinuated that a person's mind could be so altered as to develop a schizophrenic personality where one personality would be oblivious to what the other had been programmed to do. It was an innovative and daring movie for its time. But that was earlier on when black and white movies were in vogue. Since then the movie has been remade, and it has been discovered that the mind really is an ephemeral and plastic entity. I don't want to frighten you, but that old movie was not far off the mark."

"So, what does that movie have to do with MKUltra?" Sarah plodded on, determined to uncover the truth.

She had discovered from past experience that there was a general reluctance to share information that at one time had been classified as 'Confidential' or 'Top Secret'. However, no matter how many times she had been given the brush-off, she stubbornly plodded along like a bloodhound on the scent. There were times she had felt like giving up, but her Taurus instincts provided her with the perseverance she needed to carry on. The matter had become personal.

"There is an old professor emeritus from McGill who I met at a week-long symposium in Washington back in the seventies who could answer that question far better than I," Larose replied. "Let me share a little about what I found out from him... about MKUltra."

"What is his name?"

"Allen with an 'e'. Allen Thomson. Hmmm... where to begin?" Kevin Larose reflected. After once again insisting upon confidentiality for personal reasons, he looked inquisitively at Sarah and in a raspy voice asked: "Did you know there is a belated Canadian class-action civil suit pending... worth millions?"

"No. My husband keeps most of his correspondence regarding MKUltra to himself."

"You should check into it," the ex-FBI agent advised.

"I will," Sarah spritely replied. "Please continue."

"Of course Allen has his regrets; he was actually quite contrite," Kevin acknowledged. "But you know... some good has come out of all of this... lives have been saved and the security of our countries has been uh-uh... enhanced," he rationalized.

"Does that justify what happened up here... in Montreal?"

"I suppose there is a reason for the class-action suit. Personally, I was appalled at the crude experimentation that had been conducted under the guise of counter-espionage and homeland security. Allen said he had reported it to the government officials who were supposedly in charge at the time - but they did absolutely nothing."

"My husband was one of the guinea pigs involved in those experiments," Sarah reminded Kevin. "I need to know what might have happened to him."

The ex-FBI agent sighed as if he had reached an inner decision that went contrary to his better judgment. He gazed steadily at Sarah as if to say: *The answer is not intended for the faint of heart.* "I can only share with you what I gleaned from Professor Thomson. Apparently Allen was actually there at the time."

Sarah moved to a straight-backed wooden chair by the window, crossed her arms and placed her feet firmly upon the floor. She personified a professional journalist searching for a front-page story. She asked probing questions and nodded her head approvingly from time to time to egg the retired ex-FBI agent on. What did she find out?

Larose recalled that, according to Professor Thomson, compromised persons such as suspected spies or prisoners of war were the preferred subjects. However, in the absence of such candidates, unsuspecting volunteers and others whose intellectual faculties and sensibilities were intact were frequently selected... for experimental purposes. The selected individuals would be isolated in a sensory deprivation chamber for months and dosed with a variety of hallucinatory drugs. Over time their minds would not be able to distinguish reality from the hallucinations.

"Really?" Sarah had responded.

With a stony look of professional indifference masking his real emotions, Larose had droned on... "The unfortunate victims were tortured until they could no longer stand the non-lethal pain to which they were subjected. The term 'non-lethal pain' is significant. In normal situations, as an instinctive reaction of self-preservation, such victims would pass out or become unconscious when the pain became intolerable. In order to prevent this from occurring, the hapless victims were infused with a solution that prevented them from passing out. The brain would then be forced to deal with a reality so sensually painful that the choice would be either – or."

"Either – or?"

"Either shut down and die – or create a phantom reality free from such pain."

Sarah imagined George being subjected to such treatment.

"When the victim is not allowed to pass out or become unconscious, the brain is forced to deal with the pain as best it can. Those that survive this ordeal are potential candidates... for specialized programming. See the similarity to what was portrayed in the movie?"

"The creation of a-a Manchurian Candidate... You don't say?" Sarah intoned quietly.

"To create such an MC requires a controllable subject with long-term potential. Someone who is healthy, physically fit, and psychologically amenable to post time-related hypnotic recall, someone fit to be released back into the general population as if he is... normal."

"You don't say!" Sarah repeated once again as if alarmed,

"Apparently such things happened back then."

"Wh-when and how did this all be- begin?" Sarah stammered.

Kevin informed Sarah that as far as Professor Thomson knew, the project had its origins at a secret meeting at the Ritz Carlton Hotel in Sherbrooke, Quebec on June 1st, 1951. The purpose was to launch a joint US-British-Canadian collaboration led by the CIA, to fund studies on the effects of sensory deprivation on human subjects. In attendance at the meeting was Doctor Hebb, the Director of Psychology at McGill University who apparently received a ten thousand dollar grant to help with the secret project. It seems that Hebb had reached far-ranging conclusions that, *unknown to him*, would later become part of the CIA's secret agenda. During his involvement he achieved a degree of professional recognition. According to Professor Thomson, seven years after Hebb published his research, the American Psychological Association along with McGill University actually nominated him for a Nobel Prize.

"Who knew?" Sarah had queried, impressed by the old ex-FBI agent's memory for detail.

"About five years after Hebb had departed," Kevin explained, "Doctor Ewen Cameron took over the project with an unstoppable will to finish what Hebb had unwittingly started. Doctor Cameron was appointed head of the Allan Memorial, which at the time was McGill's psychiatric treatment facility. He received a salary from McGill but was medically responsible to the Royal Victoria Hospital."

"And..." Sarah prompted.

"Dr. Cameron's research was based on his ideas of re-patterning and re-mothering the mind. He proposed that mental illness was a result of an individual having learned incorrect ways of responding to the environment. These learned responses created neural pathways that led to repetitive abnormal behavior. Dr. Cameron proposed that a patient's mind could be de-patterned with the application of highly disruptive electroshocks twice a day... as opposed to the norm of two or three times a week. According to Cameron, such treatment would de-pattern the brain by severing or disrupting all incorrect brain pathways. Doctor Cameron called the process *re-patterning the brain*."

"Incredible. How was this accomplished?" Sarah queried.

"First of all, to prepare them for the de-patterning treatment, the hapless patients were put into a state of prolonged sleep for about ten days using a variety of drugs; afterwards they were given electroshock therapy that went on for another fifteen days or so. And this was only the first step."

"Some first step!"

"Following the softening up and de-patterning treatment, came what Cameron called the 'psychic driving' process where re-patterning supposedly occurred. It was very time-consuming, often continuing for months and months. "Negative messages about the patients' lives and personalities interspersed with selected positive information were played over and over on tape recorders. These messages could be repeated up to half a million times or until the re-patterning seemed to be taking."

"You have a very good memory of all this," Sarah had commented when the ex-FBI agent paused as if he had forgotten something important.

"We agents are trained to remember details... I wish my medium-range memory was a little clearer," he regretfully sighed.

Sarah refocused when the retired FBI agent straightened up as if his medium range memory had suddenly been refreshed, and he spritely asked: "Ever heard of Kubark?"

"Kubark? Can't say I have," Sarah replied.

"The CIA compiled most of the effective techniques of torture into a manual called the *Kubark Counterintelligence Interrogation Handbook*... that was one of the by-products of Subproject 68."

"Techniques of torture!"

"Following 9/11 in the US, the Bush Administration changed the rules of the interrogation process and once again the Kubark came back into vogue in shady offshore torture facilities."

Kevin Larose shook his head sadly. Had he said too much? He abruptly rose to his feet. "Has this been helpful?" he asked as an indication that the discussion had come to an end.

Sarah nodded her head and forced a sombre smile. She had found out far more than she could have foreseen or anticipated. "What did they do to my poor husband?" she thought.

Sophie Larose followed her husband to her feet and stretched her legs, "Thanks for the help, the tea and cookies... "She hesitated when the front door opened and George sauntered in nonchalantly.

"Why don't you stay and join George and me for supper?" Sarah responded brightly. "Your kitchen will be impossible to use with all the unpacked dishes and utensils... and we have plenty of food. In fact I must insist that you join us!"

"What do you think, dear?" Kevin asked Sophie out of consideration for her wifely duties as chief cook and domestic decision-maker.

"If it is not too much trouble..." Sophie replied graciously.

After a sumptuous meal of fried chicken, boiled baby potatoes, broccoli, and banana cream pie for dessert, Kevin and Sophie moved into the living room while George and Sarah cleared the table. When the dirty dishes were neatly stacked in the dishwasher, George excused himself to meet with his friends at the local Irish brewpub. Sarah dried her hands on the fluffy cotton towel hanging on the oven door, made her way into the living room, and sat down on the padded chair adjacent to the sofa where the FBI agent and his spouse had made themselves comfortable.

"That was a lovely meal," Sophie commented. "Your hospitality is overwhelming. Once we get set up you and George will definitely have to come over for supper some evening."

"Will your husband be returning soon?" Kevin asked politely.

"He will be out for at least two hours or more. That will gives us plenty of time to discuss what ah-ah... could have happened to him," Sarah said with a smile.

"I take it that you would like to-to continue with our previous discussion?" The ex-FBI agent glanced toward his spouse as if looking for some sign of moral support.

"This is Canada," his stately-looking wife prompted. "You can speak freely."

Sarah got up, went into the kitchen, and returned carrying a bottle of white wine and three glasses. She filled the glasses to the brim and offered each of her guests a glass. "To freedom of speech," she raised her goblet. The three goblets clinked.

"So, to continue with what we were discussing before supper...?" Kevin offered.

"Why," Sarah began in a quiet voice, "did they treat the inmates at the Allan Memorial Institute so inhumanely?"

"It was done, to uh-uh... to dehumanize them, to render them powerless and impotent. It is an important step in the brainwashing process that is an integral part of the mind-control program... justified as being in the interests of homeland security," he replied while slowly sipping from his goblet of white wine.

"Intriguing. There is a process?" Sarah asked in a quavering tone.

"Indeed there is. The information varies somewhat, but in general the process involves four basic steps that overlap and are essentially inseparable," Larose candidly replied, his tongue having been loosened by the alcoholic beverage.

"What are they?"

"The first step is referred to as Disorientation. The prisoner, terrorist, or victim is usually isolated in a dark cell or windowless room. It is known as *sensory deprivation*. The inputs from the five receptor senses are minimized."

"Why is this done?"

"All the stimulation received by the brain is received by our five receptor senses via our vertebrate nervous system. For example, a sound vibrates against your eardrum. This vibration is transmitted to your brain. It is just a nonsensical vibe; it could be any kind of sound. Your brain synthesizes the vibrations into a noise that has meaning, like a dog barking, or a gunshot, music etc. Similarly your other four receptors only transmit meaningless vibrations. Your brain interprets them and makes sense of them. Your brain lives in a reality of such sensory input. Get it?"

"I-I'm a bit confused"

"To put it simply, without inputs from the vertebrate nervous system the biological brain would exist in isolation. The tricky part is to force the sensory-dependent brain into transforming itself into a metaphysical entity called the mind. I use the term 'metaphysical' because this process is not properly understood at this time – but nevertheless it seems to work."

"And how is this accomplished?"

"This leads us into the second step where the brain is made to hallucinate. This often happens naturally during step two if a victim is left in an isolation chamber for months on end. The process can be enhanced by the use of hallucinogenic drugs like LSD. Steps one and two are quite commonly used when interrogating uncooperative prisoners or suspected terrorists… because the victim is not being *physically* tortured."

"I see. There would be no evidence of physical torture on the victim's body."

"Correct."

"What about step three?"

"Step three involves torture. You sure you want to hear this?"

"Try me." Sarah hardened herself.

"Once the will has been weakened and the brain disoriented, the victim is ready to be mentally and physically softened up. What I'm about to divulge may sound far-fetched, but let me assure you it is fact. At the time I was still involved, the CIA grudgingly released a list of six advanced interrogation techniques instituted in March of 2002 and used on a dozen or so top Al Queda targets incarcerated in isolation at secret locations on military bases as far flung as Asia and Eastern Europe. Only a handful of CIA interrogators are trained and authorized to use these extreme methods."

"What are they?" Sarah asked with a rising sense of incredulity that caused her to stare at the retired FBI agent as if to say: *Why are you willing to divulge such sensitive information… to me?*

It was her pathetic look of quiet desperation that encouraged him to continue. "The six techniques are couched in the most benign and mundane language possible. The first three in order are the *Attention Grab*, the *Attention Slap*, and the *Belly Slap*. It takes a perceptive and experienced operator to known when to proceed from one step to the other. They are only preludes to the next three. The fourth, known as *Long Time Standing*, is designed to physically weaken the prisoner and to make the victim physically compliant."

"How is this accomplished?"

"It is accomplished by handcuffing the prisoner and shackling the feet to an eyebolt cemented into the concrete floor. The hapless prisoner is then made to stand on the hard surface for more than forty consecutive hours." He looked up at Sarah: "How long do you think you could stand on one spot?"

"Maybe five or six hours… or perhaps eight or nine tops," Sarah estimated; "never for more than twelve hours. I don't think my feet or legs could handle it."

"Forty consecutive hours may not sound like much… until you try it yourself. Usually after that amount of time, exhaustion and sleep deprivation yield a more submissive and compliant prisoner. The prisoner is now ready to be *dehumanized*."

"What did you say?" Sarah asked as if she could not believe her ears.

"Are you sure you want to hear this?" the psychologist turned FBI agent inquired sympathetically.

Sarah nodded her head with a grim determination that caused Larose to remark: "Perhaps it might be better if you just put this matter behind you… and let it rest."

"I just need to…to understand… for-for my own sanity and peace of mind. Please continue."

"The unfortunate victims are subjected to the most abusive and inhumane treatment imaginable to deprive them of any shred of dignity or integrity. In short they are treated worse than dogs. At Abu Ghraib you saw photos of prisoners, naked except for their dog collars, being led about on leashes and made to pose in the most demeaning postures. It was all done as part of the secret process conducted by CIA officers, outside contractors, and the personnel of the 372 Military Police Company."

"And the CIA admits to all of this?"

"Not on your life! The buck never stops being passed. It should be noted, that Brigadier General Janis Karpinski, commanding officer of all Iraqi detention facilities, has adamantly denied any knowledge of the abuses, claiming that her superiors authorized the interrogations and that she was not even allowed entry into the interrogation room. The question is: *Was she just a sacrificial patsy?*"

"What happened to her?"

"She was demoted to the rank of Colonel on May 5th, 2005."

"Unbelievable," Sarah sighed and shook her head. "What about the fifth technique?"

"It is called the *Cold Cell*. It does not sound all that cruel, but it is. The prisoners are forced to stand naked on the cold hard floor of a cell in which the temperature is kept near or below fifty degrees F. Throughout this ordeal the prisoners are constantly doused with ice-cold water until they either break down and capitulate, or pass out. A few specially selected prisoners are now ready for the sixth or final treatment."

"What is it called?"

"Some refer to it as *water-boarding*."

Sarah had never heard of water-boarding. She had heard of snowboarding and skateboarding - but those were athletic activities. "Water-boarding!" Sarah exclaimed as if suddenly alarmed by the seemingly innocuous connotation of the term.

"It sounds like it could be something akin to snowboarding or skateboarding," Larose explained, "but believe me, it is far from being fun! It is actually an extreme technique reserved for only a handful of pre-selected prisoners. It is used because it leaves little or no physical evidence that the victim has been actually tortured. The most useful candidates are those who can be turned into potential MCs."

"Robot assassins or Manchurian Candidates like in that old movie by that name?" Sarah inquired.

"Yes. Perhaps that is where the label comes from."

"How are these robot assassins created?"

It is essentially a non-lethal process, a specialized technique utilized to force the brain into an extreme use of its free will. When faced with death, the survival instinct automatically kicks in; the human brain of its own free will... will do whatever necessary to survive. This last point is very significant: *of its own free will, the brain will do whatever necessary... to survive!*"

"Of its own free will... the brain will do whatever necessary to survive," Sarah repeated to make sure she understood what the ex-FBI agent was saying. "How is this done?"

"The unfortunate prisoner is bound to an inclined wooden board with his feet at the higher end - and his head at the lower end of the board. A wet towel is placed loosely over the immobilized victim's face. In this posture when water is poured on the towel, some of the water flows into the victim's nose, eyes and mouth triggering an involuntary gag response."

"Why is that significant?"

"A very important question. As you know, gagging is an involuntary reflex survival response or IRSR. It is instinctive. Consequently the will is negated, and the victim instinctively reacts as if drowning and death are imminent and inevitable."

"Imminent and inevitable!" Sarah echoed.

"Sometimes cellophane is loosely draped over the prisoner's face instead of a towel to enhance the feeling of actually being drowned. In addition the torturer intimidates the victim by telling him in no uncertain terms that he is a... *good-for-nothing useless fucking liar...* and deserves to die!"

"Diabolical to say the least!"

"The objective is to terrorize the victim into actually believing that death is imminent – even though it isn't. The hapless victim strapped to the water-board is totally at the mercy of the person pouring water over his face. Sometimes the torturer goes too far or gets carried away and accidents happen - the hapless victim is drowned!"

"What an inhumane practice!"

"The result is what is important," the old man plodded on in a monotone voice. "Faced with terrifying fear and imminent death, the hapless victim is confronted with an either-or situation: *either deny the reality of the predicament – or succumb to it.*"

"Either deny the reality of the predicament – or succumb to it?" Sarah queried.

"That is the key moment that the experimenters find most intriguing. The IRSR or survival instinct usually kicks in and the *mind* in some cases, faced with an absolutely untenable situation, is able to deny the reality of the moment by splitting of its own free will and creating a schizoid or separate identity... *a phantom personality.*"

"Sarah was stunned into silence. She thought of her husband. Her eyes misted over momentarily. She drew in a slow breath. "Did you say splitting of its own free will?" She asked incredulously.

"Yes, and creating a phantom personality. It happens. The reasons why it occurs are not as yet properly understood." The aging psychologist shook his head as if to clear his vision. "Under the duress of imminent death the human *mind* will do whatever it has to... to *survive.*"

"What is a phantom personality?"

"It is a personality that is able to survive by denying the life-negating reality associated with the victim being tortured."

"What about the victim?"

"Incredibly, the victim undergoing the water-boarding, upon being resuscitated, is not aware of the *phantom.*"

"What?"

"The real personality... is not aware of the existence of the phantom personality. You might say the phantom exists subliminally."

"Is the phantom personality aware of the real personality?" Sarah adroitly asked.

"*It thinks that it is the real personality,*" the retired agent whispered as if such information warranted it.

Sarah lapsed into silence. After a moment she parroted: "*It thinks that it is the real personality.*" She imagined George methodically cleaning his German luger at the dining room table.

"Yeah. As such, it is amenable to hypnosis and post hypnotic suggestions. In this manner a *real* Manchurian Candidate can be created."

"What is a real Manchurian Candadate?"

"That is a human being whose conscious brain exhibits all the characteristics of having free will. However, when it receives a given signal, which could be a photo, a sound, a number, a code name - the possibilities are endless, the post hypnotic suggestion is triggered and acted upon by the phantom personality."

"Abominable!"

"The conscious non-phantom brain has no awareness of what the phantom personality does; it is in fact oblivious of the existence of the other personality. In this way a suspected terrorist-prisoner, for instance, can be secretly programmed and quietly allowed to integrate back into a terrorist cell, and when the circumstances are appropriate, given the trigger word by phone for example, to carry out the assignment. If caught, the Candidate has no recollection of committing such a crime and claims to be innocent."

"Sounds, well... almost unbelievable," Sarah confessed.

"That is the beauty of it. Hardly anyone gives any credence to such cloak and dagger stuff. It all sounds too incredible. But mind you, it really is not all that far-fetched... is it?" Larose paused and looked down at the floor.

"Not at all," Sarah confirmed while nervously twirling her wine goblet. "I am reminded of ah... someone like-like Lee Harvey Oswald."

"He claimed he was a patsy - but who knows? He was conveniently dispatched... perhaps by another MC, before he had a chance to testify in a court of law. There is a lot more cloak and dagger stuff I could share with you," Larose whispered, "but I think you have enough information to digest for the time being. Perhaps you could drop over to our place after we have had time to settle in and we can continue our discussion. I find it refreshing, and-and somewhat therapeutic, to talk to someone without the fear of worrying about whether or not she might be wearing a wire.

"This is Canada, you know," Sarah spritely replied.

* * *

A fortnight from the date of their initial conversation, Sarah Brown, wearing a three-quarter length brown suede coat over a semi-newish green dress with a high neckline and short sleeves, made her way along the sidewalk toward the retired FBI agent's townhome. When she reached the entrance she hesitated. "What am I doing here?" she asked herself as she rang the doorbell.

Before she could answer her rhetorical question, the door opened and the old retiree graciously ushered her in. "Glad to see you again," he began with a happy smile on his aging countenance.

Sarah removed her coat, placed it beside her, and sat down demurely on a greenish sofa by a narrow two by four window with a bottom opener. The putrid green of the sofa clashed horribly with her beautiful dress – fortunately Sarah could not see herself.

"You look lovely today," Kevin Larose remarked, "that green dress really suits you."

"Thank you," Sarah replied self-consciously, flushing beet red; she was not used to such compliments.

"My wife went out shopping... so we have the place to ourselves this evening," Larose explained. "Can I get you something to drink?"

"No, I'm not thirsty." Sarah crossed her legs and sat primly on the edge of the sofa.

The gracious host plunked himself down on a wooden chair across from his guest and stared up at the stippled white ceiling. A long moment passed. The retired FBI agent looked at Sarah with understanding eyes. "You know... as Shakespeare once wrote: *there are more things between heaven and earth than are dreamt of in your philosophy.*"

"There are?" Sarah spritely queried.

"I used to have these long discussions with an old confidante of mine who was a journalist; he once served as a foreign correspondent for a public broadcasting organization. Between the two of us we attempted to make some sense of the irrational behavior of the historical development of what he referred to as the globalization of the Christian influence." In a softer tone he added, "It might make you feel a little better if you realized that in this miraculous world in which we reside, religious brainwashing is really... nothing new."

"Religious brainwashing?" Sarah asked with a solemn face.

"When I realized this, I felt a little better about what we were doing in those days."

"I'm somewhat confused," Sarah admitted. "Please explain."

"Consider this question: What is survival all about?"

"I have never given it much thought."

"Neither did I until I got involved in this business of brainwashing. Do you want to know what I think... now?"

"Of course."

"Religion is just a subtle form of social and psychological brainwashing. Being trained as a psychologist, I found this idea to be quite fascinating at the time... and still do." Larose leaned back and gazed at Sarah contemplatively.

"Religion is a subtle form of brainwashing?" Sarah parroted.

"Yeah. The converts are all culturally, socially, and religiously indoctrinated, whether they know it or not, to accept a certain preconceived dogmatic view of reality."

"I have never thought of brainwashing in that context before!"

"What does the term 'survival' mean to you?" Larose asked.

"Hmm, it means something like... attempting to stay alive?" Sarah replied with a doubtful inflection.

"To a normal human being *survival* connotes a natural life-affirming desire for continuing earthly existence. However, to the religious with heavenly aspirations, survival connotes something paradoxical, like dying in order to gain eternal life. In the western part of the world most believers are culturally and socially conditioned to believe in a genocidal religious doctrine that is counterproductive to their survival instincts."

"Did you say genocidal?" Sarah queried, her ears perking up.

"Think about it." The elderly man gazed speculatively at Sarah. "Are you a Christian?" he inquired.

"Why do you ask?"

"I don't want to offend you. Christianity is very big in the United States."

"I used to be in my younger days – but now I claim the right to-to... reserve judgment," Sarah cautiously replied.

"Okay. See if this makes any sense to you. Once when I was participating in a top secret combined FBI-CIA think-tank along with a host of brilliant and high-minded thinkers, it became evident that the point of the exercise was to figure out how to use our public and religious institutions along with the mass media to manipulate the gullible public into believing in a-a... cause worth dying for."

"*A cause worth dying for*?" Sarah inquired with bated breath. The word 'terrorist' popped into her mind. "What cause did you come up with?"

"Religion combined with political fervor."

"Say again."

"Religion combined with political fervor produces the most fanatical and most incredibly powerful '...ism'."

"What 'ism' is that?" Sarah asked, her curiosity piqued.

Larose looked quizzically at Sarah as if gauging her level of credulity. He turned and looked out the front window, as if searching for a reason to change the topic. He looked back at Sarah.

"You seem rather reluctant to..."

"Blind patriotism, imbued with righteous religious belief!" the old man expostulated as if uttering a profanity, is the 'ism' that produces the kind of *true believers* who are willing of their own free will, to die for their beliefs."

"What!" Sarah was stunned into silence. A sickening feeling of disbelief washed over her. She thought of her patriotic husband. She thought of the maple leaf on the Canadian flag. She recalled standing at attention when the national anthem was played whenever Canada won a gold medal. She knew that deep in her heart she was a proud Canadian. Nothing could change that! "Did you say *patriotism?*" she challenged fearlessly.

"I said *blind* patriotism... *imbued with righteous religious belief.* I know," Kevin responded empathetically. "I know how emotionally disturbing it can be when you first hear it. But nevertheless... it is a cold, hard fact. Take a hard, objective look at what is happening in the Middle East. We in the FBI and CIA had to face up to it. And the beauty of it – if that is the right word - is that in the Western world, the Judeo-Christian-Muslim faithful have already done the so-called *religious brainwashing!*"

"Unbelievable!" Sarah pronounced incredulously.

"I know, but it is unfortunately, the case. Millions of true believers have been religiously brainwashed or programmed to believe in a reality-concept that belies the rational, empirical evidence gleaned from their receptor senses. It is as if a collective *phantom personality* has already been created, and is potentially susceptible to being imbued and reinvigorated with new meaning and purpose... as we speak."

"A collective phantom personality?" Sarah queried.

"It was just there staring us in the face: the potentiality, an opportunity to take control of what has existed institutionally in the Western World since shortly after the Protestant Reformation."

"How so?"

"By covertly manipulating the manipulators. Easier said than done – I know. But as you know, human beings are susceptible to persuasion, intimidation, and influence by a vast assortment of economic, political, social, and psychological means. Some agents argued that it was a misuse of our moral authority to even try to influence the manipulators. Some were simply offended. Some were conflicted. Some said that if we did not do something – others far less scrupulous would.... and probably are. In the end we were split about even. No decision was reached... as far as I know. But nevertheless, the opportunity was, and still is, there."

"To do what?"

"We had to figure out how to-to secretly infiltrate the various established socio-economic-religious-political institutions... and become the mouthpiece for the *One and Only*."

"How devious!" Sarah exclaimed, astounded by the concept.

"Imagine the millions who presently pray for guidance while under the spell of secularized religious dogma, and who accept the pronouncements and opinions of their leaders without question." Larose paused to search his mind for a more explicit illustration. "*Imagine a staunchly Protestant Germany; imagine the rise of a demagogue; imagine Nazism. Now imagine...*" Larose paused to give Sarah time to imagine, "*six million dead Jews!*"

"Incredible!" Sarah admitted. "It happened."

"Indeed it did! When it comes to religious belief the gullible can be manipulated into doing almost anything."

"Anything?"

"It is amazing how righteous the righteous can be! The righteous will do anything, I mean anything, to be right. Who straps grenades around their waist and pulls the pin in a crowded public place? Righteous belief enables the true believer to do the unbelievable!" Larose looked up and pursed his lips as if pondering whether to continue or not.

Sarah sagged back on the green sofa. The idea presented was so unimaginable and so frightening it left her speechless. The ramifications were... scary. She drew in a deep breath and exhaled slowly. She sat up straight and stared at the ex-FBI agent.

"Shall I continue?" Kevin asked in a concerned tone.

"Please do," Sarah replied with a grim expression masking her feelings of insecurity and doubt.

"What enables religious fanatics of any stripe to commit outrageously oxymoronic acts of divine-political-terrorism?"

"You tell me," Sarah asserted.

"Blind patriotism inspired by dogmatic political and religious fervor. In their own minds, such believers are willing to sacrifice their mortal existence here on earth in order to gain everlasting life in a sublime reality described as paradise or heaven," Larose lowered his voice, stared toward Sarah with secretive eyes, and continued in a whisper, *"as did the patriotic religious fanatics piloting the passenger planes that crashed into the Twin Towers."*

"That does seem to make sense," Sarah reluctantly admitted.

"Indeed it happened – did it not? Given that the terrorists were not *born* terrorists - the real important questions become: *How did once innocent human beings become so brainwashed? Who manipulated them into doing this? Whose agenda were they following... and why? Was it really God's?"*

"Huh!" Sarah exclaimed, surprised by the astuteness of the old fellow's questions.

"I-I didn't mean to offend you," Larose apologized.

"Not at all... I get it. It is just that it seems so-so diabolical, if that is the right word."

"It is." Larose stood up and shuffled his weight from his left leg to his right. He cleared his throat as if preparing himself for a crucial utterance of utmost significance. "Our response to the nine-eleven attack was - how should I put this... not very sophisticated. It was almost as if – as if we too... were being manipulated!"

"What do you mean?" Sarah could scarcely believe her ears.

"Some of us old-timers were appalled to say the least. We, I mean the coalition-of-the-willing led by the US, retaliated in a simple-minded, vindictive, and vengeful manner. Why? We did nothing to defuse the situation – in fact we-we inflamed it beyond anything the terrorists could ever have dreamed of! Look at Afghanistan, Iraq, Iran, Syria, the entire Middle East, and Europe. In fact our war on terror has engulfed most of Western Christendom. You could say our response was like... like pouring gasoline on a smoldering fire!"

"Why couldn't the elected officials in Washington and London see it? Were they really that unaware... of what they were doing?"

"At this time it seems that the unvarnished truth must forever remain varnished… because the integrity and credibility of those who pretend they know better is at stake. All that can be proven is that huge profits were made. I mean huge profits. Gargantuan profits! Simple greed has no conscience. It seems the material world is fashioned out of our conceit, vanity, and religious predilections. All is not what it seems. There are some very rich, very powerful, and very smart people pulling the strings that make the patriotic puppets dance." Larose stood up and began pacing about the room.

Sarah stood up and began pacing along side the retired FBI agent. Around and around the living room they went like a couple of old folks out for a meditative stroll.

"It seems that in the international world of institutionalized religion, high finance, and intrigue… national insecurity provides those who think they know better, with security!" Kevin stopped pacing. Sarah stopped with him.

"It is just beginning," Larose announced.

"What is just beginning?"

"The insidious cyber attacks. The cyber attacks on our newly digitized institutions. And what is not digitized these days? It has quickly become global in scale. Any geek with a computer can indulge." Larose sighed as if dismayed by his own prognostications.

"It-it seems unbelievable!"

"I don't blame you for saying that. I know, all this cloak and dagger stuff… it is as real as it is delusionary. I sometimes have to shake my head; the stuff of my dreams seems less convoluted than this. Some of the disillusioned old-timers like myself facetiously refer to our collective roles in all of this as… *a conspiracy of fools*."

Sarah shook her head in disbelief at what she had just heard. "A conspiracy of fools, eh?" she parroted. In her personal pursuit for information regarding her husband's participation in a top-secret operation, she had discovered far more than she had come in search of. She felt withered by the burden of *knowing*. She felt uniquely privileged.

"You have shed a great deal of light upon a very dark and secretive matter. I am beholden to you for being so gracious, honest, and forthright."

"Don't mention it."

Sarah Brown slowly put on her suede coat, gave Kevin Larose an appreciative hug, smiled feebly, opened the front door, and stepped out into the dim light cast by the last rays of the setting sun. She paused pensively, drew in a deep breath, exhaled slowly and began walking homeward with glassy tears blurring her vision... following the elongated shadow cast before her.

* * *

O *Kanata*
We hear your plaintive cries
And your monumental sighs
In the vastness of resilient skies
Above the wilderness that stretches
Into the beyond where in our hearts
We pledged our allegiance
As native sons
And daughters we stood proudly
Beneath the shimmering glow
Of the aurora borealis
Like immortal spirits reincarnated
From your wounded past
Rejuvenated
By the vibrant warmth
Of the Chinook winds sweeping down
From the eastern slopes of the rugged Rockies
Chasing the drifting snows of winter
Across the windswept prairies
Where in springtime rainbow raindrops
Glistened upon golden fields of plenty
While countless rivers and streams
Crawled north, east, west and south
Like hoards of tiny lemmings streaming to the seas
To be swept away by icy Arctic currents
Or the windblown waves washing inland
Along the Atlantic seaboard
And receding reluctantly

From Pacific shores
                    Silently witnessed
By the trembling treetops
Quaking in quiet forests
Standing stoically beneath starry heavens
Providing solace for the heartfelt anguish
Of melancholic dreamers left behind
With immortal memories
Of a poignant past where once upon a time
A crimson maple leaf fluttered
And we sang your praises
O *Canada*....

                    - LB

CHAPTER SEVEN

MORTAL MEMORIES

It is simply amazing
How the humorous
Can be so serious.

The Motley Five were present: Lenny and Lana Bruce, Father Bertolli, Cathy Schneider, and Rabbi Letenberg. They gathered around Father Bertolli's majestic mahogany desk covered by a mess of papers, pamphlets, and books. If they could have exchanged the electric lights with candles, and worn cloaks instead of sweaters and jackets, they could have passed for a motley crew of alchemists searching for the elusive Philosopher's stone of antiquity, or a group of illuminati filled with esoteric knowledge they had gleaned from the passing ages.

"October 30th, Steveston, British Columbia, Canada," Lana wrote on her yellow notepad. She clicked on the tape recorder.

"Glad you all could make it," Father Bertolli said. It had snowed lightly the night before, and the good Father had worried that the meeting might have to be postponed because West Coasters were not adept at driving in snow; most did not even own a set of snow tires, including himself. Consequently he had dutifully contacted them all by phone that afternoon and they all confirmed that they would be there. He himself was particularly anxious because he knew that his good friend the Rabbi had done a great deal of research and was hoping that he would get the opportunity to share the product of his efforts.

Father Bertolli waited until everyone was comfortably seated before he began. "It is so nice to meet together like this. We have a wonderful group here of open-minded individuals… who do not mind speaking their minds."

"Ahem," Rabbi Letenberg cleared his throat, drawing attention to himself. "Hopefully we can all agree on one thing," he offered.

"And what is that?" the good Father queried.

"All my life I have looked for certainty. The only certainty I ever found was that… there is no certainty. I know I'm probably sounding like a religious skeptic, but if there is one thing I am certain of, it is that we are all as fallible as we are mortal."

"What about your belief in God?" Father Bertolli challenged.

Rabbi Letenberg smiled and asked, "What about it?"

"Are you not certain about your beliefs?"

"I am certain that they are 'beliefs'. I want to make certain that we all agree that what we will be discussing here are just beliefs - not necessarily the 'truth'."

"You do have a point there," Father Bertolli conceded.

"Let me open the discussion by sharing with you my limited understanding of how the Hebrew belief in the notion of God came to be," Rabbi Letenberg began.

"You mean the monotheistic God that all Jews, Christians, and Muslims presently worship as the One and Only true God?" Lenny asked.

"Yes. I say Hebrew God, because Abraham, Issac, and Jacob, known as the Patriarchs, are the spiritual and biological ancestors of what became known ultimately as Judaism, from which both Christianity and Islam later developed. It is therefore the root or source of the modern day institutionalized Jewish-Christian-Muslim monotheistic religions; as such it deserves special attention. Judaism is all about 'belief'. It is a belief based primarily upon a mysterious entity that defies utterance… but because we have to refer to this mysterious entity in some manner, it has been rationalized by Jewish scholars to be a Tetragrammaton."

"What is a Tetragrammaton?" Lana asked.

"It simply means 'four letters'. Tetra means four, and gramma means letters or graphemes."

"What four letters?" Lana persisted.

"THVVH."

"Isn't that five letters?" Lana zeroed in like a prosecuting attorney.

"It is a five letter tetra-grapheme which consists of a total of three different letters. The five letters THVVH are pronounced 'Je-ho-vah' or 'Ya-h-weh'," Rabbi Letenberg shook his head and waved his hand as if clearing the air. "Anyway," he continued, "let's not get bogged down by the pronunciation – it is the meaning that counts. *THVVH*, Jehovah, and Yahweh are all pseudonyms for an unutterable entity."

"An unutterable entity with utterable pseudonyms. That is a strange thing for a Rabbi to be admitting," Cathy commented.

"I am a rabbi by religion, not by faith," Rabbi Letenberg pointed out, and continued on as if that ambiguous statement had clarified the matter. "The god we are talking about here is the God of Abraham. The important question for Judaism is: 'How did Abraham come to this understanding about an unutterable mysterious Tetragrammaton that has become reduced to three letters that represent *dog* spelled backwards?'" The good Rabbi attempted to inject a sense of levity into the discussion.

Sensing Rabbi Letenberg's apprehension at his poorly timed attempt at humor, Father Bertolli laughed, "Ha-ha-ha," and turned the spotlight onto himself by saying, "A sense of humor is always refreshing especially when discussing such a-a... serious religious matter."

"A serious matter indeed!" Lenny followed up. 'Dog' is a simple three letter word. But that word differs vastly from 'god'. We know what a dog is. We know what a dog looks like. Who is to say that the invisible voice in Abraham's head wasn't dog spelled backwards... in Hebrew? And what is that? What is dog spelled backwards in Hebrew? Could it be THVVH?"

"A profoundly witty point, I must admit. I suppose you could say that the idea of an invisible 'god' existed long before Abraham was born... but doesn't that just further validate the idea? Your candor is much appreciated," the Rabbi replied before continuing. "The genesis of Abraham's belief in his mysterious THVVH begins in the city of Ur in Babylonia around 1800 BCE. Information is skimpy, but some details have emerged. His real name was Abram – not Abraham. He was the son of an idol merchant named Terach or Terah."

"His father made and sold idols?" Cathy exclaimed in disbelief.

"Yes. But rather than following in his father's footsteps as an idol merchant who made his livelihood by making and selling idols of various gods - young Abram sought a different path."

"What path?" Lana asked.

"Being reasonably intelligent and perceptive, young Abram could plainly see that the idols his father was making were just made of clay and had no special powers. As he grew older Abram began to question his father's staunch belief in idol worship. He felt that there had to be some other mysterious power beyond mere clay idols, and that that mysterious power did not reside in things, but was the creator of all things. However, to espouse such heretical views to a domineering father who made his living making and selling clay idols - was unthinkable."

"So what did Abram do?" Cathy asked, her curiosity mounting.

"The more he thought about it, the more convinced Abram became. Every time he watched his father creating clay idols as if they had special powers... he just knew that he was right! *How could mere clay objects, no matter how intricately shaped and skillfully manufactured, be worthy of worship as if they were gods?* It seemed self-evident to Abram, naïve as he was, that his father was deceiving himself. However, what was self-evident to Abram was far from evident to his father! How could Abram convert his father, Terach, from idolatry - to a belief in some invisible, mysterious, magical, non-material entity that no one else could see or hear… and that only he, Abram, gave credence to as being real?" Rabbi Letenberg paused and looked up. "That was the crux of Abram's problem."

"It is a conundrum that we all, as human beings, need to acknowledge," Father Bertolli began. "We are talking here about the formative origins of a simple idea that arose in the mind of a young lad as if well, as if no one else had ever thought of such an idea before."

"Why is Abram being credited with being the originator of this grand idea? Lana asked. "Did not human beings long before then have similar notions?"

Rabbi Letenberg looked up to the ceiling and shrugged, "No doubt thousands of others have conjured up thousands of other imaginary gods – but as I said previously, this only validates the existence of such an idea. As you all know, history is always written retrospectively so to speak. A lot depends on who is writing it! In this case, Moses might have written it - although most Jews believe that it was either dictated or written by Yahweh himself. That aside, in Terach's time the Torah had not yet been written… in which it is noted that he was the nineteenth patriarch in direct descent from the first man ever to walk upon the earth on his two hind legs."

"And that 'first man' was created from clay! So what does that make THVVH? Could Adam's Creator be considered to be a maker of clay icons like Terach?" Cathy spritely responded.

"The passage of time dulls the memory," Letenberg continued, ignoring Cathy's asinine allegation. "Abram was twentieth in line behind his father, Terah. For your information the line of descent goes something like this: 1-Adam, 2- Seth, 3-Enoch, 4-Kenan, 5-Mahalalel, 6-Jared, 7-Enoch, 8-Methusalah, 9-Lamech, 10-Noah," Letenberg paused to inhale a breath before rattling off "11-Shem, 12-Arphaxed, 13-Shelah, 14-Eber, 15 Pleg, 16 Reu, 17-Serug, 18 Nashor, 19 Terah, and 20-Abram. This covers a span of some nine hundred and thirty years after Adam's demise."

"You rabbis needed to memorize a lot of stuff, eh?" Lana inquired, impressed by Letenberg's recital. "From what you have said, it seems to me as if man's genealogical relationship to the historical roots of Abram's THVVH seem tenuous at best."

"Actually, there seems to be a major change in the narrative after Noah," Father Bertolli admitted. "After the great flood, the roots of all living life-forms including man, had to be traceable to Noah and his magnificent wooden ark. The narrative of what had occurred prior to the flood was subject to the vagaries of Noah's memory!"

"Wasn't he illiterate?" Cathy brazenly asked.

"I'm just the storyteller here, not the author. Admittedly there are a lot of inconsistencies and errors – but hey, who is perfect?" Letenberg retorted. "After the flood, Noah became of god-like importance and THVVH receded into the background and was almost forgotten... until he resurfaced within Abram's guilty conscience."

"Hmm," Cathy speculated, "Let's say that I, for example, had conjured up such a god. It would go without saying that such a god had to have existed *before* I conjured it up... or else it would not be the creator - *I* would be the creator."

"Indeed that could be the case. I'm not saying it isn't. I'm just telling it the way it was presented to me. Anyway, according to legend, in spite of his son's most cogent arguments, Terach stubbornly stuck to his idolatrous ways; after all, it was the source of his livelihood."

"Understandable," Lana piped up.

"One day, so the story goes, in a fit of frustration young Abram took a hammer and smashed all the idols in his father's store except for the largest one. He placed the hammer in the hand of the largest idol. When his father arrived at the store he was horrified; he glared accusingly at his son and demanded: '*What happened to all the idols?*'"

'*They got into a fight*', Abram lied, '*and in a fit of jealousy the big one smashed all the little ones*', he calmly explained.

"His father shouted, '*Don't be foolish! You know these idols have no power; they can't do anything!*'

"'*Then why do you worship them?*' Abram bravely asked." Rabbi Letenberg paused and looked about to see if there was any reaction.

The Motley Five stared at each other.

"A clever argument," Lana commented. "What did his father say?"

"The point of the story was to demonstrate his father's ignorance and his son's cleverness. Naturally his father was dumbfounded," the good Rabbi replied.

Lenny cleared his throat to draw attention to himself. All eyes turned his way. "What if Abram's father had argued that he was fully aware that the idols he sold were made of clay - but that they became transformed by the owner's *power of belief*? And that they were only as powerful as… the power *imbued* into them by the owner?"

"Yeah, just as Christians *imbue* the crucifix and other sacred man-made relics with power," Lana added.

"Good points," Father Bertolli responded. "Yes, indeed, what if Abram's father had said, 'You imbue some mysterious, invisible entity with omnipotent powers - while I do the same with tangible clay idols. What is the difference? We idolaters are not as stupid as you think!"

"That seems to be the nature of all worship," Cathy joined in. "Sun worshippers, for example, *imbue* the sun with mysterious powers. It is all about *imbuing*. Whether it is an invisible force, or an unutterable word, or a concrete object, the chosen items become as mysterious as our belief in them. We *imbue* whatever we worship with supernatural powers – and then pretend that we are the powerless ones."

A stony silence ensued. Lenny opened his mouth as if to say something, but decided to keep quiet. It seemed as if all five members of the Motley Five needed time to reflect upon what Cathy had said. The silence dragged on and on until Rabbi Letenberg declared with a laugh: "Phooey, you guys. You are ruining a good story."

The Motely Five inhaled as one.

"Please continue," the Motley Four encouraged as one voice.

"Admittedly, it does sound rather far fetched. But let me assure you, I am not making this up!" Rabbi Letenberg exclaimed before continuing. "Abram came to believe in the reality of this supernatural entity, and began to develop a personal relationship with it."

"A personal relationship?" Cathy queried.

"Sort of an intimate and private dialogue… much in the fashion that we pray to our invisible *Father who art in heaven*," Father Bertolli chimed in.

"Eventually Abram became a sort of a loner, a recluse who could be heard talking to himself at odd times during the day or night. It was as if he was actually conversing with some mysterious personality. Naturally the mysterious entity came to be associated with the person who gave meaning, significance and credence to its existence. The invisible *entity* came to be known as the '*God of Abram*'," the Rabbi stated.

"To think that the invisible God of Abram would eventually become the basis of so much religious conflict in the world!" Cathy exclaimed.

"Since it is supposed to be an unutterable word, modern scholars use the abbreviation G dash D for the word God," Father Bertolli reinserted himself once again. "It is amazing that from such humble origins, the god of a curious youth in rebellion against the idolatry of his father has, over the centuries, been transformed into The One and Only True God of the Judaic-Christian-Muslim hegemony that now dominates the modern world!"

"I, too, find this story to be... well, incredible, but it is what it is," Rabbi Letenberg resumed. "Unfortunately, you have usurped the ending prematurely and practically ruined my biblical story of God," he complained good-naturedly. "Permit me to complete what I have begun. To make a long story short, eventually the invisible voice that Abram heard in his head became a *real personality* in his own mind; it communicated with him on, let's say, a psychological level."

"Seems to me to have Freudian implications," Cathy pointed out.

"Abram eventually came to believe that arguing with his biological father would get him nowhere. His father believed in the power of idolatry – whereas Abram came to believe that the voice in his head was the voice of *God*. As he began to develop a personal relationship to his invisible God, his relationship with his father deteriorated. Eventually Abram came to a momentous decision: in order to be true to himself he could not remain in such an idolatrous environment."

"He must have been conflicted with a sense of loyalty and betrayal; he must have been loaded with guilt," Cathy surmised.

"Abram convinced himself that if he left the home of his idol-worshipping father, and went forth on his own - then his beloved God-father would bless him and make his offspring into a great nation of believers."

"If someone believed such a notion today, people would say such a person was delusional," Cathy interjected.

"But, it was not today – it was in biblical times," Father Bertolli offered in support of his beleaguered friend.

"Perhaps it was simply the cognitive application of discursive logic to resolve an irrational existential conflict. If Abram did what the mysterious voice in his head commanded – then this mysterious entity would bless him and make his offspring into a great nation. This covenant established the relationship between Abram, his offspring, and his beloved GD.

This covenant or b'rit as it became known, is fundamental to traditional Judaism. It implies rights and obligations on both sides." Rabbi Letenberg paused and gazed about as if wondering whether or not he should continue.

The Motley Four knew the subject was dear to Rabbi Letenberg's religious convictions. No one wanted to indicate that the topic was getting somewhat boring, so they sat in stoic silence until the good rabbi broke the tension by saying, "To be a Jew is not an easy thing."

"Please continue with your story of the Jewish people. It is very interesting," Lenny spoke on behalf of the Motely Four. The other three perked up to demonstrate their support.

"I will attempt to be brief," Rabbi Letenberg resumed, re-energized by Lenny's encouragement. "When Abram and his beloved wife Sarai, grew older and still remained childless, out of compassion for her husband, Sarai offered Abram her maid servant named Hagar, who was younger and more importantly, fertile," the Rabbi pointed out.

"Who today would be so considerate, and so - so unselfish?" Lana could not refrain from commenting.

"Hagar was the offspring of a Pharaoh who gave her to Abram as a helpmate during his travels in Egypt. Hagar bore Abram a son named Ishmael. According to both Muslim and Jewish understanding of this sensitive historical matter, Ishmael is the founding father of the Arab peoples."

"If the Arabs and Israelis are blood relatives," Cathy interjected, "then the squabbling could be called a form of sibling rivalry."

"Perhaps if more of them realized this, they would be a little more civil to each other... and a little more cooperative about sharing the Temple Mount. Anyway, getting back to what I was saying, when Abram was one hundred and his wife Sarai was ninety, something extraordinary happened," Rabbi Letenberg plodded on.

"What happened?" Lana asked.

"G-D or GD promised Abram a son by Sarai."

"So a hundred year old man had intercourse with a ninety year old woman?" Lana inquired, her prurient interests piqued.

"It is believed that people lived a lot longer in those days," Father Bertolli explained.

"Yes, in those days people remained fecund into very old age," the good Rabbi concurred. "As I was saying, GD promised Abram and Sarai a natural born son – but there was a condition: first Abram had to change his name to 'Abraham', meaning Father of Many, and Sarai, which meant My Princess had to change her name to 'Sarah' which meant Princess."

"Sounds picky, but as we all know, GD works in mysterious ways," Cathy quipped.

"Keep in mind that in those ancient days the religious beliefs corresponded, as they do today, with the collective level of knowledge. By the time Sarah begat a son named Isaac, or in Hebrew, Yetzchak, the invisible GD of Abraham had morphed in the minds of the believers into something much more tangible than an unutterable tetragrammaton. GD became personified as an omnipotent paternal figure. And to summarize a long and poignant story: because Abraham, as a test of his belief, was willing to sacrifice his precious son, Isaac, on the altar of blind faith, and at the age of ninety-nine, as a covenant of his faith, was willing to be circumcised as demanded by his GD, *Isaac lived to become the ancestor of the Jewish People – while his brother Ishmael became the ancestor of the Arab People*," Rabbi Letenberg lowered his tone to emphasize the statement.

"So the Jews and Arabs are connected by religion, by history, and by blood? Ishmael is the ancestor of the Arab People – while his brother Isaac, is the ancestor of the Jewish People. They share a common DNA. They are blood brothers! And they now share a common homeland," Cathy dramatized.

"You said it!" Rabbi Letenberg exclaimed. "Few people today who agonize over the ongoing conflict in the Middle East are cognizant, as we mentioned earlier, of the historical significance of that ongoing rivalry. It is existential at its very core."

"Knowing this should elicit more empathy, understanding and compassion amongst those struggling to co-exist peacefully in the Middle East," Lenny commented.

"Indeed. But again we have jumped ahead of our story. Let me briefly summarize the ancestral connections that take us up to the enslavement of the Jewish people in Egypt," the Rabbi pressed on. "Isaac married a woman named Rivka or Rebecca, who bore him fraternal twin sons: Jacob or Ya'akov, and Esau, between whom there was a great deal of competition. Jacob eventually changed his name to Yisrael or Isreal; this is significant because he managed to father twelve sons between the years

1759 BC to 1739 BC by four different women named: Leah, Belhah, Zilpah, and Rachael. These sons became known as the Twelve Children of Isreal."

"Do you know their names?" Lana asked.

"In order of birth they are: Reuben, Simeon, Levi, Judah, Dan, Naphtali, Gad, Asher, Issachar, Zebulun, Joseph, and Benjamin. The most famous of the twelve was Joseph because of the many- colored- coat incident, which resulted in him being sold by his jealous brothers into slavery in Egypt. Due to his uncanny ability to interpret dreams, Joseph earned a place in the Pharaoh's court, paving the way for his eleven brothers and their families to settle in Egypt. Ironically, the siblings who sold Joseph into slavery in Egypt eventually became enslaved themselves, beginning a surreal four hundred years of abject servitude."

"The so-called Babylonian captivity," Father Bertolli added.

"Which lasted until Moses led them to freedom by crossing the Red Sea." Rabbi Letenberg concluded with a flair.

"The history of the Jewish peoples and of the GD of Abram as written in the Torah, has had such a major impact on the Middle East, Europe, America, and the world, that it behooves us to make ourselves more knowledgeable of it," Father Bertolli commented.

"The JCM hegemony has become a powerful and influential force throughout the capitalistic world," Lenny added.

"This has been a very informative and, may I add, edifying, discussion," Cathy appraised.

The others all nodded in unison as they rose to their feet.

Father Bertolli turned out the light in his study. The Motley Five went out the front door and emerged into the magical glow cast by a full moon on a crisp autumn's night... as if it was Halloween.

* * *

"Man's brute existence is an undeniable fact," Brad Bradley thought one quiet evening when he sat beside the fireplace in his comfortable hunter green leather swivel rocker with matching ottoman. His wife had gone to see a movie with her friend Suzy Okuda, and so... he sat alone beside the electric fireplace with fake burning logs and sagely reflected. "Throughout recorded time man has sat beside lonely fires and cogitated upon the great mystery of existence." It made Brad conscious of the spiritual aspects of his brute existence… as if he were responsible for the tending of his own immortal soul.

It was this sentiment that made Brad, in spite of his legal status, into a sort of religious-type of person – not in the repugnant sense that was so suffocating and life-negating that it caused the founder of modern psychology, Sigmund Freud, who had resided in the staunchly Christian city of Vienna from 1856-1939, to describe the affliction as *"the universal obsessional neurosis of humanity."* Indeed Freud was insightfully profound for a person born, raised, and nurtured in such circumstances.

Unlike Freud, Brad's religious sentiments represented an innate yearning for altruistic freedom because he, in his own inimical way actually seemed to care for the souls of humanity. It was a positive, life-affirming attitude – unlike that of those who had to overcome or transcend themselves in order to free themselves from the abominable religious influences of their times. C G Jung wrote on page fifty-five of his *Memories, Dreams, and Reflections* - which Brad had read in the last year of his baccalaureate studies - *"… slowly I came to understand that this communion had been a fatal experience for me. It had proved hollow, more than that, it had proved to be a total loss… 'Why, that is not religion at all,' I thought. 'It is the absence of God; the church is a place I should not go…. It is not life which is there, but death'."*

Certainly not a sentiment dear to the hearts of Brad's Christian friends! As a lawyer he knew it was prudent to keep such sentiments to himself – but Carl Jung was not a lawyer; he was a famous pioneer in the field of analytic psychology. He understood the sexual secrets of the 'Id' couched in the figurative language of the *Old* Testament and regurgitated in the *New;* he was familiar with the Oedipus complex and consequently held no grudges against his father who was a pastor in the Swiss Reform Church. He knew where he stood: on hallowed ground conditioned like Pavlov's dog by centuries of dogmatic beliefs that made it as treacherous as quicksand. He had to tread softly - he was not the one carrying the big stick!

Still Jung had the courage of his convictions which proved to be stronger than his fear of a vindictive and vengeful 'One and only', or the intimidation of a prurient society where celibacy was preferable to intercourse. And Jung enjoyed intercourse. If Carl had had his spiritual epiphany earlier in life… perhaps his Freudian ego and super-ego would not have been so conditioned by the time he realized that the Church was essentially a tomb of perpetual atonement.

A tomb in which hung the graven image of a crucified Jew wearing only a loincloth and a crown of thorns... and before which penitent sinners groveled and prayed for the forgiveness of their unforgiveable sins – forgetting that once upon a time their kindred spirits had cried out 'give us Barabbas', when they had been given the freedom to choose the fate of their redeemer, Brad somberly reflected.

It was all there in his mind's eye: *behold, they partake of the sacraments... a pagan ritual reconstituted from long-repressed urges when they were cannibalistic parasites eating of human flesh and drinking of human blood in order to absorb the virtues of the deceased through ingestion. Indeed times had changed... the cave had become a cathedral, and the shaman now wore a long black robe and deposited tiny compressed white wafers on the tongues of those with their mouths open.*

"Why, that is not religion at all," Jung had insightfully concluded. Perhaps his old friend and mentor, Sigmund Freud, was right after all. It was an *obsessional neurosis.* Brad knew that he too had been affected: contaminated by the sins of his ancestors.

Carl Jung, like the famous German philosopher Fredrick Nietzsche who preceded him, had to over-react in order to withstand the overwhelming religious predilections of his era. Like Nietzsche he literally cried out for a breath of fresh air in a stagnant milieu filled with the halitosis of centuries past. Reason and logic struggled feebly like anemic flowers in a field of noxious weeds.

"Who can blame people like Nietzsche and Jung if they over-reacted a little?" Brad exclaimed. "They were up against the most powerful currents of irrational dogma the civilized world has ever known. They represented a spark of sanity in an oppressively neurotic culture where the neurosis was the norm," Brad commiserated.

It was obvious that Carl Gustav Jung was slightly ahead of his times. He had attempted to overcome himself and the repugnant, life-negating sentiments of his time. Oh, how he longed to be free from the repressive and domineering influence of the 'One and only'. How he struggled valiantly in his recurrent dreams. How he wrestled with the religious images and memories that loomed up out of the repressed recesses of his personal unconscious. How he, like Nietzsche, yearned for a single breath of fresh air, a single breath of freedom in a stuffy and stagnant society where he felt suffocated!

When he was a young boy Carl's devout parents regularly took him to Church. When he matured and became a responsible adult he was able to remove the child from the Church. But, try as he might, it was all but impossible to remove the Church from the child; the brainwashing had been profound. It was all there engrained in his conscious, subconscious, and unconscious mind, and manifested in the poetic prose and graphic images reproduced in a large red book he called *Liber Novus* like a fairy tale of what used to be, replete with scary premonitions.

Thus, it was with good intentions that Brad Bradley stoically tended his soul on a quiet evening while his spouse was away at the movies. He considered himself to be one of the fortunate, a Canadian citizen who had been a little luckier than the average person. Sure, he had accumulated more than his fair share of the bounty harvested from the vast hinterland that made Canada the envy of resource-starved nations. In his own mind he had been incarnated there to serve the people - people like his client George Webster Brown, a proud and patriotic Canadian... an ex-serviceman who had stumbled along the way, and needed to be saved.

* * *

It was like a slow flashback: a latent memory, if there is such a thing. It occurred soon after George left the Allan Memorial Institute in Montreal and continued intermittently long after he had left the armed forces. He had been warned to expect something like this, but not so frequently. "Variations on a theme," the nurse with the kindly demeanor had pointed out at the time. "They will come and go depending on your readiness...."

Sometimes he heard a low-pitched voice that seemed like a distant echo. The voice said, *"You need to be ever vigilant, ever vigilant. There are enemies everywhere, everywhere. Beware of the vociferous. Remember... remember..."*

And then on the 23rd of November the tenor of the voice changed. It was confusing. He was filled with a deep-seated feeling of ambivalence. Was it the same voice? Or was it the voice of his *higher self*? It sounded unearthly, like an echo from a greater distance. The voice resounded within his mind. It said: *"Look within rather than without. The noise you are making is not harmonic – it grates against the music. The universal music is an altruistic symphony. It is a melding of everything there is: a singularity, a whole. You have been there. You know!"*

George struggled to make sense of what he heard – but his enculturation and his religious views all worked against him. There was too much *dissonance*; it clogged his mind with discordant noise; his head throbbed. He was filled with doubt, confusion, and dread. He struggled like a drowning rat immobilized upon an inclined wooden board floating precariously in the middle of a man-made pond... dreaming about salvation.

It was ludicrous to say the least; once George actually dreamt he was a rat caught in the dark vortex of a swirling pool! *Save me! Save me!* he cried as the swirling water engulfed him, *I can't breathe!* How can a sinner save his sinful self? *Help!* he yelled, *I can't hold my breath much longer!* He might have drowned... if Sarah hadn't grabbed him by the hair and shook his head.

"Wake up!" she demanded. "What on earth is bothering you?"

"I thought I was drowning!"

"Go back to sleep," she commanded and rolled over so she would not have to face him.

George got up and went to the bathroom. He sat on the toilet and urinated like his spouse. He flushed the toilet, opened the medicine cabinet and located the aspirin bottle. He took two aspirins with a glass of cold water. He scampered back to the comfort of his bed. He leaned over and stared at Sarah's sleeping face. Was she really his helpmeet as the Bible said? She looked so angelic with her eyes closed. He shook his head vigorously as if to clear his vision. *Had she really 'saved' him?* The aspirins helped. He fell asleep. He dreamt of happier times.

When he was a child, George liked to pretend that Santa Claus was real. He was really disappointed when he saw that old geezer with the Santa outfit sitting in front of the liquor store ringing a bell and asking for money. "Are you really Santa?" he had asked in dismay. "Scram, kid!" the old man said. He knew it was just some old codger in a costume. But still he liked to pretend anyway. Santa was real to him - more real than God. Santa brought him presents every Christmas.

Every Christmas Sarah set up a small Christmas tree and under it placed several gifts 'To George from Santa'. Since they never had any children, George played that role on Christmas day. He got up early. He was so happy, like a child. He examined every present… and was so grateful for every gift Sarah had so carefully purchased and gift-wrapped with fancy Christmas paper.

Sarah enjoyed playing the role of the enabler. She enabled her husband to pretend. She was the ground wire, finite and mortal, which grounded him to the earth and kept him from flying off with the hallucinations in his head that came to him out of the blue. She was considerate, understanding, empathic, and consoling - but there was only so much she could do. The rest was up to him.

* * *

"It's up to you," Brad had said when George took the stand.

What on earth did Brad Bradley, lawyer for the defense, expect of his downcast client? Why was he putting him on the stand? Was he that incompetent – or was he wily like a fox?

Ruskolnikov Kublinsky, the prosecuting attorney knew from experience that it was most likely the latter. He leaned forward on his elbows anticipating his opportunity to cross-examine.

George took the stand. He swore to tell the truth. He looked pale and anemic like an undernourished POW with a fractured memory of things past remembering. Anxiety oozed from every pore on his face. His haggard appearance was enough to elicit a twinge of sympathy from a hard-hearted jury of his peers.

So much time had passed, as if the only thing it could do was pass. It was confusing - the passing of time - as if it were something tangible, solid, real. As if those images from the past had substance, as if they were something more than memories. And what are memories? Time passing as if it had length, width and depth, as if those memories represented something worthy enough to be regurgitated in a court of law as if they had some significance.

George turned to look at the twelve men and women who sat in judgment of his heinous crime. They looked smug and righteous as if they knew a secret they were not at liberty to share.

In the background he could vaguely hear Brad's hypnotic voice: *"Just tell it like it was George. Think back... to that period when you were a guinea pig for MKUltra."*

Perhaps it was that word *guinea pig* or was it *MKUltra* that did it. George stared at Brad and then at the judge. He shuddered involuntarily and turned his gaze upward as if time transcended space, and in his mind's eye the courtroom suddenly became a room in the Allan Memorial Institute in Montreal, Quebec!

Brad was practically orgasmic with euphoria. It was like an episode from the *Twilight Zone...* Brad was the director. The scene was set, the script written. Brad skillfully massaged the narrative. The story unfolded as if in real time. The jury was the audience: it was like they too... were there... in that room in the Allan Memorial Institute, fixated in a hypnotic trance.

Once again George was there! Sitting on a sofa with his head in his hands. *"Not to worry,"* Brad was saying – except his voice sounded rather feminine.

It was the way Brad looked at him with those all-knowing eyes that seemed to look right through him into the beyond, as if 'she' knew exactly what he knew, and was only pretending to be ordinary for his sake, that induced him to relax and feel more secure.

"You need to believe, George," he heard Brad saying - but it wasn't Brad – it was her!

Suddenly George realized why he was so despondent; it was because of his lost innocence. Gone. And there was no getting it back. The loss was everlasting. "Once you know," he whispered sagging back on the witness stand with his arms dangling listlessly at his sides, "you cannot return to your former state of ignorance!"

"You can't?"

George stared at Brad inanely as if to say, 'Haven't we been over this before?'

"Who-who are you?" Brad stammered timidly as if afraid to ask.

"George Webster Brown, volunteer. I work here in conjunction with the Sleep Room."

"In conjunction with what?"

"The Sleep Room. That is where we put patients to sleep for days and weeks... even months. We erase and rebuild the psyche by the use of electric shock therapy. Sometimes it takes dozens of shocks along with a variety of drugs to achieve the results that Doctor Cameron is looking for.

"Does it work?"

"Once a few years back there was a young woman admitted here who had five small children. I personally thought that she was suffering from after-childbirth depression. She was administered... I lost count, over a hundred electric shocks."

"Over a hundred?" Brad ascertained.

"Yup. I had to help hold her down. Almost turned her into a vegetable. I felt sorry for her. Afterwards she couldn't even remember the names of her kids... she couldn't recall anything. She had been completely brainwashed, so to speak."

"So that is what goes on in the Sleep Room, eh? Have ah-ah you ever been in there... as a-a patient?" Brad queried.

"It was part of a process that I am not at liberty to discuss. I signed papers. Anyway such information may interfere with my on-going treatment."

"What treatment?"

"Well, let's just say that I was privileged to participate in a very important project... number sixty-eight, I think it was. What is happening now... is referred to as reorientation therapy."

"Reorientation?"

"Think about it this way, they restore my confidence, faith, and belief in doing... what they referred to as my 'patriotic duty'. At first I felt lost and confused. I could not stand to be in the dark so to speak. I needed to regain my self-confidence, hold my head up, take in a deep breath and-and... get on board."

"Get on board for what?"

George paused, shook his head in bewilderment, and stared at Brad. He gazed inanely about the courtroom. "I need to believe in myself... in what I have to do."

"In what you have to do?"

"It is very important that I believe that."

"How so?" Brad asked with a baffled expression.

"By believing in it. By accepting the obvious. By letting it happen."

There was a surreal quality to the conversation that made the courtroom feel like a room in the Allan Memorial Institute.

"You all right?" Brad asked. "You don't look so good."

There was an empty glass on the table. Someone handed him the glass as if it was filled with water. George recalled drinking from that glass... and taking a tablet. It felt like déjà-vu.

"You sure that was vitamin C you gave me?" he asked.

"Suspicion only makes things worse..." Brad suggested as he reached over and retrieved the glass. "You need to believe that what you've just heard is the truth," he commented as he turned to face the jury.

The jurors looked on in quiet amazement.

"The truth?" George reflected, "Yes, it is all about the truth."

The Judge sat with his mouth open as if he was on the verge of saying something. After a while he lowered his gavel and called for a recess... because for a brief moment, it seemed as if George Webster Brown had told the truth, the whole truth, and nothing but the truth.

It was hard to tell where George was just by looking at him as he left the stand and slumped back into the wooden chair next to his lawyer. His face was flushed and his dark eyes darted about as if in REM mode – only George was awake with his bleary eyes wide open. Saliva slowly dribbled from his lower lip; mucus accumulated beneath his nostrils.

Two armed guards walked George out of the Courtroom and into the van that transported him back to his drab prison cell. One of the guards named Jeff got him a tall glass of water. "Here, drink this," he said, "It might help."

George sat down on the hard bunk adjacent to the brick wall. He drank the water, returned the glass, and lowered his head into his hands.

"You gonna be okay?" the other guard asked.

George raised his head and nodded feebly. The guards left him alone to contemplate his predicament.

Hours passed like minutes. Space and time combined to produce another place and another time – and yet there was familiarity. He felt older... many months... and more months, perhaps years? He sagged back into the cushioned bunk. He closed his eyes. The bunk bed morphed into a sofa chair. A flood of images rushed by as if in fast-forward mode, and time had been condensed. His hearing became acute.

He could hear the nurse patiently breathing as she waited. He relaxed. After a while he heard a compassionate voice that vibrated in his eardrums like a whisper. *You have been there... you have approached the event horizon... you have experienced the source of awareness: consciousness; it is your own. There is no other.*

"I think I've heard you say something like that... before," George reflected.

"Very good. You need to believe... in what I am saying. You really weren't out there, you know? You were here. Right here in this room. It is confusing but that is just the way it is. You were way out there... *in your mind.* Just accept it... like everyone else does."

George laid his head back against the padded headrest built into the sofa chair. He closed his eyes. He could still hear the nurse breathing. "Sounds," the concept eased into his consciousness, "they at least remained real."

"Just listen," the nurse said. "Keep your eyes closed and just listen."

George listened intently. He heard a hollow but empathetic voice; it sounded vaguely familiar. It echoed within his eardrums. *You have been there ... you have approached the event horizon... You have approached the source of awareness: consciousness... your own... your own... your own. Consciousness is the First Mover.*

"Yeah," George confirmed, nodding his head.

"You need to believe in the paradox. You really were not physically out there – you were here, right here in this room," the nurse reiterated. "You were only out there in your mind. The mind knows no physical barriers – but your brain does."

"What are you implying?" George queried.

"Hmm," the nurse pondered. "You do have some residual retrospective reality reflex - the four R's as the Doc calls it. Let me level with you. Think about that description you gave us of that singularity. You only experienced that in your mind's eye. All that time you were right here in this room. Yet to you - it felt as if you really were - elsewhere. It could be said that... you existed in the black hole of your mind."

"Black hole?"

"Yeah. The Doc analyzed your experience this way... look at the Milky Way galaxy. It swirls about a so-called black hole into which, according to the physicists, everything will eventually disappear, drawn in by an enormous gravitational force. All the light energy of the galaxy will be drawn into that black hole."

George nodded as if in agreement.

"Indeed, eventually all the black holes of all the galaxies that constitute the entire cosmos will be drawn by the force of gravity into one singularity. It will be filled with the light of the universe – even though it may appear to be nothing but a black hole. And, inconceivable as it may sound, all of that exists – not out there," the nurse paused and stared meaningfully at her patient, "but in the macrocosmic mind of your microcosmic brain."

George looked up at the nurse like a lapdog looks up at its master.

"You know it exists… because you exist. Your experience cannot be denied. It happened. Right?"

"Seemed real to me," George mumbled.

"I'm glad to hear you say that… because that indicates that your ability to differentiate has not been compromised." The nurse paused, cocked her head to one side and stared pensively at George, "You experienced something… something spiritual, didn't you, George?" she surmised.

"It was a unique moment." George solemnly stared back into the nurse's hazel eyes with speckles of starlight dancing within them. "I was out there," he said matter-of-factly.

"In the darkness there is light. Even paradoxes can be rationally explained."

"I see."

"The Doc says that the kind of experience that you had comes under the category of 'schizophrenic dementia' - as if that label explains anything! In your *mind* you really were there, weren't you?"

"Yeah."

"You were out there. I mean, way out there." The nurse lowered her voice and said, "*The mind knows no physical barriers.*"

"I'm so glad to be back," George replied as if he really had been out there.

"The Doc was worried because this was unexpected. It could have opened up neural pathways that ah-ah… let's just say that you were on your own out there. We thought for a while that we might have lost you. But thank god, you came back. It was truly a great relief to all of us. The Doc said you were a-a… an anomaly… an over-zealous and 'defective' candidate, as he calls them."

"A defective candidate?"

"It is just a term the Doc uses for patients who elicit abnormal psychic qualities. We were glad just to get you back."

"It is so nice to be back... you have no idea!" George exclaimed.

"What is it like to be back?" the nurse glanced up at George with an inquisitive look.

"Like-like a second chance. You know, like being given a second chance when you are convinced that there is no going back. I feel so very grateful."

"Hmm," the nurse cogitated while peering closely at her patient. "I see the effect is beginning to wear off."

"What effect?"

"The effect of the debriefing drugs. It helps bring you back."

"Back to earth?"

"Like I said before, you never left."

"Sure seemed like I did."

"How can I explain this? This is still experimental stuff we're dealing with. Let's just say that you did have an experience. You cannot take it back and pretend that it did not happen; it happened, just like Roswell happened. We just hope it isn't going to interfere with your program... because you really tripped out. You had a unique experience that could be called *spiritual*. You had us worried."

"Did you just say *Roswell*?" George piped up, raising his eyebrows.

"Just an example of something that happened. Forget I mentioned it."

"Weren't some aliens captured alive there?" George persisted.

"That stuff is so top secret. It could get me in a real fix if you mention it to anyone. Consider it a slip of the tongue."

"Slip of the tongue, you say?"

"Yeah, sorry," the nurse sounded genuinely contrite.

"You know, this might sound idiotic, but-but at times I feel somewhat like an alien of sorts," George confessed.

"Unfortunately you cannot take back such experiences and pretend they did not happen – all you can do is rationalize them. You seem sane enough for me. I'm going to recommend that you be released, subject to proper de-programming. You have been very cooperative and you did sign the papers... You know we mean well."

"I can appreciate the need for secrecy – but for my own peace of mind, could you give an inkling of what – if anything - went wrong in my program?"

"Can you keep a confidence?"

"Sure."

"If we could do it all over... we most definitely would not have given you such a large dose of LSD... that first time. The first experience is usually the most profound. You really were way out there. It was beyond the pale of psychiatric understanding. Carl Jung alluded to such archetypical imaginings. From what we understand you have had a sort of a born-again experience."

"Sort of like a second chance...?"

"Yeah, like a second chance to-to... put things right. We are all capable of learning from our mistakes. No one is perfect – even though some of us think we are. Believe me, we are doing the best we can with the knowledge we currently have. Does this help make you feel any better?"

George shook his head while gazing down at his feet. From head to foot he felt a deep-seated bewilderment. Were those his feet?

The man's feet were planted firmly on the concrete floor that had been painted grey and his hands rested palms-down on his emaciated thighs. His sunken chest rose and fell so imperceptivity it appeared as if he were holding his breath. His head was bowed as if in perpetual prayer and his glassy eyes were filled to overflowing with tears on the verge. He was alone in the universe: a *singularity* existing in a time and space that had no meaning. He cocked his head to one side as if to shift his brain into a more relevant position. He shivered as if suffering from hypothermia. He stared up at the barred window near the ceiling. A narrow shaft of sunlight illuminated the gloom. *Second chance*, he thought. *What have I done to deserve... second chance?*

"It has to do with state of mind, Your Honor," he remembered Brad saying. *"State of mind is crucial in this case. What was George's state of mind when his finger twitched involuntarily and - and... Lenard Bruce was shot dead?"*

* * *

It was a dream that engulfed Lenny so completely that he felt he was actually there, in the moment. He was five years old and black. He was crying despondently. The tears kept coming. It was hopeless. There was no respite. None. Zero.

His black parents stood beside him humbled and stoic as the day is long. He turned to face them while wiping the tears from his bleary eyes smearing the grime from the back of his right hand. His eyes were dark pools of despair just like his parents'. He drew in a stuttering breath and looked up at the deep azure sky above them. He closed his eyes momentarily before asking in a barely audible child's voice.

"Why us – and not them?"

The question hung in the air as if it were frozen there.

There was no answer. His parents shuffled their shoeless feet and stared at the ground. They were slaves. Their parents before them had been slaves. Captured and brought over from Africa in stinking slave-ships and sold at auction to white Anglo-Saxon plantation owners for money: coin of the realm. Owned by Christians to do their bidding. To work from dawn till dusk like beasts of burden. Dehumanized, degraded, used and abused. What kind of human beings would treat other human beings thus?

"Why us - and not them?" the child asked in a little louder tone. "What have we done to deserve this? What have I done?" the inflection was still hopeful... still curious.

There was only silence. The child's parents gazed down at their only son, an innocent child born into abject slavery. A human being of infinite worth... owned by a self-professed 'sinner' of a different race and color as if... as if they were a different species. What had their precious son done to deserve this fate?

There was no answer. No explanation. It was just the way it was. The little child began to cry pathetically. He stared up into the glassy forlorn eyes of his parents. He saw a lifetime of angst. He saw not a single glimmer of hope. He saw a void so deep... he had to turn away.

Tears ebbed into the pillow beneath Lenny's head. He was that five-year-old black American child. He was standing there beside his black American parents on that cotton plantation in Southern Virginia.

"Why us – and not them?"

There was no answer. Only silence. The silence endured for what seemed like a lifetime. And then he heard a voice like an echo from a distant past. It eased into his dream and rattled about in his consciousness as if it were real. "Many others have felt the same way. Like them, you can dream. Like them, you can make believe. Take heart! All is not as hopeless as it may seem." And then Lenny awoke feeling baffled and confused.

It was the twelfth of November, the day after Remembrance Day. Lenny remembered it well because it was a day worth remembering. He had just awakened from his dream feeling despondent and forlorn. He recalled it was 3:42 am on the bedside digital clock. He had gotten up to urinate. He went back to bed, carefully climbed in beside Lana, rolled over and had just dozed off when Pena intruded as if he had something worthy of being shared.

"Many people have felt as you did in your dream... over the millennia. Your dream indicates that you are ready," Pena stated matter-of-factly.

"Ready for what?"

"I'll be brief. I do not want to belabor the point. It is a sensitive matter to many, so I will endeavor to be concise and to the point... with regards to the significance of your dream. It is symptomatic of the story that has been recorded in the Torah and in the Old Testament. Imagine a destitute little Hebrew child enslaved in Egypt asking his parents: "*Why us – and not them?*"

"Who can answer such an existential question?" Lenny asked.

"Listen carefully to this. It is the key to understanding the Hebrew state of mind at the time when the Hebrew people made their great escape from slavery to freedom."

"The key you say... to understanding the Hebrew state of mind at the time when Moses courageously led his brethren out of... the clutches of the mighty Pharaoh of Egypt?"

"At the time Moses was leading his people to freedom, did they know the answer to the question: *Why us – and not them?* In other words, were they aware that they were the Chosen People?"

"Why is that significant?"

"If the Hebrew people knew they were the Chosen People, if they knew that they were being tested by God, if they were aware that their suffering was meritorious, if they truly believed that if they suffered stoically, penitently, and humbly for an entire lifetime – then God would reward them with eternal life in the Hereafter. If that was the case - why then, would they thoughtlessly jeopardize over four hundred years of doing penance by... escaping?"

"Adroit! If they knew that they were the Chosen People – then it would not have been in their self-interest to attempt to escape... unlike the blacks enslaved on miserable plantations in the Southern USA. Because to them suffering was meritorious!

"I appreciate the subtlety of your laconic wit. But perhaps this is not the time for it. This is serious stuff. Suffice it to say at the time of their exodus, Moses' brethren were not aware of their status as the Chosen People. Like their latter-day black counterparts in the USA, they were simply long-suffering slaves who wanted nothing more than to be free!"

"I get your point. At that moment in time the Hebrews would rather have drowned in the Red Sea - than continue surviving as slaves in Egypt. Why? Because prior to the Exodus, they were not aware that they were the fabled Chosen People?"

"Correct."

"And after leading his people to freedom, Moses gratefully went up to Mount Sinai to give thanks... and to ponder the ignobility of the fate that had befallen his people."

"Imagine him somberly reflecting upon the meaningless tragedy that his people had experienced and wondering: *'Why us – and not them?'*"

"*Why us – and not them?* I imagine many Black Americans have asked themselves that very same existential question, eh?"

"Instead of being assassinated like Martin Luther King by those opposed to him, Moses was enlightened with a grand vision."

"It was the answer to the question?"

"Yes. In the absence of pen and parchment, Moses wrote it down on clay tablets and carried them down from Mount Sinai."

"And that was the impetus for the writing of the five books, of the Pentateuch?"

"Indeed it was. Thus the history of the Hebrew people was belatedly written by learned scribes in an attempt to legitimize Moses' grand vision of his people as being the... Chosen People.

"Makes sense."

"A believable genealogical record had to be fashioned that provided the history of a proud and tenacious tribe of nomadic Hebrews living in the Middle East. There were a plethora of mythological and legendary materials like Gilgamesh that spoke of a great flood and the building of a large ark that provided flesh for the bones of a grand biblical epic. A history was redacted to justify the conclusion, ending with the beginning, that is, with the creation narrative where the mythological Fall of Man occurs that justifies the need for atonement and repentance as experienced generations later by the twelve Tribes of Israel." Pena inhaled dramatically.

"Wow."

"One of the mysterious authors has been identified by scholars as the Yahwist or 'J'. Since this extraordinary author is unknown to us by name or gender, it is impossible to say whether the writer is male or female. In any case the author has been called the greatest writer in the Hebrew language. Evidently the Yahwist wrote the crucial portions of what we now call Genesis, Exodus, and Numbers sometime between 950 and 900 BCE. The Book of 'J' is now embedded in the Genesis to Kings structure assembled by the redactors around 550 BCE, well after the Babylonian Exile. The Torah had to be belatedly back-written, since Moses was born on or about 1393 and passed away around 1273 BCE. The historical evidence indicates that the Torah was written after Moses' demise, as the authentic history of the Chosen People. But the real genius of it was in presenting it as the *immutable word of God*. The immutable word – that morphed into infallible scriptures institutionalized as religious dogma, and canonized as being beyond the critique of-of... mere fallible, sinful mortals, like us."

"Sheer genius! And look what it has spawned!" Lenny exclaimed.

"Judaism, Christianity, and Islam, and a host of other religions that can trace their roots to the unutterable word."

"Look at what has become manifest today in the Middle East and elsewhere in the world where blind faith supersedes reason and logic?"

"Look at the vast Judaic-Christian-Muslim influence that presently encircles the capitalistic world of trade and commerce!"

"Look at you and me and all who have been incarnated into this mortal moment of eternity...."

The two waxed on eloquently into the night as if they were kindred spirits.

* * *

They trudged along
Nonchalantly
        In the moonlight
Following fading footprints
Left behind by fellow trekkers
Struggling to decipher
Unutterable words
        Written
In the snow trampled upon
By those who in centuries past
Had penitently struggled
On and on and on
In a vast universe of discourse
In search of meaning.

        -LB

CHAPTER EIGHT

ONE GRAND REALITY

Within the scope of eternity
An infinite essence
Mysteriously identified
As everything-there-is
Confounds humankind
With a mystery
That resonates
Universally.

There was not much happiness in the Brown household. Sometimes they felt as if their life story was a tragedy told by some old illiterate veteran suffering from post war trauma: full of wishful thinking about some paltry old-fashioned mystery about '*Who done it*'.

Since his *return*, so to speak, George and Sarah settled down to a routine that some would call mundane. They were both retired so they could pretty well do as they pleased within their financial limits.

They usually went to Church on Sunday looking for some uplifting semblance of joy and happiness. But all that the minister had to say was "*Repent for the Day of Judgment is at hand! Get down on your knees and beg the Lord for the forgiveness of your abominable sins. Do it now… before it is too late… too late to make it through the pearly gates. Or would you rather roast eternally in the burning fires of Hell?*"

Perhaps for them, it was already too late. The minister said: "*The wages of sin… is death!*" He did not mince his words. It was the Sunday prior to New Year's Eve and the congregation was looking forward to a message filled with hope - but no cigar, not even a cigarette - just doom and gloom and hell-fire and damnation.

Fear tactics plain and simple. But they worked wonders amongst the great unwashed where insecurity lurked around every dark corner of the material world. The collection plate was filled to overflowing with the offerings of a multitude of guilty consciences scared out of their wits by a shifty-eyed little fellow ordained with good intentions.

"I've heard better," Sarah commented after they left the church.

"He has to eat," George replied with a show of sympathy and consideration for the preacher. "Them guys don't make much. I talked to him last Sunday and he told me he wanted to send his three kids to a private school but they couldn't afford the tuition… so they had to attend the public school."

"You and I went to public schools," Sarah pointed out.

"Yeah," George replied shrugging his shoulders. "I told him as much. He just looked at me as if to say, '*So what?*' I just left it at that."

The Browns left many things unspoken. Time passed unnoticed. They grew older together. Signs of feebleness appeared as if it was natural. Still Sarah could vividly remember the very day her husband was formally released from the Armed Forces as if… as if it was not that long ago.

George had come directly home to the small apartment that Sarah had found near the university campus in Montreal.

He was tired, disheveled and depressed, a shadow of his former self. When he opened the door she hardly recognized him. He looked emaciated and contrite. He just stood there with his right hand extended as if expecting her to shake it.

"It's me," he said listlessly when she gazed at him with her mouth open. She leaned forward and gave her husband a gentle hug, before leading the way into the living room where they sat side by side on the tan vinyl couch.

"I've just been released," he whispered as if ashamed of himself for being the bearer of such lifestyle altering information.

"Released?"

"My army days are over," he added despondently. "I'm sorry, dear. I can't say much about the circumstances... cause I took an oath."

"What happened?"

"They let me go."

"What?"

"They released me."

"Just like that... after all those years you put in at the ah-ah Allan Memorial Institute?"

"Time to get you out there," the Personnel Officer said.

"Time to get you out there? Out where?" Sara queried with a frown.

"Back into civil society, I suppose. Yeah. They called me in and-and thanked me... especially for my participation in MKUltra. 'Top secret' was stamped across a bunch of release documents I had to sign. 'Just routine paperwork,' they said."

"What about your pension?" Sarah demanded with a deepening frown, feeling as if the rug had just been pulled from under a secured retirement.

"'We'll keep in touch,' they said."

"Geez, you only had a few more years to go! You couldn't have hung in there? What in the hell is wrong with you?" Sarah demanded, her own sense of insecurity getting the best of her.

"They said they'd keep in touch!" George reiterated.

"What does that mean?"

"I-I think I'll be getting some kind of stipend of sorts from some anonymous financial institution, a type of retainer."

"You don't say?" Sarah inquired, perking up.

"I've said too much already, but I think you get the drift. They said not to worry about it: "We've got you covered.""

"Easy for them to say," Sarah remarked as she turned and looked over the man sitting beside her on the couch.

There was more to George than met the eye. Her dear husband had been a bit of a subdued loner, and a righteous believer with a predilection for being inconsiderate. Sarah had tolerated such behavior because… well because George was reasonably intelligent and sometimes showed indications of having compassionate feelings. Most of the time he was nice to her. Near the beginning she actually thought that over time he would change for the better. The army would straighten him out. It didn't. If anything it seemed to magnify his minor flaws.

While in the Canadian Armed Forces, George developed a reputation for being dogmatic, and excessively opinionated. Such behavior eventually led the Personnel Officer involved to insightfully suggest: "Wouldn't George make an excellent candidate for the Mk-Ultra experiments in Montreal?"

After they moved back to B.C., the Browns found and rented a small one-bedroom and den condo in Vancouver. *It wasn't much better than the apartment in Montreal,* Sarah recalled nostalgically when reflecting back on those days. Eventually the Browns lucked into a lovely two-story townhome in a quiet enclave in the city of Richmond. They were able to purchase it with the untouched savings accrued from the sale of the Royal Bank stocks they had purchased decades ago when they sold the old bungalow that George had inherited from his parents. "Best investment we ever made!" George had exclaimed. Life took on a more secure feeling after they moved in.

It was at that inauspicious time in their lives that George secretly purchased an old WW II German luger in mint condition from a local gun collector at a gun show. They met in the parking lot. George paid three hundred US dollars. It was worth every penny. It made him feel like the commandant of a Nazi death camp. He had a vivid imagination when it came to such decadence.

"Don't worry," he assured his spouse when he brought the gun home and extracted it from the inside pocket of his black leather jacket. "They just increased my pension," he said inanely, as if that justified the expense. He recalled someone from the National Rifle Association in the US once saying: *The best protection from an evildoer with a gun – is a good guy with a gun.* It made sense… to George. "We'll be much more secure now," he stated confidently.

Did he not realize that he was not residing in the US? Sarah shrugged and looked up to the ceiling as if that reaction spoke for itself.

As domestic life began to take on a complacency that approached boredom, George took to hanging out with a small group of pseudo right-wing fanatics. George fit right in. There were four of them, all retired, or on social assistance. They were, in their own minds, the "Good Guys"; they fed off one another, building each other up with tough talk about how they were going to clean up the neighborhood of crime and drugs along with all left-leaning Jews whom they blamed for the community's economic ills. They were cunning and secretive; they made imaginary plans that never came to anything because they could never agree on how to execute them. They enjoyed the bullshit and bravado more than anything else. It made them feel tough and righteous.

They never heard of Lenny Bruce until one of them named Ari, which was short for Arizona, picked up a pamphlet in Minoru Park. It was a coincidence: the pamphlet was lying on a picnic table along the path that Ari was walking. It was called: *Final Draft*.

"Take a look at this," Ari said the next time the group met for coffee at their favorite coffee shop adjacent to the Park. He passed the pamphlet around; it stopped at George. He looked it over. He frowned as if disturbed by something.

"Mind if I take this home to read?" he asked.

The other three grunted as if to say, '*Why do you ask*'?

George took the copy of *Final Draft* home and read it over. Many of the ideas intrigued him. But it was not the content as much as the name of the author that seemed to have a mesmerizing effect upon him. "Hmmm" he wondered out loud and closed his eyes.

Time and distance vanished. He was back in Montreal at the Allan Memorial Institute. An irrational echo from the past induced a state of mind not unlike a post hypnotic trance. It was like déjà-vu; he could hear a voice… a name being spoken over and over. It sounded like the name of that not so funny Jewish American comedian… that communist shit disturber… *what's his name*?

* * *

"Want to hear something far out?" Lenny Bruce casually remarked one evening after supper."

"Far out, you say? I suppose you've been communicating with that nocturnal advisor of yours?"

"Yeah, you know, that Chilean fellow I mentioned some time ago?"

"Eldorado Pena?"

"Yeah, he told me about the One Grand Reality, or the OGR as he calls it."

"OGR?" Lana queried, her curiosity piqued.

"This is rather far-out stuff so you will really have to-to keep an open mind," Lenny advised.

"Try me," Lana challenged.

"Here's the way Eldorado put it: there is only One Grand Reality, or OGR. It includes everything anyone has ever conceived of: quantum theories, string theories, parallel worlds, multiverses, plus anything that constitutes knowledge. Everything, period."

"What about Heaven and Hell or all those other dimensions?"

"Did I not say 'everything'? They are all relative aspects of the One Grand Reality. We can only become cognizant of the relevant aspects of the OGR in accordance with our biological and spiritual capabilities. Even though all the other dimensions of reality co-exist here, now... we are only aware of the particular dimensions that are relevant."

"Relevant to our level of conscious awareness?"

"Yes".

"So I assume that each level of awareness can be broken down into smaller degrees of cognition... as is evident here in this space-time dimension where some folks are not nearly as aware as others. It seems to me that intelligence might have some bearing upon one's relative degree of awareness," Lana conjectured.

"Indeed it does. IQ measurements are basically a crude indication of a person's potential level of awareness, the higher the intelligence quotient, the greater the potentiality for awareness. But alack, even the keenest intellect can be encumbered by a social and cultural blanket of dogma and doctrine, reducing and restricting the scope of intellectual freedom to the level of a small and narrow-minded neurotic who is unable to see the forest for the trees."

"So why are we all here now... in this four dimensional space-time membrane of forces?"

"We are here, now… because Everything-there-is is here, now. The One Grand Reality is here, now. We just participate in the appropriate membrane of forces relative to our level of conscious awareness."

"Could you say that every human being has been incarnated into a reality membrane of forces relative to or in accordance with their karmic disposition?"

"Indeed, that is why they are here, now. It has taken each individual soul countless years to progress to this point. It is a subjective experience for each individual. It provides individuals with experiences in line with their karmic status. They can progress, remain static, or regress. They have free will. They are free to be."

"I see… so even though I am ensconced in the One Grand Reality, I am only aware of that four-dimensional aspect of it that is commensurate with the scope of my intellectual and spiritual consciousness. All the other dimensions, including my dreams, are also here, but except for my dreams, I am not able to tune them in… yet."

"You are perceptive," Lenny praised his spouse. "To use the radio analogy, you are like a biological receiver that is set to tune-in AM frequencies. The FM frequencies are also available, but as far as you are concerned, they may as well be non-existent. However, if you were able to expand your capabilities to include the FM frequencies, wouldn't that be a pleasant awakening?"

"Enlightening."

"Eldorado says that as our spiritual and intellectual consciousness expands, our 'reality quotient', as he called it, increases relative to our level of awareness."

"Reality quotient, what is that?"

"It just seems to be a technical term Pena uses to denote the degree to which we are able to comprehend and participate in the One Grand Reality. The OGR, according to Eldorado, consists of Everything-there-is or ETI as he called it. The ETI is self-descriptive. As our consciousness expands, so does our 'reality quotient', or relative degree of awareness of it."

"Did he say what our reality quotient is?"

"I'll get to that a little later, but first let me elaborate a bit further. The concept of a reality quotient is based upon a postulated scale, something like our weights and measures. All measurements are relative to something or other. Infinity makes all measurements meaningless…

so in the face of the absurd, we postulate limits. To illustrate... what is time?"

"A segment of an eternal duration?"

"Astute. All knowledge only makes sense within a defined space-time. Mortality provides us with the finite bookends within which actual knowledge can have meaning. So, to make a long story short, some ingenious mortals who are way ahead of us with regards to their level of karmic awareness, have devised this reality quotient based on a scale that goes from zero to one thousand. Apparently relevant data is collected and fed into complicated algorithmic formulas processed by super computers. The results provide a fairly reliable picture of the membrane of forces or dimensions which correspond with a specific outcome designated as a reality quotient."

"Sounds like a glorified scale of awareness. Complicated stuff, but I think I'm getting it," Lana proclaimed proudly.

"There is a spiritual essence to all aspects of reality that becomes submerged in a materialistic mindset. Scientists and mathematicians spend so much time attempting to objectify the universe that they become victims of their own mindset." Eldorado became slightly emotional when he pointed this out. He said that, "*You're like that fabled baboon who sticks his little hand into a narrow crack in a tree to retrieve some tasty nuts lying in a pocket therein; once he grasps the nuts his fist becomes too large to be extracted. His greed prevents him from letting go. He is trapped by his own selfishness and lack of awareness.*"

"Is he saying that we are trapped in a materialistic mindset by our own greed and stupidity?"

"I think so. You know, letting go can be very difficult for a greedy materialist. Especially for a greedy and righteous materialist! Most will stubbornly hang on to those nuts for dear life, placing greater value in their material possessions and religious dogmas than in their innate spiritual essence."

"Right on!" Lana expostulated. "They are unaware that in many ways they are their own worst enemy."

"Here on earth people by and large have very little interest in discovering who they really are... because they already know who they are."

"So... who are they?" Lana queried.

"Sinners. It is just something they take for granted. Consequently they conjure up all kinds of inane, irrational, and mostly self-aggrandizing myths and superstitions about the purpose and consequences of their earthly predicament."

"Did you say predicament?"

"It seems like a predicament to those who feel that they are innately flawed, sinful creatures who have been banished here for their disobedience... and are in dire need of being saved. Collectively they are loath to let go of this righteous belief. In short they are loath to let go of the nuts! Some of them will righteously hang on for dear life! Ironic – eh?'"

"I see the irony. If their desire for righteousness is greater than their longing for freedom... they will cling ignominiously to their materialistic version of reality. What a dynamic description of a-a sinful sinner!" Lana insightfully replied.

"Unfortunately, like the fabled baboon, if they wish to be free, they must let go... of the nuts. But what else can sinners do – but hang on for dear life? It is like that wise old saying points out: 'You can only take with you what you give away.' And yet we selfishly decimate the earth and hoard material wealth as if we can take it with us when we pass on. How short-sighted is that?"

"It seems that we are just not in synch with our intrinsic spirituality or with Nature."

"Eldorado is a patient man – but even he is frustrated by our performance to date. He said: 'Reality per se is a spiritual matter. Reality is simply your own conscious level of awareness manifested. If you believe you are sinners... you will behave like sinners. You reap what you sow... it is karma.'"

"Forthright, to say the least," Lana breathed.

"I must admit I was a little taken aback by his tone. Sensing my reticence he empathetically responded, 'Even with your limited scope of awareness, I am certain that you can fathom *this*!' He said *this* with such definition that I felt intimidated. Of course I was obliged not to make a liar out of him."

"The way you are explaining it to me makes a lot of sense - so you must have grasped what he was saying."

"Thanks." Lenny looked gratefully toward his wife. "Getting back to your previous question...."

"Yeah, what did Pena say about our 'reality quotient'?"

"He fidgeted and said: *Your particular reality quotient is a work in progress. Over the millennia, due to the idiosyncrasies of the human condition, even with the use of quantum computing, the results have been somewhat indecisive... in the past there have been unexpected regressions.*

"Quantum computing? Regressions?"

"Yes. According to Eldorado, in the distant past human beings once knew more than we do now. Because we do not know any better, we think we must be the smartest, most advanced species ever to inhabit this reality. For example, in our digitized world, computers operate within an arithmetic protocol of zeros and ones, where the zeros and ones are-are separate and distinct from each other. Pena called that the 'abacus' mode. In quantum computing the protocol is based on zero-ones, or one-zeros, yielding results that are geometrically astounding. And as you know progress is not uniformly even — there are minor blips, and temporary reversals."

"I must say we are an egotistical and vain lot," Lana scoffed. "We think we are so high-tech — but are probably fledglings vaingloriously fiddling with the 'abacus' mode of computer technology."

"Pena said that there was such a wide variance in the intellectual awareness data from this plane, that it was difficult to get a reliable read at this time. I personally think he has some idea what it is, but out of consideration for my vanity and earthly level of emotional development, chose not to divulge this information to me. I pleaded with him to at least give me a ball-park estimate."

"And what did he say?"

"He hesitated and thoughtfully replied, 'Well, this is just a ballpark guess as you say, so don't take it too seriously. On a partial scale, your reality quotient... would probably be close to one hundred.'"

"That high!" Lana exclaimed jubilantly.

"That high considering..."

"Considering what?"

"Considering that one hundred is the upper end of the entire scale."

"Upper end?"

"Like you, at first I was elated. But then I realized that he had said that the actual scale went from one to a thousand."

"And we think we are so smart!" Lana exclaimed.

"Eldorado said not to get hung up on our RQ. It is all relative. What is more important, he said, was our lack of understanding of the concept of One Grand Reality."

"And our participation in it – eh?"

"According to Eldorado, even some hazy comprehension of this concept by the general population would substantially reduce the religious and superstitious misunderstandings and conflicts that plague our planet - and would enable us to cooperate, harmonize, and share the bounty we have been blessed with. In addition he thinks it might provide the karmic impetus required for most of us to realize an increased degree of awareness."

"So there seems to be hope for us yet, eh?"

"As our collective vibrations become more life-enhancing, rather than life-negating, our manifested reality will reflect this healthier attitude. We will hopefully, therefore, eventually be able to realize a reality deserving of our intellectual potential."

"Deserving of our intellectual potential?"

"This modern materialistic reality in which you and I presently reside, exists because we created it of our own free will… and we will reap what we have sown."

"It seems to me that we are underachieving. Our spiritual aura has been tragically tainted by our religious belief in original sin, which unfortunately, has negatively impacted upon our intellectual potential," Lana adroitly pointed out.

"I think Eldorado would agree with you. Before he departed he sighed lamentably and concluded: *'I am sorry to say, but in my humble opinion, you folks could be your own worst enemies! All this political bickering and righteous terrorism is indicative of your current state of awareness. Unless you smarten up soon, by way of cyber warfare you could ignominiously decimate your highly technical and digitized information base… and unconsciously trigger a genocidal regression into a void of righteous ignorance."*

* * *

There was a great deal that had been done: the decaying boardwalk had been replaced and many of the old buildings and wharves that dotted the shoreline had been carefully restored. The past had been preserved as an historical site with its memory preserved on information placards. But once upon a time it actually existed as the Salmon Capital of the World. It could be touched, tasted, heard, smelled, and seen. It was real.

It existed, just as sure as the tourists who flocked into Steveston during the summer months to walk up and down the historic boardwalk and admire the placidly flowing Fraser River as it slowly made its way out to the mighty Pacific. They became aware of the fishing and cannery history that put Steveston on the map. It was from the Britannia wharf on July 1899 that the two hundred foot clipper called the Titania had set sail for the United Kingdom with the first shipment of Pacific salmon caught, gutted, cleaned, cooked and canned in Steveston, British Columbia.

When the tourists clomped down the boardwalk and stopped to read the information signs posted at the historical sites, they became aware that many human beings had trod down that path before them: Chinese, First Nations Peoples, Japanese, and an assortment of Europeans and other nationalities. Most of them worked for the canneries that made Steveston the salmon canning capital of the world.

In early autumn the Pacific salmon, mostly coho, chinook, and the much sought after sockeye, congregated at the estuary of the Fraser while acclimating themselves to the fresh water, prior to beginning their miraculous ascent upriver to their spawning grounds in the interior. After four years in the Pacific, swimming as far north as Alaska, the sockeye returned instinctively to the spawning streams where they were hatched to reproduce their species. After completing their life cycle, the exhausted sockeye turned topsy-turvy and floated upon their backs for a while before passing on... leaving their rotting corpses behind as reminders of the fleeting nature of all mortal life forms.

When their ever-curious daughter, Kitty, was eight years old Lenny and Lana took 'the little intellectual' to see the salmon run. What they wouldn't do for that precious incarnation who represented a mortal expression of their immortal dreams! Of course she needed to see the world famous salmon run in the Shuswap. They drove up through the Hell's Gate Canyon where in 1918 a landslide had blocked the river and prevented the salmon from reaching the Shuswap. The salmon population was decimated for years to come. Eventually a fish ladder was installed to enable the salmon to get through. Kitty saw that fish ladder.

The Bruce family stayed overnight in Kamloops before journeying up to Roderick Haig-Brown Provincial Park to see the salmon run. The lady working at the Park informed them that a major run was underway. "Major runs only occur every four years, symptomatic of the 1918 landslide," she explained to Kitty.

Kitty was amazed. Her big brown eyes absorbed the spectacle. She was speechless. The streams ran red with countless numbers of sockeye swimming upstream in search of the location where they were hatched four years earlier. What motivated them to behave in such a manner? Were they driven by a collective intelligence en masse to achieve a common goal? Did the achievement of that goal produce a grand sense of joy and happiness? It was an incredible sight to see thousands of crimson red sockeye with hooked green snouts striving to reach their respective spawning beds so they could reproduce... and die.

"It is a marvel of nature," eight-year old Kitty sagely remarked as they trudged along the winding path that led to the parking lot.

It gave them pause to be aware of such a spectacle. "You know, Dad," Kitty said as they were leaving the Park, "there does not seem to be anything marvelous about our life-cycle. We don't seem to have a common goal. We don't share a common color. We don't return to the place of our birth. We just grow old and feeble... and die."

"Ah," Lenny sighed sympathetically sensing the concern in his little daughter's voice. "So it seems, eh? But there is an inner beauty in all things. When we share that common inner beauty together - like we are doing now - life seems to be a divine expression."

"Thanks, Dad," Kitty said with a self-conscious smile of appreciation. She attached herself to her Dad by curling up possessively against his left leg.

"Kitty-kat," Lenny purred endearingly while patting his little daughter on the head, "you are such a divine expression of joy."

Lana smiled enigmatically like Mona Lisa. She focused her camera and took a picture so that they could lock that memory in their minds forever. They were so very, very blessed.

* * *

Lenny was sitting on his favorite bench on the east side of Phoenix Pond on the afternoon of May 29th with a divine expression of joy transfixed upon his face. The sky was crystal clear and the ducks were sitting in a neat row on a large log protruding from the southern shore. He was sitting there meditating when he felt a light tap on his left shoulder. He turned around, and there they were: Father Bertolli and Rabbi Letenberg. "What are you two old geezers doing out here?" Lenny asked in surprise.

"Just out for a stroll," Rabbi Letenberg replied.

"Yeah, what a beautiful day," Father Bertolli added.

"Please join me." The motley three sat side-by-side on the wooden bench and stared across the shimmering pond toward the graceful arch of the footbridge in the distance. They enjoyed the serenity and the wonders of nature surrounding the little pond. The beauty spoke for itself; the spoken word was redundant. They lapsed into a meditative spell.

The magical moment was interrupted by the cheerful sound of a woman's voice: "What are you three old codgers doing out here?" It was Cathy Schneider.

The motley three could not say, "Join us", because there wasn't enough room left on the bench... so they all stood up respectfully. "Just enjoying the moment," Lenny replied on behalf of the group.

"I am on my way back from town," Cathy explained, "needed some milk and instant coffee. Say, why don't you guys join me for coffee? I just live over there." She pointed to a nearby condo building.

The motley four trundled off down the paved pathway toward the condo. Cathy led them up to her door and they all entered. The three old codgers stood beside the front window and gazed out. "It's just a view," Cathy said as she put on the kettle to boil, "a blind person wouldn't even know it was there."

The motley four made themselves comfortable in the spacious living room. Len sat on the leather sofa-chair by the fireplace. The Rabbi made himself at home on the mauve colored recliner-rocker, while Cathy and the Father seated themselves on the beige leather couch. After the kettle boiled, Cathy made four cups of instant coffee embellished with Irish Cream liqueur. She also provided little chocolate cupcakes with white icing. "Better than Starbucks," Lenny commented.

"This is nice," Father Bertolli sighed as he sagged into the luxury of the leather sofa. "Just think of it?" he asked with a thoughtful pause... "While millions are starving and suffering from malnutrition and disease – we four sit here with coffee and cupcakes in hand admiring the view."

"It's all about money," Lenny offered as an explanation.

"Money, money, money," Cathy echoed, "It seems the world as we know it is fabricated from money."

"Since our last group meeting the good Father, Lenny, and myself have been doing a little research on the medium of exchange known as money," Rabbi Letenberg pointed out for Cathy's benefit.

"Money is a relatively new development as far as the history of Man is concerned," Father Bertolli commented.

"Well as you all know, Jews and money go together," Letenberg commented with a wry grin. "Ever since the biblical Jesus drove the Jewish moneylenders from the Synagogue in a wrath of self-righteous fury, Jews as a race have been associated, for good or bad, with money. Two noteworthy examples come immediately to mind: Shylock of Shakespearean infamy, and in recent times the fabulously rich Rothschilds."

"Nice intro," Cathy commented. "Please continue."

"Money is basically a man-made commodity. It is essential, as a simple medium of exchange in the present economic system of free enterprise. And yet, the most astute economists and financial experts are confused by its relationship to what is currently assumed to be 'wealth'. The economic downturn of 2008 caused near panic amongst the worldly bankers who watched in horror as their precious 'wealth' disappeared as if into thin air. Where did all that 'wealth' go?"

"A very good question," Cathy intoned.

"Poof! It disappeared, leaving those who thought they were wealthy... bankrupt," Father Bertolli added.

"And then what happened?" Cathy prodded.

"Let us not get ahead of ourselves. A lot happened between the time that paper money first came into vogue and the year 2008. Two seemingly disparate things happened. The printing press was invented, and the powerful new religious movement known as the Protestant Reformation was proclaimed. The combination of these two events - to make a long story short - eventually led to the printing of paper money... on which someone in the newly hatched Christian Republic called the United States of America, wrote... *'In God We Trust'.*"

"Indeed that was significant because the world's most accepted medium of exchange, the US dollar, which was once backed by its worth in gold, is now backed by nothing more substantial than a religious slogan and the reality of the Free Market system," Lenny added.

"In a nutshell," the good Rabbi continued, "this development represented the culmination of an existential yearning for security in an insecure world. It began with an unwritten social contract based upon sharing and cooperation... and now it has been warped into a worldwide economic system tainted by pious self-interest and greed."

"Well put," Father Bertolli stated, following up on the Rabbi's astute remarks. "But what is it that motivates and drives a capitalist to accumulate and hoard more and more material wealth while knowingly depriving his fellowman of the basic necessities of life? What purpose does such behavior serve?"

"In essence it is self-serving and in general life-negating. The deluded capitalist may believe that he has been favored by God and is therefore amongst the chosen few destined to be saved when the entire Earth is consumed in flames. The bigger his or her stash, the more self-evident the favoritism. This belief justifies the selfish behavior and condones the greed," Rabbi Letenberg said thoughtfully.

"And since it is in essence life-negating and does not enhance the survival of the human species, or any other species for that matter, it cannot be good – can it?" Cathy inquired.

"It certainly cannot be said to be good, when one greedy individual can hog billions of dollars worth of goods and services – while ignominiously polluting the earth and relegating millions of souls to a life of malnutrition, starvation, disease, suffering, and death. On what moral grounds can such an economic system be ethically justified?" Lenny inquired.

"Justifiable or not, the world's largest and most powerful economic and religious Democracy, the US of A, paradoxically and oxymoronically aspires to promote the life-negating objectives of those who desire to sustain and spread an ideology that supports an authoritarian status quo founded upon religious dogma, self-interest, greed, and righteousness... as if it is God's will!" the good Rabbi solemnly concluded.

The motely group lapsed into silence as if to meditate upon the implications of such an economic reality. Cathy got up and went off into the kitchen to put on the coffee maker. "I think I'll make real coffee this time," she announced. When she retuned a short time later carrying a tray with four steaming cups, they all sat down around the coffee table with a sense of expectancy. Three pairs of eyes gazed in the direction of the good Rabbi, inadvertently implying that just because he was Jewish, he was the harbinger of greater economic wisdom.

"Ahhh," the Rabbi sighed as he sipped his coffee thoughtfully, "Where to begin?"

"Where you left off," Lenny offered with a grin.

"The rise of a monetary system based upon securing one's basic needs through sharing and cooperation gained impetus in the early days because in its infancy it was pragmatic; it worked. Even though the vast majority of the players – just like the general public today – did not have a clue as to how the system worked, they still participated because... what else was there in those days?"

"Still a valid question today," Cathy intoned.

'Indeed. Who understands the whys and wherefores of what motivates us human beings to do what we are presently doing? We seem to be swept along by a tide of socio-economic events over which we have very little control and even less understanding." Lenny added.

"Although the social contract that presupposed the rise of our modern economic system may have been founded upon wishful notions of fairness, equality, and social justice, as if such ideals were inherent – unfortunately, they were not!" the good Rabbi laconically continued.

"So what happened?" Cathy asked.

"Initially the system existed for the good of the participants. This insured that those participating in the social contract would benefit from the so-called 'wealth' that was created from the fruits of their labor and ingenuity. The economic system existed for the good of those who created and sustained it. It had pragmatic value. However, with the introduction of money, a new dimension of wealth was created that required the ownership and use of capital as a medium of exchange, as if it was wealth per se – which of course it wasn't." Rabbi Letenberg paused.

"So what happened?" Cathy persisted.

"Well now, let me think. To reiterate... when the economies based upon the exchange of coins manufactured from precious metals grew and expanded, it became apparent that the scarcity of such precious coins inhibited the growth and expansion of the economy; thus it became expedient to issue paper notes or IOUs that were backed by their value in precious metals like gold or silver. This was the origin of paper money. The USA and Canada for example were on the gold standard while Great Britain was on the silver standard. However, as the use and demand for paper money became international, there was insufficient gold and silver to back the demand so some nations based their paper money on their Gross National Product, which represented the total value of all the goods and services produced by the nation concerned."

"Adroit," Lenny commented. "The use of paper money presented the bankers with an incredibly easy way to create profits out of sheer greed. Usury was integrated into the economic system of exchange as if it was a necessary part of the exchange per se, thus creating a natural inflationary sense of monetary growth."

"Very profound point. Usury, or the charging of interest on money, insured that the moneylenders were guaranteed a profit. When the marketplace became global, there was a need for much more capital to service the inflationary needs of the system," Rabbi Letenberg responded. "Consequently, as much paper money was issued as was deemed necessary to keep the erratic and floundering economic system from collapsing…"

"And the use of this new medium of exchange led to the development of modern capitalism… like-like a monstrous ponzi scheme," Cathy remarked.

"Although it may seem old to us, this relatively young monetary system is based upon a belief and trust in the validity of the prevailing ideology, an ideology that contains a certain ethical underpinning, as pointed out by the famous German Philosopher, Max Weber, in his great work: *The Protestant Ethic and the Spirit of Capitalism*. The spirit of capitalism in combination with the Protestant work ethic produced the ethical milieu in which money became the means and the medium whereby man could secure his wellbeing and survival. According to the Bible, love of money is the root of all evil - but in Western Christendom in particular, money became man's social security blanket… and the route to his salvation."

"You previously mentioned the Rothschilds. I presume you mentioned them for a reason?" Lenny queried.

"Indeed I did," Letenberg confessed. "There is one name tied to the international growth of banks and the usurious power of money that is as mysterious as the spirit of capitalism itself. That name is Rothschild. Take note of it. It is a name clothed in as much secrecy, intrigue, and conspiracy as the CIA."

"I am astounded by your knowledge of such matters," Father Bertolli admitted. "Tell us more about these Rothschilds."

"Excuse me," Lenny interjected. "Would you mind if I called Lana and asked her to join us? I think she'd like to hear about the Rothschilds."

"Do call her," Cathy responded. "We could use another female point of view."

Lana arrived wearing a stylish cotton yellow dress accented by a lacey purple shawl. She ushered herself in like a breath of fresh air in a stale room. She poured herself a cup of coffee and drew up a chair from the dining room and set it next to her spouse. "Thanks for thinking about me," she said.

"Glad you could come," Cathy replied. "And now let us continue our discussion about the mysterious Rothschilds."

"Unbelievable as it may seem," Rabbi Letenberg began, "the name Rothschild is as real as the money it manipulates and controls for its own purposes. How much economic power are we talking about here? Ownership and control of over two hundred and thirty central banks in over two hundred and thirty of the wealthiest countries of the world, or about half of the monetary wealth generated by the capitalistic system to date. What do these modern central banks have in common? The ability to create wealth, that is, money... out of thin air."

"Are you sure you're not just espousing some biased conspiracy theory?" Cathy forthrightly challenged.

"Look in your wallet. What do you see?" Rabbi Letenberg asked.

Cathy got out her wallet and extracted a twenty-dollar bill. She crinkled and examined it as if checking to see if it was counterfeit. "Seems real enough," she pronounced.

"What is it?" the good Rabbi queried.

"What is it?" Cathy repeated thoughtfully while re-examining the twenty-dollar note. "It could just be a fancy piece of paper with the number twenty on it. I guess that I have no option but to trust in its value or worth and in the system that validates it."

"Why?" Lenny inquired.

"What else is there? This is the reality in which I was born and raised. I had nothing to do with its creation. It simply exists like all of you exist here in this mortal moment in the twenty-first century. In this global economic reality, money is the only medium of exchange that is used. I have no option but to believe that it has exchange value, that with it I can provide for my basic survival needs. Without money what do I have? In *this* culture it seems that money is everything!" Cathy emphasized the 'this,' and waved the twenty-dollar bill as if fanning herself.

"It seems that in this economic bubble of modernity money is everything," Lenny followed up on Cathy's pronouncement. "How did this come about? Tell us more about these mysterious Rothschilds," Lenny requested, as if he were moderating the discussion.

"Hmm." The Rabbi solemnly cogitated as if the facts of the matter were a weighty Jewish burden.

"These are the facts of the matter… as far as I know. Mayer Amschel Bauer was born in Frankfurt, Germany in 1743; he was the son of Moses Amschel Bauer, an itinerant moneylender and goldsmith who operated a counting house on Judenstrasse or Jew-street. Over the door leading to the shop Moses placed a large red shield emblematic of the red flag representing the revolutionary aspirations of the Jewish intelligentsia in Europe. Moses hoped to have his son, Mayer, trained as a rabbi - unfortunately his own untimely death put an end to such aspirations."

"What happened to Mayer?" Lana prompted.

"Shortly after his father's passing, Mayer Amschel Bauer was able to purchase the business his father had established in 1750. The red shield was still displayed prominently over the front entrance. Recognizing the symbolic significance of the red shield, Mayer morphed Red-shield into Rothschild and adopted it as his own name. Henceforth he became known as Mayer Amschel Rothschild, a surname that has become associated with banking and the pursuit of money."

"So Mayer changed his last name from Bauer to Rothschild, interesting," Father Bertolli commented. "What happened next?"

"In 1770 Mayer Rothschild married a seventeen year old girl named Gutele Schnaper. The union produced ten offspring: five girls and five boys. However in that era only the sons were encouraged to follow in their father's footsteps. What legacy did Mayer leave to his five sons? Mayer was an economic visionary who was ahead of his time. It was his insight into the mysterious power of money as a usurious medium of exchange that set him apart from his peers at that time."

"Usury!" Father Bertolli exclaimed, "A man-made convention that enabled money to grow... as if it were a living thing."

"For his time... Mayer Rothschild was an economic genius and visionary?" Cathy suggested.

"No doubt there are plenty of analysts with an anti-Semitic bias who are prone to say that Mayer Rothschild was a greedy Jewish moneylender with a frugal Protestant work ethic that gave rise to ambitions that later provided renewed impetus for the so-called Zionist movement," Father Bertolli added.

"It was his understanding of the power of usury and the compounding effect of interest on the medium of exchange that was his genius," Lenny offered.

"Lenny has hit the nail on the head. The amazing thing about Mayer Amschel Rothschild is that as early as 1780, he realized that in the new world order being fashioned in Europe after the Protestant Reformation, the key to economic prosperity lay in the little-understood economics of the compounding affects of the accrued interest on the medium of exchange," Rabbi Letenberg commented in support of Lenny's assertion. "Mayer astutely foresaw that fabulous opportunities for controlling the marketplace and becoming extremely rich and powerful were within his grasp."

"Who knew?" Cathy piped up as she carefully put her twenty-dollar bill back into her wallet and sauntered into the kitchen to pick up a freshly perked pot of coffee. The others waited until she had returned and replenished the empty cups, before continuing with the conversation.

"There is a longstanding association between money and morality," Father Bertolli offered, "that has created a sort of ethical dissonance that has serious religious ramifications for the wealthy."

"It is easier for a camel to pass through the eye of a needle than for a rich man to enter heaven," Lana astutely paraphrased.

"Indeed, prior to the Rothschilds' mysterious ascent to power, money was denigrated as being 'filthy lucre'. But to Mayer it was far from being 'filthy' – it was something to be coveted," Lenny added.

"He was nobody's fool!" Cathy piped up.

"At that time in the late eighteenth century, Mayer was unique in his secular understanding of the marketplace," Rabbi Letenberg intoned. "When others were busy accumulating the material manifestations of power and wealth like land, food, shelter, armies, weapons, precious metals and gems etc. - Rothschild realized that the ownership of all such things was contingent upon and expedited by the medium of exchange: *money*. Rothschild understood, even at that early stage in the development of modern capitalism, that the control of the medium of exchange: capital, combined with interest, was the formula that would enable his family to own, control, manipulate, and influence all that capital represented. And that was practically everything money could buy."

"Incredible!" the listeners mouthed in unison, in awe of such a revealing revelation regarding the capitalistic power of the man-made medium of economic exchange: *Money*!

"With the foresight of an economic prophet, Mayer Amschel Rothschild cleverly established branches of the House of Rothschild in the five major business centers in Europe and placed a son in each branch. Thus, Nathan was dispatched to London where the headquarters of the House of Rothschild was established and remains to this day, Amschel went to Berlin, Solomon to Vienna, Jacob to Paris, and Karlmann Rothschild to Naples."

"Wow!" Lana breathed.

"From this simple beginning evolved the privately owned secret cartel of Rothschild-controlled banks and financial institutions that quickly spread like the tentacles of a gigantic octopus to reach into the wallet of everyone enamored with the possession and ownership of money... and all that it can purchase," Rabbi Letenberg paused and gazed around at the motley group. "Hard to believe, eh?"

"It has been said," Father Bertolli wryly commented after a thoughtful pause, "that there are three types of human beings: (a) those who make things happen, (b) those who wonder, and (c) those who wonder... *What happened?*"

"What happened?" Lenny asked.

"Following their economic conquest of Europe by the mid 1800s, the Rothschilds cast their eagle eyes to the most precious gem still available in Western Christendom: the second nation in history that had been constituted with the Bible as its law book. Its constitution was specifically designed to limit the power of government and to keep its citizenry free and prosperous. Its population was mainly composed of God-fearing immigrants: pilgrims who yearned to breathe free. The United States of America looked like easy pickings," the good Rabbi explained.

"Indeed," Father Bertolli interjected, "the American Constitution has been praised for its protection of democratic principles – but in its early days did anyone understand the economic complexities involved regarding the government's control of the medium of exchange?"

"It is important to note that prior to this period of time the House of Morgan operated by US banking scion J. Pierpont Morgan functioned as a quasi-US Central bank from the corner of Wall Street and Broad. It is purported that the powerful House of Rothschild that dominated banking in Europe preferred to work anonymously in the US behind the façade of the J. P. Morgan Company," the Rabbi whispered as if sharing a secret. "The year 1913 was particularly important in the history of American banking, for in that year J. Pierpont Morgan passed away and… the Rothschild controlled Rockefeller Foundation was born."

"A whole lot of behind the scenes skullduggery occurred, eh?" Cathy commented. "It seems the rise of modern capitalism as we know it was aligned with rise of the United States of America."

"By December 23rd, 1913, the fabulously rich Rothschild Cartel was ready to pounce. When most of the members of Congress went home for Christmas, the Federal Reserve Act, carefully named so that the gullible public would not think it actually served as a Central Bank, was presented for passage before a depleted U.S. Congress."

"What happened?" Cathy asked.

"There is some contention that a quorum was not present… but who was counting? Somehow the Federal Reserve Act was passed and became a legal entity. Subsequently the Federal Reserve Act provided the legal framework for the creation of the 'Fed' or Federal Reserve System, which in turn set up the Central Banking System of the United States and granted it the legal authority to issue Federal Reserve Notes, that is Government backed IOUs, and the right to use such Notes as legal tender, or money." Rabbi Letenberg inhaled deeply. "In short, the Fed had the right to manufacture real legal tender: *money.*"

"Really?" Lana exclaimed as if dumfounded.

"I thought the so-called Fed was publically owned?" Cathy interjected as if speaking up on behalf of her American neighbors.

"The Fed is an ingenious man-made concoction that gives the illusion that it is a public institution operating in the interests of the government which it pretends to serve. In reality it is an oxymoronic public cartel... of private banks, operated in the interests of the owners of the private banks... whose shadow lurks ominously in the background."

"So how does this monetary system actually work?" Cathy asked with dogmatic curiosity. "Please try to keep it straightforward."

"It is a complicated financial matter, but I will try." Rabbi Letenberg sighed as if the request was mentally taxing.

"Please do," Cathy responded.

"The operating process is known in banking circles as fractional reserve banking," the Rabbi responded. "The term fractional is particularly significant."

"How does this work?" Lana inquired.

"It is an ingenious operation that entails the creation and disbursal of the medium of exchange: money. In simplistic terms it operates in accord with the following five steps:

(1) The Federal Open Market Committee approves the purchase of debt-securities or IOUs such as the taxpayer-backed government bonds, on the open market.

(2) This enables the Fed to purchase as many such bonds as is deemed necessary.

(3) The Fed pays for the bonds with credits that show up as numbers on the seller's balance sheets; these credits are based on a belief and trust in the viability of the system per se;

(4) The Fed uses these bonds as their fractional reserve; that means that they can loan out, with appropriate interest, *10 times* the face value of that reserve to privately owned Banks;

(5) The Banks in turn can loan out *10 times* the fractional reserve they have on hand to the general public... of course, all with added interest! And of course, unregulated private financial institutions are free to charge whatever interest the market will bear."

"I see!" Father Bertolli exclaimed as if a light had come on in his head. "If the Fed has a fractional reserve that consists of a bond worth one billion US dollars, it can loan with added interest, ten-times that amount, or ten billion dollars to national or state banks. Each of these privately held banks in turn can use the loan they receive from the Fed as their fractional reserve, magically mushrooming the original taxpayer-backed bond worth one billion dollars, into a bonanza of one hundred billion US dollars, based upon nothing more than trust and belief in a monetary system operating in the interests of the private owners. And here is the real kicker: at every level of the free market, interest can be usuriously manipulated, further compounding and inflating the value of the man-made wealth that has been artificially created out of thin air."

"A very clever monetary system… provided it can be controlled, sustained and perpetuated on a worldwide basis," Lana chimed in.

"Do we have any other options at this time, but to put our trust in this convoluted economic scheme?" Cathy ascertained. "Little wonder the US dollar has 'In God We Trust' inscribed on i

"It seems we are all beholden to those who pull the strings from behind the scenes. Hopefully our financial future is secure. After all, who knows money better than the Rothschilds?" Rabbi Letenberg posed the question somewhat facetiously.

"If the worldwide monetary system collapses, the medium of exchange, money, will mysteriously reveal its actual value: a bunch of worthless paper promissory notes with numbers on them! It nearly happened in 2008. The panic was palpable. No one knew exactly what to do. In the end the rich got richer and the poor got poorer. In 1989 there were only a paltry 41 billionaires in the US of A – by the year 2012, in spite of the near economic collapse of 2008, that number had increased ten fold to over 425, due to inflation and the continued non-regulation of the financial institutions. And at that rate it will soon reach beyond 4000 super rich individuals who will control over 99% of the wealth, "Father Bertolli speculated.

"It is in their own self-interest for the Mega Rich, who secretly manipulate the money markets of the world, to pragmatically maintain the economic health of the system for as long as they can. Ironically, by sharing the bounty that cleverness, selfishness, ruthlessness and good fortune has enabled them to accrue, they can infuse the system with greater economic vitality. Hopefully they are motivated by something more than simple-minded greed," Rabbi Letenberg wistfully concluded.

"Ah – there is the rub!" Lenny exclaimed. "At the present time the filthy rich are loath to share the bounty. As Father Bertolli has stated, the number of billionaires has increased exponentially. The rich are getting richer – while the poor are getting poorer. Greed knows no limits. Like in a cut-throat game of Texas-hold-'em, eventually someone will end up with most of the chips... and the game will forecast its own demise."

"It seems to me..." Lana suddenly perked up as if her befuddled brain had suddenly tuned into something quite alarming, causing the others to turn in her direction. "It seems to me..." Lana repeated, following up on her husband's remarks, "that the idea represented by the concept of money has evolved into something that some people are now willing to kill and die for... *as if money really is everything.*"

The smell of money permeated the luxurious confines of Cathy's condo. The Motley Five stared at each other. Silence filled the room with a sense of helplessness. "We exist in a capitalistic bubble of our own creation where our survival is dependent upon the possession of money," Cathy confirmed.

"Money presently represents something much more complicated than a-a... simple economic medium of exchange. Money is more than just a number digitized in your bank account," Lenny stated.

"Lenny is indeed perceptive. All of this," the Rabbi waved his long spindly arms about as if encompassing the entire room, "represents a reification of our collective unconscious desires made manifest by money. Everything that presently surrounds us, including this building and this city, is all man-made... cemented together so to speak by the magic of money."

"In truth, money had enabled us to reap the whirlwind of our desires, like thousands of worker ants mindlessly going about their business... creating a reality in line with their collective consciousness."

"You said a real mouthful there, Lenny." the good Rabbi commented. "Obviously you have been doing some-some serious thinking about money!"

"So?" Lana prodded, "What have you been thinking?"

Lenny gazed around at the motley group. "I have been thinking about this for some time," he confessed. "As you all know we modern, technologically advanced human beings exist in a fragile socio-economic environment that floats like a chimera upon an ocean of paper money that supposedly represents wealth. In Canada and the United States our present and future well-being and security is represented by such wealth."

"And what is the point?" Lana prompted.

"Ahh...yes. What is the point?" Lenny inhaled deeply and gazed about at his curious associates. I have been doing some research into this amorphous matter. Of course, there is a-a lot of speculation involved - but when you are attempting to predict or forecast the economic future?" Lenny held up his hands.

"Some uncertainty is understandable," Cathy empathized.

"As you probably do not know... in recent years the CIA has been involved in a practical endeavor motivated by an inbred insecurity about the fragility of the economic system that nearly crashed in 2008. As part of this endeavor they have developed a keen interest in the possibility of cyber-attacks on the New York Stock Exchange where money is represented by stocks, derivatives, bonds, treasury bills and other forms of digitized paper wealth. Such man-made wealth can disappear overnight, poof, as if it never existed."

"As trillions of such dollars vanished in 2008," Cathy added.

"In that instance, the US had terrorized itself by allowing the wealthy some very ignominious concessions: first, they passed legislation allowing the mega rich to lobby democratically elected officers of the government and secondly, they allowed big US corporations to move their headquarters off-shore in order to avoid paying their fair share of taxes on taxable income that should have been re-circulated within the US economy. And in addition they deregulated the banks. These unbelievably stupid concessions short-circuited the natural cycle that enabled the American people to share in the bounty, and created a class of super-rich parasites. Excessive greed and profit-taking was and is undermining the American dream."

"You seem to have developed some strong opinions on this matter!" Cathy exclaimed.

"It seems I may have." Lenny smiled. "But for what it is worth... some very intelligent, dedicated, and perceptive people work for various private and public agencies. The insightful among them could plainly see that basically the US was terrorizing itself with a paranoid sense of financial insecurity. They watched as the Fed cranked off trillions of new dollars to replace those that had vanished into thin air in 2008. They noted that the value of such American dollars was being artificially propped up by the Oil Cartel which specifies that the US dollar is the only medium of exchange that can be used for purchasing OPEC oil, and in addition they noted that the US dollar was being arbitrarily promoted as the most secure medium of exchange for international trade and commerce... when in fact it is the lack of a satisfactory answer to the question, '*What is the option?*' that is keeping the US dollar in place."

"Is there a viable option?" Rabbi Letenberg inquired.

"Well, to make a long story short," Lenny responded in a subdued tone, "that is the problem! A few astute Wall Street operators realized that the US had papered the world with their dollars as if such paper money represented real wealth... when in fact such wealth was as tenuous as say... the artificial price of OPEC Oil!"

"In that context, America's abiding self-interest in the oil producing nations in the Middle East seems a little more understandable, eh?" Lana declared in support of her husband's conjectures.

"Many of the world's leading economies at the time were, and still are, being held hostage to the American dollar. Investing in the US dollar seemed like a good idea," Lenny continued. "Consequently, the Chinese for example, in a vain attempt to stabilize their own economy, purchased a great portion of the American debt. At the time it probably seemed like a secure investment. But in the face of an ever increasing American deficit?"

"How can the US pay off their seemingly insurmountable debts?" Rabbi Letenberg inquired.

"One option the Fed is considering is to dilute the debt by printing trillions of new dollars and inflating the money-markets of the world... and presto, without anyone paying a dime, see their debt diminish." Lenny scratched the left side of his head as if massaging his memory.

"So what are the Chinese doing to counter this possibility?" Lana asked. "In order to protect themselves, the Chinese and other nations like Russia who hold such securities, are secretly selling them and buying gold, because gold is a lot more substantial than paper money."

"Secretly selling off American securities, eh? Who is buying the American debt?" Cathy inquired.

"This is the mysterious part. Belgium."

"Belgium!" the Motley four exclaimed in unison.

"Obviously a little country like Belgium does not have the finances. However, unbeknownst to most folks who participate at the G-8 and G-20 economic summits, a secret cartel of mega-rich and very powerful folks who control the International Monetary Fund, is apparently supposedly buying up part of the US debt!" Lenny revealed.

"Why?" Cathy inquired.

"Why indeed? Are they secretly hedging their bets? Are they preparing for a new economic world order based upon their vision of what the future may bring?" Lenny pondered. "This is where the mystery really becomes mysterious! Based upon the economic reality of what is presently happening in a world-wide marketplace confronted by global warming, terrorism, and huge migrations of refugees, many plausible scenarios become evident: (a) remain in denial, do nothing and attempt to maintain the status quo, (b) prop up the US dollar for the time being and react to increasing economic, social, and climactic problems as they happen or (c) begin laying the foundation for a new universal and hopefully more equitable monetary system in anticipation of future global, political and economic instability."

"It seems to me that options (a) and (b) might be the most appealing to the one percent at the top of the economic scale," Father Bertolli pointed out. "We are mostly a conservative lot. We like to hang on for dear life to what we have..."

"When we factor in climate change," the good Rabbi soberly commented, "it seems to me that the third option becomes the most viable."

"Climate change." Lenny gazed about at the curious faces that surrounded him. "It could be a game changer."

"Lenny my boy, you know how to keep our interest piqued," the good Rabbi commented.

"When the astute amongst the forecasters factor climate change into the equation they realize that massive geographical, political, economic and population changes could occur. To illustrate, as the oceans rise, vast land areas will become submerged, and as the temperature increases areas that now are life-sustaining, for instance California, will rapidly become parched and uninhabitable, necessitating large population shifts toward more life-sustainable habitats."

"This could happen far more quickly than most people believe..." Cathy quipped, "like moving from winter into spring; it is like the end of February... the snow is rapidly melting."

"Who has not experienced such seasonal climate change? Of course it seems natural... on a seasonal basis," Lana added.

"Global warming is something else! It will place immense pressure upon the artificial lines drawn upon maps demarcating ownership of the land," Lenny resumed. "Over time large areas that are now covered with ice and snow will become habitable, triggering a natural movement of life forms into these areas. Of course it is obvious that the status quo will not only be threatened, but also challenged in every way. In such a fluid situation anarchy could easily become a reality as massive populations are forced into survival mode. In such an ongoing period of change and adjustment a secure transferable and universal medium of exchange will be vital to the preservation of a civilized sense of stability, decorum, and security... in the midst of unprecedented global upheaval."

"Climate change forces the mega-rich to focus on the real issues, issues submerged beneath the veneer of an economic system based upon a medium of exchange that is based upon nothing more than simple trust in the system," Rabbi Letenberg pointed out.

"However, as you know, in spite of the obvious, there is a natural tendency to attempt to protect the status quo. In 1969 when global warming was considered to be a red-herring, the International Monetary Fund was created to stabilize failing third world economies and to bolster the main medium of exchange, the US dollar," Father Bertolli added.

"I can see the importance of maintaining a secure, global medium of exchange," Cathy remarked.

"Since then it seems that the IMF has essentially morphed into a world bank disguised as a fund," Lenny resumed. "It operates as a world banker of last resort. Since the crash of 2008 the IMF has spent billions propping up beleaguered Euro participants. It has even taken upon itself the right to issue monetary credits known as Special Drawing Rights or XDRs: X for Special, D for Drawing, and R for Rights, a fancy name for phantom money."

"Could it be that with climate change becoming more and more prominent the foundation for option 'c' is actually being insidiously implemented?" Cathy astutely ascertained.

"What was option 'c'? Lana asked with a frown.

"The implementation of a new global monetary system," Cathy refreshed Lana's memory.

"The IMF is very secretive about its banking practices," Lenny continued. "As yet the so-called *XDRs* are not backed by anything - except for the cluster-intelligence that manifests the behavior that enables

– 258 –

the economic system to endure. 'Manna from heaven,' some critics call it. It exists because the economic system requires it… without a viable medium of exchange, what do we have?"

"Good question," Cathy commented. "What do we have?"

"Nothing. Sheer anarchy!" the good Rabbi stated. "The demise of a modern materialistic civilization that has, in the blink of an historical eye, risen as if by magic from the Protestant Ethic and the Spirit of Capitalism to encompass the world."

"And… a super-secretive international association of financial wizards manipulated by the long arm of the Rothschild cartel, is going to save us from this pending catastrophe?" Cathy asked with a hint of skepticism.

"Indeed," Lenny began to every one's surprise, "apparently the top executives of the International Monetary Fund have already been carefully vetted - to reflect an international attitude and deportment - worthy of world-class-bankers on the verge of…"

"On the verge of what?" Cathy interjected.

"On the verge of creating a centralized *World Bank*!"

"A what?" Cathy followed up.

"A *World Bank* ready to hastily step in and take control when the US dollar falls from grace, and the pressures from climactic change along with increased pressures for geographical realignments obviate the need for political, social, and economic changes."

"In order to preserve a semblance of civilized decorum," Lana finished off her husband's thought, "and perhaps most importantly, to avoid sheer anarchy."

"This conversation is getting a little too heavy. Let's take a break and stretch our legs," Cathy suggested standing up and flexing her arms.

"Good idea," Father Bertolli seconded, rising to his feet with a groan while motioning Lenny and the Rabbi to join in. The Motley Five stood around the coffee table and stretched and limbered up encouraging the blood flow to their brain cells.

"Ah, that feels better," Rabbi Letenberg sighed sitting back down. The others followed suit. "Now, where did we leave off?"

"Getting back to what you said before about some secret cartel in Belgium buying up part of the US debt. For what purpose?" Father Bertolli asked, resuming the discussion.

"Perhaps it is a last ditch attempt to sustain the unsustainable, to prevent or forestall the hundred trillion dollar market crash that is being predicted as being imminent and inevitable, given the lackluster behavior of the US Treasury. Or perhaps it is a behind-the-scenes transfer of monetary wealth and control, a passing of the torch, so to speak, from the US to the-the... mysterious mega rich manipulators anonymously lurking in the background," Lenny suggested.

"Ominous!" Lana exclaimed.

"The masterminds behind the secret cartel that controls the IMF are nobody's fools... they are able to speculate as well!" Lenny asserted. "They are aware that in the face of a world-wide redistribution of land and resources created by climate change, eventually there will need to be a re-evaluation and globalization of the mindset associated with the medium of exchange. In order to stabilize an increasingly chaotic international marketplace, a secure medium of exchange will be required that most, if not all, of the essential players will buy into, a medium of exchange more synonymous with the old concept of wealth."

"And what could that be?" Cathy inquired.

"A gold-backed currency."

"A what?" The idea seemed so ludicrous and obsolete that it caused the Motely Four to turn toward Lenny and expostulate in unison: "A gold-backed currency!"

"The medium of exchange needs to be anchored by something substantial that symbolizes Wealth. Gold is a precious metal that has always had such universal appeal. It elicits ah... spiritual sentiments, because of its purity, and perhaps because it reflects the golden vibrations of the primordial sun? Since all of the big players already have large gold reserves," Lenny explained, "it would be a no-brainer, in the face of pending anarchy in the financial markets, to simply back the XDR*s* to some extent with gold, and issue XDR notes as a universal gold-backed medium of exchange for a worldwide system of trade and commerce. In other words, it would be a return to the oldest standard of economic security ever known: gold."

"Sounds like a refurbished tune with yesterday's dance steps," Rabbi Letenberg observed. "But it could work. Something needs to be done. So far we have been dancing to a tune that has brought us to this sorry pass. Some of us like to pretend that we know what is going on. But what do we really know?"

"We know that due to climate change, northern countries like Canada and Russia with large natural reserves of land and water will probably accrue more and more real value – while those countries without such reserves will struggle to survive," Cathy contributed.

"When it comes to survival, our powerful southern neighbor will eye our water and natural resources with jealousy and envy. Necessity may eventually provide the impetus for a USA-Canada sharing of resources. After all, no one really owns the land in perpetuity; we only get to use it for a brief mortal moment. We have to get over this selfish idea of ownership and learn to share," Father Bertolli sagely added.

"Hopefully those who are pulling the strings realize that in the face of something as inevitable and catastrophic as global warming, excessive greed could bring the entire system to a grind," the Rabbi astutely pointed out.

"Ironically, it is in the best interests of those involved in the Secret Cartel to somehow find a way to keep the system relevant," Lenny stated thoughtfully. "Perhaps common sense will prevail, and the economic reality to which we have become accustomed will gradually transform itself into a more sharing and caring system."

* * *

Was it not light years ago
That you cried irreconcilably
When you relinquished ownership
Of the burden that weighed you down
With the dross of your own ignorance
Long forgotten along the Great Chain of Being
Receding back into time immemorial
Where by accident of birth
Mortality imbued existential meaning
Upon immortality
As you gradually became aware
That you were not at all
Who you thought you were?

- LB

CHAPTER NINE

ALLEGORY OF THE FISH

Like goldfish in a glass bowl
We swim about ignominiously
Thinking we are in the great ocean.

When he was little his dad told him to, "suck it up and be a man." He was in grade four at the time and some bullies had taunted him by calling him a sissy and other worse names. "Georgie Porgie puddin' and pie," they often yelled, "kissed the girls and made them cry." And when he ran off and hid, they would add, "When the boys came out to play, Georgie Porgie ran away!" It was very unpleasant and what was worse, his behavior seemed to personify the meaning of the silly rhyme.

Childhood is a precious time, and it was with good reason that both Freud and Jung placed such great emphasis on early childhood experiences. They tend to form the basis of our personal unconscious and subconscious mind and bring into play the dynamics of the psyche that, according to Jung, enables the collective unconscious to relate to archetypes of: *father, family, child, hero, maiden, sage, animal, joker, primordial man, self, and God.*

Exactly who did little Georgie Porgie think he was? He was born, baptized, and raised as a God-fearing Christian. Given the social and cultural influences, was it any surprise that by the age of seven he thought of himself as being a sinner... and behaved accordingly?

He definitely was not unique in this. There were billions of others like him in Western Christendom. There actually was something to the concept of *synchronicity* that Jung had promulgated. The concept resonated amongst the collective unconsciousness of the rich and powerful, the sophisticated upper class, the intelligentsia, and last but not least, the common people: the humble, the meek, the downtrodden, and the gullible. George was definitely not alone.

The perverse idea that he was a sinner had long family roots. He inherited this life-negating self-concept from generation upon generation of ancestors who simply accepted the dogma as truth. Who could blame George for inculcating such a belief? Was he not just an innocent victim of the circumstances?

His parents had him baptized at birth – he had absolutely no say in it. Zero. They made him go to Sunday school, and they took him to church when he got older. He was one of the masses who prayed for forgiveness for their sins on Sunday morning... and spent the rest of the week accumulating more.

It can be said unequivocally, that although George was not born a sinner - he had no choice but to become one. In fact it would have been unnatural in such an environment, if he had remained untainted, so to speak.

And so it came to pass that George Webster Brown, *needed to be saved*. Being a sinner, he did not have the moral integrity to *save himself*. Therefore he needed someone else who was not tainted by sin to save him. Who could that 'someone else' be?

Throughout the two thousand year history of Western Christendom, the identity of that 'someone else' has been of utmost importance to those who need to be 'saved'. At the Council of Nicaea organized in 325 AD by the pagan ruler Constantine the Great in order to consolidate his influence over the Roman Empire, three hundred and eighteen Bishops were called together to amalgamate all the dissident, fledgling, and developing Judeo-Christian faiths under the umbrella of one *Roman* catholic church.

A new Creed had to be surreptitiously created that would enable the 318 Bishops with the support of the great unwashed who identified with those who had ignominiously cried, "Give us Barabbas", to transform the beleaguered *son of man* - into the archetypical *Son of God:* the Christ, their Lord and Savior. The transformation was not at all miraculous. It was calculated, manipulated, secretive, and self-serving.

Unfortunately, due to the complicity of the Roman Catholic Church, few modern day Christians, Muslims, and Jews are aware of the religious and historical significance of what took place in 325 AD at the Council of Nicaea. In that year the old existing gospels were purposefully re-written, twisted, and reconstituted to suit the dogma of a newly created *Nicene Creed* that transformed the humble son of a carpenter into a deity... and like magic, eighteen long years of the shortened lifespan of the enlightened individual who called himself the *son of man* vanished... into the bonfires that raged on and on consuming every incriminating bit of pre-history in an attempt to create a 'new' testament of faith: a single Gospel that would enable Constantine the Great to consolidate all the dissident faiths into one 'catholic' Faith over which he – not Pope Sylvester - would rule supreme.

Synchronicity happens all the time. Few people are aware of it. We all live in the same time and space. We all breathe the same molecules of air that make up the atmosphere. We exist in the same universal mortal moment. There is a fluidity that enables people existing in the same time-space to experience the same vibrations.

"In all recorded history, this is the first time that a religious dogma became so socially and politically entrenched as to render it static or immutable, so to speak!" Eldorado Pena had emphasized on an occasion when Lenny was engaged in a particularly erotic dream and had shouted out loud: *Don't bother me!*

"Have you ever wondered why the JCM Faiths seem archaic, primitive, and dogmatic? It is simply because these religious faiths have become institutionalized or *varnished.*" Pena seemed particularly incensed as if the consequences had negatively affected him personally. He assumed Lenny was listening.

"As you know most ideas are allowed to, grow, develop, evolve, and change over time in accord with man's ever changing level of understanding. For example, look at how the scientific idea of the multiverse has evolved: at the time the Roman Catholic Church was being constituted, people believed that the world was flat and in the center of the universe. Look at how that belief has changed over the centuries – in spite of the Pope's attempts to condemn and suppress Copernicus' ideas." Eldorado drew in a deep breath as if the thought had necessitated such a reaction.

"However, unlike your scientific ideas about the shape of the earth and its place in the heavens – your religious beliefs regarding Creation, Morality, Immortality, Heaven, Hell, Justice, God, Truth and other such concepts have not been allowed to evolve, change, grow, and develop over the centuries in line with man's intellectual understanding of such concepts and ideas. Unfortunately in the era that preceded the Dark Ages, the religious-truth has been sealed in a veneer of institutionalized piety. When the Bible became holy, the religious-truth became fixed, static, varnished, and institutionalized as the *immutable word of God.*"

Eldorado had spoken as one who was incredulous that such an event had actually come to pass... and that after the passage of millennia, so many were still tragically unaware that in order to facilitate this historical *varnishing* of the truth, all irreplaceable authentic hand-written sacred old bibles - over two hundred were still available at that time - and other precious documents that did not support the newly concocted Creed, had to be destroyed or burned! The deception had to be as immaculate as the impeccable virgin birth of the new *Christ* who rose like a phoenix from the flickering ashes of the mortal *son of man*... to become the immortal *Son of God,* the Lord and Savior, the Redeemer of all the penitent sinners... that his *Father*, in a fit of vindictive rage, had condemned so long ago!

In order to protect the extraordinary claim made by the Creed and reinforced by the Nativity pageant, eighteen of Jesus' most crucial developmental years - the years from age 12 to age 30 when the self-professed 'son of man' matured into the enlightened individual who returned to his homeland in hopes of freeing his countrymen from an obsolete belief in 'ancestral sin' - were carefully expunged from the historical record... *as if they never happened.*

And irony of ironies... the archaic dogma that Jesus had hoped to free his people from became entrenched in the guilty consciences of those who called him 'Lord and Savior'. The old archaic Hebrew dogma of ancestral sin became renewed, invigorated and promulgated via the epistles of the founder of modern Christianity, Saul of Tarsus, and *Christianized* as the 'Doctrine of Original Sin'.

The 'new-bible' had to focus only on those events that supported the Doctrine and justified the Nicene Creed. Consequently the newly created *Gospels* were focused almost entirely on the Nazarene's brief three-year ministry, a ministry that lasted from the time of his *return* at the age of thirty from *somewhere*, until his untimely death at the age of thirty-three.

Incredibly, after such a long and poignant absence, not a single person in the New Testament had the curiosity to ask: *"Where have you been for the past eighteen years?"* Didn't anyone care?

Apparently not, as far as the New Testament gospels are concerned. For over two thousand years the faithful have been deliberately kept in the dark with regards to those eighteen missing years. The eighteen years just vanished like smoke in the raging bonfires at the Council of Nicaea. It is an indisputable historical fact. It happened. It came to pass. Unfortunately Jesus had absolutely no say in this matter. None. Zero. After all, he had been crucified 325 years earlier. At that time he had graciously said: *Forgive them... for they know not what they do.* Was he prophetic... or what?

Most Christians, in general, are unaware of this historical event. For sure, it is not something they want to hear. But it did occur. The bonfire of the vanities burned for days on end until nary a shred of contradictory evidence remained. The powerful Roman Catholic Church has never condemned this sacrilegious act - because without it, there would be no *Roman Catholic Church!*

Unfortunately, neither George nor any of the people that he associated with knew anything about the Council of Nicaea of 325 AD. Space and time religiously endured and over the centuries morphed into a vast hegemony of dogmatic belief that billions of converts accepted as being the *word of God.* They argued, squabbled, fought, killed, and terrorized each other in the name of a primitive deity whose relevance had become increasingly obsolete, as man's level of intellectual awareness expanded. Ignorance can be somewhat blissful. So George just carried on as if such behavior was natural and he was normal.

What is normal? In the state of nature the wonderful world of the *collective unconscious* is essentially a man-made phenomenon. The collective unconscious consists of vibrations collected from the brain waves of human beings who have evolved hand in glove with their karmic memories.

Whatever dreams, desires, thoughts, and ideas that once vibrated within the collective minds of men and women, now resonate within the *Collective Unconscious.* It is just there, something like the *cloud* of information and knowledge that services the Internet is *there* for all users to tap into. Modern technology has made the hypothetical cogitations of Carl Jung seem ingeniously real. Cloud computing exists out there in the modern world as a practical manifestation of the collective unconscious; it is purely a man-made creation that inhabits the state of nature like a shadow upon the landscape.

When George was born there was no such thing as the Internet, let alone the Cloud. Those ideas were yet to come, along with the host of high-tech gadgetry and the network of satellites, computers, servers, and drivers that are now ubiquitous. It all happened within George's lifetime. It just materialized, as if it was natural, just like George himself. It happened. And is happening.

So Georgie Porgie puddin' and pie did not kiss the girls and make them cry - instead he shot poor old Lenny the Bruce… and made him die. In the accidental rhythm and rhyme involved, could the outcome be rationalized as being poetic justice? Or was it just plain murder?

There is a lot of prose, but not much poetry in the world of sin. Sin is such a life-negating concept. Freud attempted to make sense of such behavior, and in so doing uncovered a psychological realm filled with repressed desires manifested as neurotic tendencies with sexual anxieties. This behavior, rationalized as being spiritually moral, became reflected in the state of nature as a superficial man-made subculture manifested upon the surface of the earth from the collective unconscious of sinful man. Ideas that resonate synchronistically can have a powerful effect upon human behavior.

In Western Christendom the seeds of the Protestant Ethic were planted when Martin Luther stood alone before the doors of Wittenberg Castle and nailed his ninety-five theses into the personal unconscious of the mighty Roman Catholic Church. "Here I stand," he defiantly stated, "*I can do no other!*" Those vibes synchronized with sympathetic vibrations within the collective unconscious of Western Christendom and resonated as the Protestant Reformation that gave rise to the Spirit of Capitalism. It is a relatively recent development in human history.

Many amazing things have come to pass since then, but one particular event stands out because it seemed so surreal that it was almost unbelievable. Nevertheless it did indeed happen; it cannot be denied: a human being intelligent enough to be able to fly a passenger jetliner with hundreds of paying customers on board, deliberately crashed it into a tower of glass, steel and concrete wherein thousands of people were working. Why? What religious beliefs and dogmas motivated him to commit such a seemingly irrational action? Could he have done other?

Could George Webster Brown... *have done other?* Or was he too... like Martin Luther?

* * *

"Could he have done other?" Brad Bradley defense counsel for George Webster Brown rhetorically asked himself. He often felt humiliated and impotent, particularly on Monday mornings when he was just beginning his week. "Of course he could have," he answered his own question and frowned. "He had free will, didn't he?"

Brad tried to be philosophical about it. He took credit for the victories – and shrugged his shoulders when things did not turn out in his favor. He had given a good summation, he thought. It even made George weepy. He could visualize it in his mind's eye.

Yes, George just sat there stoic-like with nearly invisible baby-tears ebbing down his anemic cheeks, sunken at the sides into shallow indentations where the wetness glistened. He sat there gazing up at His Honor with blurry eyes... isolated, afraid, alone.

How could anyone be unmoved by such a pathetic sight? A lump formed in Brad's throat just thinking about it. Sometimes an image like that was worth more than a dozen carefully thought-out summations.

The outcome could depend upon such a moment. The moment is such an ephemeral and fleeting thing. It comes and is gone, never to return, except in subconscious memories reflected, as in one of Carl Jung's archetypical drawings in the *Red Book,* a mosaic of the life of an ordinary person pretending to be a sinner and acting like a Christian - or was it vice versa? The question never occurred to George while he sat in his cell... waiting.

Brad Bradley, counsel for the defense, gingerly rubbed the fingers of his right hand over his right eyebrow as he sat patiently in his office pondering upon the age-old slogan: *innocent... until proven guilty.* However, in George's case, he sanguinely reflected, was it actually a matter of *guilty... until proven innocent*?

It was a matter of faith. He had to believe in himself. He gazed pensively toward the narrow white-framed windows on the north wall while stoically waiting for the phone call that would alert him to the fact that at long last the jury was preparing to return with the verdict. How many times had he waited thus?

How many times had he risen to his feet and nervously driven over to the courthouse? On how many occasions had he jumped jubilantly to his feet and quietly whispered, "Thank you, God!" How many times had he sat morosely in his chair, while his client bowed his head penitently and wept as if there were no tomorrow?

* * *

"Belief is perhaps the most powerful motivator that exists. Over the centuries it has enabled ordinary human beings to accomplish the seemingly impossible. People have been known to cure themselves and others of terminal illnesses. They just have to believe in their own divinity, in their own power." Eldorado's voice echoed in Lenny's mind as if his brain were hollow. Lenny knew it was Pena; he could feel his presence.

"Altruism!" Pena exclaimed in a voice so loud Lenny was afraid it would awaken Lana, "is the modus operandi or the ghost in the machine, to use one of your mechanical ways of imagining such concepts, that imbues the entire universe with purpose and meaning. Altruism is the spiritual essence that results in what you refer to as an idea. It is the First Mover, as Aristotle would say. And yes, he was quite correct when he said that 'happiness is the end that all men seek'. Happiness results when sentient beings give assent to altruistic tendencies and sentiments."

"Hold on there!" Lenny demanded. "What the heck are you babbling about? You have this tendency to just burst in here and expound upon some esoteric topic as if... as if it is of special interest to me."

"Well, isn't it?"

"Never mind..." Lenny gazed up to the ceiling. "Are you saying that happiness is an altruistic expression?" he asked with a puzzled frown.

"One of the reasons I sometimes mention Aristotle and of course Plato, is that they both existed at a time when the collective unconscious was uncontaminated by the Christian Doctrine of Original Sin. Consequently they both were able to give expression to ideas based upon reason and logic – rather than dogma and doctrine."

"Ah, I see your point. So when Aristotle says that happiness is the end that all men seek, and Plato talks about apprehending the good... they are both in pursuit of the unvarnished truth. Right?"

"I know that this is a difficult concept for people who are basically unfamiliar with such a notion to comprehend. When I was down there, historically speaking, I had trouble myself. Before the Spanish conquistadors arrived, Chileans had no such life-negating self-concept as Original Sin. It was a foreign concept, as foreign as the greed that drove the conquistadors to devastate our culture and country in search of little bits of inanimate yellow metal."

"Imagine what might have happened... if the Spanish had been Buddhists – instead of Christians!" Lenny interjected.

"Indeed, what if?" Pena raised his eyebrows. "What amazes me to this very day is that intelligent people all over the world still behave in much the same manner as the greedy conquistadors. Have they learned nothing in all that time?"

"Learned nothing? How can that be?"

"Since the American Declaration of Independence, the world as you know it has experienced a very unique and disturbing blip in its evolutionary development."

"A blip, you say, as if it is an unexpected aberration of some sort?"

"In the context of say, the last million years or even the last ten thousand years, it is indeed a blip. Unfortunately the historical evolution of a particular religious belief has warped your collective westernized view of man's nature from being intrinsically sacred to being tragically flawed, and this neurotic aberration has profoundly changed how you relate to yourselves and the environment in which you exist." Pena paused to give Lenny time to grasp the profundity of what he had just said.

"Continue," Lenny urged.

"Here is the key to understanding your present or modern existential predicament, so listen with both ears."

"I am."

"As I mentioned previously, no one knows exactly how or even when the ancient Hebrew myth known as the creation narrative as expressed in the book of Genesis came into being. What is known is that the creation narrative exists as part of the Torah. Someone wrote it down retrospectively, *after* Moses had led his enslaved brethren to freedom... as if to provide a rationale to explain why the newly freed Israelites had to ignominiously suffer over four hundred years of abject slavery. And the belated *history* was then made available to Moses on Mount Sinai as if it was the immutable word of God."

"I see. The timeline seems to justify such an interpretation. Little wonder there is a great deal of speculative confusion about a story that seems more like-like a myth or a fairytale – rather than the sacred word of God," Lenny admitted.

"What is known is that in the year 325 AD the *New* Testament was juxtapositioned with the *Old* Testament, and institutionalized in a single document presented as the *Holy Roman Bible*. At that time the narrative became fixed. It became frozen in time and dogmatized as the *immutable word of God* - and therefore prevented from evolving along with man's ongoing spiritual and secular development."

"Immutable - huh? Are you saying that the so-called 'word of God' has been preserved at the cognitive and spiritual level of believability commensurate with the epoch in which it was written?" Lenny queried.

"You constantly astound me with your perceptiveness," Pena commented with a smile. "Yes, to illustrate: the five books contained in the Old Testament known as the Pentateuch which includes Genesis, were written long before Charles Darwin, who was born on 12 February 1809 AD, wrote the Origin of the Species; consequently the writer or writers who wrote the words attributed to God, were not aware of the theory of evolution and therefore could not have included such ideas in the creation narrative."

"Seems obvious. If they were writing that narrative today, it would be a far different story!"

"The Creation Myth was written for and by people who lived in an age when the world was flat and the cognitive level of awareness matched the supernatural ideas presented in the creation narrative. In short, the story of creation was written for a primitive people to whom such an explanation actually made sense... and seemed believable."

"So... what is the point?"

"Once the Torah and the Bible along with the Koran became sanctified as being *Holy,* they became inviolate: they could not be challenged or changed. They became immutable religious dogma designated as being *the word of God. Who would dare to tamper with or challenge such sacred words?*"

"I see!"

"They became *institutionalized* as the literal Truth. It is as if the truth became varnished with a fixative that preserved it at the cognitive potential of the ancient Hebrews for whom it was originally intended. Promulgated throughout the world as the Word of God, the varnished-truth has produced a varnished mindset with a varnished modus operandi to match."

"That is a whole lot of varnishing!" Lenny laconically lamented.

"You said it," Pena shrugged. It is so frustrating to have to stand by and witness such-such..."

"Life-negating behavior?"

"When has such a collective neurosis ever affected so many at once? Billions just accept the word-of-god as expressed in the Bible... as if it is a *given*. It is very disturbing, and like I said, very frustrating to have to impotently stand by... and just watch."

"Your empathy is very much appreciated," Lenny replied on behalf of those unaware that such a conversation was even taking place. "In spite of spectacular achievements such as the unraveling of the human genome and our cosmic understanding of the quantum universe of light and dark matter, we cling pathetically to the primitive status of our institutionalized religious beliefs; religious beliefs that as Freud and Jung would say, resonate within the collective unconscious and produce synchronistic behaviors."

"Reality mirrors the irrational psychological conflict and existential angst that is created when... devout devotees attempt to manifest their beliefs."

"Like behaviors that resulted in..." Lenny paused to gather his thoughts, "such an oxymoronic declaration as a-a *war on terrorism?*"

"Oxymoronic is the key word there. Freud called it neurotic behavior."

"Are you suggesting that a simple religious belief regarding man's nature could be the underlying cause for eliciting such irrational behavior by seemingly intelligent human beings?" Lenny queried.

Eldorado lapsed into momentary silence. "Let me leave you with this parting thought," he whispered ominously. *"I am saying that within the scope of the last millennia the biblical version of man's ignominious fall from grace as depicted in the Creation Narrative has become entrenched as possibly the most life-negating religious dogma ever to contaminate the human psyche!"* Pena stated this with such conviction that Lenny felt a chill run up his spine.

* * *

"A lot of people, including myself, thought that Lenny the Bruce was somewhat radical in his thinking, Your Honor," the man identified as Tennyson Davies said in a booming voice. He spoke with an English accent.

Ruskolnikov Kublinsky had called him to the stand as a witness for the prosecution. Davies was a tall man by most standards, but when he walked by the prosecutor who had risen to his full height, he was dwarfed by the White Russian giant in spite of the fact that he wore cowboy boots with two-inch heels.

Tennyson Davies had dressed up for the occasion. He wore black denim trousers, a black polyester shirt along with a shiny black leather vest. The only thing missing was his black Stetson. The fringed dome of his hair gleamed under the florescent lights. He was a barrel chested man with slightly bowed legs. His parents had emigrated from Liverpool when he was thirteen. He had played some rugby in his days in England and took some pride in being manly.

"Could you tell us to the best of your recollection what happened out at Garry Point Park on the occasion of Lenard Bruce's tragic demise?" the Prosecutor requested.

"I was out there along with some of my buddies. I must admit we had had a few beers – but we were not drunk... perhaps a bit unruly, but definitely not drunk. We kind'a took exception to some of the remarks the deceased had been makin'. We thought it would be fun ta ridicule him and kind'a rough him up a little... you know, ta sort of smarten him up." The witness looked toward Ruskolnikov for reassurance.

"Okay, fine. So what happened next?"

"A bunch of people surged toward the stage. The flimsy contraption collapsed and the speaker fell to the ground."

"And?"

"All hell broke loose. We had no intention of... really hurtin' him."

"Tell the jury exactly what took place after Lenny fell to the ground."

"Well, all of a sudden, this fella…."

"Is he in this courtroom?" the prosecutor interrupted.

"Yes."

"Could you point him out?"

Tennyson pointed his right index finger toward the table for the defense, where Brad Bradley sat patiently waiting for a chance to pounce. To his left sat the accused, George Webster Brown.

"Let the record show that the witness has identified the accused, George W Brown," Ruskolnikov announced triumphantly.

Brad rose as if to protest, but thought the better of it and sat back down beside his client whose pale complexion seemed to exude an aura of guilt.

"Please continue," the gigantic prosecutor urged.

"Hmm," the witness cogitated as if verifying the facts in his mind. "All of a sudden this fella is standin' over him with his foot on his back."

"You mean George Webster Brown was standing over Lenny Bruce with his foot on Lenny's back?" Ruskolnikov clarified.

Once again the defense lawyer rose to his feet as if to object, but sat back down without saying a word to defend his client.

"Yeah, that fella over there," the witness pointed out the accused once again, "that fella pulls this gun... I think it was a German luger - out of his jacket pocket and-and... points it at the back of Lenny's head!"

"And?" the prosecutor prompted as a hush fell over the courtroom.

The jurors turned as one to stare at Brad when he rose to his feet: "I object to the way the Prosecution is leading and prompting the witness!"

"Objection denied," the Judge declared, anxious to hear what Tennyson had to say.

"I couldn't believe what I was seein'! Who pulls a gun on-on a helpless man lying flat on his face?"

The jurors inhaled as one... awaiting the answer.

"And?" the giant prosecutor, whispered caught up in the drama of the occasion.

"Suddenly everything changed. Like in a panic. Some people closest to the accused were desperate to get out of there. Others strained to see what was happenin'. There was a lot of pushin' and shovin' goin' on. Someone in a shrill and demented tone of voice yelled, 'Shoot the little bastard!'"

Brad exhaled and rose to his feet as if anticipating the worst. The jurors leaned forward.

Tennyson Davies stood tall and spoke with an authority beyond reproach: "There was a deathly moment of silence... seemed like a-a second or two."

"And after that?" Ruskolnikov asked with bated breath.

"Bam!"

"Just like that?"

"It wasn't that loud. More like the sound of a firecracker... sort of a poppin' sound."

"What happened next?"

"He just stood there."

"You mean the accused?"

"I vehemently object to this line of questioning!" Brad leapt to his feet, glad for a chance to be of service to his client. "The Prosecution is leading the witness."

"Objection denied," the Judge declared. "You may answer the question."

"Yes, it was the accused. I think he threw up or somethin'. There was an eerie feelin' as if - as if somethin' catastrophic had happened."

"And then?"

"All I can say is that the moment passed," the witness soberly announced. "It was sickenin'! I know right from wrong. I charged into him. Knocked him down and wrestled the gun away. He didn't struggle much. He was white as a sheet. I got him in a full Nelson and waited for the police to arrive. It didn't take long 'cause they were on site monitorin' the events."

"What happened when the police arrived?"

"They asked me what happened. I tol' them what had happened. They put cuffs on George and put him in the back seat of the police cruiser. The officer in charge asked me to come down to the police station to give a statement. So I went down there after I went home and cleaned up a little. When I got there they asked me if I wanted a lawyer present. I tol' them I had nothin' ta hide."

"Any further questions?"

"No, Your Honor," Ruskolnikov replied with a satisfied smile.

"Do you wish to cross-examine the witness?" the Judge asked Brad.

"Not at this time," Brad said, keeping his options open.

"You may step down," The Judge directed the witness, who glowered malevolently in George's direction as he left the courtroom.

The prosecutor rose to his full height and smiled.

Brad Bradley glanced furtively toward the jury, His Honor the Judge, the giant prosecutor, and then at his client, George Webster Brown. *"Guilty... until proven innocent,"* he reflected sanguinely.

* * *

It was three weeks before Christmas. The wispy skiff of snow that had fallen the previous day had all but disappeared leaving ghostly remnants here and there along the walkway. Two old retired pensioners sauntered side by side, chatting as they went, their grey heads bobbing up and down in synch with their lackadaisical gait. They felt secure within themselves; money was the least of their worries. They were in no hurry. Mortality had drained them of their youthful exuberance.

As they sauntered along the waterfront from the downtown core of Steveston, Lenny cleared his throat of some residual phlegm, symptomatic of a deteriorating cold, spat it into the stubborn quack grass growing beside the walkway, and interrupted Cathy Schneider's mindful silence by asking "What did you do before you retired?"

"I worked at a University lab."

"What did you work on?"

"Immortality."

"What?"

"I'm a gerontologist."

"A what?"

"A gerontologist. We study the aging process. Because we are all mortal… we all age… until we die. Some refer to it as senescence."

"Senescence?"

"Or sens for short. It is the study of the aging process with the objective of extending life indefinitely."

"Is that possible?" Lenny asked coming to an abrupt stop and turning to face Cathy.

"Some gerontologists like Aubrey de Grey, for example, foresee a time when humans could live for a thousand years or more."

"A thousand years seems like a long time compared to our present life expectancy. It is such a long time that most people probably have trouble relating to it."

Cathy paused, gazed reflectively at Lenny as if indecisive, and then replied, "Many gerontologists that I know believe in the mechanistic theory: they assume that the human body is just an anatomical construct, a mechanical vehicle like a computer or a car; it is susceptible to the ravages of time. Eventually parts wear out or break down, and the vehicle grinds to a halt. However, if the susceptible parts could be replaced or prevented from wearing out or breaking down, the vehicle could run on forever. This mechanical view assumes that the biological vehicle is simply comprised of the sum of its parts."

"But, what about those people who say that the whole is greater than the sum of the parts?"

"Those people probably espouse the philosophical notion that there is a ghost in the machine - or soul or spirit to use religious terminology - that resides in the biological vehicle while it is functioning or alive; this notion transforms the sum of the parts into a conscious whole. I'm kind of partial to this view."

"Did you say conscious whole?"

"The consciousness is an invisible or immaterial presence in the machine. It is the ghost in the machine."

"Where did it come from?" Lenny asked while squeezing the tip of his nose.

"A very astute question. For months I wrestled with this conundrum! I became obsessed. I argued vehemently with my colleagues at the university who all had their own pet theories and opinions. I just couldn't let it go. And then one night at 4:32 am, it just came to me. I remember the time precisely because I glanced at our luminous clock," Cathy sighed as they sat down on one of the vacant benches along the way.

"My best thoughts come to me at night too," Lenny commented. "So how did you resolve this matter?"

"There, you said it. It was all about matter. The essential question is: What is matter? Consider this: all the matter that presently constitutes our solar system was supposedly once just a flaming mass of gaseous material torn off from the sun by a passing object. At the highest vibratory levels this energy is immaterial or without substance; it is invisible like dark matter – yet when it vibrates at frequencies amenable to our sensate sensibilities, it miraculously becomes manifest as light. Suddenly, we are conscious!"

"Boy did you ever say a mouthful there!" Lenny expostulated, shaking his head with credulity. "That single statement takes us beyond the pale of rational scientific thought."

"I know. That is why I never did share it with my colleagues at the university. Most of them would have just scoffed."

"You have my sympathies. Please continue."

"The key conundrum as I see it is simply this: we assume that only we the living are conscious. On the contrary, all matter is conscious. In fact everything there is, is conscious. Together we make up the conscious whole which some refer to as the Cosmos.

"So why is it that we seem to be more aware of being conscious, than say a rock?"

"It is all about vibrations: the higher the frequency of vibration, the greater the consciousness. Over billions of years, the light from the sun was transformed into a gaseous material that cooled and condensed into planets that presently revolve about the light-source from which they were torn."

"Grade five Science," Lenny pointed out with a smug smile.

"What most fifth grade teachers fail to point out is the importance of the transformation of the very high energy vibrations of the light into very low level vibrations associated with solid material like lava or rocks. Matter per se is simply the physical manifestation of vibratory solar energy. All matter, whether solid, liquid, or gas, vibrates at a specific atomic frequency relative to its constitution. These invisible vibrations could be said to be the ghost in the machine," Cathy paused to give Lenny time to reflect upon this thought.

"Giving rise to spiritual sentiments associated with the highest vibratory frequencies the light of consciousness can emit," Lenny conjectured.

"These ghostly vibes constitute a universal form of consciousness. Everything vibrates; therefore everything is conscious. The level of conscious awareness is relative to the frequency of vibration. Even rocks have a miniscule form of awareness. Why? Because they *exist*; and therefore they vibrate with invisible energy. Consequently, they exude presence... just like we do."

"Astute."

"However, there is a vast difference in the vibratory frequency of light-infused organic material - as compared to inorganic material. This is the crux of the matter... as far as gerontologists of my bent are concerned."

"Yes?"

"The difference between living and non-living matter appears to come down to the little understood process known as photosynthesis, whereby the radiant light-energy from the sun combined with water and minerals in the presence of chlorophyll, synthesizes inorganic matter into organic or living matter. This photo-synthesized organic matter is able to synthesize or reproduce itself in kind, a pro-creative process so amazing that we still refer to it as being magical, miraculous, and even sacred."

"It seems we are still in grade five when it comes to understanding the incredible process of photosynthesis," Lenny laconically remarked.

"How about kindergarten?" Cathy countered. "Anyway, after billions of years of evolutionary development, light-infused organic matter transformed itself from a single-celled organism that wriggled out of the primordial slime... and gradually morphed itself into a multi-million celled life form called homo erectus."

"And what is so special about that?" Lenny asked as if he were still in grade five.

"Over the eons, a fabulously intricate biological organ evolved called a brain. It vibrated with synapses of light-infused energy reminiscent of the source of its vibrations: the sun. The brain is still evolving. On earth two legged parasites called homo sapiens, incapable of performing photosynthesis, have become the biological vehicles in which inorganic matter has reached a vibratory frequency that makes concepts like *soul*, *spirit*, or a *ghost in the machine* meaningful."

"Homo erectus became vaguely aware of the primordial power of the sun from which eons ago he evolved," Lenny added.

"Yes, the sun was the source of the light, and to primitive man, sun-worship seemed natural. Homo erectus evolved to that organic frequency where the brain became innately aware of the affinity between light and conscious awareness. Apparently you and I have reached that level. However, it is assumed that dogs, cats, and perhaps even monkeys still have a long way to go before they - like us - can quibble about whether or not there is a *ghost in the machine*," Cathy gazed up at the fluffy clouds that slowly drifted by in a light-infused sky. After a moment of quiet reflection she said, "According to some gerontologists there seems to be a direct relationship between conscious awareness and longevity."

The implications of the statement caused Lenny to inhale deeply before turning to stare at Cathy. The concept had a special significance to both of them because they were both old, relatively speaking. "Please elaborate," Lenny replied, intrigued by the possibility that there could be a direct relationship between conscious awareness and longevity.

"This concept is only a theoretical work in progress, so at this stage it could seem to be somewhat convoluted, so it would be nice if you could suspend... critical judgment."

"You're beginning to sound like me," Lenny laughed. "I'm usually the one who says that."

"As you know, our ancestors were not nearly as aware as we are. They were not aware that germs caused disease and infections, or that there was such a thing as ethics. So they bashed each other over the head and stole each other's food. Naturally like Thomas Hobbes stated, their lives were 'short, nasty and brutish'. As time passed they came to realize that sharing and cooperation greatly enhanced their ability to survive, and that invisible germs caused sickness and disease. Consequently, as their ethical and hygienic practices improved, so did their longevity. We learned that by sharing, cooperating and, by washing our filthy hands before eating, our life need not be short, nasty, and brutish. Over time, Man's longevity increased in accordance with his growing understanding of medicine and the functioning of the human body, providing further definition to what constituted a mortal lifetime".

"That is a very insightful statement!" Lenny exclaimed as if he fully comprehended it. "Let me see if I got it right. What you are saying is that our longevity as a species is relative to our knowledge, and the more knowledgeable we become, the longer we as a species can expect to live."

"Yes, over the last century we have doubled our life expectancy. But, because our level of awareness has also expanded, we do not find our increased longevity boring even though we now have twice as much time to endure. Why? Because our cognitive level of awareness expands to fill the space-time parameters of our mortal status."

"You said another mouthful there. So if we were able to live for say, ten times longer than we do now, we would be able to endure through that expanded length of time as if it were normal. Our longevity is relative to our level of awareness."

"Yes. Our life expectancy would expand ten-fold commensurate with our increased level of awareness."

"Incredible!" Lenny enthused.

"However, before you get too carried away," Cathy cautioned, "there could be a finite threshold to the our longevity in accordance with our existential status,"

"How so?" Lenny asked wrinkling up his nose.

"The threshold to our longevity as a parasitical species is determined by our relationship with the life-forms upon which we depend for sustenance and survival. There is a symbiotic relationship here. We need to learn how to share and to cooperate with the other organic life forms that feed, nurture, and sustain us… if we hope to further prolong our own mortal existence. Once we fully comprehend this symbiotic relationship and realize the extent of our interdependence... our longevity will increase in conjunction with such an understanding."

"That is a very big 'if' – isn't it? At this time in our evolutionary development we do not seem to realize the basic existential fact that we are parasites - parasites dependent for our survival upon the sustainability of the life-forms that are able to perform photosynthesis," Lenny soberly acknowledged as he rose from the bench, extended a hand to help Cathy to her feet, and recommended walking homeward.

As they sauntered along Lenny stared up at the seemingly limitless sky as if peering into a giant crystal ball.

"A penny for your thoughts, Cathy offered after a prolonged silence.

"If we are genetically incapable of photosynthesis because of the biological limitations imposed by our DNA, could we not grow genetically modified humanoids with artificial intelligence capable of such?" Lenny offered speculatively.

"What makes you think it hasn't been done?"

After they had reached the footbridge that spanned the estuary to Phoenix pond, Lenny looked at Cathy with respect and admiration. "Are you insinuating that it already has been done?" he queried.

"It is an ongoing debate..." Cathy paused, and gazed at Lenny with twinkling eyes, "You've heard of Roswell haven't you?" she inquired.

"Who hasn't?"

"As you know a UFO crash landed at Roswell. The debris was quickly whisked away from prying eyes by the military. The entire incident was highly controversial – and still is. Apparently some little greenish, spindly, short-legged creatures with large dark oval eyes survived the crash. Do you know what happened next?"

"The aliens were captured and the cover story as reported in the local newspaper was hastily changed from being the crashing of a UFO - to the crashing of some weather balloons. How gullible do they think the public is?"

"Perhaps they had discovered something truly remarkable that in their opinion had to be kept secret," Cathy speculated.

"I assume you have an explanation?"

"Why do you think the little alien creatures are greenish?"

"Perhaps because those particular alien creatures... are actually humanoids?" Lenny guessed.

"Yes, and like plants they are green because they can perform photosynthesis... and possibly reproduce themselves."

"I see. What about the so-called Greys? Do they represent some form of less sophisticated artificial intelligence?" Lenny inquired, demonstrating his knowledge of the subject.

"I'd say that is a distinct possibility. Once the difference between mechanical and biological becomes blurry, the distinction between what is artificial and what is not, becomes a matter of-of..."

"Pure speculation?" Lenny queried.

"It seems that in the end we are left with the conundrum: *what came first, the chicken or the egg?*"

"Who knows, perhaps we ourselves are a biological form of self-replicating artificial intelligence transplanted here from - who knows where? And being genetically engineered and monitored by much more advanced, god-like forms of intelligence," Lenny's imagination went rogue.

"Just speculation," Cathy reminded Lenny with a grin as they continued their walk homeward, "nothing more."

* * *

Lenny loved to speculate. It was his favorite pastime. It was during the long tedious hours he spent as a janitor sweeping, washing, and waxing floors that he developed the habit of staring ahead as if looking for some invisible particles of dirt, while his curious intellect tirelessly searched for the reasons why he ended up becoming what he became: a custodian with a humorous bent and a predilection for satire.

In his own nerdish manner Lenny attempted to be funny because... wasn't Lenny Bruce the name of an infamous American comedian? With a name like Lenny Bruce, would not it be expected that even his most serious thoughts would be laughable? But to a perceptive minority who could read between the lines, there was a lot more substance to his literary babblings than just a bunch of words.

Thinking was what Lenny did best; it was a natural product of his intellect. Did it eventually make him into the persona non grata the public so loathed that they angrily tore him from the open stage at Garry Point Park? Was it all because of his grand concepts and unique ideas?

Lenny had many misgivings about his own natural abilities. To think that a custodian could write something of merit, like the essay Lana published in the June edition of *Final Draft*, was remarkable.

"Too bad," George thought after previewing the entire essay with furrowed brow, "that high-minded title: *Lofty Thoughts For Lofty Minds*, will probably put most readers off." Ironically, it was the title that drew George's attention because sometimes he sort of felt that way... sometimes he felt good about himself: he felt *intellectual*.

He had surveyed the pamphlet carefully. There were seven short sections. He had skimmed over them as if he knew what he was looking for. George refocused on the sections from (III) to (VII). Something there attracted him like a lonely moth to a porch light.

(III) What is Cluster Intelligence?

Sharing enables similar fragments of intelligence to cooperate with many others to form a 'cluster' that is greater than the sum of the parts, yielding a reality corresponding to such a combined level of awareness. On Earth examples of this sort of cluster intelligence are evidenced in the collective behavior of schools of fish, flocks of birds, colonies of ants, and social/political networks of humans. For example, thousands of individuals working alone in isolation can only create simple individual works – but the same individuals sharing a common ideal and working cooperatively together can construct gigantic skyscrapers of glass and steel, great cities, or vast civilizations. What a cluster can achieve is much greater than anything that can be achieved by a far greater number of separate individual parts, working alone.

This concept is brought home to roost in the *cluster intelligence* apparent in the manner in which millions of tiny cells work in synch to manifest a distinctive biological creation, such as a fish, a dog, a monkey, or a homo-erectus... which make up parts of the Whole.

(IV) What is the Whole?

The *Whole* is 'Everything-there-is'... and due to its *wholesomeness* is not epistemologically amenable to definition by a bunch of words conjured up by human brains. At best it can be abstractly described as being something miraculous: a Grand Omnipresent Divinity, an Altruistic Mind that is eternally perfecting itself, and thus becoming increasingly more aware of itself.

It could be said that all the grand theories and ideas Mankind has ever cogitated upon, are simply attempts by a limited form of intelligence to make sense of, or rationalize, this eternal and miraculous process of *Self-realization*.

(V) How is Man Connected to the Whole?

The 'part' is intrinsically connected to the 'Whole' by its brute existential status. Such an existence cannot be denied… because it simply 'is'. All knowledge is dependent upon this solipsism. The biological part that encompasses the *micro-brain* is capable of intuiting the infinite *macro-Mind*, which represents the Whole. The Whole is made up of the sum-of-the-parts. The relationship is symbiotic as is evidenced by the free will accorded to the parts by the inherent Freedom of the *altruistic* Whole.

(VI) What is Altruism?

Altruism is the modus operandi of the Whole (or Everything-There-Is). There is no higher operating principle.

Altruism is best described by two words: 'freedom and sharing'. Freedom is 'shared' vicariously by the Whole with the myriad of parts that make up the sum-of–the-parts.

This altruistic endowment of the parts with free will enables the parts to collectively participate in the definition of the Whole, of which they are a 'part'.

In this symbiotic manner the Whole is beholden to the 'sum-of-the-parts' for the realization of what it is constantly becoming. This makes the entire ongoing process inherently meaningful, significant, harmonic, and *wholesome*.

When human beings become aware of their unique role in this on-going process, it gives rise to feelings of gratitude, joy, love, and happiness… such an experience is realized spiritually as enlightenment. For human beings who are capable of approaching this level of conscious awareness, it is not only edifying, but also transformative.

(VII) How Can the Part Relate to the Whole?

At our current level of cognitive awareness, exemplified by the JCM hegemony, such spirituality needs to be personified and presented in the persona of a personality with whom one can relate. The cluster intellect of such a group manifests a reality commensurate with such a level of awareness. It is very difficult for those ensconced in such a cluster to see beyond the manifested-reality of such a limited vision. Religious sentiment represents an attempt to give expression to the *parts' symbiotic relationship to the Whole.* Inevitably, the participants will reap... whatever they are sowing.

When George Webster Brown first read the June edition of Final Draft, for some unconscious reason he felt uplifted. There was something there, that however obtuse, spoke to him. He thought he would share it with his friends at the local pub.

Somehow they did not get it. "Just bullshit," they scoffed while laughing sardonically. They had a strange sense of humor. George laughed too because... was he not one of them? For some inexplicable reason, he felt the need to laugh the loudest.

* * *

Lenny knew that the older one got, the quicker time seemed to fly by. It seems that way because each passing day represents a smaller and smaller portion of a lifetime spent. Over the ensuing months Lenny noted that the other four members of the Motely Five seemed to have aged. They seemed a little more subdued and frail. Their short-term memory often failed them. Sometimes they repeated themselves without knowing, or were at a loss for words... as happened on the balmy evening in late April that the Motley Five had assembled around Father Bertolli's magnificent mahogany desk.

On that particular occasion they had nothing in particular to discuss so they all settled in with cups of green tea Father Bertolli had provided, and nibbled on the cookies Cathy Schneider had brought with her. The silence was becoming a little awkward when Lenny piped up and said: "We need to be ever mindful of being mindful."

"Mindful?" Cathy perked up. "Is it not a term often used by Buddhists to indicate a higher degree of awareness?"

"Yes," Rabbi Letenberg joined in, "in the Judaic tradition we use the term to indicate an awareness of our relationship with God."

"As a Catholic," Father Bertolli interjected, "mindfulness is a state of moral awareness; it has ethical dimensions."

"To me as a member of the no-name-brand," Lana laughed, "being mindful means something like being consciously aware, like in the saying, 'be mindful of your 'p's and 'q's.'"

"And you Lenny?" Cathy asked. All eyes turned toward Lenny. No one knew what he was going to say, or how profoundly insightful it would turn out to be.

Lenny cupped his hands about his teacup and slowly raised his head to meet the expectant gaze of the motley four assembled about him. "You know, this business of being mindful has been something that I had just taken for granted for some time, but then about a week ago I had a glitch while working on the computer: there was a 'spool.exe application error'." Lenny spelled it out for them. A little memo popped up which read, 'spooler subsystem app has encountered a problem and needs to close'. It seemed as if there was a little homunculus in the computer who was minding the computer. And there I was minding the homunculus."

"What is an homunculus?" Lana asked.

"A little imaginary person inside the computer who is aware of what the computer is doing," Rabbi Letenberg clarified.

"And there I was," Lenny continued, "thinking to myself that I myself functioned in somewhat the same fashion. My brain is the homunculus that is aware of how my body is functioning. It gives me messages like: I'm hungry; I'm tired; I'm bored; I'm sick, and so on. My brain is mindful of my body."

"So… the next question would be, 'Who is minding your brain?'" Father Bertolli added insightfully, rubbing his hands together in anticipation of the answer.

"The answer to that question…" Lenny paused to inhale, "is what gives impetus to religious or spiritual sentiments. The microcosmic brain intuitively relates to the macrocosmic Mind, but has immense difficulty in rationalizing the scope of the difference. The greatest brains that have ever existed have grappled with this conundrum to little or no avail. They always fail to grasp the essence of their existential predicament and end up feeling frustrated, dejected, nauseated, and overcome with a depressing sensation akin to suffocation. Little wonder mankind in general cleaves to irrational dogmas in blind faith, because they offer a modicum of solace in a sea of mystery."

"Clear as mud!" Cathy exclaimed. "Could you elaborate further?"

"Mud is certainly opaque!" Lenny admitted. "Is it even possible to clarify such muddy waters?" he asked himself rhetorically before beginning. "Let me share with you a-an esoteric vision that has been developing in my mind for some time... I call it the Allegory of the Fish. Perhaps it will enable you to comprehend the scope of the existential conundrum in which we are all entrenched like goldfish in a bowl."

"Allegory of the Fish? Sounds intriguing," Rabbi Letenberg commented while rubbing his hands together in anticipation.

"Great thinkers like the so-called joint Fathers of modern Existentialism, the introspective Danish-Christian thinker Soren Kierkegaard, and the much maligned German philosopher Fredrick Nietzsche, along with the famous psychologist Carl Jung, all struggled to make sense of the feeling of angst and spiritual suffocation they respectively experienced during their lifetimes," Lenny began. "They were all born, raised, nurtured and acculturated in an all-pervasive culture of religious piety... like goldfish in a glass bowl."

"Little wonder they felt suffocated." Lana breathed.

"All three, especially Carl Jung, spent their lifetimes attempting to overcome a nauseating sense of suffocation they could not shake off. Nietzsche and Jung came near to a kind of psychosis of the spirit or madness which they were able to transcend via their respective writings: Nietzsche penned *Thus Spake Zarathustra*, while Jung produced his *Liber Novus* or *Red Book*. Kierkegaard related his struggles in *Either/Or*. They were all monumental exertions of the human soul in search of an existential freedom... they seemed incapable of realizing."

"Why?" the curious Rabbi asked with raised eyebrows.

"They were analogous to goldfish that were hatched, raised and nurtured to maturity in a large glass bowl. Their biological DNA had encoded their previous experiences associated with the time when they swam freely in the great ocean – but the reality to which they had to relate was limited to their experiences in the glass bowl. Even if they tried to describe or explain the primordial recollections stored in their collective unconscious, they would have to do so in terms of their experiences in the glass bowl. Imagine attempting to explain or describe primordial memories of the freedom experienced in a vast ocean of life, in terms of a lifetime enclosed in a glass bowl?"

"I'm sorry, I'm still a little confused by your analogy," Cathy confessed.

"Ah, let me see," Lenny pondered. "Instead of a goldfish consider the predicament of the landlocked sockeye salmon known as kokanee".

"I've been to the Adams River to see the world famous salmon run in the Shuswap," Cathy related. "The little streams ran red with sockeye returning to spawn and reproduce the species. It was one of Mother Nature's natural wonders."

"Indeed it is a miraculous sight to see. And even a more miraculous feat to ponder upon," the good Rabbi sagely commented on behalf of the motley four who lapsed into silence while waiting to learn more about Lenny's Allegory of the Fish.

"It is a fishy allegory," Lenny began with a grin while rubbing his hands together. "You are all familiar with the life cycle of the sockeye salmon... I presume?"

The motley four all nodded in unison.

"Imagine two battered and bruised red sockeye salmon with green hooked snouts making it back from their long sojourn in the Pacific Ocean to the little stream where they were hatched four years previously. The female salmon lays her eggs while the male fertilizes them. In that mortal moment the primordial memories stored in the cascading strings of their immortal DNA is passed on to their offspring. Shortly thereafter they turn topsy-turvy and pass on."

"Indeed, that is what happens," Lana confirmed.

"Now suppose two identical sockeye fry are hatched from those particular eggs. When they are able to, the little fry swim down the little stream that flows into the Adams River which empties into Shuswap Lake," Lenny continued. "There they grow into minnows capable of swimming to the Thompson River that flows out of the western end of Little Shuswap Lake. Along the route one of the little fish becomes disoriented and is not able to make its way out of the freshwater of the Shuswap to the saline waters of the mighty Pacific Ocean. It must remain in the Shuswap, along with hundreds of other such unfortunate minnows, where it grows to about twelve or thirteen inches in length and remains silvery-grey in color till spawning time."

"A mere shadow of its true potential," Cathy noted.

"On the other hand its twin brother swims hundreds of miles down the Thompson River which flows into the Fraser River which empties into the mighty Pacific Ocean at Steveston. From there it spends the next four glorious years of its life foraging, maturing, and exploring, travelling as far north as Alaska and growing to a length of about two and a half feet. After four incredible years of freedom in the vast Pacific, the mature sockeye, twenty to thirty inches long, returns to the estuary of the Fraser River where it acclimates itself to the fresh water and gradually turns a crimson red with an olive green hooked snout."

"What an amazing transformation," Lana noted.

"Instinctively the sockeye begins its long and arduous assent of the Fraser and Thompson rivers to Shuswap Lake and from thence to the mouth of the Adams River. During his lifetime he has experienced both the nurturing security of an inland freshwater lake and the vast freedom of the saline waters of the mighty Pacific Ocean. After spending four glorious years abroad, the red sockeye salmon with the hooked green snout finally reaches the place of his birth... where by sheer luck it encounters its stunted, long lost brother!"

"Some coincidence!" Lana exclaimed.

"If the two salmon could communicate, how could the landlocked kokanee salmon relate to his brother's vast experience in the saline waters of the mighty Pacific Ocean - when all he has experienced is life confined to a small inland body of fresh water?" Lenny asked.

"How indeed!" Father Bertolli exclaimed, impressed by Lenny's metaphor.

"The effects of nature and nurture are dramatic. Although they have the same parents and the same DNA, who would know that the two salmon were actually brothers?" Cathy exclaimed.

"The two brothers are bonded by a common birth experience and a common genetic inheritance. For thousands of years, and generation after generation, the brothers' ancestors have experienced the freedom of the mighty Pacific and returned home to procreate their species," Lenny elaborated.

"If their ancestors had failed in this endeavor, the two brothers would not presently exist!" Letenberg adroitly pointed out

"The land-locked salmon's primordial DNA occasionally provides the kokanee with intuitive glimpses into his past when he too, like his ancestors, once swam freely in the great ocean of life - but alas, he can only relate to such memories in terms of his own personal life-experiences. The kokanee can only dream about such karmic memories. He is haunted by instinctive feelings and desires that make him yearn for a greater freedom that cannot be found in the fresh waters of a confining inland lake." Lenny related.

"I get it," Cathy replied enthusiastically, "Like the landlocked kokanee... Jung's, Nietzsche's, and Kierkegaard's immortal souls were incarnated into the confines of a sort of inland lake of conscious, subconscious, and unconscious Judaic-Christian-Muslim dogma. Consequently their mortal personas were tainted, stunted and restricted by the cultural reality in which they found themselves."

"And in which they had few options, except to become kokanee – in spite of an innate yearning locked within the fabric of their DNA, to realize a far greater freedom," the Rabbi astutely completed Cathy's thought.

"Indeed," Lenny responded. "Their destiny was conditioned by circumstances that limited them to a degree of awareness that corresponded with their social, psychological, religious, and spiritual experiences. Intuitively they realized that there was a greater freedom for which they instinctively yearned; however, try as they did to overcome themselves, they could only do so in terms of the reality in which they existed - like the little silvery-grey kokanee that remained landlocked in the fresh waters that flow into the Great Ocean."

"What an insightful realization!" Cathy commented. "Their growth and development was restricted by influences beyond their control, that reduced them to being analogous to..."

"It seems as if they had no option but to become *kokanee*," Lana sagely noted while drawing in a deep breath as if she herself felt suffocated.

"If all one has ever known is baptism in a little pond of inland water – how is it possible to relate to the exuberant freedom that exists in the vastness of the saline waters of the mighty Pacific Ocean?" Cathy inquired.

"To the kokanee, the sockeye would seem to be an alien species from some mysterious far out place invading their freshwater habitat. And yet... the sockeye are only *returning home!*" Lana exclaimed taking the liberty to enhance her husband's allegory.

"It would be very difficult for later generations of such landlocked kokanee to believe that in past incarnations they too were once sockeye. Of the thousands of kokanee perhaps a paltry few might be able to vaguely intuit the primordial memories stored in the spiraling strands of their DNA. Would not such enlightened kokanee seem to be liars or blasphemers, a dire threat and affront to the status quo?" Cathy insightfully inquired while gazing about at the group.

Father Bertolli had sat listening with furrowed brow. His head was slightly cocked to the left and his body language depicted a person experiencing some mental discomfort. He sighed and adjusted his posture into a more upright position. The conversation had had a transformative effect upon him. He looked up at Cathy and smiled feebly as if feeling slightly embarrassed. "Yes," he said quietly, "they would."

All eyes turned expectantly toward the good Father.

"I-I would like to believe that I am among the-the... 'paltry few'," he slowly began. "Until this very moment I have felt somewhat like-like Kierkegaard, Nietzsche, and Jung," he confessed, "I felt existentially suffocated and stifled... I yearned for a deep breath of freedom – but the atmosphere about me was polluted with the halitosis of those who maintained the status quo. I was constrained to experience the ancestral sins embedded in the collective unconscious, subconscious, and consciousness of those who presently constitute the billions who exist in the confines of the Judaic, Christian, Muslim hegemony that circumscribes us like the imposing shores of an inland lake. We are like kokanee swimming about ignominiously attempting to convert other fish to our limited point of view rationalized from our predicament as kokanee!" Father Bertolli inhaled deeply as if suddenly freed from an asthmatic condition.

"Father Bertolli has spoken forthrightly and sincerely," Rabbi Letenberg empathized. "I too can relate to Lenny's Allegory of the Fish. I too can appreciate the predicament that Jung, Nietzsche, Kierkegaard... and my good friend the Father, have struggled to transcend." The Motely Five lapsed into a meditative silence

"The good Father and Rabbi have both been very honest, gracious and insightful; their sentiments are much appreciated," Lenny humbly acknowledged. "They have given credence to a malaise that has persisted like a sickness unto death over the centuries. As you know,

Nietzsche spoke of a need to overcome the self, to rise above the staleness of centuries of religious indoctrination and dogma where the human spirit was suffocated by an all-pervasive, doctrine of Original Sin. He was mindful of all of this and he railed against it with all his intellectual might. But in the Protestantism of his day, he was looked upon as a spokesman for the Anti-Christ and his intuitive insights were later regurgitated out of context to fuel Nazi propaganda about Aryan supremacy and anti-Semitism. Like Zarathustra, he had come... too early."

"It is unfortunate that individuals who are ahead of their times are so often maligned, misunderstood, and censored," Rabbi Letenberg sighed regretfully.

"Yes," Lenny agreed. "These astute scholars had intuited the innate grandeur of the human spirit. They were mindful of having once swum in the mysterious waters of a fabulous Ocean of Freedom."

"I have not come across such a credible explanation for the conundrum that keeps us babbling and squabbling like a bunch of idiots about things beyond our mortal experience. Your allegory of the fish clearly explains why it is such a struggle to acknowledge and relate to the primordial experiences ingrained innately into the DNA of our biological essence," Father Bertollli sagely commented.

"In *Either/Or*, Kierkegaard describes how it felt to be a true believer. He spent a mortal lifetime attempting to come to terms with the religious beliefs that reduced him to the existential status of a kokanee. In the end after a great deal of introspection, he reluctantly gave up his love for the woman of his dreams and remained a stunted, celibate goldfish ensconced in the glass bowl of his religious beliefs," Lenny espoused demonstrating his understanding of the said work.

"Kierkegaard is a lonely and solitary example of the choices that confront many of us celibate priests," Father Bertolli sanguinely revealed. "Many of us have rationalized our behavior in a similar fashion. Kierkegaard's writings demonstrate the deep inner feelings of uncertainty and angst that precede such a commitment to God. Sexual abstinence, as any male or female knows, is not a natural inclination. It is in fact a most unnatural prescription, if that is the right word. It appeals especially to a troubled minority who come to the Faith to find solace from social and sexual prejudices and negative attitudes toward homosexuality and other so-called deviant sexual desires. Regarding such tortured individuals you could say, the more obsessive the affliction, the greater the personal courage and commitment required to sublimate and transcend," Father Bertolli's voice diminished ominously. "To successfully overcome oneself is an act of piety of the highest order... and there are more than a few such pious individuals who have demonstrated the motivation and fortitude required to rise to the highest ranks of holiness within the Church," the good Father confessed as if clearing his conscience of an oppressive burden.

"From what you have said it is understandable why the Roman Catholic Church has been and still is so-so secretive, and reluctant to deal honestly and forthrightly with the plethora of serious allegations relating to the sexual abuse of innocent little children!" Cathy exclaimed.

"We are like kokanee living in artificial lakes of our own creation and being suffocated by our own delusions and ignorance," the good Father concluded.

"There are millions of others like us swimming about in the delusional waters of religious dogma," Rabbi Letenberg concurred. "And yet, we are mindful that deep down inside, in the DNA of our primordial instincts, there is a nearly forgotten memory, an aching recollection... *that once we too swam in the Great Ocean of Freedom.*"

* * *

We reach out
Like divine expressions
Submerged in murky waters
Where the sunlight is diffuse
And dreams are hazy recollections
Of mortal moments sublimely reflected
In the sacred waters of freedom
Ever flowing into the great ocean
Where in the solitude of our mortality
When the heart aches
And the soul yearns...
We reach out.

-LB

PART THREE

HOME FREE

CHAPTER TEN

THE PROTOCOLS

Imprinted upon the ages
Like ghostly footprints
The past mitigates upon the future
As if it is the present.

Only once did George get to swim in the saline waters of the mighty Pacific Ocean. He was nine years old at the time. The family went down to English Bay on July the first, wearing their bathing suits under their ordinary clothes. George helped pack and carry the picnic basket. They all wore sandals. It was one of the 'funnest' times George ever had.

They took the bus to the beach. When they got there hundreds of skimpily clad folks were sprawled all along the sandy foreshore. They all looked so grub-like and unhealthy without their clothes on; they reminded Georgie of the larvae that existed under rocks.

They made their way past an assortment of thin and fat grubs comatose on their backs, sides and stomachs, dehydrating in the sun. Eventually they made it to the waters' edge. His father was the first one in. "Last one in is a rotten egg!" he yelled while entering the water with a huge splash.

This rather juvenile remark embarrassed George, but he laughed and pretended it was funny. "Hold your horses!" he responded, surreptitiously looking about to see if anyone else that he knew was lurking about.

"Come on in," his father challenged, "don't be a sissy!" George was rather reluctant because the water was quite cold. He cautiously waded in up to his waist while his father waited impatiently out in the deep where the water came up to his armpits. His mother sloshed about in ankle deep water.

Suddenly a big wave rolled in over his father's head. When it hit, George jumped up and started dog-paddling furiously. He made it out to where his father had been swamped. He had lost his footing. He actually could not swim.

George grabbed him by the hair and yanked his head above water. When his Dad regained his footing he was subdued to say the least. On that day George came of age. He was only nine, but he knew what it felt like to be a hero.

"Imagine," his mother would tirelessly reiterate so that her husband would remain contrite: "Little Georgie saved your life!" It was a stretch to put it mildly, a joke of sorts, nevertheless his mother, who had witnessed the entire happening, decreed hero status on her only begotten son; it was the next best thing to being a saint.

It took years and years. But decades later that nine-year-old heroic little boy would some day become a stalker. There did not seem to be anything in his childhood or adolescent years that may have predisposed him toward becoming such. Nor were there any indicators in his early adult years that may have alerted his spouse to such behavior. It appeared to be something that developed after George had been released from the Armed Forces and returned home.

Home, to both George and Sarah was their townhome near the historic fishing village called Steveston, where coincidentally, Lenny and Lana Bruce resided. Something happened shortly after the Browns had settled there that seemed to affect George's behavior in an unseemly manner. What was it?

It was shortly after he read his first edition of *Final Draft* that George began developing a morbid interest in reading it. Copies were usually available at the convenience store on the corner of the block where he lived. Sometimes special editions appeared unexpectedly, but mostly it came out on the first Thursday of the month, written by someone called Lenny Bruce, and edited and published by Lana Bruce.

Something about the contents of "that rag", as George called it, seemed to attract him like an incandescent porch light attracts moths. He was like the obstinate moth that kept hovering about so near the hot bulb that it jeopardized its own health and wellbeing. The behavior seemed as irrational as a death wish, yet something beyond his conscious control pointed him in that direction. Would the light he instinctively sought eventually consume him?

The name 'Lenny Bruce' seemed intriguing. Lenny's ideas as presented in *Final Draft* were the light. They drew George out of his mental lethargy. Beneath the veneer of his pious convictions a disturbing awareness began to rise like the early rays of the morning sun. They conflicted with the dogmatic darkness to which he had become accustomed. There was dissonance.

Something in the depths of George's subconscious made him feel uneasy, suffocated, and sometimes even nauseous. He couldn't put his finger on it. It was just there; a deep-seated feeling of angst that stirred the dissonance into a cloud of doubt and insecurity. As the months grew into years the dissonance increased with his growing awareness.

It was everywhere, the neuroticism; it seemed natural, as natural as pretending to be one of the 'saved' destined to go to heaven. "Believe and ye shall be saved", the preacher had said. Most, if not all of his friends 'believed' – so why not him? There was comfort in numbers. Still the angst remained buried in George's subconscious where from time to time it manifested itself as irrational outbursts of anti-social behavior.

Like Pavlov's famous dog, shivering with indecision and frozen in an approach-avoidance dilemma, George was drawn toward the light of reason that seemed to be emanating from the ideas in *Final Draft*. It was a classic approach-avoidance conflict: light versus darkness, reason and common sense versus blind faith. He skulked about the fringes of society looking for some resolution to his dilemma.

One day by sheer coincidence, George saw Lana Bruce when she was delivering copies of *Final Draft* to the corner convenience store. She was such a petite, clean-cut, Christian-looking woman that George suddenly felt a twinge of empathy for her, a sense of macho manliness, as if she needed his protection. The fact that her husband's name was Lenny Bruce, combined with the fact that he was the author of the articles published in the pamphlet, triggered a long forgotten memory - a deep dark memory that emanated from within his subconscious of time spent at the Allan Memorial Institute. It triggered a vague feeling of dissonance that caused George to shiver uncontrollably. He shook his head as if attempting to disburse the lingering shadows.

George stealthily followed Lana all the way to her home. He watched her get out her fob and open the front door. He stood on the street and stared at the front entrance for about ten minutes. "So that is where Lenny lives," he said to himself. "He doesn't deserve such a nice, decent Christian-looking woman." He scowled menacingly and wandered off in the direction of the back alleyway.

After that George began hanging around Lana and Lenny's residence. "Lucky little Jew bastard to be living there with such a pretty woman," he lamented. Day after day he came to the neighborhood and pretended he was just casually strolling about. When he got tired he'd sit on a nearby bench and conjure up fantastic images of the homely little Jewish nerd with the petite Christian-looking wife.

He never took the same route two days running; in addition he changed his apparel daily so as to remain incognito. The dark sunglasses were an authentic touch. He had learned a great deal about the act of surveillance from watching television programs. He imagined he was a secret agent working on behalf of national security. He frequently reminded himself of the famous words spoken right after 9/11: '*You're either with us - or against us!*' "So true," he thought, "...so true."

One day Lana Bruce emerged from her home with a male partner. He did not look at all like the homely Jewish nerd that George had conjured up. "Can't be her husband!" he exclaimed to himself as they strolled hand in hand past the very bench he had plunked himself down on twenty minutes earlier. "Looks more like a *goddamned Scotsman*," he decided.

He followed them all along the street into town. They went into a coffee shop. He went there too. They ordered two fresh brewed coffees. He ordered one. They sat down outside at a square table. After picking up a copy of the free daily newspaper, he sat down at a nearby round table and carefully opened the paper, which he hid behind. They began sipping their respective coffees. George sipped his. They began talking. George's ears perked up.

"Don't you think it is about time we edited the various copies of *Final Draft* into book form? I know what you're thinking, Lenny; you're thinking, 'who would want to publish it' – right?"

George was all ears. *"So that is her husband!"*

"Okay, go ahead and get started. You are far better at that sort of thing than I am."

"Quite a few people are reading our paper," Lana remarked.

"It is all your doing," Lenny commended. "You've done a remarkable job with that newsletter format. Makes it seem as if the author is somebody important."

"You are important, Lenny... someday you might even be famous."

"Should I live so long!"

"You are in very good health. Your prostate cancer has been successfully treated. I'm sure you will live a very long and fruitful life."

"We are all 'born to die'," Lenny stated philosophically. "Death is inevitable."

"Why so pessimistic?" Lana asked as a cold breeze caused her to shiver when unbeknownst to her, George folded up his newspaper and skulked off across the street.

"Who's that?" Lenny asked gazing across the street as if by instinct. He spied a hunched figure scurrying across the road.

Lana stared across the street. She spotted a man pulling up the collar of his blue denim jacket and bending his head downward as if attempting to hide it. "You know?" she began auspiciously, "Hasn't that guy been hanging about in the neighborhood?"

"You sure that's the same guy?"

"Gives me the creeps."

"Trust your intuition. There certainly is something creepy about that guy. Look, he's running now. You know... he ain't no jogger."

* * *

Unlike her husband George, who often seemed to be in a mental fog, Sarah Brown was quietly alert. On sunny days she liked to take long quiet walks contemplating the unpredictability of life and the events that had brought her spouse and herself to such a seemingly ignominious and meaningless retirement.

She was somewhat fearful of new technologies. They baffled and confused her; they also made her feel ignorant and insecure. So she avoided them and carried on as long as she could with her old-tech ways. She probably would have continued to struggle along without any appreciation for the computer age - if she had not become suspicious about what might have happened to her husband at the Allan Memorial Institute in Montreal, Quebec.

From the moment he returned home after his years of active service in the army, there was something about the forlorn and needy expression in his demeanor as he stood awkwardly in the doorway upon his arrival that hinted of a need for understanding and empathy. It was there day after day, month after month: George hanging about without anything worthwhile to do. It was as if he was waiting... for something to happen.

"What on earth are you waiting for?" Sarah blurted out one rainy afternoon, as her husband lay sprawled out on the sagging couch.

"Nothing... that would concern you," was his abrupt reply.

But it did concern Sarah. Something seemed slightly out of synch. It grated on her protective instincts. "My dear Georgie," she mouthed to herself at the time, "what on earth have they done to you!" Sarah's curiosity was piqued. It was a healthy curiosity: it kept her mind stimulated and her instincts honed.

It was the librarian at the local public library who provided the motivation Sarah needed to brush up on her computer skills. "MK-Ultra?" she pondered... "Hmm, now let's see," she typed the word into her computer. "You know?" she looked up, "You can probably find out all about it on the Internet."

"My computer skills are negligible, and I don't have a computer at home."

"There is a free computer course that begins tonight at the Seniors Centre. I helped set up the computers," the librarian remarked.

It was the word 'free' that made all the difference. Sarah smiled confidently as she left the library. She would not have to ask George for money.

Sarah went. She sat behind a tabletop computer and placed her right hand on the mouse just like the instructor told the class to do. She clicked her right index finger and behold, the screen flickered and the words, "Welcome to the computer age" appeared on the monitor. She was amazed. She suddenly felt empowered; and as if by magic, she actually was... empowered.

She cajoled George into buying a secondhand computer. She attended every free computer course available at the Seniors Centre plus a few that she actually paid for, which were put on by the local Adult Education Program. She became very proficient in a very short period of time because she already knew how to type.

What intrigued Sarah the most about the computer age was the working of the Internet. At her last Adult Education computer course, she asked the instructor, who happened of all people, to be a practicing Buddhist Monk, to explain how the Internet worked. He gave the most edifying explanation any member of the class ever heard.

He began: "I could give you a high tech response that would leave you baffled and confused – or I could give you a simple analogy that you can relate to. Perhaps I should give you a little of both?"

The class nodded in unison.

"The internet or ethernet as some now refer to it, is all about communication. It takes two or more people, as does any communication. We have progressed from the beating of drums to smoke signals, to telegraph, to telephones, to television, to computers and now, the Internet. It is all about communication... and what is communication? The exchange of information. The Internet represents a high tech reality of communicative networks. To understand the Internet, it helps to look at it as a system with two main components. The first of those components is the hardware, the second, the protocols.

"The hardware consists of the machinery like cables, routers, servers, cell-phone towers, satellites, radios etc., in short, all the devices that create the network of networks that enable communication to take place. That network of networks is inter-connected: the result is the *'Inter-net'*. Get it?"

There were smiles and bobbing of heads.

"The protocols consist of the sets of rules that the machines follow to complete tasks. Without a set of rules that all the machines must abide by, communication between devices cannot take place. The protocols provide both a method and a common language for the machines to use to transmit or communicate the data. The transmitters and receivers of the data are called 'end points'."

The instructor took in a deep breath and said, "So much for the technical aspects of the Internet. "Now consider this analogy that evolved out of my Buddhist mindset. The hardware is your *brain*, and the protocols are the *mind*. Normally we use the terms 'brain' and 'mind' interchangeably as if they are one and the same. For the purposes of this analogy, a distinction must be made.

"How does the mind differ from the brain? The brain is the hardware or biological mass that represents the command center for the vertebrate nervous system. The mind represents a non-biological set of protocols that enable the brains to communicate. How do we know that such a mind actually exists?

"There are scientifically proven cases where patients have died on the operating table. The EKG monitor flat-lines, indicating that the patient is technically brain-dead. And yet, when the patient is miraculously resuscitated, the patient can recall or remember the events of her near-death experience. If the brain flat-lined, where were such memories stored?"

"In the mind," the class responded as a chorus.

"The mind represents the protocols that enable memory to exist – even when a single brain or personal computer is turned off or unplugged... the Internet continues to operate. In other words, even when a brain or single PC is turned off – the Mind or Internet still continues to exist and to operate." The instructor paused to give the class a moment to contemplate this idea.

"Like... when one of *us* passes away - life still goes on!" Sarah blurted out.

"Our biological brains are plugged into a universal Mind. That Mind represents the sum total of all experience... something like the *collective unconscious* or even the mysterious *Akashic Record*. As individual brains, we each in our respective manner contribute to the infinite memory of the universal Mind... and share vicariously in its infinite knowledge."

"Incredible!" Sarah exclaimed out loud on behalf of the incredulous class.

"Our connection to the Mind is as tenuous as a PC's connection to the Internet. The tenuousness is relative to our notion of our relationship to that connection. Who makes up the Internet? The Internet is 'us'. The Internet is simply a network of networking human beings. And so is the Mind. It represents the paradoxical truth of the statement: *the whole is greater than the sum of the parts*.

"Think about that the next time you get on the Internet. Without users like you and me... there would be no Internet. And without brains like yours and mine... there would be no collective unconscious... and no *Mind*. Make sense?"

"Edifying," Sarah said to herself as she left the College's computer lab and headed back home. When she opened the door she found her husband snoozing on the couch with his prized German luger resting on his hairy belly, which had become exposed when his black T-shirt with the skull and crossbones had pulled up. He looked so innocuous with that childlike grimace on his face. In the dim light he looked... *surprisingly handsome*, Sarah thought. On television, a commentator was reading the evening news in a nasal tone. Sarah turned the television off, thereby accentuating the sound of George's spasmodic snoring.

She bent over and gingerly picked up the hefty metal luger and dropped it as delicately as she could on the adjacent glass coffee table where it landed with a crunch that left a tiny bruise on the mirror-like surface. When this happened George's right index finger twitched involuntarily as if he was dreaming one of his recurrent dreams where someone fired a shot... 'Bam!' and he froze in his tracks in disbelief that such a god-awful thing could actually happen.

* * *

Perhaps it was Eldorado's comments regarding immortality and the importance of reason and common sense, along with Cathy Schneider's intellectual ruminations on aging that inspired Lenny to give expression to his ideas on mortality. Perhaps it was his preoccupation with his own sense of being 'mortal'.

He was lounging under the leafy canopy of the fake deciduous tree in the corner of the living room when the essential nuances of the idea struck him. He recalled Pena saying: *the real miracle is... being mortal in an immortal universe.* He hastily scribbled down some notes so he would not forget.

He forgot about the notes for about three months... until Lana discovered them on the floor behind the wooden pot holding the fake tree when she was cleaning up. "What is this?" she asked at the time. When Lenny arrived home after his morning stroll she said, "These must be yours."

After re-reading his notes, Lenny incubated on the ideas for two more weeks before he felt inclined to expand upon the words he had scrawled. He laboriously rewrote the rough draft five times before turning it over to Lana. She proudly published it in the January issue of *Final Draft*. It warmed up the bone-chilling month with some heated debates amongst the readership.

George W. Brown was amongst the readership. "Radical!" he had proclaimed at the time. Who knew he would actually get it?

The Miracle of Miracles

Under the Bodhi tree
Of your immortal mind
You sit in quiet meditation
As the sun rises inexorably
Illuminating the heavens
With one paradoxical thought:
How is it that
In this infinite, eternal
And immortal universe
I am... mortal?

Mortal Moments

The essential question is: In an eternal, infinite and therefore immortal universe – is not mortality impossible?

Yet who can deny it? Mortality exists! It is an undeniable existential fact. The evidence is all about us. We see others all about us grow old, feeble, and die. We pay our last respects to an immobile corpse. We know the corpse will rot and decay, and the organic material will eventually turn into inorganic matter: *ashes to ashes, dust to dust.* The empirical evidence is overwhelming.

Whatever happened to good old so-and-so? Where did she come from? Where did she go?

Is it possible that she is still here... here in the *eternal-now* where she has always been? Could it be that she did not come from anywhere – or go anywhere? That she has always been here in this eternal time-space... as if she simply woke up as if from a dream of memories past, vaguely remembered? Is it possible that the dreamer does not have to come from somewhere or go anywhere, that the dreamer is always present? Could it be that we are actually immortal dreamers *pretending to be mortal...* so that we can exist for a mortal moment in eternity?

Is not that mortal moment everything? Does not that mortality provide the *finite bookends* that make our existence meaningful and significant within an infinite and eternal universe? Is not mortality *everything...* to us? Is it not the *miracle of miracles*?

The Mortal Miracle

After thousands of years of evolutionary development many of us are still not aware enough to respect the miracle represented by all mortal forms of life, past and present. Do we realize that organic fuels like crude oil and coal provide indisputable evidence of the passing of countless numbers of living organisms? In a short historical timeline we have progressed from the Stone Age, to the Bronze Age, to the Iron Age, and now to the age of Plastics. Except for the plastic age, all the other ages have been fashioned from inorganic materials like stone, copper, and iron. Plastics are made from the residue of trillions of trilobites that once lived on this miracle planet... just like we are now.

Oil provides empirical evidence of the miracle of photosynthesis that transformed a desolate landscape into a living planet. It takes millions of years to produce a single drop of oil – and only a fleeting *mortal moment* to burn it up. So, what are we doing?

Unfortunately many human beings believe that they have been given *dominion over the earth,* a religious dogma that has given rise to a vanity and conceit that is unique amongst the mortal. Coupled with the simple biological fact that human beings are not able to perform photosynthesis, this righteous entitlement places over seven billion of the most voracious warm-blooded mammals to ever inhabit planet Earth into the category of self-serving, avaricious *parasites*! It seems we are, as yet, too preoccupied with our own sanctimonious importance to fully appreciate the significance of the countless numbers of mortal life forms that *must die - in order for us to live.*

Are we shamefully sowing the seeds of our own mortal demise? We need to think about that every time we sit down at the table with knife and fork in hand, or visit a fast-food outlet and inhale our meal without a pretense of appreciation for all the mortal life forms that gave up their precious lives in order to sustain ours. This uncaring attitude is what is fuelling an unhealthy materialistic trend toward obesity and diabetes with accompanying liver, kidney, lung, and heart ailments, not to mention a host of other related diseases like cancer. In order to counteract this alarming trend, an assortment of expensive diet plans, exercise programs, and nutritional supplements are being adroitly marketed to the gullible public. Of course huge profits are being made – but unfortunately the problem continues to get even worse. Why?

The problem is imbedded in one's personal religious beliefs and one's attitude toward one's self and one's sacred relationship to Mother Earth. What are we doing to ourselves and to the earth? Why do we curse and denigrate our *miraculous mortal status*?

Immortal Memories

The interface of the biological brain with the eternally infinite Mind manifests *memories*. One remembers that moment by mortal moment, one created one's own level of mortal awareness. Such *awareness* is created from one's memories. Memories, being immaterial, cannot be destroyed – they represent the *experiences* from which our remembrances are cultivated, and from which our karmic identity and destiny is constantly being fashioned. We exist on the cutting edge of such a creative process; it provides us with our *human condition*. The condition involved is a time-space related existential conundrum: as soon as one becomes aware of something, it becomes a past event, a mortal moment: a *memory*.

Memories provide the individual with an ever-developing identity. It is especially important to be cognizant that such memories can only be fashioned from meaningful *mortal experiences*; and that each *immortal soul* has been inculcated into this four dimensional space-time membrane of forces to create new memories... *from the old.*

How is this done? Our *mortal* status provides us with an awareness of the space-time reality membrane of forces into which we have been magically incarnated as if we belong here, now. In such a reality paradigm our *free will* enables us to impact upon old memories and magically reconstitute the 'old' into the 'new'. Nothing is created or destroyed - only recycled, reconstituted, changed or renewed... like fashioning new dreams from old memories. There is an innate instinct to move in the direction of perfection. All human beings the world over, regardless of their race, religion, or cultural environment, naturally yearn to perfect themselves: to progress from being ignorant and selfish to being more unselfish, enlightened and altruistic. Why is this natural?

The perfection of the altruistic *Whole* is a work in progress. In a nutshell, that is why we, human beings, as parts of the *whole*, have been incarnated on this miracle planet as *parasites*, so we can learn to appreciate and help to create a more wholesome and perfect *Reality*.

Therefore it behooves us to act in accord with the Universal Principle of Self-realization. *Consciously behave in such an altruistic manner as to be constantly creating wholesome, life-enhancing memories.* As *immortally mortal* beings we have the free will required to participate in the realization of what many refer to as our *destiny*.

"*To be immortally mortal!*" George breathed upon first reading Lenny's article. The thought triggered something that brought a strange expression to his countenance. It was a countenance that spoke of nearly forgotten memories poetically expressed as if in a drug-induced trance...

> *An unforgettable remembrance...*
> *Crept in from an eternity*
> *Of dark spaces*
> *Folded like endless planes of origami*
> *Transformed with one unique cut*

Into everything there was
A singularity of one consciousness
Ever so humble and contrite
Insinuating presence
Into the confines of a symbiotic reality
Where altruistic vibes
Imbued ambient shades of freedom
Upon divine expressions speaking in tongues

"It is so nice to be back," it recalled
Withered by a deep-felt appreciation
For the mundane and the obvious
When it shuffled in from the infinite
And shed a quiet tear as it sat down
On the saggy sofa-chair by the entrance
Overwhelmed by the realization
That it had been given yet another
Second chance...
Another miraculous opportunity
To be itself.

* * *

The name Jigme Singye Wangchuck rose to the conscious level of Lenny's cognitive domain on the evening of June 27th when he was slouching lackadaisically on the sofa with the TV remote clutched in his right hand. He was surfing the "Guide", pausing at his favorite Public Broadcasting channels, when his eye caught the letters "GNH" in conjunction with the word "Bhutan". In the far reaches of his memory he dimly recalled someone once saying: "Keep an eye on Bhutan". Of course this sage advice had slipped Lenny's mind because... *who cares what is going on in the obscure eastern Himalayan country of Bhutan?*

"Keep an eye on Bhutan," the nearly forgotten advice caused his index finger to twitch and presto, a documentary program appeared on the screen dealing with the concept of "Gross National Happiness". The concept piqued Len's fancy and he sat up and absorbed the information like a dry sponge in water. For some obscure reason he was reminded of Mount Kailash and the sublime "lake of the mind" at its base; it resonated in his subconscious as if he had been there eons ago.

Afterwards he retired to the den where he immediately set pen to paper. Lana later edited and published the article in *Final Draft*. It was entitled: "The Enlightened Philosophy of Jigme Singye Wangchuck". Who ever heard of Jigme Singye Wangchuck before reading the August edition of *Final Draft?*

According to Lenny's article the phrase "Gross National Happiness" was coined by Jigme Singye Wangchuck, the fourth Dragon King of Bhutan, who had ascended the throne at the age of seventeen, shortly after the demise of his father, Jigme Dorji Wangchuck in 1972. The term was used to signify his commitment to building a modern economy that would serve the needs of Bhutan's unique culture, a culture rooted in the spiritual values of a Buddhist population of approximately two million human beings. With the assistance of a Canadian health specialist named Michael Pennock, a sophisticated surveying instrument was developed at the Center for Bhutan Studies under the leadership of Karma Ura, to measure the population's general level of well-being.

Prior to that, the youthful fourth Dragon King had studiously examined the "have" nations of the developed world and concluded that such rampant, self-serving greed was not only unsustainable, but did not lead to the goal which all human beings desired: happiness. He noticed that in countries where people and governments strove for material wealth, that only a very small percentage of the population achieved an affluent and comfortable life-style. He was particularly disturbed to observe the downside: the vast majority of the population was marginalized to levels of poverty and misery where basic health and survival needs were inadequate. In addition he perceived that in the relentless search for bigger profits, huge parts of the natural environment were decimated without much thought given to sustainability. And to top it all off, this type of behavior was carried out on purpose and condoned as if it was good in itself.

Jigme Singye Wangchuck the Fourth decided that this "greed is good" approach to life created more unhappiness than happiness for the vast majority of the inhabitants who embraced such an economic approach. The GDP or Gross Domestic Product of the wealthiest nations, while yielding a higher standard of living for the affluent, produced an economic footprint upon the world's precious renewable and nonrenewable natural resources that was not only unsustainable, it was damaging to future generations.

Nevertheless the idea of "Gross National Happiness" as the primary objective of a modern economy seemed ludicrous, ridiculous, and even plain stupid to those from cultures dominated by capitalism where more is rarely considered to be enough.

The ancient Greek Philosopher, Aristotle, stated that *Happiness is the goal that all men seek.* The primary goal of GNH synchronizes with Aristotle's idea that *all men seek happiness.* The *pursuit of happiness* is also an ideal enshrined in the American Constitution

Happiness happens when conditions are appropriate. The GNH provides an ideological umbrella under which the people are empowered to interact in synch with each other – like entangled particles in a quantum universe - to achieve happiness. All economic, social, and political development must be consistent with this over-riding altruistic endeavor. Under such conditions, a free market economy can serve as the practical and pragmatic means by which such a glorious end can be realized. The social and political structures in place in Bhutan enable the people to enjoy a common spiritual and cultural tradition based upon compassion and an unselfish attitude toward sharing and generosity... carried out in the altruistic spirit that their *ancient ancestors* may have condoned.

The King himself set an example for his people. In the year 2006 the fourth Dragon King of Bhutan of his own free will handed over sovereignty to his subjects. In 2008 Bhutan elected its first representative government thus making the people responsible for their own happiness.

"Gross National Happiness. What a beautiful idea," Lana sighed when she had finished typing the final page. "Too bad it only exists in Bhutan."

* * *

Over the years, droplets of happiness accumulated in George W Brown's memory like drops in the proverbial old bucket. The drops accumulated, and in the blink of an eye the bucket was well over two-thirds full. In the translucency of each drop, flashes of memory glimmered in moments when George lay in bed reflecting upon the good old days when he was a child… and it was Christmas.

To little Georgie Christmas had nothing to do with sinners and penance doers. It almost had nothing at all to do with being a Christian in good standing with the Lord. It was all about Santa Claus, Christmas gifts, Christmas trees all decorated with colored lights, Christmas carols, and all sorts of happy Christmas festivities. It was more like a *potlatch* of sharing: an outburst of happy unselfish vibrations. Christmas was George's favorite time of year. He had so many fond Christmas memories.

It started when George was in grade one. That was the first year that Santa Claus actually came to the Brown's home. Unbeknownst to little Georgie, that was the year his dear mother said to her husband: "I remember when I was Georgie's age, Christmas was such a big deal. Before George gets any older… we need to-to make it seem real to him."

"Okay," George's father agreed, "If we are going to do this, let's go all out, and as you said, make it a really big deal." And so it came to pass….

George fondly recalled the time he was six years old and in grade one. It took so long for Christmas to arrive. He helped decorate the tree his dad had put up in the corner of the living room by the brick fireplace. It was so much fun! He put on some of the multi-colored transparent glass balls and silver icicles. His mom put the angel on the very top of the tree while his father held the ladder. When they turned out the room light and lit up the tree it was so beautiful. That night George could hardly sleep… waiting for Christmas to arrive. *How long is a fortnight?* he wondered.

The next day his dear mother hung three long red socks along the fireplace mantel. The middle one was his; it had the letter 'G' embroidered across the top in white. "You better be good or Santa might not come," his mother warned.

Little Georgie was real good. He made his own bed and he even offered to help wash the dishes. "Why don't you just go outside and play?" his mother asked thoughtfully.

When he got back in and was waiting for supper, his dad arrived home from work. "Have you written your note to Santa yet?" he asked.

"No."

"Why don't we sit down after supper and I will help you compose a letter? If Santa doesn't know what you want – how will he know what to bring?"

After George helped to clear the table, he sat down with his dad with pencil and paper in hand. "Dear Santa," he wrote in his best grade-one printing. "I have been very good." With his father's prompting he changed it to: "I have tried to be good."

"You must be truthful or Santa might not come!" his dad reminded him.

"You can bring me… whatever you like," a chastened little boy carefully printed with hope. He signed the letter, "Your good friend George." He folded the note in half and placed it in a white envelope addressed: *To Santa – North Pole.* His father said he would mail it.

The next day when his dad got back from work, the first question George asked him was: "Did you mail it, Dad?"

"Nope, I forgot," his father joked.

Little George remained silent. He turned away so his dad could not see, and started to cry.

"Cheer up. I was just kidding!" his dad admitted scooping him up and parading him about the room.

From then on until Christmas Eve, when the family enjoyed a special fondue supper with all kinds of good things to cook with long forks, George was real good. He attempted to shovel off the front sidewalk whenever it snowed, and did his best to be useful around the house.

"You should be out playing with the other kids," his mother suggested when he always seemed to be hovering about trying to be helpful.

"I sure hope Santa comes," George would wistfully reply and look up to his mom with large luminous eyes.

"You have been so good, I am sure that Santa will come this year for sure."

"But he hasn't been here before… has he?"

"He might have been – but you were probably too young to notice," his mother explained with a sigh of regret. "Remember last year when you got those new pants?"

"Were those from Santa?"

"I think so. Santa often brings things that you really need."

"I sure hope he comes this Christmas," George reiterated.

Both parents had such a grand time buying gifts for their only son that they vowed to make every Christmas just as memorable from then on. At a downtown department store they found exactly what George has been asking for: a metallic six-gun and holster along with a black plastic mask, just like the Lone Ranger's. It made them very happy just imagining how thrilled their son was going to be.

George was the first one up on Christmas morning. It was still dark out. He crept out of bed and slowly made his way into the living room. The tree lights were still on. The stockings were stuffed to overflowing; and under the tree presents of all shapes, colors, and sizes were neatly arrayed.

George stared with amazement at the fireplace hearth where he had left a note along with half a glass of milk and two fresh oatmeal-raisin cookies that he had helped to bake. The note read: *In case you are hungry... your good friend George.* All that remained was an empty glass and a few crumbs on a pale porcelain plate. Little George was awestruck.

In the dim light he could see the shiny angel gleaming on the treetop. He stood there in silence. He never touched anything: it all looked so perfect. He quietly went back to bed and snuggled into his warm comforter. He never felt so happy. He closed his eyes, placed his little hands together and whispered with heartfelt sincerity: "Thank you, Santa... for coming to our house."

* * *

Lana Bruce liked to think of herself as being somewhat of an enlightened optimist. She often had to cajole her husband into cheering up after he had conjured up a particularly unsavory view of the modern capitalistic world. She felt it was her role to assuage her husband's rather high-minded views with a more down-to-earth vision of the status quo.

"We should be thankful that we can count ourselves to be amongst the 'haves' of this world," she would say, especially at those times when their only daughter Kitty was hovering about. "There are so many who are far less fortunate than we are. We have been blessed."

Somehow Lana's positive attitude rubbed off onto Kitty. She grew up to be a bubbly, effervescent young lady with an infectious sense of understated humor. "Cheer up, Dad!" she would admonish when he was looking particularly morose, "you are still alive and breathing."

To Lenny, Kitty represented all that was good in the world. He doted on her hand and foot. "No can spoil," he would say when Lana would object to his over-indulgent ways. In Lenny's mind there was no more precious human being on the whole planet than his little daughter.

On the day Kitty left for the University of Victoria with battered suitcase in hand, Lenny glanced empathetically over to his spouse who stood in the hallway with tears in her eyes. Kitty had matured into a beautiful young woman with high cheekbones and smiling eyes that always seemed to be twinkling. Lenny took a hasty photo of her standing in the doorway with the sunlight cascading over her.

"She looks like an angel," Lana remarked after the photograph had been developed. "I hope she has a good life," she had whispered wistfully as their only offspring left the protective shelter of her home to venture forth into the great unknown to engage in what Socrates referred to as the highest virtue: *the tending of one's own soul.*

Time seemed to pass as quickly as the arrow shot from the crossbow held by the Ancient Mariner. Fortunately no albatross was thoughtlessly dispatched. On the contrary, omens of good fortune seemed to abound, substantiated by the many epistles sent from their daughter over the years highlighting her journey from innocent to mature young lady with worldly knowledge. The latest epistle was a belated Christmas card post marked from Boulder, Colorado, USA.

Kitty had moved there along with a young man from Utah whom she had met while snow skiing at Silver Star near Vernon, BC. Shortly thereafter they had joined up with the adherents of a wandering group called the 'Sacred Fire Community.' They wandered south of the 49th parallel like the aboriginals of old used to do when following the vast herds of buffalo. Except the hoards of buffalo had been replaced by endless lines of cars zooming past the remnants of a distant dream that had been defended to the death by the indigenous peoples at Little Big Horn.

Fortified with an honors degree in Philosophy, Kitty represented the altruistic hopes and dreams of two old folks residing in Steveston, British Columbia, Canada. Along with her friends, Kitty had set out to discover her own *brave new world.*

The Christmas card contained a note that read as follows.

Greetings Mom and Dad.

Hope this note finds you both in good health and good spirits.

As you probably are aware, we are now entering into the end of a five thousand year cycle; the time of the winter solstice of the year 2012 marks the end of the Mayan Calendar… and the rising of the sixth sun. This will indicate not the end of time but the beginning of a new era of hope and renewal.

Here in our little hamlet in Colorado, people gather on the winter solstice to remind themselves of the ignorant behavior of those who presently approach Mother Nature as if she is an adversary to be wantonly plundered, polluted, and wasted and is only a means to a selfish end. It is time for those among us who share a more benevolent attitude toward Mother Earth to come together and rejoice in the ending of an era influenced by attitudes condoning selfishness and greed.

Like Dad has often said, we are presently living in a civilization that has manifested a human tragedy where the sanctity of life is secondary to the ambitions of a privileged few who condone war, poverty, disease, and human suffering in order to make more and more money! Dad has always harped on the lack of awareness of his generation and the ones preceding it… and for good reasons, I'd say.

For thousands of years Mayans have walked through the ravaged mountains of their sacred homelands like ghosts reluctant to leave this miracle planet… until their memories can be restored with happiness. Happiness is the goal which all men seek. Did not Aristotle say something like that – eh Dad?

The Zapatistas of Chiapas have long espoused the view that we are at long last about to enter into the beginning of a peaceful era on the world stage… beginning with the ascendancy of the Sixth Sun. The indigenous peoples' calendar, which existed long before Jesus was born (and upon whose incorrect historical date of birth the present calendar is based), alludes to times backwards and forwards in time immemorial. The Mayan Calendar is a celestial calendar. Where did this vast degree of awareness, rationality, and knowledge originate?

Did you know that descendants of the ancient Mayans like the Hopi of the Southwestern States have an age-old prophecy that lives like a memory in the heart of every human being? In due time, we will learn the vital lesson for which we have been placed like children upon Mother Earth, to learn. We have a choice; there are two paths: one grows corn – and the other is barren.

For too long we have been treading the wrong path! There is still hope for all of us. We are the generation of promise. We are the children of the Sacred

Fire that burns in every heart; it is the spirit of altruistic Freedom… the fire that never burns out.

On cold wintery evenings when they were feeling a little fatigued and despondent, Lana would get out Kitty's letter and hand it to her husband. "Read it out loud," she would say. And Lenny would quietly inhale and exhale while affecting an indulgent little smile… and begin.

* * *

In later years, after George had been discharged from the Armed Forces, the flashbacks from his earlier years fused with those from his army experiences to create a surreal world of paranormal dimensions. Sarah proved to be a stalwart helpmeet. In the dead of night when George woke up in a panic, Sarah's presence would be consoling. It was always a relief to awaken to a comforting reality of bed-sheets and Sarah's reassuring voice saying, "It's only a dream."

"Thank god you're real!" he'd say and hug Sarah so tightly she could scarcely breathe. George would cling to his spouse like a frightened little boy hiding under the covers. At other times he would make inane comments like, *'It just takes one more step'.*

"What step?" Sarah would ask.

"One more," he would reply as if in a daze.

"Snap out of it!" Sarah would command, feeling slightly frightened and confused.

"It's so nice to be back!" George would declare as if pointing out something incredibly obtuse. *"There is no going back,"* he whispered ominously on one occasion as if, for some strange reason he had been given something he referred to as a… *second chance.* Why? Did he need it?

It seemed he was just grateful to be back… in the here and now. Being back was comforting. He was grateful to be back where he belonged. It was where he, George Webster Brown, could relate to what was happening…

What was happening? It was confusing. Was it all about attempting to make a difference of some sort? Otherwise what was there? Just phantoms lurking about: meaningless shadows scurrying hither and thither searching for something elusive.

Sometimes practically an entire acid trip flashed back and George would cling to Sarah as though, if not for her, he would just disappear into the void. It was hard on Sarah. She was his anchor. Without her, where on earth would he be? Out there? Somewhere way out there alone in the universe? Sarah had her role. It was far more important than she realized.

It was around Halloween that Sarah began to sense a feeling of detachment emanating from George. It developed after a strange and ominous phone call that he had received early one morning. It was about seven-thirty. She remembered it because... it made her feel anxious and frightened. She recalled her husband's eyes: they seemed to glaze over... and after that he became even stranger than he had been. He seemed distracted by something. Whatever it was, it made a significant difference in his behavior. He seemed to find various excuses for getting up each morning and going out.

In many ways it was refreshing to get him out of the house. In other ways it was disconcerting because his behavior evolved from simply being obsessive to being somewhat paranoid. He behaved like a robotic zombie programmed to react to a given stimulus, like Pavlov's dog.

Who can blame such an animal for its behavior? A "conditioned response", they called it. Was it really that simple?

Most evenings there were two people living in the house, but each felt alone. The loneliness made the house feel empty like a shell, an empty shell in which two people 'played house'. There was little either could do about it. "Just me, myself, and I," George once remarked to himself one evening as he stood by the kitchen counter loading the dishwasher.

"What did you say?" Sarah had responded hoping her husband was open to further communication.

"Oh, nothing," he replied absentmindedly.

Sometimes Sarah felt as if George had become a phantom who lurked about the house like a ghost; he could have passed for the phantom of the opera without the opera. Sarah had seen the movie version twice. It always made her feel sad and vaguely depressed. Now she understood why... it was the hopelessness. Sometimes she just felt like crying.

* * *

"Where to begin?" the person responsible for the prosecution of George Webster Brown asked himself as he lounged about in the glass bubble of his comfortable office in the building that represented the physical presence of law and order in the province of British Columbia. Ruskolnikov Kublinski stared at the mound of papers he had removed from the residence of the accused, George Webster Brown. Among the mound of papers he had found several copies of *Final Draft* that he had read with due diligence. "Interesting, to say the least!" he had concluded at the time of reading. He was searching for something that might provide a motive for the gruesome murder, something that hinted of premeditation and warranted a charge of *murder in the first degree.*

There was a lot of food-for-thought condensed in the literary efforts of the recently deceased. He had trouble visualizing George actually reading such an esoteric publication. But nevertheless, in so far as he was able to discover via interviews with a number of George's associates - George had read it with morbid interest. Why? Being a man of considerable intelligence and psychological insight, Ruskolnikov had mumbled under his breath with a prescient sense: "You can kill the man – *but have you killed his ideas?*"

The ideas expressed by the deceased percolated within the inquisitive caverns of Russ's intellect and synchronized with his preconceived biases and predilections with an alacrity that caused him to say: "Courageously insightful!" Never before had he read such outspoken views on matters that he had carefully kept to himself for fear of being revealed as a… a social misfit, a radical, an anti-establishmentarian. He had to be careful of how such ideas reflected upon his public image.

The Crown Prosecutor stared out of the magnificent glass windows that gave him an unimpeded view of the building next door. In spite of the floor to ceiling windows he felt confined and stifled. Still he was glad to be indoors – mindful of the early frost and the bone-chilling wind factor.

Before he left his house the broadcaster on the morning news had mentioned that some fragile old homeless person had succumbed overnight to the bitter cold. "Too damn bad," Ruskolnikov thought as he swiveled his padded leather chair back around to his desk. "Somehow we have lost our unselfish nature, our instinct to share the bounty with our fellow man."

Russ had read a similar point of view expressed in the April issue of *Final Draft*, and in a May issue he had read about the First Nations Peoples… *The Aboriginal Peoples shared. In the dead of winter when food was scarce and starvation loomed, if a skilled hunter managed to kill a noble animal like a mighty elk, he would take it back to the village and there would be a communal feast. In times of plenty there would be a Potlatch where the greatest honors would be bestowed upon individuals who displayed the most unselfish attitudes. But we civilized folks who righteously enforced a generation of cultural genocide upon them by taking their children and enrolling them in residential schools, banned the potlatch and called it an ignorant and gross display of paganism. From our perspective, the hunter who killed the elk should have cut it up in pieces and hid it under the snow and ice, to be secretly gloated over whenever he selfishly partook of the bounty - while his tribesman died of malnutrition and starvation.*

Ruskolnikov sighed and gazed out the window with a perturbed look etched upon his pallid face as if to say: *Little wonder we have abject poverty side by side with unseeming opulence… right here in Vancouver. A status quo that many of us are prepared to defend to the death!* The thought caused Russ to lean back and gaze up to the ceiling as if looking for answers amongst the florescent lights that hung there.

* * *

Sarah and George Brown were both snuggled-up in their cozy queen sized bed on the verge of awakening to a gorgeous early fall sunrise. The golden rays of the sun were skimming across the tops of the trees and out over the Fraser, all the way to the Gulf Islands. They were both unaware that it was Halloween, a day on which pranksters liked to play scary tricks on unsuspecting victims.

The time was 7:28 am. The phone rang and rang. Sarah reached over and picked up the offending instrument. "Hello – hello?" she responded sleepily.

"Is George W Brown available?" a male voice asked.

"He's still sleeping."

"Could I please speak to him?"

"Why?" Sarah replied groggily.

"It is very important that I contact him about his time in the Canadian Armed Forces."

"Okay, just a moment." Sarah passed the phone over to her husband who had rolled over next to her. "Wake up George! Someone wants to talk to you about your time in the army."

George grabbed the phone and placed it near his left ear. "George here," he muttered.

"Is this the George Webster Brown who spent some time at the Allan Memorial Institute back in the early 1960s?"

"Who's asking?" George replied suspiciously.

"My name is Tom Smith. I am following up on your participation in a MKUltra experiment. Sub-project number 68, I believe."

"What experiment?" George cautiously inquired, his brain scrambling to re-establish connection to old memories.

"The classified use of long term mind control," Tom replied candidly. "In the interests of National Security... of course," he hastily added. "It was nice of you to volunteer."

"I was glad to be of service."

"Saved us a ton of obtrusive background checks and time-consuming paperwork. Identified you as a true believer, a real patriot. Patriotism is more important than ever these days. It instills pride... eh? It enables one human being to righteously kill another... and be labeled a hero to boot," Tom pointed out facetiously attempting to interject a modicum of levity into a humorless situation.

George lapsed into momentary silence stunned by the sudden intrusion of past memories into the present. "Did you say *long term mind control?*" he inquired as the ramifications of what Tom was insinuating began to dawn upon him.

"We are primarily interested in its effectiveness. We need to know... if it actually works. I believe you were one of the candidates who was being... surreptitiously monitored as a test subject."

"I was?" George queried, his suspicions mounting.

"Yes you were," Tom hesitated as if cogitating about his responsibilities in such a secretive operation. "I guess there is no need for us uh-uh... not to be honest and forthcoming... at this time. It is all being done, as you probably know, under the MKUltra provision. Homeland Security takes precedence over individual rights and freedoms... as was indicated in those papers you signed. And you did sign them – right?"

"I-I was not exactly sure what I was signing. I was just anxious to be of service."

"But you did sign them... and your name is George Webster Brown, isn't it?"

"Of course."

"We need to be sure. Is your Social Insurance Card handy?"

"It's in my wallet."

"Could you get it?"

George slid out of bed and dug his wallet from the right back pocket of his rumpled trousers discarded on an adjacent chair. "Okay, here it is."

"Could you read the nine-digit number?"

"Okay." George read off the nine-digit number in groups of three.

"Could you repeat that?"

"Sure." George carefully reread the number.

"Good. Now listen very carefully. Are you ready?"

George switched the phone over to his right ear. "I'm ready." An eternity lapsed as if it were only a mortal moment.

"... *MC – 68: Code Black!*"

The phone slid from George's grasp. The dial tone filled the silence.

"Who was that!" Sarah intruded, suddenly wide-awake.

George's eyes glazed over. He was no longer good ol' George Webster Brown, retired Army veteran. He was *a Manchurian Candidate.*

* * *

Sometimes in somber moments
As fleeting as the air we breathe
We vaguely recollect
    Distant memories
Of a time when we once soared freely
High above the clouds
In realms where the past fused with the future
To create a mortal moment
As miraculous as the present

- LB

CHAPTER ELEVEN

DREAMS AND SCHEMES

The truth is often
Staring us in the face
Like a fugitive
Hiding in plain sight.

There was a low stuck off the Coast rotating in a counterclockwise direction that brought in wave after wave of icy cold Arctic weather. For two days the wind blew in sheets of fine drizzle that misted Steveston with a dampness fit only for ducks and green winter flora. Lenny waited two days for the weather to cooperate – it didn't. So, in spite of the intermittent wind and rain Lenny Bruce, dressed in his blue plaid lumberjack coat, Blue Jays' baseball cap, and tan leather gloves, appeared on the scene carrying a rolled-up black umbrella.

Why would any elderly person walk down a boardwalk with his hands clasped meditatively behind his back like an old Chinese sage? It suited Lenny's demeanor and frame of mind; there was solace and a kind of recalcitrant poetry infused in the mortal moment. He ambled along, *a movement and a rest* inculcated into every gentle step forward: heel and toe pause, heel and toe pause, heel and toe....

Like a gentle breeze upon an ambient landscape, poignant memories slowly drifted by with each heel and toe step. Lenny thoughtfully ambled into his past. It was like magic. In his memory he was once again a curious young man with a purpose. What purpose? Had he always been on some sort of subconscious spiritual mission? Had the mission become any clearer... as the passing years transformed his hair from mousey brown to peppery white and the spring in his footsteps slowed to a movement and a rest?

All those wonderful thoughts and ideas accumulated over the decades from thousands, if not millions, of other sentient beings – including his nocturnal advisor Eldorado Pena... they were all there, intermingled with his own ideas and manifested in the space-time endured with every step. A mortal lifetime nostalgically remembered in a passing parade of memories drifting by with each heel and toe pause.

Thus Lenny the Bruce could be seen on solemn occasions, a solitary figure slowly making his way along the plank boardwalk that once had extended as far as the now defunct Chinese store at the far end.

There was a time when the boardwalk bustled with life... before the visible-minority dubbed "enemy aliens" were uprooted, their boats and property confiscated and sold for next to nothing to pay for their internment in wretched camps hastily set up in the interior; before the canneries closed down; before BC Packers gave up the foreshore and the waterfront. Before the condos and the clutch of townhouses were built on the fourteen-acre site that once was home to a cultural mosaic of almost every possible variety of humanity. They all worked and lived there until Prime Minister Mackenzie King patriotically unfurled the dreaded War Measures Act.

The passing away of historical Steveston happened right under Lenny's nose, but he was too preoccupied with more mundane things to smell the decadence of its passing. He had vague recollections from his childhood, and as a teenager he recalled only the sadness assuaged by the passing of time. People grew up, matured, and moved on; it just happened like the rising and ebbing tide. Was there a turning point when the rising tide began to ebb?

It took a long time for Lenny to realize that he was old. When he first retired he still felt useful and productive, but as time passed there was noticeably less and less bounce in his step. People treated him with deference, as if he were an *old man*.

He did not think of himself as really being 'old' until he took a crowded city bus to go to the Richmond Center shopping mall. A kindly young man jumped up and offered him his seat. "Is it that obvious?" he asked himself as he sat down gratefully. He did not feel as old as he probably looked. Oftentimes in his mind as he ambled slowly down the boardwalk, he was a vigorous young man with plenty of time to waste... so why hurry?

A lifetime of memories circulated as he strolled aimlessly along the boardwalk toward the sun that was attempting to break through the stubborn clouds. The rising sun reminded him of the time when he and his dad got up early in preparation for their journey to Pincher Creek, Alberta. It brought back poignant memories of the early rising in the quiet of the pre-dawn, the rattling of breakfast utensils, and the dim glow of the kitchen light. Early morning risings, especially in late spring or early summer, always felt like that to Lenny: as if he was preparing for a long journey. *What was so special about that journey?*

A sentimental feeling of nostalgia washed over Lenny as he sauntered along past Asayo and Otokichi Murakami's refurbished boat-shop and beautiful flower garden. He sat down on the wooden bench across the walkway. The flowers reminded him of the colorful purple and yellow pansies that grew adjacent to the driveway of his aunt's cottage in Pincher Creek. There was a young teenaged girl... yes, the comely girl with the red bathing suit whom he had saved from drowning: the one he could picture in his mind's eye as if she was still perched upon that rocky outcrop at the Canyon swimming hole preparing to dive into the shallow pool. He shivered as he re-lived the poignant experience. All his adolescent longings flooded into consciousness.

It was like an awakening. The moment was imprinted indelibly on his memory. It happened long ago in a little foothills town in southern Alberta called Pincher Creek.

He remembered the parting. In particularly he remembered his father returning in the fall to pick him up. What could he do? He was just a teen-aged kid; he had no control over the matter. He had to go back to Steveston. He recalled the heart-felt goodbyes, the silent tears, and the solemn drive west toward the setting sun. Next summer... was such a long way off.

That moment was locked indelibly in Lenny's long-term memory. It lingered on and on because there were powerful vibrations involved that resonated throughout the years. During his meditative strolls down the rickety old boardwalk the vibrations often filled his heart with a yearning to... return.

If he had, he might have met a withered old woman with long, wispy shoulder-length hair who now lived in the very cottage he had painted during that memorable summer. Everything was kept almost exactly as it had been when he was there. The yellow and purple pansies still bloomed cheerfully next to the lilac bushes adjacent to the driveway. The gardener was meticulous.

No doubt it helped to ease the inexorable passage of time... when she knelt prayerfully on her knees in the soft loam... tending her soul. She had stoically waited year after year after year... for his return. It would be a surprise. She often pictured it in her mind's eye when she gazed off into the distance: *A youthful Lenny riding his bike up the lane.*

Who knows the longings of the human heart?

She had waited... the young girl who dove into the canyon pool and struck her head on the rocky bottom. The one he had carried from the water with blood streaming from her hair and on whom he had frantically performed mouth-to-mouth resuscitation. The one he had anxiously prayed over, cried over. The one he had willed with all his might... to breathe. The one he had saved from drowning. She patiently waited for his return. She dreamed of it. She grew old... dreaming.

But Lenny never returned. Not once. Sometimes out of the blue he felt a sense of desperation as if time was running out and he was immobilized by inertia. And on those occasions he was often inundated by premonitions of a melancholy so profound he often felt like weeping.

Who knows how quickly time can traverse space? Is it not instantaneous? Are not the invisible vibrations of the human spirit synchronistic?

Perhaps someone in Pincher Creek felt like weeping too? Perchance that person was nostalgically gazing toward an ornate wood-burning fireplace on the mantel of which was situated an old windup clock that solemnly ticked away the seconds into years. Only in Alberta it would be an hour later.

* * *

Unbeknownst to most of his peers, Brad Bradley actually meditated once in a while. There was a spiritual side to his personality that most of his friends overlooked. He considered himself to be a freethinking individual with a mind of his own.

A number of influential service clubs and other societies sought his membership because he was a well-known lawyer with a true-blue Anglo-Canadian surname. After hearing him pontificate on obscure subjects such as the Philosopher's Stone and Alchemy, some of his peers harbored suspicions that he might be associated with the infamous *Illuminati*, a secret society supposedly banned in 1784... because in those olden days individuals and groups who based their ideas on reason and logic, instead of blind faith, were considered suspect by the Church. His peers were mistaken.

Neither was Mr. Bradley a member of the Free Masons, an all male fraternity that once attempted to recruit him. But he declined because he was not a joiner of clubs of any kind. He was sort of an aloof and introspective type of individual. He enjoyed his privacy. But that was not the quality that set Brad apart from his fellow lawyers. Brad had a certain demeanor that invited people to cozy up to him; even stray dogs and cats caught the vibe that caused them to look up at him with trusting eyes. Brad had a most generous spirit.

Generosity was not a trait that was prevalent or relevant in a dog-eat-dog capitalistic civilization where there was 'no free lunch'. Everything had a cost-factor attached... soup kitchens, thrift stores, and all types of social welfare included. Nothing was free. The concept of 'ownership' made the concept of 'sharing' almost redundant. Greed made the private hoarding of material wealth into a social virtue.

Such behavior amongst the affluent was accepted as the norm; thus Brad's wealthy peers were able to accumulate vast stores of economic wealth in the forms of real estate, stocks, bonds, and precious metals. Collectively, they controlled millions and millions of dollars that they secretly gloated over in private moments when they carefully scrutinized the balance sheet. They weren't exactly misers, but they had difficulty being generous. Thus Brad was able to garner the greatest share of accolades for doing the most pro-bono legal work for the firm.

What hastened Brad Bradley's evolution toward becoming such a generous spirit occurred in a dream that took place on his forty-ninth birthday. His wife bought him a new Toyota Solara with convertible top, and Brad was feeling unusually self-satisfied when he went to bed and enjoyed a sustained session of coitus before drifting off to slumber land. The excess sugar in the chocolate cake mixed in with three shots of single malt scotch produced a stupor that resulted in a most vivid nocturnal experience. Brad dreamed he had died and gone directly to the admittance-facility located just inside the pearly gates, which were actually made of wrought iron.

It was one of those slightly embarrassing situations. Brad sat in the waiting room that had "Admittance" painted over the entrance door. He was the only person in the room. It was a sterile, white room with no windows. The chair he was seated on was white plastic. In contrast, the opulent-looking dark brown leather briefcase he had brought with him seemed to be incongruent with the sanctity of the surroundings.

On a counter to his right was a wire bin with a sign that read: *"Please place all items into the bin that you did not have in your possession when you were incarnated into the Miracle Planet."*

Beside this sign there was a larger sign that read: *"Warning!!! Those who refuse to cooperate will not be admitted. When they are ready to give up those things that burden their spirit with the dross of ownership, they will be free to re-apply for admittance."*

Brad sat on the white plastic chair with his feet planted firmly upon the white ceramic floor tiles. He had brought title to all of his most coveted material possessions with him, possessions that had taken him a lifetime to accumulate. They were neatly organized in the expensive leather briefcase that he clutched securely on his lap.

After the passage of what seemed like a mortal lifetime, he carefully opened the briefcase and looked inside: everything was there: certificates, titles, and deeds to all his hard-earned stocks and properties, the proceeds of his life's work. He stared at the contents for what seemed like an eternity. His gaze fixated upon the large rolls of hundred dollar bills he had so carefully counted and secured with red rubber bands. He was especially loath to give them up. He clutched the briefcase as tightly as he had ever clasped anything. His knuckles gleamed white with tension and his mouth was set with grim determination. He sat stoically clutching his briefcase for what seemed like forever.

Slowly... ever so slowly he raised his head and gazed up at the white ceiling. Only it wasn't a ceiling. It was a white canopy, a canopy of light: an eternal light. His spiritual essence levitated into the light. He looked back and there he was, hanging on for dear life to his leather briefcase... like a drowning man clutching a golden anchor.

Suddenly his entire body began to tremble and shudder; tears of remorse streamed from his eyes. How could he have been so blind? Had he not come into the world with nothing? Had he not been given everything? Was not his existence a divine expression: a mortal miracle? Had he not been gifted with the free will to further perfect himself? To realize a greater freedom? And what had he done? Ignominiously encumbered himself with a *belief* that made the contents of his briefcase more important than the tending of his immortal soul.

When his tears subsided he was overcome with a deep-seated sense of shame... for being so gullible and so ignorant. He squirmed with embarrassment. It all but consumed him. With the innocence of a contrite little child staring up at his benevolent parents, he slowly rose. With trembling hands he carefully placed his precious briefcase into the wire bin. He solemnly removed all his expensive garments and placed them on top of the briefcase. Brad Bradley stood there as naked and vulnerable as the day he was born.

Beside the wire bin was a simple white plaque inclined on a metallic gold stand that he hadn't noticed before. It was rectangular and trimmed with gold. Etched in simple gold print were the words: '*You may take your memories with you*'.

Brad humbly bowed his head with his hands clasped prayerfully before him. A mortal moment passed when he drew in a quiet breath. And then as if from a great distance he heard an empathetic voice quietly say: "*Well done, my son...*" and then he woke up.

* * *

Lenny the Bruce woke up with a yawn and a snort, rolled out of bed and sauntered into the bathroom. He looked at himself in the mirror and grimaced before disrobing and stepping into the shower. He turned on the water. The hydrotherapeutic effect of the pelting aqua revitalized his aging anatomy. He felt rejuvenated until he shut off the water, toweled off, and returned to the bedroom.

"You know?" Lana Bruce greeted her husband as he emerged from the bathroom like a hairless ape with shorter arms. "It is amazing that a primitive looking specimen like you has a brain that seems so advanced."

"You don't say." Lenny responded.

It really did seem quite odd, the integration of such a brain in such a primitive looking body. *Incongruent*, Lana thought, like integrating gold with a leaden alloy. She looked away feeling slightly embarrassed.

"Incongruent, eh?" Lenny asked, returning her gaze.

"What?"

"Sometimes your thoughts are uh-uh rather transparent."

"So... what else was I thinking?"

"Perhaps something to do with alchemy?"

"Close enough. It wasn't that long ago that long-bearded alchemists pondered the mysteries of the deep."

"You know?" Lenny reflected as he selected clean underwear from his dresser, Nostradamus was interested in alchemy."

"He was more of a star-gazer," Lana pointed out, "perhaps somewhat akin to the Mayans who gazed at the same skies an ocean away in Central America."

"When Nostradamus looked up at the heavens he saw more than was sanctified by the world-view of those entrenched in positions of Papal infallibility. He had to be careful of the manner in which he depicted what he saw, and the meaning of what was written in the constellations.

J T SAWADA

Consequently he drew complicated diagrams and wrote poetic quatrains with ambiguous meanings that foretold future events."

"He was a visionary who was ahead of his time."

"The vast universal sky was like a macroscopic mind entrenched in a fortune teller's crystal ball; when he peered into it he could see what had been, what was, and what would be. It was all there in the timeless heavens. *Nothing is created or destroyed, only changed or transmuted*: it was all there written in the stars… as far as Nostradamus was concerned."

"He made some astounding end-of-time predictions that the passage of time has given credence to," Lana commented.

"Nostradamus predicted that when the sun aligns with the center of the Milky Way Galaxy, this confluence of forces could have a dramatic effect upon the four dimensional reality membrane of forces that constitute the present or what-is. The tiniest change in the delicate balance of cosmic forces could result in cataclysmic consequences. Tweaking the membrane could change the balance and counter-balance of forces dramatically… resulting in something as dire as a polar shift."

"A polar shift, you say?"

"This type of galactic alignment occurs once every 26,000 years. And it was 26,000 years ago that the dinosaurs perished."

"Sounds ominous," Lana retorted. "Numbers like that are hard to dispute. They give us a feeling that there is a predictable uniformity and harmony in the universe that can be rationally understood."

"Symbolically we have used the circle to represent our concept of unity because a circle is complete in itself with neither beginning nor end. The circle encompasses a mathematical universe."

"How so?"

"Consider the mathematical concept known as 'pi'."

"Grade ten math." Lana boasted.

"It is a mathematical constant whose value is the ratio of any circle's circumference to its diameter."

"Which is precisely the same value as the ratio of a circle's area to the square of its radius, the radius being half the length of the diameter," Lana expounded showing off her grade ten math.

"The ratio of a circle's circumference to its diameter is 22 to 7. This ratio represents the mathematical constant known as pi. Pi is an irrational number which means that its value cannot be precisely known because its decimal representation never ends… making it a transcendental number which implies that no finite sequence of algebraic operations on integers such as powers, roots, sums etc. can represent its absolute value – simply because it does not seem to have an absolute value. Try it; divide seven into twenty-two," Lenny urged.

"I tried it," Lana replied, "and I got 3.14159265… and on and on into infinity with no end in sight, so it seems. As far as I know the current record for the decimal expansion of pi stands at five trillion digits!"

"You know Lana, there is far more significance to this concept of pi than most folks are aware of?"

"There is? Please elaborate."

"When we realize that pi represents the imperfection of the circumference, area, and volume of a sphere - or for that matter the entire universe - we awaken to the possibility that the never-ending decimals of pi are analogous to our expanding universe. It represents in numerical fashion, the logical conundrum of creation.

"Of what?"

"Creation."

"Please explain!" Lana exclaimed.

"The mathematical formula that provides us with an inkling of what is entailed in the creation process, is logically represented by the cascading decimals of pi. The amazing thing is… *pi only exists in the minds of people like you and me.*"

"Unlike apple pie, you cannot touch, taste, or smell it."

"Exactly. It is only an abstract idea - an esoteric thought conjured up by human beings with large brains, a mathematical formula that boggles the minds of all rational thinkers by being irrational. It is this mysterious irrationality, manifested in quantum physics as the Uncertainty Principle, that constantly plagues rational man's feeble attempts to quantify the universe with mathematical formulas that are as precise as the mathematical constant known as pi."

"Humble pi," Lana retorted, as she got up from the bed and went to make breakfast.

"The concept of pi is indeed humbling," Lenny replied as he slowly pulled on his trousers. "Perhaps it is analogous to the ever- expanding universe of knowledge that unravels before us."

"Somewhat like our karmic destiny... forever unraveling like the cascading decimals of pi, in search of ever more significant memories of an ever elusive dream of perfection?"

"Yeah. Something like that."

* * *

Lana was something of an introvert as a teenager. She kept her thoughts to herself mainly because she felt that her pseudo-devout Presbyterian parents were a little out of touch with the times. What did they know about intimate sexual matters, the very hint of which turned their faces beet red? Dare she approach them for advice?

In grade seven Lana walked around like a hunchback endeavoring to disguise the overt signs of her sexual development and maturity. Who knew she was now ready for sexual intercourse? Of course Lana knew... and instead of being proud of her newly emerging womanhood – it caused within her a dissonance that filled her with an embarrassing sense of shame. This personal sense of embarrassment connected to anything of a sexual nature, became the bane of her existence as she matured into a healthy biological life form - a life form that recent DNA analysis has scientifically confirmed; she was a distant descendant of the extinct Neanderthal with whom one of her ancient ancestors must have had coitus. And here she was, a splendid specimen of *Homo erectus* struggling for survival amongst the fittest, and ready to reproduce the species... in Richmond, British Columbia, Canada.

This embarrassing, life-negating sense of shame followed Lana wherever she went. It weighed upon her like a protective suit of shiny armor that guaranteed her virginity - until she met her future husband to be: Lenny the Bruce. Somehow he made her feel proud. How fortuitous! And she was only a senior in high school at the time. Fortunately she was open-minded.

In later years, long after they were married with a child - and most of the shame and embarrassment had worn off - they were able to discuss the topic in a sensible and adult manner.

"Your neurosis is analogous to transmuting gold into lead", Lenny had pontificated late one night after Lana had awakened from a particularly embarrassing dream in which she had gone to school wearing only her white sneakers!

The thin line of esoteric logic that connected Lana's Freudian fixation to the Philosopher's Stone was tenuous at best, but once she heard her husband expound upon it, the seemingly far-fetched actually seemed to make sense. "You've been encumbering yourself with a primordial concept that equates anything sexual with sin," he had said. "Via the alchemy of Original Sin the purity of your spiritual nature has been insidiously transmuted into something flawed, corrupted, vile and sinful."

"Let's not get too carried away, dear," Lana cautioned.

"A point well taken," Lenny responded as if he were a lecturer in a class full of seminary students. He paused and looked at his spouse before recommencing. "You could say that your sexual neurosis is an existential illusion."

"An illusion?" Lana parroted.

"Yeah, an illusionary self-concept regarding your existential status as it has evolved in the collective unconsciousness of Western Christendom. It lurks about in your dreams and pervades your behavior. Your inhibitions are an example of the influence of the concept of Original Sin on your psyche. There is a dissonance there that results in your personal embarrassment about perfectly natural biological functions."

"I see," Lana acknowledged.

"As you were born and raised in this society it is little wonder that you associate natural biological functions relating to urination, defecation, and, copulation with sin. Subconsciously you relate these functions with feelings of guilt and degradation. In Western Christendom this is not at all uncommon. Millions of folks have similar feelings. You are far from being unique in this matter."

"That is somewhat consoling."

The trigger event that finally enabled Lana to get a handle on such an amorphous neuroticism occurred when she was watching the late news on CBC and her favorite news-anchor, Peter Mansbridge, reiterated the tragic story of a slightly older than middle aged Canadian citizen, an immigrant from Afghanistan and a devotee of the Judaic-Christian-Muslim tradition. According to Peter, the man concerned, along with his only son, had drowned his three beautiful teen-aged daughters because they had become an embarrassment to him.

"Some embarrassment!" Lana mouthed aloud at the time. It gave her an inkling as to how deep-seated her personal embarrassments might be.

If the story had been a fictional novel, most publishers would have rejected it out of hand as being too far-fetched. But it was not fiction. The killer - a wealthy Canadian citizen - carried out the cold-blooded, premeditated murders with a clear conscience and a righteous demeanor. Why? Because as his three precious daughters grew up to become comely teenagers in a multi-cultural Canadian environment, they began to behave like normal, healthy Canadian teenagers: they attracted boyfriends!

"Boys, who probably found such beautiful girls to be sexually desirable," Lana conjectured.

In the dogmatic depths of their father's righteous religious convictions such behavior was an intolerable embarrassment: a sin of unforgivable magnitude. As an upstanding devotee of a religion that could trace its roots all the way back to the twelve tribes of Israel in ancient Egypt, the father of the three innocent Canadian teenagers performed his righteous duty: *he made the ultimate sacrifice*!

What he had done was a *sacrifice* reminiscent of God's request that Abraham sacrifice his precious son Isaac on Mount Moriah as an ultimate test of his faith – only in this case there was no burning bush, no respite – only the righteous doing of one's sacred duty... *before the One True God.*

"The main difference between the two situations is this," Lenny had pointed out; "we cannot be absolutely sure that Abraham – unlike his latter-day Islamic counterpart - would have had the courage of his convictions to carry out the ultimate sacrifice. Perhaps as his knifed hand hovered above Isaac's heart he might have said: *"No God of mine would command me to commit such a sacrilege!"*

To the vast majority of those listening to the solemn intonations of Peter Mansbridge, such behavior was evaluated in terms that had nothing to do with the moral implications associated with Abraham's biblical performance. And yet it happened, as did 9/11 years before: a premeditated act, carefully planned in advance, and executed with courage, determination, and commitment to the *One True God* came to pass. Why? The 'burning bush' of reason had been snuffed out by centuries of religious indoctrination.

Shocking? Yes. But throughout the ages other atrocities have been righteously committed in the holy name of the *One True Monotheistic*

God of the Judeo-Christian-Muslim tradition. Countless numbers of innocent victims have been tortured, burnt alive at the stake, drawn and quartered, crucified, shot, gassed, and exterminated by the millions in death camps by righteous sinners piously performing their 'duty'.

And over the centuries only the pagans, the heathens, the excommunicated, the blasphemers, and the ignominiously discredited like Galileo, Copernicus and a handful of other free-thinkers, have bolstered up the courage to question the immorality inherent in such impious acts of retribution and sacrifice, that in the cultural milieu of their times… *had been condoned by the powers that be.*

"What is wrong with us?" Lana asked with a growing sense of exasperation, speaking up on behalf of the three murdered teenaged girls, and all Canadian women. "Are we that unaware of who we really are? Or are we just that ignorant? That ignorant… and that gullible!" she added for emphasis.

* * *

Pena dropped in on January the fifth for a brief but important visit. It was 2:27 am. He always arrived when Lenny was asleep. "When you are asleep your consciousness is more in tune with incoming vibrations," he once explained.

Lana was curled up on her left side spasmodically snoring in fits.

Lenny heard the disembodied voice. His ears perked up; at least he thought they did. Sometimes Lana's snoring interfered with incoming vibes. "That you, Eldorado?" he said.

"Who else? Just popped in to give you some advice."

"About what?"

"You've been praying a lot lately, haven't you?"

"How'd you know?"

"I hear things."

"I'm not the only one who prays. People all over the world pray. It seems natural, especially when one is faced with great adversity. So what is your advice?"

"Think about what motivates you to pray."

"Motivates me?" Lenny inquired as if the question was asinine.

"Did you know that prayer is at the heart of all religious sentiment?"

"I never thought of myself as being all that religious – but I do pray a lot," Lenny confessed.

"All religious sentiments are born of insecurity, doubt, fear, despair, and a mortal awareness of the nihilism of death. Death hovers over every mortal being like a phantom question to which there does not seem to be a rational answer."

"And so we are motivated… to pray?"

"Prayer is an acknowledgement by man's microcosmic brain that there is an omniscient macrocosmic MIND of which it is a miniscule part, and to which it is beholden. Prayer is mostly motivated by man's self-interest and inspired by hope."

"You don't say!"

"It is in this context that prayer is a meaningful behavior. Prayer is a holistic endeavor that brings into play the relationship between freedom and free will, and between free will and belief. Prayer is related to one's beliefs. It gives rise to what has been referred to as the placebo effect of believing; it manifests the subjective power of one's beliefs. In large groups, such as in churches and congregations, the vibes can be psychologically uplifting and edifying. Ritualized prayer combined with religious dogma amplified by the collective hopes, desires, and dreams of the true-believers can be very powerful indeed."

"Imagine the collective economic, political, and spiritual influence of the collective known as the JCM hegemony that presently dominates the West and is making major inroads into the East, especially China. Imagine all those people praying!" Lenny exclaimed.

"Imagine the collective power of their prayers."

"What are they praying for?" Lenny asked as if suddenly alarmed.

"Prayer brings into play what has been called the *Law of Attraction*. What is presently being manifested upon the face of the earth… is all man-made. Think about that. Why this particular competitive, parasitic, consumer-driven, neurotic, materialistic version of reality?"

"You get what you hope and pray for?" Lenny threw out a wild guess.

"Like I said before, you are no fool. Look about you. What do you see?"

"Vast economic disparities; opulence in the midst of abject poverty, disease, malnutrition, starvation, and death; terrorism, war, and religious conflict; the ravages of pollution and climate change; a world that seems to be oxymoronically praying for its own salvation while hastening its demise."

"This being the case it is important that you learn how to pray properly!"

"What?"

"You haven't learned how to pray properly - yet."

"I haven't?"

"You're always demanding or asking for things. And even worse, you usually start your sentences with the word 'I'."

"I do?"

"You say: 'I want this', or 'I would like that'. Your prayers are a proverbial litany of 'egotistical-I' statements."

"Sor-ry. I had no idea my prayers were coming across in such an egregious manner."

"You know that old saying: 'Gimme, gimme, never gets'?"

"I used to say that to my daughter."

"There is actually something to it."

"You don't say! So, how should I pray?"

Eldorado hesitated a moment as if in thought. "It surprises me that a perceptive character like you has not twigged onto this long before now, but I suppose just like everyone else, you are far from perfect."

"You hit the nail on the head there," Lenny humbly acknowledged. "So how should I pray?"

"Always begin by giving thanks and being grateful," Pena stopped and waited for some response from Lenny.

After about fifteen seconds Lenny asked the simpleton's most effective question: "Why?"

"Gratitude begets gratitude. It is the universal Law of Attraction."

"Huh?"

"In a universe of infinite probabilities, the Law of Attraction is the modus operandi: freedom begets free-will, which begets belief, which begets prayer, which begets the placebo effect... of prayer. It is fundamental to the concept of karma: you reap what you sow. This includes the contents of your thoughts as well; remember that."

"Profound indeed! I never conceived of the concept of karma as being that simple. We attract our own destiny: we reap what we sow... only most of the time we are unaware of what we are sowing. We sow greed and selfishness – and expect to reap generosity."

"Like I said, you are a perceptive person, so it is no surprise that you find this to be illuminating."

"So… how exactly should I pray?" Lenny asked timidly.

"Do you need me to actually demonstrate how you should pray?"

"I may not be as smart or as perceptive as you think I am," Lenny pointed out with a self-effacing smile. "I am prone to making stupid mistakes that fill me with embarrassment even months and years after I have made them. I don't want to put you on the spot, but I would greatly appreciate it if you would just … demonstrate how I should pray."

"You want me to tell you… exactly what to say?"

"Yes I do. It's possible that I am that dense!" Lenny replied contritely.

"That dense," Eldorado drew in a deep breath. "Hmm… the problem is… words are morphemes that can convey a multitude of nuances, feelings, attitudes and meanings. The same words can mean different things to different folk. Prayer is much more than just words!"

"I see the difficulty," Lenny acknowledged. "So in general terms, how should I pray?"

"Well, to begin with, it is of ultimate importance that you clearly understand that praying is a creative endeavor."

"A what?" Lenny inquired.

"A creative endeavor. It entails the existential-essence of the karmic relationship between your free-willed microcosmic brain and the Freedom of the macrocosmic Mind."

"Huh?"

"Prayer is an expression of free will. And what is free will? What is Freedom? What is the difference?"

"You tell me," Lenny replied with a baffled expression.

"Ever heard that phrase: *the same difference*?"

"What?"

"First of all, Freedom is a pseudonym for ETI or *everything-there-is*. ETI is made up of an infinity of parts, which constitute the whole. Prayer represents the spiritual connection between the microcosmic part, and the macrocosmic whole. When one prays, one must be mindful of this relationship.

"Now I understand what you meant when you said that words are morphemes that can imply a multitude of meanings etcetera," Lenny acknowledged with a shake of his head. "And yet we need to use words to express meaning."

"Meaning! You said it. It is all about meaning! The relationship between the part and the whole is all about meaning. That relationship is constant. Constant," Pena reiterated. "It is constant and essential. Why? Because the part... is part-of-the-Whole and is therefore constantly involved in the process of creating a more wholesome Whole. Get it?"

"Sort of... it has to do with intention. It is the sentiment that counts."

"You are certainly nobody's fool, my friend," Pena appraised. "In short, when you pray... you are unwittingly praying to your *wholesome-Self.*" Eldorado paused to give his friend time to assimilate the sublimity of this idea.

"Somehow something that simple – escapes us! So, again, how should I pray?" Lenny asked, undermining Eldorado's appraisal of him.

"Gratefully. Gratitude is what becomes manifest as the placebo effect of belief..."

"Placebo effect of belief?" Lenny interjected as if confounded by the notion.

"What is belief? Think about it. Belief gives meaning to meaning. It is what provides rationality to consciousness. It is implicit in all meaningful human experience. It imbues the whole with significance, which in turn imparts meaning to the parts. It is that which predisposes sentient beings to pray... prayer being a creative endeavor."

"I see," Lenny responded like a blind man whose sight had been partially restored.

"Remember, you will reap what you sow; so when you pray, ask yourself: What am I sowing?"

"I see the difficulty. If, for example, I *ask for something*, especially material things... I am sowing the seeds of *neediness* - right?

"And you will reap neediness!"

"Makes sense," Lenny acknowledged.

"Be aware of what your prayers represent: they represent who you are and what you desire to become. You are constantly creating your wholesome-self."

"I will inevitably reap what I sow..."

"Indeed you will. You are free to experience the freedom of being your own creation."

"Say again!"

"*You are free to experience the freedom of being your own creation!* In other words, you are always becoming what you are praying for! After all, the *Whole* is made up of the sum-of-the-parts… and you are one of the *parts*. So… what are you, as one of the participants, creating?" Pena lapsed into silence.

"This?" Lenny asked with eyebrows raised.

"What else?"

* * *

Lana had an attractive backside that she liked to accentuate by wearing dresses that pulled in at the waist. She wore such a dress on the occasion that Rabbi Letenberg gave his noted soliloquy.

"Lovely dress," Father Bertolli had noted when Lana arrived with her husband in tow. The comment made Lana blush because she was not used to receiving such compliments.

"Oh, it's nothing… just something I found in the back of the closet. Haven't worn it in years. Should have donated it to the Thrift Store long ago… but here I am… wearing it," Lana replied in a self-deprecating tone as if she needed to humiliate herself.

"You look exquisite tonight!" Cathy chimed in as she approached. "New dress, eh?"

"Well, not exactly…"

It happened near the beginning of a meeting of the Motley Five, before Lenny had poured the wine that liberated the free flow of ideas. After the compliments about Lana's dress, someone had quoted a sentence from the Gospel of John that stated that *In the beginning was the Word, and the Word was with God, and the Word was God.* There was a lot of animated babble that filled the room with a heightened sense of expectation.

During this interval Rabbi Letenberg had sat silently in meditative composure. When there was an appropriate lull in the conversation he stood up. It was evident that he had been thinking deeply about something that elicited his unusual behavior. He had a Hamlet-like demeanor. If he had begun, 'To be or not to be…' it would have seemed appropriate. Instead he rubbed his hands prayerfully together and said, "Before we begin the evening's discussions, let me share some thoughts with you, thoughts that I have been harboring for some time now. You are probably the only motely crew who might find my thoughts to be somewhat, uh, edifying." He sat back down.

A hush fell over the group. They knew when to shut up and listen.

"In the beginning there was something called the 'Word'," Rabbi Letenberg began. "As you all know 'words' are abstract symbols or memes that convey meaning. It took billions of years for intelligence to evolve to the point where there could have even been a 'word'. That 'word' represents the beginning of what is now known as abstract thinking. According to evolutionists, it took over fourteen billion years for such a fundamental level of consciousness to evolve."

"That long, eh?" said Lana, turning to face the Rabbi who was sitting beside her.

"The 'word' as it is expressed in the Old Testament of the Holy Roman Bible, simply denotes the evolutionary status the human brain had achieved at that critical juncture of our development. It represents a level of awareness known as symbolic consciousness. Such a level of consciousness enabled one human being to communicate on a symbolic level with another using words. The awareness encapsulated within one skull could be shared with another, creating an ever-expanding universe of discourse, something like the ever-expanding decimals of pi. This universe of discourse was filled with abstract meanings that had neither mass, density, or substance."

"You are talking about *ideas* – right?" Lana clarified.

"One of these abstract ideas, as expressed in the universe of discourse that we are presently ensconced in, is spelled *G-d*, in English. In the beginning there was only the meme or unit of meaning, a universal sentiment that, according to Jewish religious authorities, some intuitive Hebrew youth named Abram attempted to give expression to as an abstract idea… even though the 'word' was considered to be *unutterable!*"

"An unutterable word," Cathy remarked. "What an oxymoron!"

"Of all the plant and animal life forms in existence, it seems that man is the only life form capable of abstract thought. In fact man has been described as the thinking animal; it is man's highest evolutionary achievement," Father Bertolli contributed.

"Thinking is an abstract process that requires symbols in order to be shared or communicated," the good Rabbi continued. "These symbols morph into morphemes or meaningful units called words, and words form the basis of language, which allows the meaning to be communicated from one brain to another. Without words, rational thought seems impossible. For example, when a baby is hungry, it does not think: 'I am hungry', because it cannot speak English. It simply cries and makes a fuss. We assume it must be hungry and feed it. The baby simply eats and falls asleep.

Dogs and cats behave like this. Dogs bark and cats meow. But a two-year old child, whose parents speak English, can eventually say: 'I'm hungry'." The good Rabbi paused and gazed about the group.

"Sounds, meaning... words, language. It seems every human culture has evolved to a level that enables this facility," Lenny commented.

"This is a tremendous evolutionary accomplishment," the good Rabbi continued. "It is the difference between being human and simply being an animal. This ability requires a brain that has evolved to a point where it is capable of being self-conscious; this awareness is the beginning of wisdom. Humans have evolved the largest brain, the only brain thus far that is capable of an entirely new level of consciousness associated with having developed an affinity for reflection."

"You have been thinking!" Cathy expostulated.

"As Lenny has intimated, thinking is an expression of abstract reasoning manifested as symbolic consciousness. Such a consciousness represents the apex of our fourteen billion year evolutionary development from hydrogen gases torn off from the sun to thinking organisms. For billions of years our evolution was seemingly arithmetic: it progressed in a linear and mechanistic manner that can be traced by examining the fossil record. With the advent of a symbolic consciousness, man's evolutionary development has progressed geometrically. This has changed the scope and breadth of our potentiality to create. Thinking enables us to realize a reality that is limited only by thought – and not by the laws of physics."

"Think about that!" Father Bertolli exclaimed impressed by his Jewish friend's exposition.

"A whole lot... of food for thought," Cathy rhymed by accident.

"On a world-wide basis, using the Internet, every brain can be interconnected to every other brain creating a collective cloud of consciousness that enables the present age to participate in a knowledge base that would have been unthinkable a scant hundred years ago," Lenny rejoined. "Such knowledge mixed alchemically with silicon can produce microchips of artificial-intelligence that can store the memories of generations of thinkers, and this worldwide storehouse of information can be accessed with the click of a mouse."

"As the ancient Mayans have predicted, commencing near the end of the year 2012 a new age of enlightened awareness will begin to unfold," Lana pointed out.

"Yes," the good Rabbi agreed. "We are in it now. It is all about us. We are part and parcel of it. I gives us expression and definition. It enables us to have this conversation. We as a species have risen to a new level of conscious awareness that enables us to-to... not only utter and discuss - but to argue, fight, murder, and terrorize each other... all in a vain and righteous attempt to ascertain the ultimate meaning of the unutterable word."

"The new age is just dawning!" Lenny concluded optimistically.

* * *

Sometimes a special type of light emerges from the unknown that belies the kind of rationality that most folks have become accustomed to as being normal. But due to his near-death-experience Lenny the Bruce was one of a very few seemingly normal humans available on planet earth who could receive epistles from beyond. Unbeknownst to Lenny, his nocturnal advisor, Eldorado Pena had vouched for him as being not only intelligent and open-minded, but also highly reliable. Reliability was very important to Pena's associates. On planet Earth there were so many closed-minded souls! Attempting to communicate with them was not only frustrating but all but impossible

So it came to pass that on the late evening just prior to Easter Monday Eldorado materialized out of the vastness of the unknown. "Peenya here," he announced.

"Eldorado?"

"Who else? Yeah it's me, Eldorado Pena. Remember me?"

"A forgettable name like that? Nevertheless it stuck in my mind, especially the Peen-ya part," Lenny replied good humoredly.

"Good on ya, as the Aussies say. Did my associate write to you yet?"

"What associate?"

"Oh, never mind. I just thought he might have by now. Anyway he will. He always keeps his word. I told him you might be able to help him set the record straight."

"What record?"

"You'll understand when you receive the epistle."

"What epistle?"

"You'll know when you get it." Pena paused as if reflecting upon whether or not he had said enough about the matter. "Anyway, it will be obvious..."

"Okay," Lenny responded robotically as if totally baffled.

"I know much of what I share with you must seem inane and baffling, even to one with your paranormal gifts. It is an awesome condition."

"What condition?"

"The human condition. It is a condition that is simultaneously mundane and miraculous. You laugh and cry; you love and hate; you live and die."

"We exist like dumb brutes with a modicum of intelligence. We have come a long way since we climbed down from the trees," Lenny pointed out.

"I must admit that you have come a long way. However, along the way you developed this dogmatic belief that has created a kind of dissonance that prevents many of your fellow human beings from reaching their full potential."

"Full potential?"

"Yeah. Most of you are not able to-to... share altruistically with good intentions."

"Share altruistically... with good intentions?"

"Easy to say, I know - but for most of you folks, very difficult to do... given your present predilections."

"You don't say."

"However, you, my good friend, seem to be an anomaly of sorts. There is an aura about you that is rather exceptional. I think it could be something as simple as your attitude... and willingness to share your ideas, that inclines you toward a higher ideal."

"Higher ideal you say?"

To me evolution denotes a progression to a higher, more spiritual existential status – rather than a fitness for brute, mortal, biological survival."

"Please elaborate."

"I'm not sure you will be able to fathom..."

"Try me!" Lenny challenged.

"All matter consists of vibrations. This energy is constantly changing: it can transmute into a higher more transparent state - or into a denser more opaque state. The Philosopher's Stone alludes to a transmutation analogous to this when it seeks to find ways to change a base metal like lead into a more refined state like gold. Like the first law of thermodynamics states: nothing is created or destroyed... only reconstituted, changed or transmuted."

"I get it. Reality is constantly changing or reconstituting itself relative to the machinations of the free-willed parts that determine what will become manifest. Right?"

"Close enough. Not so long ago this process was referred to as alchemy. Using that paradigm you could say that in recent millennia, human evolution has become somewhat… regressive."

"Indeed, there seems to be a lot more lead around here – than gold."

"Unfortunately there has been an evolutionary *descent* toward the low vibratory status of crass materialism, which at this time in your karmic evolution… seems natural."

"Natural – eh?"

"It seems natural to most of you – but to me, well, I've been there, done that… so it is nothing new."

"You've been here… and done what?"

"I've seen the spiritual consequences of-of those burdened by the crass materialism of lead – attempting to embellish themselves with the refinements of gold."

"Are you implying that there could be, or could have been, other less materialistic-oriented lifestyles… other than what is presently being manifested here on earth?" Lenny cautiously inquired.

"There are many various styles-of-life that human beings have the capability of manifesting. They range from the opaque grossness of a dense materialistic plane of existence to the sublime spirituality of a more ethereal plane. In between lies an infinity of mortal states of cognitive awareness. What you become conscious of… determines your existential status."

"And what are we currently conscious of that is causing us to manifest this?"

"Your beliefs. Especially your belief in Ancestral Sin. As you know… when I was there, some righteous, pious believers took our gold and called us sinners and ignorant pagan savages. They callously murdered, plundered and destroyed our civilization in search of material wealth. Who were the real savages? Who were the fools besotted by little golden pebbles of metal? It was, as they say: *fools' gold*! Believe me. It came to pass. It is locked indelibly in my memory!" Eldorado vented.

"You have my complete sympathies," Lenny commiserated.

"Pardon my outburst," Pena apologized. "Some things just stick in your craw. My memory is chock-full of esoteric ideas, but some ideas become emotionally charged, especially if an injustice is perpetrated."

"Understandable."

"Speaking of *justice*..." Eldorado paused pensively as if he had just remembered something of vital importance that he needed to clarify.

A pregnant silence filled the room as if ready to give birth to an outlandish idea. Lenny was filled with anticipation. "Yes?" he prompted impatiently.

Pena gazed steadily at his nocturnal friend. "I've been thinking of late that it would be *just* if ah-ah you would treat all of these ideas that we have been discussing as if..."

"As if what?" Lenny interjected.

"Well as if... *as if they were yours*," Eldorado whispered as if sharing a confidence.

"But they aren't mine – they are yours!" Lenny protested vehemently, caught off guard by the ridiculousness of the proposition.

"Of course they are yours," Pena countered solemnly as if he had already given sober thought to the idea.

"How so?" Lenny asked, flabbergasted by the notion.

"I don't exist."

"What?" Lenny followed up.

"I'm just a phantom in the night, a figment of your imagination, a disembodied voice, a personified thought, an abstract idea..."

"Don't try to bamboozle me with such verbosity!"

"Believe me. I'm serious! Given the skeptical nature of most folks when it comes to paranormal events - suffice it to say... most folks would not take you seriously, if you mentioned the likes of me."

"Of course you are kidding."

"They would probably just heap laughter and ridicule upon you – rather than consideration and understanding..."

"Yeah..." Lenny acquiesced as it dawned upon him that his mentor could be right.

"That is why I need to ask you to do me one very kind favor."

"No problem... just mention it," Lenny replied soberly.

"Like I said before... could you take credit for... ah... all of these various ideas we have been discussing as if... well, as if they are yours?"

"But they aren't mine - they are mostly yours!" Lenny reiterated.

"Think of it this way." Eldorado paused to cogitate. "Your dreams are your own - right? Therefore the contents of your dreams are also your own. I am only a part of the contents. Make sense?"

The logic slowly illuminated the opaque depths of Lenny's limited awareness. He looked up toward his mentor with baleful eyes and opened his mouth as if to reply, but was inexplicably overcome with feelings akin to experiencing the death of a kindred spirit. Suddenly tears began to well up and dribble down his cheeks unimpeded. A great sorrow descended as he bowed his head as if standing by the graveside of a beloved comrade.

The moment endured until Eldorado softly whispered, "This is not the end of our association. You, my dear friend, have been gifted with free will. Like I said, you are the creator of your own dreams. Look on the bright side. Perhaps together we will be able to manifest a beautiful dream. My prayers and best wishes go with you."

* * *

Free will is divine
Because it enables one to create
Something out of nothing
And call it an 'idea'
That exists
    Independently
From the creator who thought it up
In the first place
    And insisted
That it really was real enough
To be taken for granted
And accepted on blind faith
As being the one and only
Immortal idea
    Ever given expression to
By a mortal being
Gifted with free will.

\- LB

CHAPTER TWELVE

PEOPLE OF THE LIGHT

In the light
Of reason and common sense
We have been able to reach
The infinite boundaries of the manifest
Where everything-there-is
Makes up the whole
Which is constantly on the verge
Of being perfected.

The autumn leaves had turned to shades of red, orange, and brownish-yellow. The ducks and geese had already flocked together and were on their way to warmer climes. The landscaper had put the flowerbeds to sleep for the winter. It was a lovely fall evening with just a hint of early frost. Lana and Lenny had invited the crew over for a potluck supper. The Motley Five assembled at Lenny and Lana's residence at 6:30 pm. It was October twenty-third. No one could have predicted that it would be the last time the Motley Five would meet together.

Lana and Lenny had prepared a succulent teriyaki chicken dish along with steamed rice and chow-mien noodles. Father Bertolli brought a baked Italian vegetable dish, while Rabbi Letenberg had made a healthy green organic salad accented with red cherry tomatoes. Cathy Schneider contributed a homemade angel food cake with white icing for dessert. Everyone was salivating by the time the Motley Five sat down at the dining room table that had been expanded with the insertion of an additional leaf. Candles were lit and ample glasses of red wine were poured to overflowing before Father Bertolli said grace.

"Thank you, dear God," he prayed, "for the nourishing food, the fellowship we share, and the loving-kindness that warms our hearts this fine autumn evening. Thank you for the compassion that vibrates around this table. May it resonate around the world. Amen."

Everyone echoed the "Amen". Lenny raised his goblet of wine and proposed a toast: "To the Motley Five: good health, long life, and much happiness!" Five goblets clinked. Lana passed the chicken around; other dishes followed. Everyone settled in, knife and fork in hand. Nothing much needed to be said for the time being.

After about seventeen minutes, Rabbi Letenberg opened the conversation by saying, "You know, I have been thinking..." he paused to sip his wine, "that the very act of thinking per se is a little understood process that has been described by terminology like 'knowing', or 'consciousness', or 'awareness'."

"Another of your deep philosophical insights?" Cathy responded absentmindedly as she filled her plate a second time. "As I vaguely recall at our last get together you waxed cloquent on a similar topic. As a matter of fact I believe I referred to it then as a 'soliloquy'. Remember?"

This remark alluding to the quality of his memory and the possible redundancy of repetition motivated the good Rabbi to continue undaunted. "Consider this if you will. We listen with our ears, we see with our eyes, we smell with our nose, we taste with our taste buds, and we feel with our fingers and skin. All of these sensations are transmitted via our central nervous system to the appropriate neurons housed in the command center of our biological body called our brain, where appropriate brain cells tune-in and process the information. But for whom?"

"Ah, I see the problem," Lenny responded. "The brain makes 'us' aware of the stimuli. But who is 'us'? Who is the 'I' who possesses the free-will that directs the brain to do whatever the brain does… and to whom the brain reports all this sensate information?"

"Exactly," Rabbi Letenberg replied, "that is precisely the difficulty that has baffled theologians, philosophers, scientists, and scholars over the ages. That unknown personality, often referred to simply as the 'beholder', to whom the entire vertebrate nervous system reports, in my humble opinion constitutes the Existent-Essence, or the invisible and immaterial Spirit-Soul that provides us with the free-will to create our respective identities."

"Indeed, you have been thinking!" Cathy exclaimed, impressed by the Rabbi's astute remarks. "But-but haven't we discussed something like this before?" she asked wrinkling up her nose. "The word homunculus comes to mind along with the concept of a ghost in the machine."

"You could be right," Lana asserted, "but at our age a little repetition doesn't hurt."

"Since the last time we met… I've been doing some serious research on the grand period of rational thought which the great German philosopher Karl Jaspers called the 'Axial Age'."

"Please enlighten us," Lana encouraged as she finished off her second glass of wine.

"The Axial Age extended from about 900 to 200 BCE. It was during that seven hundred year period that the 'I' turned inward and gave us what some have dubbed the 'wisdom of the ages'. During that pivotal period, the spiritual development of homo sapiens took a giant leap forward into a greater dimension of awareness. Since then, it seems we have sadly… regressed," the Rabbi lamented.

"That would be about 2500 years ago," Lenny calculated.

"Yes, about that," Rabbi Letenberg concurred. "That was the period of intellectual rationalism in Greece, monotheism in the Middle East, Daoism and Confucianism in China, Shintoism in Japan, and perhaps most significant of all, Hinduism, Buddhism, and Jainism on the Indian subcontinent."

"The intellectual and spiritual influences from that exciting age still resonate strongly with those open to the wisdom of the ages," Father Bertolli added, while munching on another leg of chicken.

"Indeed, this was the inspiring era of Aeschylus, Socrates, Ezekiel, Isaiah, Lao-tzu, Confucius, Siddhartha, and the Upanishads. Since then, we have never surpassed the existential and spiritual insights of the Axial Age!" Rabbi Letenberg pronounced. "The early Upanishads gave us the first inkling of the depths of the psychological insights these earlier thinkers were capable of. Long before Freud or Jung, they were bent on finding the 'ghost in the machine', so to speak, or the 'true self'. According to one of the most perceptive of these early wise men named Yajnavalkya: *'You can't see the Seer who does the seeing, and you can't hear the Hearer who does the hearing; and you cannot think with the Thinker who does the thinking; and you cannot perceive with the Perceiver who does the perceiving'*," the good Rabbi's eyes sparkled.

"So who or what is it that is aware of all of this?" Cathy asked.

"The supreme awareness is referred to as the Atman. The Atman is always there behind the scene at the heart of reality," the good Rabbi replied.

"Is the Atman a person?" Lana inquired.

"The Atman is a transcendental concept – not a person. It just so happens that in the English language the word 'Atman' contains the word 'man,' giving most Westerners the impression that the Atman is a person like Superman. The 'man' in Atman is no more significant than say... the 'man' in 'manure'; it is just the way the word is spelled in English."

"Nice comparison," Lenny commented as he finished off the last of the organic green salad with a relish. "Sounds like the Atman signifies the highest state of human awareness, or as you say, what lies at the 'heart of reality'."

"So what happened... that placed a damper on this great age of spiritual advancement?" Lana asked innocuously, causing everyone except the Rabbi to sit up a little straighter.

Rabbi Letenberg hunched over his plate as if he were still hungry. "A very good question," he intoned as he looked up at the others. "You know at first I hated to admit it - probably due to my religious upbringing and indoctrination."

"Admit what?" Lana pursued.

"That the primary idea that placed a damper, as you said, on this wonderful age of spiritual advancement was the promulgation of the archaic Judaic concept of Man as being a creature with a tragically flawed nature. For years and years I sat stubbornly in denial," Rabbi Letenberg admitted sheepishly – "but the historical facts spoke for themselves!"

"There is no denying that the Council of Nicaea occurred in 325 AD – even though the Catholic Church has been loath to admit its complicity in it. The Dark Ages soon followed," Father Bertolli added. "The sins of our ancestors washed over the great unwashed like a tsunami wave upon vast populations of mostly illiterate and beleaguered peasants, destitute villagers, indentured serfs, and the sick and diseased in dire need of otherworldly hope," the good Rabbi continued. "The newly formulated Christian theology appealed to the slave mentality of the great unwashed of the world. And most importantly its message was simple, unequivocal, and all-inclusive."

"How so?" Lana inquired.

"Everyone had a simple choice: believe in the recently fabricated Nicene Creed and be *saved* and enjoy everlasting life in heaven – or reject the Creed and be *damned* to burn eternally in the fires of hell. There were no exceptions: it was either – or. Who wouldn't choose to be saved? It was a no-brainer. Such was the persuasive power of the discursive logic inherent in the newly created Christian theology."

"Well said," Cathy interjected. "Every sincere Christian needs to verify this information for themselves because it is important that they know what really happened at the Council of Nicaea in 325 AD and thereafter. Anyone can validate what the good Rabbi has said on the Internet. I did. The truth is out there."

"The Judaic-Christian-Muslim monotheistic theology spread like a sickness from the Middle East to Europe, Asia, North and South America, and the entire world, snuffing out the Axial light of spiritual enlightenment and replacing it with a religious dogma that threatened any dissenters with a fate worse than death," Rabbi Letenberg plodded on. "What you see around the capitalistic world today is a far cry from being enlightened behavior. The Atman within has been repressed, stifled, and spiritually stunted by the overwhelming influence of the Judeo-Christian-Muslim theologies."

"Man, did you ever say a mouthful there!" Father Bertolli exclaimed as he refilled his wine goblet.

"Tragically we have lost the clarity of this earlier insight into the untainted spirituality of our human nature. The earlier sages, through deep meditation and introspection, discovered an innate altruism at the heart of reality. This spiritual notion did not accord with later conceptions of sin, greed, and selfishness, nor even with Darwin's theory regarding the survival of the fittest. Evolutionary theorists have anticipated a trend toward Man becoming more selfish, greedy, and egotistical – and less and less unselfish, generous and altruistic."

"If you examine the reality we have created about us, it is plain to see that human beings have become increasingly selfish and greedy. Many staunch capitalists even claim that greed in good!" Cathy pointed out in support of the Rabbi's statement.

"And sad to say," Father Bertolli sighed resignedly, "the fundamental concept of human nature upon which the Judaic-Christian-Muslim notion of morality is based, instills a very self-serving motive: to save oneself – even if the entire world is destroyed. Darwin's secular theory of the survival of the fittest seems to provide a rationale for this self-serving type of behavior. When the world is consumed in flames, what group will survive?"

"The fittest?" Lana offered.

"In their own minds the saved think of themselves as being the only ones *fit* for survival. They believe that they will be taken up and rewarded with everlasting life!" Father Bertolli adroitly answered his own question.

"A decade ago I would have felt much more constrained," Rabbi Letenberg confessed. "But today I must admit, I agree one hundred percent with what the learned Father has just said. From the JCM point of view the *saved* are the fittest. Why? Because they will survive eternally... in heaven."

"For a Rabbi, I must say you have demonstrated an unusual candor," Lana rejoined.

"Who said Rabbis can't be open minded?" Father Bertolli responded. "Labels like Rabbi and Father aside, we are just ordinary human beings searching for the Truth, just like the rest of you... you know? When I removed that white collar I felt liberated. Until then, I always felt like a dog on a leash tethered to the Vatican. But now, I speak my mind as I see fit."

The others clapped. Lenny proposed a toast: "To a more tolerant, compassionate, and enlightened world," he said with a benevolent smile. All glasses were raised, clinked together, and guzzled.

Thus ended the potluck supper. The motley five never met again as the Motley Five. They came together once more at a funeral, but on that sad occasion one of them was deceased. After that, they were the motley four… but it was never the same… without Lenny.

*   *   *

Lenny casually rolled over to his left side as if subconsciously attempting to amplify the clarity of incoming vibes. His biomass radiated an aura of gratitude and humility. His eyes flickered about as if in search of something profound. An enigmatic smile creased his countenance. Was it a premonition? Was he about to learn something stupendously significant? He resembled a curious little child with the covers pulled up to his chin.

Eldorado gazed upon Lenny as a concerned teacher looks upon an earnest student, with patience and understanding. After a long pause he began in a quiet and subdued tone, "Did you know that at one time in pre-recorded history, there were intelligent beings who existed on planet Earth who had been able to expand the scope of their awareness to a level where they were able to see the energy fields called auras that surround all vibratory life forms?"

"Pre-recorded history – eh? So how is it that you know this?

"A prescient sage with a scraggily white beard and long shoulder-length hair to match once appeared to me like I supposedly appear to you, and informed me about this-this uh… ancient historical happening. Consequently it is now a part of my long-term memory of things past, and soon it will become part of yours. Memory is non-material; therefore it endures. It has karmic significance. Hopefully we all can learn from the information that is shared with us… and move on."

"Sounds fascinating," Lenny wrinkled up his nose as if anticipating something worthy of such a reaction.

"I'll be as brief and as concise as I can, so concentrate on what I am saying. I think you will find this quite interesting. I sure did."

"I'm all ears," Lenny replied his eyes lighting up with anticipation.

"Thousands of years before this little bubble of modern, high-tech, civilization appeared, there were some highly evolved spiritual beings living in the area you now refer to as Tibet or the northern Himalayas."

"Where did they come from?"

"It is speculated that thousands of years ago their ancient ancestors had migrated from an unspecified location associated with what some of you folks refer to as a spiritual vortex."

"Certainly sounds mysterious. There has been some speculation of late concerning the existence of other possible dimensions of reality eliciting concepts like wormholes, and time travel. There are so many possibilities that come to light."

"There you said it!"

"Said what?" Lenny asked with a puzzled look.

"You said... *come to light*. What light?"

"The light of-of the sun? The light of day? The light of life?" Lenny speculated.

"All this speculation is meaningless unless there is a consciousness to whom the light is relevant," Pena pointed out.

"Very good point."-

"The ancient ones eventually came to believe that they were divine expressions of that light. They conceived of themselves as being the People of the Light."

"What difference did that make?"

"A world of difference: it changed their attitude toward the significance of the sun, and to the earth to which they owed their mortal existence and survival. They developed a spiritual outlook and a grateful attitude that enabled them to live in harmony with all the other life forms that were manifestations of the light."

"What did they look like?"

"The People of the Light were a sublime, happy, tranquil, and radiant lot. They were slender, with rather short legs, long dark hair and elongated skulls that contained a brain with a more evolved thalamus core. They were hardy and ethereal-looking folks who somehow managed to survive and multiply at a time so distant, it now seems more like the future – instead of the past."

"Sounds rather far-fetched," Lenny skeptically intoned, "but carry on."

"These ancient people enjoyed a serene and peaceful pastoral existence around a beautiful fresh water lake called Manasorovar at the base of a towering pyramid-shaped mountain historically known as Tise by the pre-Buddhists, Astapada by the Jains, Kang Rimpoche by the Tibetan Buddhists - and most recently as Mount Kailash."

"You don't say?" Lenny remarked, impressed by Pena's knowledge of the particulars.

"Lake Manasorovar is also known as the Lake of the Mind because of its placid spiritual beauty and life-enhancing qualities. A short distance away a crescent-shaped lifeless salt water lake named Rakshastal provides a sombre contrast."

"So these early peoples lived an idyllic life at the base of a mystical mountain where they had both fresh and salt water at their disposal. Perhaps that combination created a special electromagnetic vibration?" Lenny conjectured.

"As you know that northern global area is not the most hospitable for human habitation. Consequently over time these people came to realize that there was a sacred trust between the sun that energized them, the earth that sustained them, and their own wellbeing. They developed a natural and symbiotic relationship with the sun and the good earth that nourished and provided for them generation after generation. Although the word parasite was not known then, they realized that - being essentially parasitical - it was only through the sharing of Mother Nature's bounty, that they could survive; consequently their modus operandi, so to speak, was to exist in harmony with What-is."

"What is?" Lenny queried with a frown.

"What-is represents the vital energy that became separated from its origin, the sun, and became a separate entity. As you know, this blob of molten energy that was once part of the sun gradually cooled down to become manifest as Earth."

"It seems that almost everything that presently exists on planet earth comes from the sun," Lenny confirmed.

"Life-forms in particular, are directly and indirectly dependent upon the radiant energy from the sun for their existence and survival. The process is known as *photo...synthesis*." Eldorado syllabized the word.

"So?"

"All life forms are directly or indirectly dependent upon this mode of utilizing the sun's radiant energy along with minerals that once were part of the sun, to produce time-bound mortal manifestations presently vibrating as organic or living matter."

"Time-bound mortal manifestations?" Lenny queried.

"To mortals, all things take place in space-time. Indeed, time is of the essence. Time endures as an infinitude of mortal moments, and connotes the possibility of eternity. Photosynthesis is an essential aspect of an eternal process denoting a mortal form of awareness."

"What does that mean?"

"Sounds rather convoluted... I know. It means that all organic matter endures within the limits of the speed of light squared, making it finite, and therefore mortal. Energy from the sun provides the light. When inorganic materials like water and minerals vibrate at the speed of light squared in the presence of sunlight, as represented by the formula $E=mc^2$, guess what?

"What?"

"As if by magic the once inorganic matter begins to vibrate at a frequency that is greater than that which can be produced by the sum of the parts. This miraculous transformation can only occur in the presence of sunlight. Now do you understand why the sun is so important to us... and why the ancient ones thought of themselves as being the People of the Light?"

"They intuited that somehow they had become manifestations of-of the light?" Lenny suggested.

"But not directly," Pena corrected his friend. "Human beings must ingest the life-giving energy from the sun... indirectly."

"Why?"

"Ironically, human beings are not able to do what every tiny little green blade of grass can do. Human beings are not able to perform photosynthesis, thus requiring them to feed off of those life forms that can."

"Why do you think that is?" Lenny asked.

"Good question. All that you can do is to-to think about it... and ask: *Why not us?*" Pena smiled and stared at his friend as if awaiting the answer.

"Why not... us?" Lenny pondered with a perturbed expression.

"Think about it," Pena exhorted. "The ancient ones, the beautiful People of the Light, they knew. It was obvious to them – but perhaps it is not so obvious to you materially advanced folks... who believe you have dominion over the earth."

"What was obvious to them?"

"You have been incarnated upon planet Earth to learn a very simple, but essential karmic lesson."

"And what exactly is that?"

"To learn to share."

"Is that it?"

"*Think about it!*" Eldorado exhorted once again as if exasperated by Lenny's obtuseness. "*Why do you think you are parasites?*"

"Let's take a short break. This stuff is getting a little too esoteric, to say the least." Lenny rolled over to face Lana's alluring backside, which at that mortal moment went unnoticed and consequently unappreciated.

* * *

"Ready?" Eldorado inquired, taking note of Lenny's compromising position.

"Don't I look ready... for further discourse?"

"Not exactly. But as they say appearances can be deceiving, eh? Anyway...a long time ago before the word photosynthesis was even known, there existed beings, as I previously mentioned, who had evolved through eons of time to a spiritual state alluded to in some of your folklore as being magical - where the materialistic reality to which you presently relate, was considered to be not only gross and encumbering... but untenable."

"What type of beings are you referring to?" Lenny inquired, his curiosity rising.

"Very intelligent beings who used to call Earth their home." Eldorado paused and gazed at Lenny speculatively as if gauging his ability to comprehend what he was about to share. "You know, progress can be spiritual as well as material. Suppose you smart folks eventually manage to pollute and decimate Mother Earth beyond recovery in the name of modern capitalism – is that *smart?* Is that progress? Does that demonstrate a higher level of intelligence?"

"To many of us... apparently it does," Lenny admitted sheepishly, "that is why we are doing... what we are doing."

"There is still time… to learn from the past. As I said, long ago there were beings who would be denigrated as being pagans by most of you so-called civilized folks."

"Why pagans?"

"They admired the sun. To them the sun symbolically and existentially represented the primary substance and energy source for all life forms on earth, and it is, in fact, the continuing source of energy that enables *What-is* to be. As I previously indicated, these ancient folks with elongated skulls had brains to match - brains that had evolved in accordance with their spiritual development."

"So why are our brains less capable?"

"Relative to them – you have unfortunately taken a-a… regressive turn in the road, so to speak. It is as if you have gone backwards in time. Hmm… I'm not quite sure how to put this. This could be very sensitive stuff to a person of your intellect… and I do not want to offend."

"Try me."

"Your brain has developed in accord with the physicality of your four dimensional space-time membrane of forces. You relate to your reality via your vertebrate nervous system, which is sensory dependent. You have evolved accordingly."

"This accounts for our smaller brains compared with the ancient ones?"

"Not necessarily smaller – but qualitatively less efficient. It is indicative of your more limited interface with the spiritual as contrasted with the material. Your intellect has evolved in a manner that manifests the finite aspects of your parasitical relationship with the material realm."

"I see. Unlike us, the ancient ones evolved in a manner relative to their relationship to the spiritual realm. We are limited by the existential parameters of our own… limited state of awarness," Lenny stated succinctly.

"Something like that." Pena ruminated for a moment before spritely responding, "Perhaps an illustration will help make this clearer."

"Especially to a person with my limited understanding of such abstract philosophical matters," Lenny felt the need to humble himself for no apparent reason.

"After the passage of billions of earthly years in Eternity, an aberration of some significance happened in the Middle East as if it was a precursor of Darwin's concept of the survival of the fittest. A very imaginative Creation-Narrative as it is known today, along with a personified notion of a supreme deity, was realized by an enslaved people at a level of believability congruent with their existential status."

"Why is this significant?"

"It is significant... because it happened. It came to pass! It became a reality. Their relationship to the Supreme Deity became fixed at the cognitive level of awareness associated with the dogma promulgated and institutionalized as being the immutable word of God."

"The immutable word of God – huh?"

"As such, the archaic master-slave relationship became religiously entrenched and immutable. The great unwashed, gullibly accepted God as being a vengeful, chauvinistic, punitive Father Figure because they could easily relate to it. It suited their collective mentality. Such a deity was integral to their self-concept as sinners. And ever since, they have behaved accordingly," Eldorado elucidated.

"They have?"

"Consider, for example, the Temple Mount with the magnificent golden dome, located in Jerusalem," Pena suggested.

"The Judaic, Christian, and Muslim faithful are drawn to that place because of its spiritual vibration," Lenny commented.

"Indeed they are. You know, there is a great deal of spirituality imbued in that golden dome. To the ancient ones, the purity of gold symbolized not only the golden rays of the life-giving sun, but also the spiritual essence of the vibrations that energize the earth."

"I see. The golden dome symbolizes the golden sun that shines down upon everyone regardless of race, creed or religion," Lenny added.

"A simple and universal analogy overlooked by those who denigrate each other and the Temple Mount with their animosity and self-serving religious sentiments. No one has a righteous claim on the glorious sun that provides the energy that enables life to exist. Likewise, the Temple Mount should be shared and cared for by all who wish to visit that particular location."

"Very good advice, I'd say," Lenny concurred.

"The Temple Mount not only symbolizes the one and only glorious sun, the sun that lights up the earth as it revolves around it; it also symbolizes unity, wholesomeness, and Oneness."

"But what do we care?" Lenny scoffed on behalf of the great unwashed. "We worship the golden dome – not because it reflects the sun - but because of its archaic institutionalized religious dogmas.

"Look at the Temple Mount from the omniscient point of view of the Sun," Eldorado suggested. "What do you see?"

"A bunch of tiny ant-like figures encircling a golden sun-like dome and bobbing and bowing as if gratuitously paying homage and giving thanks to some deity."

"So it would appear, eh?" Pena smiled ironically. "But how do you actually treat those who respect the sun that provides the energy that photo-synthetically enables the miracle of life to exist on earth?"

"We denigrate them as being primitive, ignorant sun-worshippers!"

"Yet, that celestial orb, that provides all living life-forms with everything needed to sustain life, is more precious to you earthlings than *anything else you can conceive of.*"

"So obvious! And yet... billions of seemingly intelligent human beings prefer to righteously argue, terrorize, wage war, and sacrifice their lives in the name of some fearsome, imaginary, invisible *god* that has punitively reduced humanity into being a bunch of tragically flawed sinners. Go figure!" Lenny responded. "Whatever happened to common sense?"

The outburst caused Pena to lapse into momentary silence. After about ten seconds he quietly replied, "Their attitudes and beliefs dictate their behavior."

"They can do no other?"

"Their religious beliefs function like a magical spell or neurosis that confounds their free-will, and restrains them with dogma. Belief is a powerful force. And blind, dogmatic, institutionalized religious belief is very powerful indeed!"

"Ah," Lenny acquiesced. "Indeed, look at what is happening in the Middle East... as we speak."

"The People of the Light had evolved in a slightly different direction." Pena paused ominously. "Are you ready to hear about this?"

"Indeed I am."

"What I am about to share with you will probably challenge your credulity - so be prepared," Pena cautioned.

"I'm as ready as I've ever been," Lenny announced.

"It has taken you millions of years of evolutionary growth to develop a vertebrate sensory system that is hardwired, so to speak, to enable you to interface with a four dimensional space-time reality membrane of forces. The ancient ones related to their environment around Mount Kailash in a slightly different manner than you moderns; it was more of an attitudinal shift than anything else. Key to their spiritual development was their attitude toward the simple act of breathing. They were mindful that breathing provided the air – you call it oxygen – that enabled the body to manifest light."

"Didn't you mention something about the importance of breathing to our health and happiness... some time ago?

"I might have, but it is worth reiterating in this context. As you know, human beings require oxygen to burn the fuel that produces the vital force that lights up their world. Once they stop breathing, the vital force diminishes and the light fades. Consequently, the ancient ones were very mindful of their breathing. Being mindful of the vital importance of breathing on their health and happiness became the basis of a prayerful form of meditation."

"A prayerful form of meditation?"

"Every breath was a miraculous breath-of-life. Breathing to the ancient ones became a silent and ongoing prayer of gratitude and appreciation."

"As of yet the vast majority of us moderns still haven't cottoned on to the vital importance of breathing to our physical and spiritual well being," Lenny lamented. "We just take it for granted."

"Eventually the ancient ones realized that breathing energized them, and enabled them to radiate energy. Breathing differentiated the animate from the inanimate. When breathing ceases – what happens?"

"The animated becomes inanimate?"

"Correct." Pena paused to give Lenny time to reflect upon this.

"So?"

"The animate breathe. The inanimate do not breathe," Eldorado stated matter-of-factly.

"So what?"

"It takes a breath to say: *So what?* The inanimate may have a zillion questions – but they must remain mute. And then... for a mortal moment they are bestowed with a breath of life!"

"For a miraculous mortal moment in eternity... they can breathe!" Lenny exclaimed.

"And in that mortal moment they become aware of their miraculous existence." The statement hung in the air as if it was a self-evident truth.

"Ah!" Lenny began after a prescient lull. "Breathing is not only natural; it is essential."

"To the ancient ones breathing became a sacred spiritual endeavor that in combination with a grateful attitude, miraculously transformed them into the People of the Light. This mindset fostered an awareness and reverence for everything. Reality was a divine expression: a miracle of miracles, a gift of transcendent proportions that cast a spiritual aura over everything."

"Everything there is?"

"The ancient ones through mindful breathing, meditation and prayer came to believe that Everything-there-is was a divine expression of who they were."

"Could you repeat that?" Lenny asked with furrowed brow.

"The ancient ones came to believe that Everything-there-is was a divine expression of who they were. They realized that they were an integral part of it."

"Like... a single molecule inside a body made up of millions of such molecules?" Lenny asked, attempting to formulate a concrete image to which he could relate.

"Not only that. Conceive of that body as being part of the Earth which is part of the Solar System, which is part of the Milky Way Galaxy, which is part of the Universe, which is part of the Cosmos, which is part of... *Everything-there-is.*"

"Boy, did you ever say a mouthful there," Lenny grinned. "I am trying to imagine this..." Lenny lapsed into a prolonged silence.

Compassion prevailed when Eldorado broke the silence. "As you know... belief is a very powerful thing. Although all are incarnated with the potential to perfect themselves - many have regrettably... regressed. Why? Because, unlike the ancient ones, they have come to believe that they are defective parts, distinctive and separate from the whole."

"And, like you said, *belief is a powerful thing!*" Lenny reiterated.

"Billions of you earthlings, and further billions influenced by those billions, have in general come to believe that some imaginary autocratic God created man apart or separate from Himself and placed man into an alien environment as a punishment for being disobedient. Accordingly many of you believe that it is up to each person to fend for her/himself: to find a way to ingratiate him/herself. As you are aware, there are many, many individuals all vying for the few spaces allocated in Paradise by God for the so-called Chosen Few. This, along with your mortal status and linear concept of time, causes the converted to squabble amongst themselves for the few available spaces God has reserved for the righteous."

"I must admit, that rather unbelievable explanation does help to make our behavior in the Middle-East and in other areas of the world dominated by the major religions, seem somewhat more... understandable. How does such a-a righteous attitude differ from the mindset of the People of the Light?"

"The key to understanding the ancient ones' mindset is in appreciating the intuitive nature of their comprehension of time." Pena hesitated as if wondering if Lenny was advanced enough to understand what he was about to divulge.

"Time, you say?" Lenny prompted.

"It takes time to breathe. Time to exist. Time to be. To the ancient ones time was magic."

"Magic? I don't understand."

"It is difficult to explain, but I'll try. Time endures... as space, creating the dimension required for mortality to exist. See the relationship?"

"Time endures," Lenny cogitated, "as space; the one is the other, and vice-versa. Like Einstein said, it is time-space, not time and space. Right?"

"I am impressed by your astuteness. To the ancient ones the past, present, and future all co-existed, so to speak, in the everlasting now. The *now* was *magic*. It was a divine expression of who they were: parts of a whole... that was made up of the sum-of-the-parts. They existed in harmony with that magic and identified themselves as growing out of the divinity in which they existed."

"I'm feeling a little confused and-and lost," Lenny admitted with a frown.

"Cheer up. You are definitely not alone. The thing that was most admirable about the People of the Light was their gratitude. They considered themselves to be part and parcel of the grand miracle of space-time. They smiled a lot and displayed a humility that reflected an attitude of eternal thankfulness."

"I wish I could be more like that."

"I like your attitude. Unlike you - most of your peers think that they are the smartest, most advanced people ever to have walked the earth on their two hind legs. Their vanity, conceit, and righteousness is-is… lamentable. I was going to say insufferable, but that would have been far too vain on my part," Pena reprimanded himself.

"Vain, but accurate," Lenny commented dryly. "In this space-time bubble of modernity, vanity and conceit have become identified as being part of our so-called fallen nature."

"Unfortunately in this cultural space-time reality, the notion of time per se has taken on a monetary value. And it has given mortal existence a crass capitalistic sheen," Eldorado announced.

"Time is money!" Lenny followed up. "Since one has only a limited amount of time to accumulate one's fair share of Mother Nature's bounty, some resort to unscrupulous means to get their fair share of the bounty. This naturally brings greed and selfishness into play. We have diminished the sublimity of our inner divinity with the dross of the spirit of capitalism. Unfortunately to many, greed has become a-a virtue!" Lenny righteously pontificated."

"Ahhha…" Pena sighed as if suddenly becoming aware of his own shortcomings and duplicity in the matter. "Keep in mind that no one is perfect, including you and me. We are all on our own learning curve." Eldorado paused pensively as if reminding himself of his role as mentor in the relationship.

"A point well taken," Lenny acknowledged deferentially.

"Remember this – even if you forget everything else that I've said," Pena stated solemnly. *"A human being is a human being, is a human being… regardless of race, sexual orientation, religion, or economic status.* We each have our own karmic destiny. We have to respect that." Pena disappeared as if he had said more than enough.

* * *

It was 3:02 am. Lenny had just fallen asleep.

"I'm back," Pena announced. "There is a lot more to this story than is recorded in your history books?"

"What story?" Lenny yawned.

"The one about the People of the Light."

"Oh, yeah, now I remember," Lenny stated groggily. He shook his head vigorously in an attempt to enhance the interface between the natural and the supernatural.

"Listen to this."

"I'm all ears."

"Based upon plain, everyday common sense, wouldn't you say that the ordinary person would eventually become cognizant that the miraculous sun that nurtures Mother Earth and to which your planet owes its very existence, was much more worthy of being deified – than say... a chauvinistic personality with a cruel fetish for vengeance and retribution?"

"You certainly don't mind telling it like it is," Lenny commented.

"Look at the miraculous sun! The omnipresent and omnipotent sun shines down upon you folk with miraculously nurturing and life-sustaining energy – and you folk scoff and call those who feel inclined to demonstrate a modicum of reverence for the obvious... primitive, ignorant, and unenlightened. What motivates you to behave thus?"

"Righteous religious dogma?"

"It is rather amazing that so many of your kin folk cannot see what is apparent."

"Maybe... they have been incarnated here in this mortal moment of eternity so-so they can learn to appreciate the obvious," Lenny conjectured. "They need time, like perhaps two or three incarnations... to think about their role in all of this."

"Perhaps they do." Eldorado reflected momentarily before saying, "You know... the ancient ones had a saying that went something like..." he hesitated as if searching his memory for the correct phrasing, "*the Sun is the husband of Mother Earth; and the offspring of the union populates the mysterious universe with the fecundity of their free will.*"

"What a lovely way of putting it."

"This was the popular belief of the People of the Light."

"Do they have a-a proper name?" Lenny inquired.

"They became known as the Wandering-Qi."

"The Wandering... what?"

"The name per se represents a form of poetic license. Of course they did not call themselves that; someone else must have made up that name… probably because it seemed appropriate at the time. Sort of like many of you refer to the aboriginal peoples of North, Central, and South America as Indians. That name was meaningless to the people so designated. Remember the genocidal slogan: *the only good injun is a dead injun?* There weren't any such *injuns*. They only existed in the minds of the fabricators of such genocidal injustice." Eldorado paused as if the thought perturbed him. "We were not injuns!" he suddenly declared with such ferocity it startled Lenny.

"I get your drift," Lenny began empathetically. "Hopefully the term Wandering-Qi denotes a much more ah-ah… appropriate connotation?"

"Indeed it does," Pena replied calmly, having recovered from his outburst. "But in actuality they thought of themselves as being the Kindly Qi. According to myth, the legendary Wandering Qi eventually became dispersed from their northern homeland… that once existed at the base of Mount Kailash. Still, the essence of their passing lives on amongst those of you gifted with vague karmic memories of things long past."

"Ah," Lenny acknowledged, pretending that Pena was referring to him.

"The Wandering Qi were mindful that they were part of the miraculous flow of energy that emanated from the Sun and became divinely manifested on Earth. That energy represented the Qi, or the divine-essence, that energized everything in the universe. Mount Kailash, Lake Manasorovar and the surrounding area shimmered like a divine mirage of the sun's vibrant energy. From your foursquare mentality this probably sounds rather far-fetched. What seems obscure to many today, as I intimated previously, was obvious to the Wandering Qi."

"Why?"

"They felt they were an integral part of *What-is.* Unlike adherents of the major religious faiths who feel alienated from the earth – the Kindly Qi felt a natural affinity for the earth along with an inclination to share the bounty; this attitude enabled them to vibrate at a higher frequency of being, as befitting their self-concept as the People of the Light."

"Amazing."

"Generosity evolved out of life-enhancing behavior. Behavior that was life-negating, such as greed and selfishness, was frowned upon. Through introspection and meditation they became aware that the miracle of life was a divine expression that shimmered and vibrated all about them.

The past, present, and future were experienced as a seamless flow of space-time that manifested the everlasting now in which they magically existed"

"A seamless flow... makes sense."

"This realization was shared amongst the majority of those living in that northern part of the world. They became sensitized to the ever-changing ebb and flow of life-enhancing energy that came from the sun with the passing of the seasons and seemed to emanate from Mount Kailash and their surroundings as if they were ensconced in a sacred vortex of divine vibrations. They identified this invisible high-level, life-affirming energy-force as Qigong... an energy-force in which all humankind participated. Happiness resulted when one was innately in tune with this vital energy. To them Happiness or Nirvana existed intrinsically, right here on Earth – not somewhere *way out there*."

"You don't say?" Lenny asked incredulously, "*Right here – eh?*" he subvocalized so loud that Lana rolled over and elbowed him in the back.

"Did I mention that some of the highly spiritualized Qi were able to vibrate at a rate that enabled them to le-levitate?" Pena stammered.

"You might have... but please continue."

"Angels really do not have wings."

"Really?"

"Primitive non-levitators just supposed that anyone who could fly had to have wings."

"You mean non-levitators like us? I'd say that those fake bird-like wings painted onto human beings wearing long white robes represent the archaic status of our superstitious gullibility," Lenny appraised.

"Don't be too critical of your peers. After all levitation is a highly evolved spiritual endeavor. Some of the more advanced Qi were able to levitate huge mass objects."

"You don't say."

"You look a little skeptical there. Let me share a sliver of far-out information with you... that might add even more fuel to your credulity," Pena added with a smile.

"Why don't you?" Lenny replied with a tiny hint of exasperation.

"Levitation is a *potentiality* that is innate within everyone. When the time is right... you will be able to vibrate at a frequency that enables you to dematerialize, and levitate. It is hardwired into your DNA molecules. The ability to levitate is in fact… natural."

"What!" Lenny exclaimed his skepticism rising. "Did you say natural?"

"Indeed I did. Through mindful meditation the Kindly Qi discovered what most sentient beings only discover after they pass on."

"And what is that?" Lenny asked with bated breath.

"You become freed from your material encumbrances. You realize that your seemingly material existence is actually immaterial."

"You do? So how did that enable the ancient ones to levitate?" Lenny asked.

"Hmm," Eldorado pondered. "Actually I have to admit that-that it is difficult to put into mere words that which is beyond your foursquare mentality. Sorry," he apologized with unexpected humility. "There are many things that are beyond the scope of my intellectual ability. There are some secrets that only the Qi have been able to comprehend…" Eldorado's voice trailed off.

"I understand," Lenny commiserated sensing Pena's frustration.

"Perhaps it might help to think about it this way. The Wandering Qi were known for the meticulous manner in which they cared for their feet."

"What?" Lenny asked surprised by Pena's seemingly inane assertion.

"All human beings stand upright on their two legs. What part of their body makes contact with the earth?"

"Their feet."

"All green life forms that are capable of photosynthesis are rooted to the earth from which they draw their sustenance. Look at the trees. Look at how they cling to the good earth that nourishes and sustains them. It is from the sun and earth that all life forms draw their life force. The Qi felt that through their feet they were able to connect with the divine vibrations of the earth, from which they had become uprooted, so to speak. They believed that their feet kept them grounded to the life-enhancing vibrations of the Earth. Consequently they developed a fetish about the importance of their feet. The placebo effect of this fetish became manifest. Wherever their feet wandered… the Wandering Qi felt at home."

"The placebo effect of belief, you say? Amazing!"

"Belief is a very powerful force, indeed. Because they believed that they were an outgrowth of the Earth, some of the more advanced Qi were somehow able to assimilate the electromagnetic force of the Earth as if... as if it was part of their free will. It all happened quite naturally."

Incredible!"

"I know. It is mindboggling isn't it?"

"So what does that imply?"

"It implies that the reality paradigm in which they existed was synonymous with their existential status. They experienced the Earth as a magical realm from which they emerged and to which they owed their existence. There was a symbiotic spirituality to the relationship that transcends conventional thinking. I know it sounds unbelievable. Don't ask me exactly how they did it, but eventually they were able to-to um... levitate, and-and to time-travel."

"Time-travel you say?" Lenny responded before lapsing into a stunned silence.

"There are limits to such time-travelling," Pena continued after an appropriate interlude.

"What do you mean?"

"As far as I know, one can only move about within the parameters imposed by one's very own holographic space-time memories."

"Did you just say *holographic*?

"Indeed I did. It is a difficult concept for folks with a materialistic mind set to comprehend. Suffice it to say, it is amenable with the concept of a dream-world... and with time travel."

"Could the phenomenon of UFOs be examples of ... ancient time travel?" Lenny asked, playing a hunch."

"The operators of UFOs come and go within the space-time parameters relative to their respective memories. Naturally some memories are much older than others. To you they may seem to have come from the future – that is because, *relative to them*, you may have regressed to a materialistic plane of existence that correlates with your four-square mentality!"

"The key phrase there is *relative to them*, eh?" Lenny ascertained.

"Indeed it is. Relativity is the key to understanding the relevance of travelling through space-time dimensions."

"Time-travel?"

"The Qi believed that, what you think of as time-travel, entailed travelling through time-space dimensions. These dimensions are all here, now. The Now is the epicenter of the vortex of all dimensions of time-space. There is no inner or outer, so to speak... all dimensions exist simultaneously right here, right now. Time travel is actually a trip through the immaterial holographic dimensions of the immortal memory."

"Amazing! In that context, who knows what phenomena the UFOs represent?"

"I like your curiosity," Pena commented.

"Is it possible these are time-travellers: ancient aliens who are returning home?" Lenny paused to cogitate. He thought of his *Allegory of the Fish*; he recalled holding forth about the amazing sockeye and how they left the place of their birth to spend four incredible years basking in the freedom of the mighty Pacific Ocean... only to return home as if passing through a time-warp, where their stunted landlocked brethren, the kokanee, had multiplied and dominated the homeland... greeting them when they returned 'home' as if they were an alien species. "Mindboggling... to say the least!" he exclaimed.

"I am impressed by your demeanor and ability to comprehend such matters. I know that at your present level of awareness most people probably find it difficult to wrap their minds around anything that is not considered to be a cold hard fact, based upon empirical evidence," Eldorado responded empathetically.

"Believe it or not – you are making a lot of sense," Lenny replied spritely, attempting to stay in tune with the higher frequency of Pena's vibes.

"Good," Pena appraised. He paused deliberately before continuing. "What I am about to share with you might be a little premature... but I think you can handle it."

"Try me!" Lenny challenged, feeling a little miffed by his nocturnal friend's apprehensiveness.

"Okay. This might help you to appreciate what is known in the vernacular as the 'great mystery': *Death*."

The change of topic caused Lenny to inhale deeply as if his brain cells required more oxygen.

"To us mortals fear of death and dying fills us with dread and anxiety. Whatever light you can shed on this subject would be most appreciated," Lenny stated soberly.

"Like I may have implied before… when you *die*, as you folks say, you will be able to dematerialize. It is innate or hardwired into the cascading memory-strands of your DNA. *Ashes to ashes, dust to dust.* The difference between the organic and the inorganic will disappear. According to Qi folklore, it will happen naturally."

"Naturally?"

"It is hardwired into your DNA. It will unfold like a miraculous dream commensurate with your karmic memories. You, that is your immaterial *spirit-soul,* will reappear or incarnate… as if you belong."

"Belong where?"

"In the here and now of the space-time membrane of forces relative to your karmic status. All dimensions of being exist here, now. *Here* is the space… and *now* is the time. It will always feel like… the *present.*"

"It will always feel like-like… the present!" Lenny echoed. "Truly edifying."

"I can hardly believe that you are getting this."

"Seems like common sense," Lenny replied, attempting to sound erudite.

"See if you can comprehend this. Most of your kinfolk are grounded, so to speak, in a materialistic mindset. To such folks materialism is natural: everything that is real is material, that is, concrete, solid, and dense. The building blocks of their reality paradigm are made up of such matter. This gives rise to a self-serving attitude that accompanies materialism. So it is that your compatriots have, of their own free-will, fashioned the vast, sprawling, polluting cities of concrete, pavement, glass, and steel in which most of you presently abide… awaiting death."

"You paint a most unflattering and disturbing picture. So what is the alternative?"

"A non-materialistic or spiritual mindset. More akin to the attitude that used to be displayed by the Ancient Peoples of North, Central and South America - that the pious amongst you denigrate as being pagan. Levitation, in my humble opinion, requires a much more altruistic mindset. One is not pitted against Mother Nature. The part is not alienated from the whole – one cooperates and flows with the invisible energy from which all physical matter is manifested; one becomes a *part* of the whole."

"So what difference does that make?"

"A world of difference. The Wandering Qi had this slightly more advanced mindset. They existed in a spiritual vortex made manifest by the placebo effect of their relationship to the earth. If they trod lightly – who knew how the earth would reciprocate? Belief is such a powerful thing. Eventually some of them could levitate and shape huge massive blocks of dense matter as if they were nothing but air."

"How?"

"To them such blocks were immaterial manifestations of energy, as insubstantial as one's dreams. And in one's dreams, how substantial are such massive blocks of matter?"

"Hard to imagine," Lenny admitted. "I am reminded of Moses parting the Red Sea. He raised his staff and commanded the seas to part! They parted and he was able to lead his enslaved brethren from captivity to freedom."

"That would have been perfectly understandable... to the ancient ones. But to you folks? A blessed miracle! From time to time exceptional people can do exceptional things."

"Like the People of the Light?"

"The Kindly-Qi were incarnated on Earth to experience the same miracle planet as everyone else... but they experienced it from a spiritual point of view. The reality that surrounded them was a divine expression, just as they were. They demonstrated a profound attitude of appreciation."

"What type of attitude?" Lenny responded as if he'd missed the last word.

"Appreciation... appreciation for what-is."

"So they did not need to change or conquer their environment – but rather to simply accommodate themselves to it... because to them it was a manifestation of a divine flow of energy?"

"Correct. Tell me what you think *progress* means to folks with a materialistic mindset?" Pena suddenly inquired.

"Hmm, let me see. I suppose it means more effective weapons of mass destruction, more powerful thirty-three-story rockets, greater technological advancement, faster computers, fancier cars and..."

"Enough. The Qi did not accomplish anything like that... and yet the progress they made enabled them to levitate and to travel far into the starry heavens where death meant: *more abundant Life.*"

"What!" Lenny exclaimed as if dumfounded.

"A good place to pause and reflect. We still have a lot more to discuss. See you tomorrow night. Sleep tight." Pena left.

"Sleep tight? What does that mean?" Lenny cogitated while rolling over and cuddling into Lana's cozy presence.

* * *

The luminous dial on Lenny's wristwatch read 4:45. Lana was snoring quietly on her back. The bedroom window was open to the night sky. Pena intruded. "As I mentioned before..." he began, "to the Kindly-Qi, death meant: *more abundant life!*"

"What!" Lenny awoke with a start, his brain seemingly suffering from overload.

"More abundant life," Eldorado paused to give Lenny time to shake out the cobwebs.

"An absolutely amazing description of a mysterious inevitability that-that fills most of us with dread. Can you explain how the Qi came to such an astounding realization?"

"To grasp this idea of death, you need to understand how the ancient ones experienced the everlasting-now wherein the past, present and future represented a mortal moment: a miniscule portion of an altruistic Whole. This notion of space-time entailed an ever evolving concept of growth or progress toward perfection."

"As compared to our linear concept that goes from *beginning* to *end*: the end being death," Lenny astutely interjected.

"And who experiences the death?"

"The subjective I?"

"The Qi conceived of the 'I' as being the core of the everlasting-now from which meaningful growth radiated in expanding circles of free will, analogous to dimensions-of-meaning within dimensions within dimensions toward a greater awareness of a greater freedom." Pena stared at his nocturnal friend and asked, "Can you visualize this?"

"You know," Lenny hesitated, "I have always harbored a notion of reality somewhat like that! Indeed, I can visualize it. I can imagine myself living in such an ever-expanding world of intrinsic meaning."

"You seem to have some Qi-like sensibilities!" Eldorado appraised.

"Th-Thanks," Lenny mumbled. For some unknown reason he suddenly felt truly humbled, as if for the first time someone had recognized him for being a person of some substance. It was a solemn moment, but it passed.

"Some of my old native Chilean kinfolk had similar sensibilities - before the Spanish came..." Pena's voice trailed off as he reflected. *"Ignorant pagan sun worshippers, eh?"* he scoffed under his breath.

"It is the radiant energy from the sun that energizes the earth and all its life forms.," Lenny commiserated.

"Indeed, the sun is everything to the earth. Everything. It is the *Qigong* or life-force that enables all sentient beings to vibrate with free will. Do you know what free will is?" Pena inquired.

"Tell me," Lenny said.

"Think of it as the Ultimate Gift: *a magical gift of freedom* from the Altruistic-Whole to each *part* participating in the miraculous process of perfecting the *Whole*."

Lenny could feel the magic swirling about him.

"Tell me more about this Qigong?" Lenny requested as if in awe of Pena's wisdom.

"Qigong became a key semantic expression that provided the cognitive basis for the Wandering Qi's self-concept: they believed that they were divine manifestations of the vital energy emanating from the sun which symbolized the freedom... to be."

"To most Christian folks that undoubtedly implies something like... *primitive pagan sun worship*," Lenny elaborated.

"Of course, but who are they? Worshippers of the most diabolical form of religious dogma ever rationalized as being believable!" Pena vented uncharacteristically. "Talk about being primitive!" he added.

"I-I had no idea that you felt so strongly about this," Lenny ventured discreetly. "But it is understandable, given how they mistreated your kinfolk."

"People with the same mentality once called us ignorant savages," Eldorado replied as if that justified his outburst.

"You have my personal sympathies," Lenny offered.

"Sorry about my emotional reaction," Pena spoke in a more subdued tone. "Somehow memories concerning shameful acts of injustice... irritate me far beyond what they should!"

"For a man of your intellect, I am sure that it must have been..."

"Getting back to the Kindly Qi," Eldorado interrupted, "they were motivated to experience the whole of which they were a part. Sharing and caring became their natural way of life. Ownership and greed became alien to their self-concept. It is generally assumed that they eventually evolved into a pantheistic society."

"A what?"

"A difficult concept for your kinfolk to conceive of, because of their emphasis upon the self. They behave as if the part is more important than the whole... of humanity. That is what makes individual acts of terrorism so self-satisfying... and it is precisely why some of them are willing to sacrifice the entire world in order to *save* their own vainglorious self."

"A hard truth to swallow!" Lenny admitted. "But it is happening... as we speak."

"In a society where the health and well-being of Mother Earth is more important than the parasites that live off of her generosity, physical appearances like one's countenance are inconsequential. The more a person radiated gratitude and unselfishness, the more prominent and more beautiful the aura. Consequently, the most revered individuals were – not those with the most money or comely physical appearance as determined by a biased subjectivity – but rather, those whose intrinsic beauty was reflected in the beatific sublimity of their spiritual auras. This became the essence of what some of your more enlightened folks presently refer to as being one's Buddha nature; it existed long before Siddhartha Gautama was born."

"Is it a subliminal aspect of man's relationship to the Whole?"

"One's Buddha nature represents an altruistic attitude toward life; an attitude that vibrates as kindness and compassion, and manifests an aura of happiness."

"Interesting. I assume that such an attitude with accompanying mindset and life-affirming outlook eventually spread far beyond the area originally inhabited by the ancient ones?"

"Because at that time the earth was essentially borderless, small groups of Wandering Qi, while still in the more primitive stages of their historical development, were able to move far beyond the confines of their northern habitat. They were keen to explore the far reaches of the miracle planet that nurtured and sustained them."

"How far afield did they go?"

"These ancient peoples - unlike the present generation - scarcely left a noticeable footprint behind to indicate their passing. Being a free-spirited people, some groups found their way to northern India where their wisdom found poetic expression in the Sanskrit of the Vedas. Small groups also wandered west to Europe, and southeast toward China and Japan. Some traces of their sojourn in the Orient can be found in the folklore of the so-called hairy Ainu of Northern Hokkaido and in the pantheistic concepts associated with the Shinto religion. They also managed to make it to the mid Pacific, all the way to the Hawaiian Islands where their influence is reflected in the spiritual magic of the Kahunas. "

"Did any of them get to the North American continent?"

"With the geological passage of time the earth cooled and the crust heaved creating a land-bridge between Northern Asia and North America. Adventuresome groups of nomadic peoples crossed the land bridge and wandered into North America. Amongst them were a substantial number with elongated skulls who could trace their lineage back to the People of the Light."

"You are talking about the *aboriginal* peoples?" Lenny clarified.

"Yes. I guess you could call them my ancient Asian ancestors. The newcomers migrated southward all the way to the tip of South America. However, the further they migrated from the epicenter of their spirituality, the more diminished their spiritual auras became. Since the arrival of the early Europeans the cultural values of the aboriginal peoples of North, Central, and South America have been further corrupted with a depraved notion of sin. The potlatch, one of the few remaining vestiges of a spiritual culture that once condoned sharing as being virtuous behavior, was banned and outlawed by the proponents of greed - and replaced with the concept of ownership of that... which was meant to be shared."

"You're not afraid to tell it like it was," Lenny approved.

"It happened – didn't it?" Eldorado paused and gazed at his good friend meaningfully. After a short interval he thoughtfully raised his head as if he had decided it was worthwhile to continue.

"You know the spirit of the Wandering Qi has wandered down through the ages from Asia across the ancient Beringia Strait, as it is known these days, and into the vast hinterland portioned off as Canada, The United States, Mexico and other lands further south. You modern civilized folks think that you own these lands. It is a materialistic manifestation of your secularized concept of sin."

"We believe we have been given dominion over the land; consequently we selfishly appropriate the land for ourselves."

"You think you own these lands – but you don't."

"Someone needs to speak truth to power... before it is too late!" Lenny exclaimed with such indignation it caused Pena to smile.

"Not so long ago someone did just that."

"Who?"

"One of the last of the aboriginals to speak with the wisdom of the Wandering Qi was the Chief of the Squamish Duwamish Peoples of the Pacific Northwest. His name was Seathl. Most folks say *Seattle.*"

"And what was the occasion?"

"As you know the US Government had been trying to force the Native Peoples onto tiny patches of land called Reservations. As part of this strategy, in the year 1854, the US Government offered to purchase two million acres of land from the impoverished Indians."

"Two million acres! That is a lot of land."

"This 'offer to purchase' as real-estate agents say today, was a foreign concept to the Aboriginals. What baffled Chief Seathl was the notion that they, the US Government, was asking him to sell something... that he did not own."

"I see the difficulty. How did he respond?"

"There are various interpretations of what he said. Here is my understanding of what he said on that historic occasion:

How can we buy or sell the sky, or the warmth of the land? The idea is so strange to us. If we do not own the freshness of the air and the sparkle of the water, how can you buy them from us?

Every part of the earth is sacred to my people. Every shining pine needle, every sandy shore, every mist in the dark woods, every clearing, and every humming insect is holy in the memory of my people. The sap, which courses through the trees, carries the memories of the Red Man. So, when the Great Chief in Washington sends word that he wishes to buy our land... He asks much of us.

This we know: all things are connected. Whatever befalls the earth befalls the sons of the earth. Man did not weave the web of life. He is merely a strand in it. Whatever he does to the web, he does to himself.

Nevertheless we will consider your offer to go to the reservation you have set aside for my people. We will live apart and live in peace.

One thing we know, which the White Man may one day discover. 'God' is the same God. You may think now that you own 'Him'... as you endeavor to buy and own the land. But you cannot.

He is the God of Man; and his compassion is equal for the Red Man and the White. The earth is precious to Him, and to harm the earth is to heap contempt on its Creator.

The Whites too shall pass. Perhaps sooner than all other tribes. Continue to contaminate your bed, and you will one day suffocate in your own waste."

"Talk about *speaking truth to power!*" Lenny expostulated.

"The *prophesy of Seathl...* lingers. The wisdom of the Qi resonated in his spirit, as it continues to vibrate in the energy from the sun that energizes us and the land that sustains us. No one owns the sun or the earth. We only share in its abundance and in its greater freedom to be everything to all things."

"Yet all too many of us pious, civilized folks scoff and refer to the prophetic words of Chief Seathl as being the words of an illiterate and ignorant injun. What do such folks know?"

"Yeah, what do they know?" Pena concurred.

"Vanity and conceit along with an abiding sense of guilt often enables us to hide the truth from ourselves," Lenny pointed out.

"The truth is staring you in the face – unfortunately many of you just cannot see it." Pena lamented. "In the vast scope of the evolution of the earth, the reality in which you presently reside has existed for only a very brief moment in eternity. In the blink of an historical eye Man's golden spiritual essence became transmuted into lead, via the alchemy of a religious belief in Original Sin."

"It might prove to be our own undoing," Lenny followed up. "A doomsday scenario is certainly not out of the question. It could be said that we are about to reap... what we have so righteously sown."

* * *

Somehow
I vaguely remember
You quietly said something
Quite profound
        Light-years beyond
"How do you do?"
When you cried reluctantly
On your Anniversary
With sorrowful eyes
As doleful as Mother Nature
Exposed
      Naked with embarrassment
Because another year had passed
Unnoticed
        While the greedy
Encumbered by the dross
Of their own undoing
Grew ever more desperate with age
From lessons unlearned.

    - LB

CHAPTER THIRTEEN

LOVE AND ALTRUISM

There is a divine existential-essence
That continues to be expressed
With each immortal breath
That measures the duration
Of an eternity spent
Giving altruistic definition
To what could be.

Serenity glistened upon Lenny's face. Passersby noticed it. Dogs of all shapes and sizes sniffed his pant legs and looked up at him with big glowing eyes. Sometimes he reached down and gently patted them upon the head. "Good doggy," he'd say under his breath. He knew they could hear him just like the deer can hear the silent deer whistles people stick on their front bumpers. Little kids almost always smiled when he grinned. He felt like petting them too, but wisely restrained himself.

He enjoyed sitting complacently on the wooden bench adjacent to a commemorative bronze statue of a little Japanese fisherman holding a large salmon. He tilted his new Toronto Blue Jays baseball cap to the back portion of his head while rejoicing in how sublimely the early morning rays of the sun reflected upon the misty waters of the southern Fraser.

He pictured himself in his mind's eye. A smirk creased the corners of his mouth as he sat and watched the warming rays of the sun cause the mist to rise like a filmy curtain over a stage where he sat like a worldly comedian.

He had attempted to be funny in a weird sort of way. It was part of a lifetime spent attempting to see the humor in the faces of those laughing hysterically at their own jokes. As the sun rose he reflected upon one of his most poignant memories of things past... the birth of his only child, Kitty. That was no laughing matter! What a miracle that was: a tiny infant bundle of pure joy. It was a miracle. He recalled saying: "She looks like the baby Buddha."

Lana never laughed. She knew her daughter was special: a divine expression of infinite worth.

How and why so many of his affluent and seemingly intelligent friends could contaminate such innocent children with the dogma of *sin*, was-was... tragic. There was not one iota of humor in it.

Kitty had no need to be saved. She was innocent. She grew up like a free spirit. It was awesome. The childhood years were a blessing. Never were two parents so doting and so happy. The years passed without their noticing. And when she left home they suffered the empty nest syndrome. Without Kitty the home became more of a house, just a place where they lived.

Kitty went to the University of Victoria to further her education. After she graduated she wandered like a free spirit across the vast wilderness of Canada searching for something significant that had real meaning to her. Such significance was and is hard to find in a materialistic society where the great unwashed already know who they are. Most people had a brand name to which they were very loyal.

"Are you a Christian?" they would politely ask. When Kitty shook her head they would stand back and stare at her as if she was some kind of a freak of nature. "Are you Jewish?" they would continue. "Muslim?

If one was not Christian, Jewish or Muslim – what was left? "Are you Buddhist?" they would persist. No cigar.

Could she possibly be one of those... those supercilious atheists or agnostics? They scratched their heads and looked askance.

Actually Kitty belonged to that vast unlabeled group known as the *NNB* or no-name brand. She was just herself: a human being of infinite worth, a divine expression of life... something like her dear old Dad. That's all.

It was a beautiful spring day in April. The sun shone golden though the last of the cherry blossoms still clinging tenaciously to twiggy branches; and the air smelled of the nearby Pacific. Lana and Lenny had just returned from a brief stroll. Just as they entered the door the phone rang. Lana rushed into the den to answer the phone. "Hello, hello," she said.

"Hi Mom... how's it going?" It was Kitty calling long distance.

"Is that you Kitty?" Lana replied hesitantly.

"Who else?"

"It's Kitty!" Lana whispered to her husband, and motioned for him to pick up the extension phone.

"What did you say?" Kitty inquired.

"Just told your Dad to pick up the other phone so he can listen in."

"Good... cause I've got some good news."

"You do?"

"I'm due in late August."

"What?" both Lana and Lenny responded in chorus.

"Are you saying that you are pregnant?" Lana ascertained.

"The doctor predicts sometime near the end of August."

"That soon?"

"I wanted to make sure before I called you."

"Wow, that is good news!" Lenny interjected. "Congratulations!"

"Thanks Dad. I think you and Mom are going to have a grandson... according to the doctor."

"I guess he'll be a US citizen, eh?" Lenny asked.

"Wow." Lana breathed into the phone. It took her a moment to accommodate the idea. It was hard for her to conceive of the notion that their little girl had actually become pregnant and was about to give birth. *But she is a mature adult now...* the thought enabled her to say "How wonderful!"

"Are you and Dad flying down?"

"Of course," Lenny interjected once again. "You can count on us to be there. We will fly down around say... the middle of August and make a holiday of it."

"Indeed, we will definitely be there. Count on it. Call us... if anything happens sooner than you expect," Lana added.

"We'll keep in touch." Kitty paused. "I guess you haven't met my husband yet... I spoke of him in some of my previous communications... remember? His name is Solomon. You'll really like him." Kitty spent the next five minutes extolling her common-law husband's virtues.

"We will be looking forward to meeting him," Lana replied.

"Anyway, I'd better be going. I've got plenty to do. Bye for now."

"Solomon, like in Ecclesiastes?" Lana asked her husband with raised eyebrows after hanging up the phone. "Do you think he was named after *that* Solomon?"

Of course their curiosity had been piqued. What did Lenny and Lana know about their son-in-law? And perhaps of equal importance: what did they not know?

They knew from what Kitty had related in earlier letters and phone calls that he was from the state of Utah, somewhere north of Lake Placid. They also found out that he was a polite and liberal-minded American citizen with a kindly disposition toward Mother Nature.

But what they did not know was that he was actually a *Jack-Mormon*; that is, a Mormon who is only a Mormon in name. His parents were a little less Jack and a little more Mormon; they belonged to a fundamentalist group called the Apostolic United Brethren. The only reason the family belonged to the Apostolic United Brethren was because the <u>AUB</u> staunchly defended Joseph Smith's outlawed practice of polygamy; and the young man's father was one horny old goat. He was scrawny with a tuft of beard.

The young man's father had three wives who, after much copulation on a rotational basis, bore him five daughters and one son. The son was named Solomon because his parents had high expectations of him.

Solomon's mother, who was said to have some native Hopi in her heritage, had emigrated up from northeastern Arizona with her parents. She was the youngest of the three wives and the prettiest. She called her son Sol. She had an intuitive bent of mind. Sol reminded her of the sun. He had a slightly darker complexion and a sunny disposition unlike his sisters. It was because of his mother's spiritual aura that he grew up to be a free spirit of sorts. In quiet moments when they were alone she would tell him: "You are special, Sol, you are like the sun, a radiant beam of divine light. You are one of the 'Peaceful Ones'... like your ancient Hopi ancestors. Do not be afraid to help make the world a better place for all people."

After he graduated from the state University as a forester, he looked about for a job that would align itself with his new fangled ideas that included a deep and abiding respect for Mother Earth. He headed for Canada because he felt stifled by all the Republicans who claimed to speak on behalf of the upper crust in his homeland. Although he wasn't upper crust he considered himself to be part of the loaf.

After months of backpacking in the Alberta Rockies, he ended up in Vernon, B.C. where he lucked into a part-time job at a nearby ski resort called Silver Star, where by sheer happenstance Kitty Bruce was on a brief skiing vacation. They hit it off like two peas in a pod.

That was the beginning of a relationship that seemed to last and last until it became a common-law relationship. It was fifty-fifty. "What is mine is yours, and what is yours is mine," Sol explained.

They moved to the United States along with other members of a Sacred Fire Community to join a group of idealistic young to middle-aged green-minded folks, near Boulder, Colorado.

On August 9th Lenny and Lana arrived in their rental car, a white Toyota Corolla sedan, at the abode of their daughter and son-in-law. It was tucked in the bush in a little community of similar dwellings just outside Boulder. "The green shack with the peaked roof and the brown carport," Kitty had said. It was rustic, but crudely satisfying. Roughing-it appealed to Lenny – but Lana was not quite so impressed.

The baby came a bit early on August nineteenth. Seven pounds six ounces of flesh and blood. His parents called him 'baby-Lenny' on behalf of his doting grandfather. Lenny and Lana's precious DNA had been extended to survive at least one more generation.

Being grandparents was an absolute joy for the elderly couple who had flown in all the way from Steveston, B.C., Canada, rented a car at the airport, and driven out feeling giddy with expectations. Lana said the baby boy sort of looked like his Grandpa. Lenny thought the little gaffer resembled the baby Buddha, because he could plainly see the aura of divinity that surrounded him like a protective shield. The little guy was their 'favorite grandson'. They could say that because, not only was it amusing; it was true. He represented the future. There was hope.

And now, like all the other memories accumulating in the microcosm of Lenny's brain, they were only recollections of things past - but there was a future there too. It sparkled in the dream world of Lenny's fertile imagination... as he sat on the wooden bench adjacent to the bronze statue of the old Japanese fisherman clutching a big fish.

Lenny the Bruce... to look at that solitary figure sitting by the Fraser River like an out of date nerd wearing a Blue Jays baseball cap backwards... who knew he was such a deep thinker? Who knew that as he sat there cogitating about his grandson's future well-being, a simple question illuminated his mind like the rising of the morning sun: *"How can I help make the world a little better place for all sentient beings... like our little grandson?"* Even in old age Lenny was an optimist.

* * *

Lenny was still alive and breathing when the mental-epistle arrived nocturnally at 4:35 am as if it had been typed on a real computer. "More information?" he thought. "Do I need more information?"

The question flooded his consciousness with a kind of ennui – until he began to read. He had no idea what to expect. His mind was open to whatever....

The after-image of the epistle remained etched upon his memory long after it had vanished. Fortunately his friend Pena had forewarned him of its arrival. But nothing could have prepared him for such a message.

My Dear Friend,

My compassionate colleague Eldorado Pena tells me you are still ensconced in the same type of four-dimensional membrane of forces that he and I used to inhabit. He told me you were handling it well. It isn't easy. I know.

Since my tragic demise, I have learned a great deal. So many words have been put in my mouth! You know how important the written word can be. Most importantly, I am now able to speak for myself!

The reason I am communicating with you is that Pena vouches for you... and I thought it was about time I set some religious matters straight. You know how it is... you procrastinate, and in the meantime some things just seem to get worse and worse.

Like my friend Eldorado said: "They need to know the truth... don't they?" It was the 'don't they?' that finally motivated me to write this epistle.

It fills my heart with deep sorrow and my soul with dismay to know that about three hundred and twenty-five years after my demise, at the Council of Nicaea those who deified me via some fictitious dogma sanctified as the Nicene Creed... deliberately expunged eighteen of the most precious years of my life from the historical record - while preserving only the three tragic years of my ministry for posterity. It is such an embarrassment to be portrayed in such an egregious manner. Nevertheless... it happened. Who can deny it?

I know that a great multitude of humble, kind, sincere and honest people believe in the Creed. It pains me immensely to have to level with them – but it is imperative for their own karmic progression that they know the truth. Let this be crystal clear: 'No one else can save you. You have the free will required... to save yourself. I am no more holy than you are.'

I left my homeland at the age of twelve and returned eighteen years later at the age of thirty. My countrymen were happy to see me. Of course their curiosity was piqued: "Where have you been all these years?" they asked. "And what brings you back home?"

I mentioned Plato's 'Allegory of the Cave'. I had learned about it while I was journeying northeast on the Silk Road. Apparently it was part of Plato's great work called The Republic, written about three hundred and eighty years before my birth. I tried to explain that I was like that fellow who left the shadowy confines of the cave and experienced the miraculous illumination of the heavenly sun. And like him, I had 'returned' to share my enlightened views. Unfortunately many of them did not understand the meaning of that allegory. The Magi had forewarned me; they had said, 'You must be very patient and understanding'. Perhaps I should have been much more patient.

It was such an idealistic endeavor... and I was a young man of thirty-some, and so full of good intentions and altruism.

Pena told me you were one of the few... who seemed to understand. It has been such a long time. Thanks for being willing to help to set the record straight. As you know, I am not the Christ. I am not the Lord and Savior. And if I were a contemporary, I would not even be a 'Christian'! I am a Jew.

I could have said nothing. But think of all the millions upon millions of people who pray to me on bended knees. Think of them. How could I not tell them? They have the power to save themselves. Is that not wonderful news? Over countless years I have heard their fervent prayers. I understand how powerful their belief in me is. I know how they yearn for my second coming. It is heart-rending and soul-withering.

I could have said nothing. I could have played along. I could have deceived them... those who trust and call me their personal Lord and Savior, their redeemer. I am no more holy than they are. Every human being is a divine expression of infinite worth. Please believe that.

During my brief time in my homeland it was obvious to me that the religious dogma that now rationalizes the historic slave status of my people, only served to diminish the divinity of their self-esteem. Consequently I urged them to emulate my example. "Follow me," I said. "Be like me... free from sin."

But as you know, four hundred years of abject slavery weighed heavily upon their intrinsic sense of identity and self-worth. The High Priests did what they had to... to preserve the mythological religious history that substantiated their existential status. There was one moment, however, when I thought reason would prevail. As I recall... the Roman Procurator, Pontius Pilate, magnanimously granted the people a free choice. Imagine that. A free choice!

For a moment I had such hope! When the multitude cried out: "Give us Barabbas," I was devastated.

They called for one of their own. Somehow instinctively my brethren intuited that Barabbas was a sinner, not unlike themselves: a fellow human being in dire need of a 'second chance'.

Sometimes I wonder: 'What if they had chosen me?

Imagine a world where the people actually followed my example. I often dream about that. Is it an impossible dream?

Anyway, after all is said and done... what I really meant to say, was simply... Namaste.

Issa

* * *

A beautiful pinkish-red glow reflected off the billowy clouds that hovered just above the western horizon in southwest Richmond at Garry Point Park. A brand new park bench had recently been installed beside the winding pathway that followed the curve of the westerly shoreline. On the backrest there was an inscription: "In loving memory of Lenard Bruce Jr."

Lana read the inscription before she sat down. She stared out at the beautiful sunset as if she was Lenny. In the past few months she had spent most of her waking hours reflecting upon his latter days.

"Just stay home and ignore them," had been her sage advice. But no... like a fool he had to go. He had to 'share the word' as he put it.

Makeshift platforms were set up in various public parks throughout Richmond that day that served as stages where various individuals and groups were given the opportunity to entertain and enlighten the great unwashed. The Green Party had asked Lenny to speak at 3:30 pm. Although Lenny was not a member of the Green Party, he had 'green ideas'. He accepted the invitation because he felt that his nocturnal advisor, Eldorado Pena, was counting on him to pass on the insights he had shared with him... as if they were his own.

When Lenny arrived at Garry Point Park a sizeable crowd had already assembled. Two members of a popular band that had just finished playing a number of country and western favorites stood to one side smoking cigarettes. A goodly number of motorcycle gang members loitered near the front apron of the stage.

After being courteously introduced by a member of the NDP who was filling in for her friend in the Green Party, Lenny Bruce cautiously made his way to the podium. An uncanny sense of apprehension quivered in his stomach and tingled his nerve endings. How was he to know that he was about to give his final speech?

For the occasion Lenny had worn his black outfit: black shirt, black pants, and black coat. Lana had quipped, "You know, except for your white sneakers, you could pass for the Man in Black; why don't you take your guitar along and start off with a song or two?"

"I'm no Johnny Cash," Len had replied.

Perhaps he should have taken his old Yamaha; perhaps he should have sung a few of his old folksongs in his imitation Bob Dylan nasal twang. Perhaps it would have assuaged the temperament of the writhing beast… and he would have lived to sing another day.

He stood tall at the podium like a smaller and slimmer facsimile of the popular country and western singer. He picked up the mike, turned it on, and tapped on it with his left index finger: tap, tap, tap. He forced a smile that distorted his features and nervously laughed before drawing in a sobering breath of clean Pacific air.

"Ladies and Gentlemen," he began. "I'd like to take this opportunity to share with you a very profound insight that a very wise person once shared with me." He paused to give the audience time to react.

Hearing only silence, Lenny continued. "All of us have been blessed with the karmic opportunity to inhabit this miracle planet. Ask yourselves these very basic questions: Firstly, why have you been born or incarnated into this particular reality? And secondly, is there a reason or purpose for your being here? What vital lesson have you been incarnated here to learn?

"Or, are you here for no reason at all… to irrationally pillage, plunder, and decimate the earth, and to shamefully suffer the catastrophic consequences of such behavior?"

There were impatient gestures followed by the nervous shuffling of feet combined with the shaking of heads. An obese lady wearing a purple flannel vest coughed ominously.

Perhaps Lenny should have paused here. Perhaps he should have cut his remarks short and left the stage. But instead he courageously continued to drone on and on as if oblivious of the mounting tension and hostility.

How could he have missed the dark cloud that passed overhead casting a gloomy shadow over the menacing throng encircling the stage?

The air grew heavy with an impending feeling of dread. It held an icy edge that cut into Lenny's breath as it issued from his lips in fading puffs of vapor. And still he held forth.

There was a moment before the uproar began when it seemed as if time had vanished into space. In the space of that immortal moment the ideas he had been attempting to communicate shattered in the mirror of his good intentions and revealed an irony that was laughable. The more he spoke the greater the agitation. It was as if the baser instincts of the Leviathan had been released to act in accord with its sinful nature. Like the lifting of a misty veil Lenny suddenly became aware of the misshapen forms lurking below him. He stopped speaking. He held up his right hand feebly as if symbolically attempting to hold back a tide of unforeseen consequences.

"Who do you think you are?" a righteous voice rose like a demented shriek from the surrounding gloom.

"Fuck you, man!" the foul obscenity spewed from the mouth of a tough looking youth with bulging eyes and muscular, heavily tattooed arms.

"Don't listen to the sacrilegious little blasphemer. He's an idiot!" a belligerent voice hidden behind dark shades of anonymity screamed contemptuously over the din, aided and abetted by a chorus of quarrelsome voices.

"Get the mike away from him!"

"Get the little bastard off the stage!"

"Let's teach him a lesson he won't forget!"

"Get him!" the voice boomed like a military command from three hundred and fifty pounds of rotund obesity resting precariously upon two spindly legs stabilized by a metal walker.

The mob grew monstrous. It writhed and seethed with self-righteous anger. It morphed into a monstrosity with a hundred angry heads.

The hardnosed troublemakers led the charge. The surly mob surged forward. Some climbed upon the makeshift stage. A scrawny fellow grabbed for the mike. Another reached for the lapel on Lenny's coat. The buttons ripped off.

A guttural howl reverberated in Lenny's ears.

More hands reached out with fierce claw-like fingers, tearing, ripping, scratching. The podium fell over; heavy leather boots trampled it to bits.

A ringed fist smashed into the left side of Lenny's face leaving its imprint. Another connected with his stomach. A sharp-nosed motorcycle-boot ascended, with serious intent to injure, towards his crotch.

It connected. The pain seared through Lenny like a red-hot poker.

"*Mercy!*"

Angry hands pushed him from behind. He tripped and fell awkwardly to the ground. Footwear of all kinds trampled him from head to sneaker-clad feet.

Lenny lay face down on the cool hard-packed ground. His arms and legs were spread-eagled. He was motionless, supine, and totally defenseless. He tried to lift his head as a black army boot landed heavily on his back.

"Kill the little bastard!" a shrill voice screamed insanely as if directing the proceedings. "Kill the rotten little heathen bastard! Kill him!"

Someone produced a handgun, a German luger, and pointed it menacingly at the back of Lenny's head where his hairline covered the base of his skull.

"What are you waitin' fer? Shoot him!"

The German luger quivered and shook.

An impatient tormentor pushed forward jostling the gunman.

A trigger finger twitched.

BAM!

Suddenly there was an ominous silence that could be heard throughout the park. Lost in a stillness that seemed to last forever, a wind swept in from the vast reaches of the ocean.

Lenny only felt the wind and the warmth and familiarity of the word 'Namaste'... as if someone was greeting him.

* * *

Beauty and truth descended like a breath of freedom upon Mother Earth... and she shivered to think that for all those years past, such injustice had prevailed. The fair sex, as they were known, had been passively biding their time flitting about gossiping, shopping, reading copiously, pursuing artistic endeavors, pondering... and thinking. It wasn't the ordinary type of thinking indulged in by men – it was 'intuitive' thinking. Most men made fun of them saying they were fanciful and romantic, and lacked the logic and discursive reasoning skills entailed in conventional wisdom. *Women's intuition*, they disdainfully muttered, *was not to be trusted*. What did they know?

During the Dark Ages malevolent males carrying big swords went on righteous crusades and participated in the inquisition of the innocent. Pious men garbed in long black gowns with matching hoods disgracefully burned intuitive women alive at the stake. What did they know?

The whimsical creatures with feminine voices, sharing and caring for Mother Earth, had to disguise themselves as fairies, nymphs, angels, and other such otherworldly creatures. They inhabited the psyches of ordinary women who had survived century after century in fairy tales and children's stories where intuition was a magical power.

Alas, Mother Nature is feeling vulnerable and decrepit despite her youth, and praying to her *sisters*. Her vibes resonate compassionately throughout the world. Her *sisters* are reduced to tears of empathy. Nothing needs to be said. They know. They love Mother Nature as they love themselves. It is the Golden Rule divinely expressed.

"Women are the gentle sex – not the weaker sex," Lana's husband had once written. *They nurture the young and care for the sick and aged. They affirm the Golden Rule in thought and action. They have endured for millennia under the yoke of a repressive chauvinistic authority that has suppressed and robbed them of their dignity. It is from the existential roots of their angst that their compassion arises like the inexorable rising of the tides or the awesome aura of the morning sun above the dark horizon. They have demonstrated the fortitude and the patience. They know that they must persevere when the unaware turn a blind eye.* Lenny the Bruce was a champion for the gentle sex.

Lana wept when her husband was suddenly dispatched, and she wept when she was deluged with flowers from all her grieving friends. She wept because the present tense impinged upon her with the wisdom of the ages. With the untimely passing of her husband had her time come... to carry the torch?

* * *

The time had come. George Webster Brown was there. How he wished with all his might that he had not been – but there he was.

Standing there wearing that black leather jacket with that *goddamned* German luger in his right hand pocket. No one could retrospectively change the facts. It happened...

The crowd surged forward and George surged with it, carried forward by the riotous impulse. "Get the little heathen bastard!" someone yelled pushing George aside to reach the makeshift stage. A big burly fellow grabbed the mike away from the guest speaker and ripped the cord from the amplifier. The podium came crashing to the ground. Pandemonium ensued. It was surreal, like a bad acid trip. He was right there when *Lenny the Bruce* was pulled from the stage; his flimsy coat ripped to shreds. "Get the impious blasphemer!" It was delusional. A nightmare descending: punching, kicking, spitting, yelling, cursing, grunting, sweating, even farting... like a grotesque herd of wild animals.

George saw him trip and fall when merciless hands pummeled and pushed him from behind. Steel-toed boots kicked Lenny into submission. "Kill the little bastard!" There was a frenzy of irrational behavior.

George was there... in the eye of the storm carried along by the insanity, the brute, dumb force of violence. He pushed. He punched. He spit. He cursed. He yelled the loudest. He was beside himself with excitement. His eyes bulged; sweat oozed from his armpits and his breath grew shallow with anticipation. He was one with the herd: the herd mentality was his mentality. It was surreal.

George frowned and circled about like a caged tiger caught up in the mortal moment that precedes the kill. And it just took one more... *just one more step.*

There were no excuses, no rationally thought-out reasons - only a hoard of bloodthirsty animals savagely attacking one of its own like a carnivorous pack of mad dogs feasting upon the vulnerable.

Lenny lay supinely upon the ground, spread-eagled in the eye of the storm. George stood over him. His shadow blocked out the feeble rays of the sun. He raised his right foot and placed his black army boot on the victim's back as he vainly attempted to lift his head; he barely heard him mumble: "*Somebody please... please help me!*" Did anyone besides George, hear?

There was a brief moment of uncertainty, a brief moment in eternity when he, George W. Brown, could have been a hero. He could have removed his foot from Lenny's back and reached down compassionately, extending a helping hand. *He could have saved him! Did he not have free will?*

It seemed as if he was frozen there in time, poised like a statue carved from ice. After what seemed like an eternity, he reached into his right hand pocket and extracted his German luger. He pointed the gun at the back of Lenny's head. His hand was shaking. He faintly heard someone exhale the words "…my god - No!" He closed his eyes.

For some strange reason the concentric color codes of awareness developed by Colonel Jeff Cooper flashed before his eyes. There were five distinct circles of color; he had memorized them. *White stood for a benign state of conscious unawareness. Yellow represented an attentive outlook. Orange indicated a direct and immediate danger. Red meant the presence of a definite threat. Black meant engagement and action.* George closed his eyes. The light dimmed. He looked into the void. He saw black!

"Kill the little bastard!"

There was darkness, the vastness of the void, the opaqueness of a black hole.

"Bang!" Nothing. *And then the light ever so gradually came back on.*

George Webster Brown stood as if he had been quick-frozen into an ice-sculpture: a patsy waiting to be apprehended. Cold sweat beaded his forehead. The armpits of his jacket were damp. He felt sick… sick to his very bowels. Was it the sickness unto death? He wretched and threw up on Lenny's head. The vomit mixed in with the oozing blood. A mortal moment passed second by second.

The hand holding the murder weapon began to shake uncontrollably. George stared at his right hand as if it wasn't his own… as if it belonged to someone else. Someone else must have done it! He could not have done it. Not him! Yet there was his black army boot planted firmly on the victim's back… and in his right hand dangled the incriminating evidence.

Someone made a citizen's arrest. He pried the gun from George's hand and wrapped it in a hanky. It was the burly fellow with the black Stetson. He was enraged. "You fuckin' idiot," he fumed.

The police car arrived with sirens screaming blue murder. Tasers were adroitly deployed, whether they were needed or not. Handcuffs were quickly placed upon his wrists. He was read his rights. Cameras clicked and flashed. People gawked and uttered obscenities. The crowd gradually disbursed. George was hauled up to the back door of the police car. An officer of the law opened the door and pushed his head down. George stumbled in. The door slammed shut. He heard the driver burble something about bringing in the suspect. The siren started up again. Inside George's skull it was deathly quiet.

George bowed his head forward until it hit the screen that separated the front seat from the back. It all seemed like a demented dream, a grotesque nightmare. "Please, please, please," he pleaded, delusional with hope. He closed his eyes. When he opened them again... would he be lying in the comfort of his very own queen-sized bed with the white satin duvet, cuddled up next to the comforting reality of Sarah's saintly presence?

The sudden and gruesome dispatching of 'Lenny the Bruce', as the newspapers dubbed him, was picked up by CTV and CBC television networks in Canada, and CNN in the United States. It made for the kind of violence-related journalism that the great unwashed had become accustomed to. Actually the term 'great unwashed' had become somewhat outdated, but the journalists of the day were happy with the phrase because it was so expressive.

There was actually footage. Someone with a video camera had captured the gruesome fatal shooting in graphic detail. The sound effects were enhanced. The results were shocking. With a victim named *Lenny Bruce*... the American viewers with long memories could relate. Gun-control advocates were outraged. The NRA was alarmed; in Lenny's defense the spokesperson was contritely quoted as saying: '*He should have been carrying.*'

* * *

It was a cold, drafty day. Lana had lingered in the foyer of the courthouse near the hot air vents to warm up before proceeding outdoors and heading back home. As she was standing there looking out the front window, she felt a slight tug on the sleeve of her right arm. She turned and gazed into the soulful eyes of Sarah Brown, wife of the accused, George Webster Brown.

Lana blinked her eyes and timidly pulled her arm away.

"Hello, my name is Sarah Brown. I've been wantin' to speak to you fer quite some time, but-but have been rather reticent to approach you."

Nervousness caused Sarah to unconsciously mimic the vernacular her spouse had lapsed into as his hopes degenerated with the duration of the trial.

Lana nodded her head as if giving consent for Sarah to continue.

"I'm not sure if I'm supposed ta be talkin' to you, as we are on the opposite sides of the legal fence... but I saw you standin' here so I thought, 'What harm could it do?'" Sarah drew in a deep breath and added, "I-I have been feelin' for some time that I should apologize on behalf of myself and my husband." Sarah's appearance and intrinsic grace had been decimated by the long ordeal, as if defiled by the wages of an archaic ancestral sin that lingered on and on like a blight upon the soul. She spoke as one whose intellect and vernacular had undergone a gradual degradation along with her social standing.

Lana leaned away as if she needed the extra space between them. She was inundated by an approach-avoidance conflict. She stared at the wizened little woman wearing a threadbare grayish black overcoat with a transparent black shawl over her head; she looked so shrunken and pathetic. Lana relented and replied, "Glad to make your acquaintance."

"I am so very sorry for your loss. I know that words are inadequate... but I thought that you should know that George has changed over the last few months. He-he asked me to apologize to you... if the opportunity presented itself. So here I am," Sarah paused to collect her thoughts. "We are both very sorry for what has happened. He saw that gruesome photo. He cannot explain it." A tear ebbed from the corner of her right eye.

Lana rummaged in her coat pocket and extracted a rumpled Kleenex, which she handed to Sarah.

"George wanted me to tell you he did not mean ta shoot your husband. He has no memory of actually sh-shooting anyone. He is very contrite and extremely sorry for what happened. It must have been an accident. I hope you can believe that." Sarah stepped back and added, "George has really been changed by this ordeal." Sarah's vernacular improved with her confidence.

"Changed? How so?" Lana inquired out of curiosity.

"He used to like to pretend he-he was this pseudo-macho, hard-nosed person... in public."

"He did?"

"Yeah, the kind represented in movies about the old South... who drove old beat-up half-ton Fords or Chevys."

"A redneck?"

"I suppose, although his neck isn't red," Sarah joked feeling a kinship with her female counterpart, "but he did once drive an old black battered up F-150. He liked people to think he was tough."

"Was he?"

"He mostly just talked tough. He was always puttin' other people down. He took an irrational dislike for your husband. He attended most of the public forums that Lenny spoke at and he developed a fetish about readin' that 'Jewish rag' as he called it."

"There was a Jewish American comedian named Lenny Bruce. My husband is Scottish – not Jewish," Lana clarified.

"George was probably unaware of that – and if he was, he probably didn't care. He referred to Jews as Christ Killers. I think that in his mind he pictured Lenny as the Anti-Christ or someone like that. He'd say the most derogatory things about him. I won't say what he said because I know you have feelin's." Sarah glanced up at the demure woman wearing the Scottish plaid scarf about her neck. "He used the word fuck a lot," she stated matter-of-factly as if the use of that term was self-explanatory.

"He did?" Lana responded, surprised by Sarah's use of that expletive.

"Yeah, practically every sentence. It was fuck this or fuck that. The term became meaningless… unless we were actually doing it," Sarah added with a hint of embarrassment.

"I get your drift," Lana stepped back and looked over the pale, emotionally drained woman who used the word fuck as if it was habitual. A twinge of empathy caused her to nod her head ever so slightly as if she understood.

"But like I said, he's changed a lot. He hasn't said fuck more'n two or three times in the last week. He doesn't sound like his old self anymore. I think the real George is beginning to break through: the shy, insecure, timid little boy who had been hiding behind George's macho bravado."

"You don't say?"

"Indeed I do," Sarah remarked, encouraged by Lana's response. "As a matter of fact it was last month that he tol' me, he said, 'If you ever see Lenny's wife, I think her name is Lana, could you please apologize on my behalf fer the terrible thing I done.' I think that was the first and only time he ever said please."

Lana stepped closer and inhaled nervously. "Is that so?"

"Naturally I agreed. He tol' me to explain that it was an accident, that he really didn't mean ta do it. He thinks that someone must have jostled his arm and his finger twitched."

"He tol' you that?" Lana asked, absent-mindedly mimicking Sarah's manner of speaking.

"Yeah, he tol... I mean told me that," Sarah self-consciously corrected her manner of speaking. "And for that he is truly remorseful. You have no idea how such a thing can prey upon a person's soul... like a-a vulture consuming carrion. George sometimes looks like death warmed over. He-he's a mere shadow of his former self." Sarah glanced self-consciously at Lana. "He-he's learned to meditate," she added.

"Meditate – you say?"

"That's where you sit cross-legged and slowly breathe in and out. George just stares at the sixty-watt bulb in his cell and weeps. That's all he does, day after day after day. He seems like a-a broken man... a phantom in the darkness of his cell... crying out for forgiveness."

"Sad."

"But still... it seems evident that he is the one who shot your husband. I totally understand if you hate him."

"You know, at first I was afraid of him – but even then, it did not occur to me to hate him. I felt sorry for him," Lana explained.

"You are an angel. I just knew you were a compassionate soul. Could I ask you just-just... one kind favor?"

"What?" Lana asked surprised by the request.

"Could you ah-ah find it in your heart to-to forgive my husband for what he has done? If you did... perhaps he could stop crying." She looked so lonely and fragile. And here she was asking forgiveness for her man. Would he have done the same for her?

Lana's heart trembled. Intuitively she knew that Sarah was a generous and compassionate soul. She instinctively reached out and grasped her hands. She could feel her trembling. They both wept. When the tears subsided, Lana whispered, "Underneath the skin we are sisters. *I forgive George... he knew not what he was doing.*"

"I thank you from the bottom of my heart."

The two women parted and went their separate ways.

In the solitary confines of a prison cell a meditating soul stared up at the incandescent light cast by a single sixty-watt bulb... and stopped crying.

* * *

It was a verification of the so-called Twin Paradox that states that two particles separated by a vast space can influence each other. It made the seemingly disparate and unconnected, meaningful and significant. Just an hour's drive north of the 49th Parallel in Pincher Creek, Alberta an elderly lady with a long memory clicked off her thirty-two inch Toshiba TV using the remote clutched in her trembling left hand. She sadly bowed her head, shed a lonesome tear, and whispered an earnest prayer. She slowly raised her right hand to the top of her head and left it there. The scars were still evident. She could feel the pain and the wet blood.

"Lenny," she sighed, "My dear, dear Lenny, my knight in shining armor. What have they done to you?"

It was a cool, overcast summer morn. A funeral memorial was being held at the site where Lenny had been shot. Hundreds of people came to pay their last respects and pass on their deep-felt condolences to Lana. She wore a neat grey pantsuit with a white satin blouse and carried a black umbrella in case of rain. Many dignitaries outdid themselves with glowing eulogies about the life and times of Lenard Bruce Jr. A Buddhist monk, after igniting a bowl of incense, conducted a gracious service. It was a mournful and solemn occasion.

Unnoticed, under a shade tree near the fringe, stood a little woman about Lana's height dressed from heel to toe in black. Her oval-shaped face was framed by long shoulder length hair that had turned a steely grey from age. Prayer beads draped over her tightly clasped parchment hands sparkled dimly in the diffused sunlight as she stared out over the grand vista of the Pacific Ocean. Her refined countenance was creased with lifelines of past memories patiently remembered. There was pain and suffering long endured, sadness and loving kindness, compassion and grief. The vibes permeated the space about her like an aura.

It clung to her like an immortal memory needing gratuitous expression: "Thank you, Lenny... thank you for saving my life," she whispered to the infinite sky above. "I-I love you," she reluctantly admitted as tears of gratitude seeped from her eyes. It was the only emotion that made sense, the only emotion that time could not diminish or destroy.

The day before yesterday she had risen early in the morning and driven all the way in from Pincher in her battered old Honda Civic.

Unbeknownst to Lenny, after he had left… she had graduated from High School in Pincher Creek, attended first year at the Junior College in Lethbridge, and then transferred to the University of Alberta in Calgary where she had graduated with a Bachelors Degree in Education. After teaching at the Canyon School in her home town for nearly seven years, she had gotten married to an older gentleman she respected. They lived in a small white clapboard house in a place just west of Pincher Creek. The marriage only lasted three years. He could sense her dissonance. They did not have any children.

She was an excellent schoolteacher. She taught kindergarten and grade one because she loved little children. She treated every child as if she or he were her own… with loving kindness. Over the years she became a sort of kindergarten saint. When she retired the school suffered an irreplaceable loss. "One of a kind," the School Principal had praised.

She had a faded picture of Lenny she had taken with her little Brownie camera way back when he was a teenager. It had been enlarged and framed in mother of pearl. It sat on the mantel above the wood-burning fireplace. She had made a bit of a shrine effect about it, as if it was a picture of a holy person or a saint. "We are kindred spirits," she often thought… "Spirits are immortal."

She loved ethereal-sounding music. When she was in her mid forties she discovered the Theremin. The Theremin was the first electronic musical instrument ever invented. It fascinated her because it could be played without even touching it! One became part of the electronic music: the left hand hovered above the horizontal volume-antenna while the right was poised near the vertical pitch-antenna. It was expensive, but she bought one. What else did she need to spend her money on? As she grew older she spent countless hours improvising, inventing, and enjoying the *music of the spheres*, as she thought of it. It brought her into communion with Lenny.

Somewhere hundreds of miles away she imagined Lenny was listening… and the empathetic vibes often brought tears to her eyes. In solitary moments did he get an inkling of something ethereal? Could he hear the soulful music?

Unbeknownst to her, actually there were times, especially in the early morning, when Lenny would awaken feeling desperate... as if time was running out – and he was frantic with inertia. It was unnatural in many ways, but it was the sacred path that she had chosen... it was her life. Who knew it would turn out like that?

As if by instinct Lana turned and glanced in her direction. In that instant she caught the vibe that radiated in ever-widening concentric circles from the source. It was only a brief moment, but that moment captured a mortal lifetime spent. It was there in the mortality of the moment: the loneliness, the sadness, the overwhelming grief, and the existential longings of a simple human being. Lana could feel the resonance even as she made her way to the parking lot. "I wonder who she is?" she puzzled as she opened the front door of her car.

* * *

When someone dear passes on, it often triggers poignant memories of days gone by. Lana had such memories stored in the deep crevices that constituted the grey matter of her brain where they could be re-lived on days when melancholy wrapped itself about her like an old woolen coat.

She really had not said a proper good bye. She recalled the last day. Lenny was getting ready to go out. "Where's my Blue Jays cap?" he had asked while looking on the shelf above the hanging coats. He found it, put it on his head backwards and opened the door. Usually she said "Good luck" or something like that. However on that occasion she said nothing. She just stood there watching as he said "See you later," and closed the door. She remembered how the room felt so quiet right after the door closed. Maybe she knew... there would be no good-byes; hadn't he said: *See you later?*

In her mind's eye she could see him wearing that Blue Jays baseball cap. It reminded her of how he looked in his high school days. He liked to wear blue jeans with a denim jacket to match. It made him look cool and somewhat macho at the same time. After school, if he thought any girls were watching, he would affect a pose worthy of some character in a classic old movie he was fond of.

"Hi Len," she'd say pertly as she sauntered by.

"Hi yourself," he'd reply as coolly as possible for a timid juvenile pretending to be someone important.

In those days it was popular to go to the movies showing at the local theatre. It took him months to muster up the courage. Then to Lana's everlasting surprise, one warm autumn day in October he said: "Ever heard of, '*Of Mice and Men*'?"

"What?" she replied.

"It's a movie," he casually replied grimacing like Bogie in *Casablanca*; he even raised his lip to moisten his upper teeth.

"Is it any good?" she asked.

"Want to find out?" he morphed into slightly shorter version of Henry Fonda.

"Ummm… why not?"

"Tonight, 7:30?"

"Okay."

That was her first real date with Lenny the Bruce. It was memorable. He was so cool, she was reminded of one of the characters in *Happy Days*. But that was a long time ago when they were both shy and young… and he was still alive.

It was touching to see Lana walking alone down the old boardwalk that led past the Britannia Shipyards with her long, grey woolen coat wrapped around her and the breeze blowing in her wispy grey hair. She looked like a memory just 'blowin in the wind'… Who knew such poignant memories were floating along the rickety old boardwalk courtesy of an old retired widow out for a stroll… for old time's sake?

* * *

A slight breeze whipped up the mottled brown and yellow leaves that littered the gritty grey pathway along the inlet that led to the remnants of Scott's Pond, where fishing boats of various sizes, colors, and styles were safely moored, protected from incoming waves by a dug out channel. Brad Bradley walked alone along the shoreline that defined Garry Point Park, the very park where Lenny the Bruce gave his last infamous public address before an unappreciative mob of dissenters. *Why do such things have to happen?*

He drew in a deep breath as he stared out toward the westerly skyway that receded into the heavens beyond, where in his imagination the spirit of Lenard Bruce Jr. hovered about as if awaiting the outcome. *What outcome?*

The question filled Brad with such an overpowering feeling of anxiety he felt slightly faint. He stepped gingerly toward the water's edge and slowly raised his arms in a circular motion as if scooping *chi* energy toward himself. He inhaled deeply as he brought his hands together above his head, and exhaled slowly as his arms descended. He repeated the motion six times before launching into a leg and arm coordinated exercise that he hoped looked as graceful as the slow-motioned movements demonstrated by the instructor. He practiced the heel and toe walk as he made his way along the sandy shore.

When finished, he sat down on the sand and removed his shoes and socks. With gnarled fingers he meticulously rolled up his white flannel trousers about halfway to his knees. After heaving himself to his feet, he carefully extracted a ripe peach from his jacket pocket. He had purchased it on his way to the Park.

Why had he wore those white flannel trousers and purchased that peach?

He zipped up the front of his blue nylon windbreaker as he made his way along the water's edge. His bare feet left damp imprints in the sand. He strolled casually along swinging his arms in a pendulum fashion with the wet sand squishing between his toes.

As he sauntered meditatively along, his mind took him back to his undergraduate years. He recalled a poem published in the year 1915 by T.S. Elliot entitled, *The Love Song of J Alfred Prufrock*. It had been one of his favorite poems back then. Two lines echoed faintly in his memory...

> *I grow old... I grow old*
> *I shall wear the bottoms of my trousers rolled...*

He began to feel vaguely like old Prufrock. He attempted to recall other lines from the *Love Song*. "Some love song!" he exclaimed. And then for no apparent reason the questions popped into his mind:

> *Shall I part my hair behind?*
> *Do I dare to eat a peach?*

He stared inanely at the peach he held in his right hand. An imbecilic grin of delight creased the indentured lines on his face. He dared! He took a healthy bite from the peach. The juice dribbled from his chin and stained the front of his trousers. He sighed and gazed down at his sand-flecked feet as he thought...

> *I shall wear white flannel trousers,*
> *and walk upon the beach.*

The poem was prophetic... or rather somehow he had managed to personify the poem. How did it end? There he was a solitary figure silhouetted against the faded sky, a melancholic figure like old J. Alfred himself, reflecting upon a mortal lifetime spent, as he plodded along the shores of eternity.

Unlike most of his colleagues at the firm, Brad had dared.... He had spent his maturing years attempting to become as enlightened as possible: the one who took on cases no one else cared for, who did his small part to help make the world a little better.

At the time, the case bestowed a semblance of notoriety upon both client and lawyer. Brad had kept many news clippings and pictures from those exciting times. There was one image that kept recycling in his fading memory as if it was a reminder of something too important to be forgotten. It was a photo: it showed the dark face of his client standing over Lenny Bruce with his foot on his back and a smoldering German luger dangling in his right hand. The only thing missing was the caption: *The wages of sin is death!*

It brought to mind one single, solitary question that remained with Brad long after the Judge's gavel resounded on the hardwood and the case was closed. "Is it possible for a person born, raised, nurtured, socialized, acculturated, and baptized to believe in the Doctrine of Original Sin - to become something other than a product of such an environment?" Brad wondered.

The all-seeing sun had eased behind a billowing cloud formation as if embarrassed by the scenario it had just witnessed: an elderly man scrupulously washing his hands in the Pacific. Brad Bradley flicked the water from his hands, stooped and rolled down his trousers. He rubbed his ankles as if he had just removed invisible leg-irons and sat down cross-legged on the sand. He sat in quiet meditation until the sun peeked out the far side of a stubborn cloud. With a groan he struggled to his feet. As if by habit he made his way to the very spot where Lenny Bruce had closed his eyes and slowly inhaled and exhaled for the last time.

There was a park bench facing the water. On the backrest a brass plate had been inscribed to read: "In loving memory of Lenard Bruce Jr." There were no dates. He sat down gingerly upon the left side of the bench, as if sharing the space with someone else.

Brad Bradley clasped his hands together as if in prayer and stared off into the blue-grey vastness of the Pacific. He could feel Lenny's presence. He cautiously looked about to see if anyone else was near. All he could see was the sandy beach and miles and miles of watery solitude.

"I grow old… I grow old," he mouthed as if reminding himself of the obvious. A faint breeze blew in from the infinite sky that illuminated the eternal…

> *We have lingered in the chambers of the sea*
> *By sea-girls wreathed with seaweed red and brown*
> *Till human voices wake us, and we drown.*

He stared down at the bottoms of his white flannel trousers… they were unrolled. He looked around as if expecting to see someone. He sighed as if overcome with ambivalence, as if the passing years had produced a reticence that kept him coming back to the scene of the crime. It was a long and heartfelt sigh. He bowed his head self-consciously and whispered as if to an invisible presence.

> *"Did you know… that George got off?"*

*   *   *

> Were you there?
> In that miraculous moment
> When freedom descended
> Illuminating mortal minds
> With reasonable doubt
> Confounding the impartial forces

Of justice with unutterable words
Vainly uttered
When you swallowed your pride
As if overcome with humility
Pretending that you knew something
Others did not.

- LB

CHAPTER FOURTEEN

EPILOGUE

"My friends, love is better than anger.
Hope is better than fear.
Optimism is better than despair.
So let us be loving, hopeful, and optimistic.
And we will change the world."

Jack Layton
August 20, 2011

"**B**am!" The gavel fell. The sound echoed authoritatively throughout the courtroom.

Ruskolnikov Kublinsky, the chief prosecutor, looked as if he had just been shot. The blood drained from his face giving him the appearance of a figurine carved from marble with varicose veins. It had been a long and tiring ordeal. Perhaps he had taken it too lightly? It seemed from the very beginning to be, what was known in the vernacular, as an 'open and shut case'. He had done his best. He looked down at his shoes as if feeling ashamed of himself for losing. He hated losing. He felt as if he had been the coach of a team that had victory in the palm of its hand – only to have it snatched away in the last second by a referee who made a bad call.

"God help us!" Ruskolnikov exclaimed out loud, disappointment searing across his weary countenance. He rose to his full height and stared in the direction of the lawyer for the defense. He nodded his head as if he was in agreement with something. It was an acknowledgement, an indication that he accepted the verdict. He pulled his shoulders back and slowly drew a deep and sobering breath. As the air inflated his lungs he suddenly felt slightly faint and light headed. He could sense a spiritual presence. It was as if... as if Lenny the Bruce was standing beside him, patting him on the back and saying with deep-felt compassion: *It's okay... George has changed. Don't you think he deserves a second chance?* Ruskolnikov forced himself to smile feebly at Brad Bradley.

His nemesis smiled back and bowed his head as if expressing a condolence.

The chief prosecutor caught the vibe; he walked over and extended his right hand. "Congratulations," he said as jovially as he could. His soulful eyes gazed down into Brad's as if looking for something more than an empty stare.

Brad Bradley shook Ruskolnikov Kublinsky's extended hand; he shook it firmly, man to man. He shrugged and self-consciously lowered his gaze as if feeling slightly embarrassed about something. Just a hint of a sardonic grin creased the edges of his mouth. "Do you think justice has been served?" he quietly asked.

* * *

George stood as white as a ghost ensconced in a void as eternal as a black hole, a singularity of one. "The mind has no physical limits," the nurse had said. It was true. The black hole was filled with light; it was like an ever-expanding universal Mind that could only apprehend its own reality from within. Paradoxically, from the outside where there was nothing; it appeared to be a black void: a so-called singularity. George had been out there. He knew. It was infinitely better... *inside.*

It was so good to be back, to be given a *second chance*, to come in from the cold, to feel the warmth of human compassion.

His Honor leaned down as if he was god almighty sitting on a wooden throne meting out justice. He had a worn and stoic expression as if he had been sitting there for ages. It was not an unkindly demeanor; there was just a hint of a plebian – or rather a patrician - sense of restrained humor: it was exceedingly wry. It was enhanced when the lips quivered ever so slightly and a sound issued that felt, rather than sounded, slightly familiar.

George had felt it once before when the nurse had said, "Welcome back." It was everything. The black hole was filled with it. Who knew it was always there? "Second chance," George thought.

Warm tears coursed down his anemic cheeks and left shiny streaks behind. He was overwhelmed with love for everything that enabled him to be there and to experience such a miraculous mortal moment. There was no other like it. It happened because he, George Webster Brown, existed in the here and now as if it was everything... because to him it *was* everything.

"I suggest that you seek the help of a competent counselor."

George nodded his head.

"You may go now."

George remained mute and unmoved.

"You may go now," the judge repeated compassionately.

George's legs quivered. He sank to his knees.

The man wearing the black flowing robe leaned down from his perch on high and gently addressed the humble human being kneeling submissively before him, as the Roman Procurator Pontius Pilate, about two millennia ago, had spoken to a penitent and bewildered murderer expecting the worst: *"You are free... free to go. You are a free man."*

* * *

Lana Bruce was there, in the *here and now*, wearing her mauve woolen shawl with the brownish-green trim. She sat on the wooden bench adjacent to the pond clutching a beautiful bouquet of yellow daffodils because… Lenny loved daffodils.

She smiled self-consciously and nestled under the shawl as if she suspected that she was being watched by someone… someone whose observations mattered. It was an innocent smile, the kind that radiated an inner beauty that matched the miracle of life that surrounded her.

Lana liked to come down to Phoenix Pond on the anniversary of her late husband's passing. She liked to come down in the early morning and sit on the weathered wooden bench where Lenny used to sit gazing out at the ducks, geese, herons, and other waterfowl resting quietly upon the half-submerged logs that floated languidly upon the surface. It gave her a melancholic feeling of being in tune with the world in which she existed.

She hummed a poignant little tune that Lenny had written in the somber days immediately after he had been diagnosed with prostate cancer. It was entitled *The Sad Faced Clown*. Somehow the lyrics seemed appropriate….

> *My soul is in your hand*
> *I'm sure you'll understand*
> *If I look a little bland*
> *When it's all over…*
> *I'll play the fool or clown*
> *Look cheerful when I'm down*
> *Whenever you're around*
> *And it's all over.*
>
> *If you catch me hanging 'round*
> *A sad faced little clown*
> *Would you laugh to see me frown?*
> *When it's all over…*
> *And should you hear me sigh*
> *A sad whimper in the sky*
> *Will you smile and wave goodbye?*
> *When it's all over.*

I love the peaceful sunlight as it filters through the trees
I love the gentle laughter of your voice amongst the leaves
And sometimes in my solitude when all the world is free
I pretend I'm just as funny as the circus clown you see.

> *When sadness comes along*
> *I'll sing myself this song*
> *As the hours hurry on*
> *And it's all over...*
> *And as the years pass by*
> *And in my heart I'll cry*
> *Will you know the reason why?*
> *When it's all over.*

There was an ominous rustle amongst the fallen leaves alongside the bench, as if someone's feet had passed through them. Something intangible disturbed the quiet. Lana felt it as a sudden awareness, an unseen presence. She swiveled her head to the left and then to the right as if expecting to see someone. Her mind swirled into the misty realm of imaginary childhood memories... *she was playing hide and seek... and out of nowhere - there was Lenny.*

"Impossible!" she thought, "Lenny's gone...."
Who can see a thought or an idea? Who can see a spirit or a soul?

"What? Is that you Len?" Lana looked about wide-eyed at the miracle that existed all about her. She stood up and waited in stoic silence.

"Is that you Lenny?" she repeated again while standing before the elements with her flimsy shawl flying askew, and the yellow daffodils held aloft as if being presented to invisible hands.

She felt the fleeting shadows of the wind.

"Home free!" Lenny yelled.

* * *

The curtain came down like a shower of northern lights descending. In the foreground a vast universal audience rose to its feet and clapped enthusiastically.

It had been a dream-like experience..., The visual effects transformed the dark spaces into manifestations of light. The narrative and dialogue gave meaning and significance to the mysterious and mundane. And the acting? So down to earth!

The entire cast emerged on stage to raucous applause and whistles. They formed a motely lineup of unique characters standing self-consciously in front of the shimmering backdrop.

When George stepped forth from the line, the applause grew to a crescendo. He stood in the spotlight mesmerized by the magic of the moment. He bowed graciously.

And then Lenny stepped forward in an attitude of supplication, with hands clasped prayerfully together. He looked up and mouthed the word 'Namaste'. He bowed ever so humbly before the great unwashed, the washed, and the immaculate. The audience inhaled as one gigantic leviathan. The protagonist and the antagonist stood face to face. The applause receded to a prescient hush when Lenny extended his arms. George shuffled toward him. They stood together in the spotlight. They embraced.

The altruistic light of kindness emanated. It filled the space with time. It endured. Human hearts trembled. Happiness emerged with the revealing light. For a mortal moment in all eternity some of the seemingly disparate, mundane and insignificant parts had momentarily coalesced to produce something worth sharing... something worth remembering.

THE END

ABOUT THE AUTHOR

J T Sawada was born and raised in Pincher Creek, Alberta, Canada. He has also written an historical novel entitled: Once A Proud Canadian, available on Amazon.com.

PLEASE SHARE THIS BOOK WITH AS MANY PEOPLE AS POSSIBLE

Original Owner: _____

DATE READER'S NAME BRIEF COMMENT

(1) _____

(2) _____

(3) _____

(4) _____

(5) _____

(6) _____

(7) _____

(8) _____

(9) _____

(10) _____

(11) _____

(12) _____

"THANKS FOR SHARING"